KATANAGATARI
Sword Tale

1

NISIOISIN

Art by take

Calligraphy by Hiroshi Hirata

Translated by Sam Bett

KATANAGATARI
Sword Tale: One

A VERTICAL Book

Translation: Sam Bett
Production: Risa Cho, (softcover only) Tomoe Tsutsumi

First published in Japan in 2007 by Kodansha, Ltd., Tokyo
Publication for this English edition arranged through Kodansha, Ltd., Tokyo
English language version produced by Kodansha USA Publishing, LLC, 2022

Katanagatari Dai Ichiwa Zettou Kan'na
Katanagatari Dai Niwa Zantou Namakura
Katanagatari Dai Sanwa Sentou Tsurugi

Previously published in hardcover in 2018.

ISBN: 978-1-64729-155-6

Printed in Canada

First Paperback Edition

Kodansha USA Publishing, LLC
451 Park Avenue South
7th Floor
New York, NY 10016
www.kodansha.us

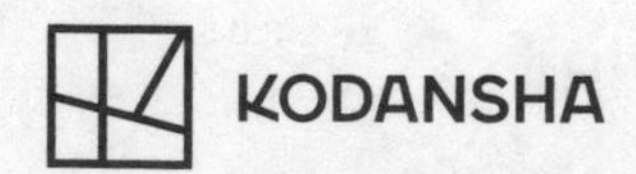

TABLE OF CONTENTS

NOTE ON THIS ENGLISH EDITION

This volume collects the first trio of a dozen-part series. The cover art was for the original Book One, while Books Two and Three's have been included as a color insert.

The footnotes appended to this translation can be ignored, if the reader so wishes, and the story encountered on its own. Not intended to be exhaustive, they give the Japanese word and its transliteration when they occur, in addition to supplying more literal or straightforward renditions in most cases. Readers with some Japanese may find them clarifying, and those with none, too, are invited to observe (for instance) many no doubt familiar terms in their native form.

Where appropriate, the transliterations add bars called "macrons" above vowels for a closer approximation of the pronunciation, including for names and words that appear without them in the main text; a syllable with "Ō" is supposed to sound more like *boat* than *bot*. A repeated consonant like "CC" should be construed in the same manner as in *Rebecca*.

The translator agreed beforehand to provide the bulk of the annotations. The author's infamous penchant for wordplay always poses a challenge, but it is the work's period setting that inspired the publisher's request. If all that it does is open a window into the difficulties of the endeavor, not just for this particular project but regarding any attempt to convey the sense of a source language, then so much the better.

Enjoy.

—Ed.

BOOK ONE

ZETTO
THE LEVELER

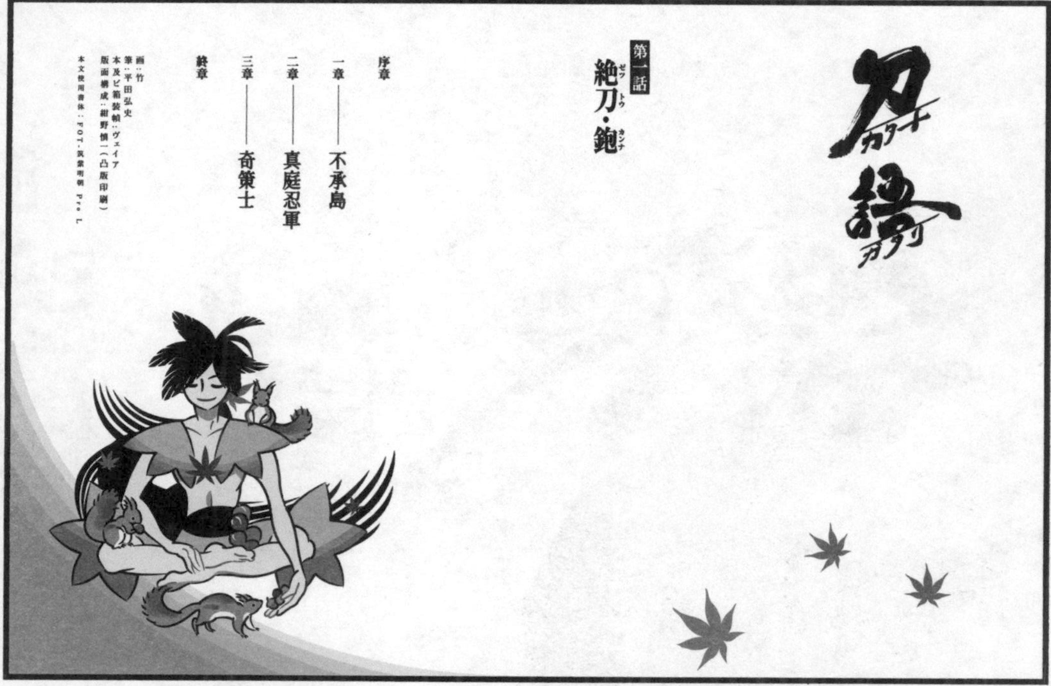

The original Book One Table of Contents spread

PROLOGUE

■ ■

In those days, the Capital[1] boasted six hundred and forty-five official schools for swordplay, great and small—but when you throw in all the unofficial schools, there were easily a thousand. Famous among them was the Hisho[2] Dojo, on the east[3] side of the city, an elite institution with strong ties to the bakufu[4] and a history extending back to the Age of Warring States,[5] and a household name for anyone conversant in the martial arts.

Within these walls, seven men faced off.

But no—to say they faced each other confuses things. In actuality, six men surrounded one man, in a circle.

Not what you would call a sporting atmosphere.

Something was awry.

Dressed in the black gi[6] of Hisho Dojo, the six men stood with their bokutos[7] at the ready. Unbelievably, the man trapped in their weir of swords was empty-handed.

This was not exactly the right time for contemplation, but the man penned by the other six was focused not on them, but on the floor, as if puzzled by the planks below his feet.

The only one without a gi, he was bare to the waist and basically in rags. While fit and long in stature—he was not what you call slender. You could say that he had just enough muscle in just the right places. His tousled hair was knotted at the back. Every movement radiated wildness.

He shook his head.

Eyes on his feet.

"What's wrong now?"

She spoke at a remove, from a corner of the dojo.

A woman in a brash, brilliant kimono leaned comfortably against the wall. The perfect vantage point for watching the seven men—that is, the six men encircling the one. She did nothing to hide her smile. While young—her long hair was completely white. No strand of black.

"If something's on your mind, just say it."

The man seemed bothered by her question.

"It's not like that—I'm just a little out of place. I'm an island monkey.

1 京の都 KYŌ NO MIYAKO phrasing of 京都 KYŌTO ("capital city") that brings out the literal meaning
2 氷床 HISHŌ "floors of ice"
3 左京 SAKYŌ "left capital"
4 幕府 BAKUFU shogunate
5 戦国時代 SENGOKU JIDAI historical period of conflict, culminating in the unification of Japan
6 着 GI attire worn when practicing the martial arts
7 木刀 BOKUTŌ wooden sword

I don't think I've ever stepped on wood so shiny."

"I suppose not."

The woman smirked.

Enjoying herself.

"Don't take the name of the dojo seriously. The floors aren't actually made of ice. Pay attention to these guys—none of them should be mistaken for expendable. Men of their ability go down in history—"

"History? Who needs it. Can't help you, can't help me," the lone man said. "All that matters is they're swordsmen.[8] And up against a sword, I never lose."

"That's some confidence. And no doubt justified. But remember, you're not up against one man. There's six."

"Six swords."

"Six is six. Even if you punch and kick and headbutt all at once, that's only five—you and your kenpo[9] are in over your head. Something must be wrong with you to face a sword barehanded. But then again, if you were any other way, you'd be no use to me."

"I want to show you. I want you to need me. I need you to. Nothing else matters."

The six men shrank their circle.

Not happy.

And why would they be? Those two were blabbing as if none of them were here—it was enough to annoy anybody, not to say the elite of a venerable dojo.

Their stirring made the trapped man raise his head.

But his words—

"Alright. Let's go."

—were endlessly aloof.

The same went for his expression.

"No use thinking. No room to move, but no room to slip—let's go. You say the word."

"Alright," the woman nodded. "Let's—"

Begin.

Before she could say the word, the six men—six wooden swords—rose to action. Swordsmen of such legendary promise could aim[10] at the same target without clashing. Sparing none of him, their swords would fall at once over his body—

Or would they?

"Ugh—what a pain..."

Even now, he showed no sign of excitement.

[8] 剣士 KENSHI swordfighters
[9] 拳法 KENPŌ "law/method of the fist"
[10] 剣線 KENSEN "line of the sword"

"I told you—this isn't kenpo. This is swordplay.[11] And *even with six*, they're short a sword—against me. Feast your eyes on this."

The Swordless Swordsman crouched—low to the ground.

"Kyotoryu[12]—Shichika Hachiretsu[13]—"

■ ■

That's as good a place to start as any.

To unroll the scroll of this war of katanas.

This swashbuckling play on swords, this piecemeal period piece.

And so we begin: the Tale of the Sword[14]♪

[11] 剣法 KENPŌ "law of the sword" homophone with 拳法 KENPŌ

[12] 虚刀流 KYOTŌRYŪ "fictive katana style" (KYOTŌ, and not KYŌTO)

[13] 七花八裂 SHICHIKA HACHIRETSU destroying seven foes pun on 八つ裂き YATSUZAKI "tear apart" and the saying 七転八起 SHICHITEN HAKKI "fall down seven times, get up eight"

[14] 刀語 KATANAGATARI (a neologism) *Sword Tale*

CHAPTER ONE

HAPHAZARD ISLAND

■ ■

In Tango, beyond the sea extending from the Cliffs of Shinso, an island sits on the horizon. Tiny, only ten miles[1] around. Few of the villagers of Shinso even knew that it was there—and those who did could care less. What was there to care about? It wasn't on any of the maps, and it had no name. Nobody felt the need to name another empty island in a string of empty islands.

Empty...or was it?

It had been, until some twenty years ago.

Twenty years back, when a family crossed over from Shinso—they named this place Haphazard Island.[2] They were the only three souls on earth with a reason to name it.

■ ■

"What a pain[3]..."

It was the crack of dawn.

Outside a ramshackle hut built near the center of the island, a man sat grumbling, dressed in rags, tousled hair tied at his neck. Still in the process of waking, he muttered over his handiwork.

A bucket.

Big and round.

Perhaps, more aptly, a barrel—and shaped with the same slapdash attitude as the hut. At first glance, you might mistake it for a roped-up bundle of sticks, but the seams lacked even the slimmest gap for water to intrude. He threw a ladle in the bucket and slung it on his back, using the ropes that bound it tight to strap it to his shoulders.

What a pain, he thought, not voicing the words this time.

He wasn't mad—had nothing against the bucket or the ladle. To him, almost everything was, by default, a pain. Waking up? Absolutely. But even closing his eyes to go to sleep at night. A pain.

"Here we go."

While not actually pausing, he seemed supremely bothered that he had to stand. Eyes bleary from sleeping, he turned and set off for the mountain—

[1] 四里 YONRI four 里 RI = approx. 2.5 miles

[2] 不承島 FUSHŌJIMA "un-assented island"
evokes 不精髭 BUSHŌHIGE, a lazy beard, and 不祥事 FUSHŌJI, a scandalous event

[3] 面倒 MENDŌ nuisance

Which is when the door to the hut creaked open.

"Shichika..."

Someone called him from inside.

Shichika Yasuri[4]...

His name.

"Where are you going, Shichika?"

"Uh..."

He turned, flustered and embarrassed, and tried but failed to look away. Eyes spinning in his head. The face of a kid caught red-handed in a prank. But Shichika was too old, though not by far, to be confused for a kid, and no kid had a build like his. Strictly speaking, he was doing nothing wrong, but when the voice from the hut—his older sister Nanami—reached his ears, he was as good as guilty.

Nanami Yasuri.[5]

Unlike her wild younger brother, Nanami was the picture of comely grace. Her face and bearing had the attraction of porcelain—but in her beauty and crafted smoothness, there was something fragile and breakable. Leaning in the doorway, wearing just a haori[6] over her slip, she watched Shichika with a cold stare.

Voice drained of feeling.

"I asked where you were going."

"It looked, uh, like we were low on water, so I figured I'd go fetch some. Go back to bed. You shouldn't come out dressed like that. You'll catch a cold."

"Says the guy not wearing a shirt. I'm fine. It's just enough to cool me down. The cold air feels nice against my skin. Besides, I was supposed to do the chores today."

"Yeah, I know. I mean—" Shichika sputtered, "I didn't know that." He was shaking in his sandals. "Does it really matter? Consider it part of my training."

"Shichika."

Her voice was cold.

Ready to refute any excuse.

It shut him up real quick.

"How many times do I need to tell you? Stop treating me so preciously."

"I didn't—mean to."

"I'm capable of fetching water. You were raised better than to be so pushy. And all this training?" Nanami sighed[7] dismissively. "Pointless."

"What makes it pointless—"

[4] 鑢 七花 YASURI SHICHIKA "Seventh Flower of the File"
seventh generation of the Kyotoryu
his family name evokes a tool capable of honing or abrading other implements

[5] 鑢 七実 YASURI NANAMI "Seventh Fruit of the File"

[6] 羽織 HAORI short robe worn over kimono

[7] ため息 TAMEIKI "pent-up breath"

"Everything. Why train when you're the end of the tradition?"

"..."

Nanami sighed again.

She could sigh with the best of them.

"No one's asking you to be a hero."

"Yeah, well, thanks for the advice. I'm doing my best. Yesterday I came up with an insane new Fatal Orchid. This one is out of control."

"Shichika."

Nanami wouldn't let him change the subject.

"...What?" he asked.

"It's been a year since Dad died. Don't you think it's time?"

"Time for what?"

"If you can build a bucket," she said flatly, pointing at the thing strapped to his back, "I'm sure that you can build a boat. Dad was the one they banished.[8] I would never make it over there, but you..."

"Don't be ridiculous." This was too much. Shichika was done humoring her. "I get what you mean. Same as you, I've been on this island as long as I can remember—but I can't just up and go over to the mainland. I wouldn't know my left from right, or up from down. I'd wind up dead in a ditch[9] somewhere."

"Still," Nanami said.

"Training may be pointless. I agree. But the school is the only thing Dad left me—I'm going to uphold the tradition as long as I can."

"Huh." Nanami smirked. "I had no idea that you missed Dad so much."

"Sis."[10]

"What? Go ahead. If you want to go fetch the water, go and get it. We can talk about this later. It's too early for this sort of thing. I'll make breakfast. Is the water gone?"

"There's a little left."

"Alright," she said. "You can show me your new move later on."

Nanami stepped back into the hut and closed the door.

Seeing her go was such a relief that Shichika heaved a sigh. And for a man his size, a sigh was not becoming in the least. His sister put him to shame.

"I knew she'd bring it up someday, and I guess today's the day. But she doesn't know what she's talking about. A bucket's nothing like a boat."

Maybe their father could have built a boat. Twenty years ago, he built the hut—with his own hands.

But Shichika? No chance.

Not without a single blade[11] on the entire island.

[8] 島流し SHIMANAGASHI marooning

[9] 頓死 TONSHI "die a sudden death"

[10] 姉ちゃん NEHCHAN term of endearment for an older sister (or young woman)

[11] 刃物 HAMONO blades of any kind

This was no exaggeration.
Shichika and Nanami were stuck here.
On this island.
Stuck to their father.
And to his school.
"..."
Did he miss him?
Did he really?
His line about fetching water being part of his training was sincere (it had to be), but it surprised him when his sister referenced his feelings for his father.
He was a great man. They called him Hero of the Rebellion.
By comparison, Shichika had accomplished nothing.
To be fair, having lived most of his life on Haphazard Island, he had yet to have the chance to perform daring feats of valor—but this gave him a lingering sense of inferiority.
Uphold the tradition—
His father had trained him up until his death.
It was his father's school. That made the training matter.
But Nanami was right. If Shichika stayed holed up on this island, the school would die off with him. She may have been the one to bring it up, but it was on his mind. Hell, even their father must have known—a day would come.
But all the same.
At any rate.
Shichika knew nothing of the outside world—
And didn't care to learn.
Why bother—such a pain.
"...Here we go."
He twisted his back to slide the bucket into place and headed toward the mountain.
Across the desert island.
Deserted as it was, Haphazard Island had freshwater—if it didn't, his whole family would have died of thirst years ago. But the water wasn't in a river or a well. It bubbled from a spring in the mountain. Because the island was a single mountainous mass, it was hard to say what was mountain and what wasn't (and in reality, outside of the beaches and the clearing where they kept their hut, almost everything was mountain), but the spring in question sat beyond an especially treacherous pass—not a place he would gladly have his sister venturing for water. In the year since their father's passing, Shichika had been quietly replenishing their supply, but it seemed that she had finally caught on. Soon she would discover all the other menial tasks he had

been carrying out in secret—but what could he do. It was a miracle that somebody as dull as him had been able to delude someone as sharp as his sister for so long.

—Her face.

She did look a little pale.

The hour was not to blame.

Only her brother could possibly have noticed, since already on normal days her complexion was not just clear and white but almost sky blue—

—Still.

What if she is sick again?

When she said the cold air felt nice, could that mean she was catching a fever?

Nanami was frail. That much was certain—encountered in the night, she would be easy to mistake for a spirit,[12] if not an actual ghost.[13] She had been doing so well—not like this was to his credit, for handling all the chores—yet now that she had caught up on his act, he doubted she would listen if he told her to stay home and rest. More likely she would overextend herself, trying to compensate. The opposite of her apathetic brother, she hated nothing more than sitting still. At first glance, you may think her lethargy shared some aspect of her brother's grumbling, but at the root, these moods were unrelated. Hers, quite simply, was a function of her sickly constitution.

She would rather be working. Always.

Sick as she was.

Or maybe sickness was the reason—people want what they can't have, and long to do what they cannot. Surely this was the case for Nanami.

But not Shichika. He hated what he had, and was loath to do the things he could.

My father—

—the hero.

Enough thinking. He closed his eyes.

His head was hurting.

Shichika was not a thinker. Reasoning was not his strength. If there was anything he hated or loathed, it was complicated explanations.[14]

That was his sister's territory.

—They were like a bow and string.

Or rather, a mended lid on a cracked pot.[15]

As Shichika would have it, things were the way they were, and whatever happened happened—period. In his view, it was best to leap before you looked.

12 生霊 IKIRYŌ "living ghost" the apparition of a living person
13 死霊 SHIRYŌ "dead ghost" a dead soul visiting from the afterlife
14 理屈 RIKUTSU logical arguments
15 割れ鍋に綴じ蓋 WARENABE NI TOJIBUTA complementary

"Huh?"

He noticed something.

Shichika knew this island better than anyone, with his father gone—and maybe even when his father was alive. The island was so small. He knew it all, down to the last blade of grass. If something changed, even slightly, he would notice.

"..."

A disturbance in the soil.

Footprints—small, but human.

They were wearing sandals. Flat ones.

Was it Nanami? Couldn't be. First off, he had no memory of making her this kind of sandal, and second, the footprints were fresh—there was no way Nanami could have overtaken him. Distracted as he was by his confounding thoughts, he had traveled in an almost perfectly straight line, but Nanami, on top of being too weak to catch up to a tortoise, was so easily disoriented[16] she was apt to set off for the mountains and wind up in the sea.

It was just the two of them, on the entire island. If these footprints weren't Nanami's, and obviously not his, whose were they?

By process of elimination—no, no matter how you thought about it, or even if, like Shichika, you didn't think, the answer was clear—*someone else was on the island.*

Not a problem.

Just a pain.

Shichika even felt that his priority was to move on to the spring and fetch water—but he couldn't let himself ignore this. His father had been on the lookout nineteen years, since being banished, watching for someone from the mainland to show up on the island. While there had been a few near misses, no one had ever come.

Until today.

Sure enough, only after his father's death.

"If Dad was here, he'd school them and be done with it. But what am I supposed to do? Welcome them? I'd better leave that to Nanami."

Talking to himself, Shichika adjusted his route. Knowing the entire island—he could guess, from the footprints, what this stranger had been thinking. They were trying to follow the easiest path. Wherever it was easiest to walk—of course, this being in the mountains, there was no path, but that aside, the steps did not suggest that whoever made them had a specific destination—or if they did, they had no clue how to get there.

Or maybe, like Nanami, they were quick to lose their way.

Shichika knew exactly where he was, but if a normal person wandered off into these hills, they would be in deep trouble, quite doomed. But then again,

[16] 方向音痴 HŌKŌ ONCHI "deaf to direction"

as far as Shichika recalled, he had never met a "normal person." Twenty years ago, when his father brought them here, he was only four years old. He lacked the perspective necessary to comprehend words like "normal" or "other." His world had only two people—his father, dead a year, and his sister, whom he saw every day. His father had taught them facts about the outside world—but facts were not reality.

Faced with unfamiliar footprints and the question of who left them, a normal person would have been more cautious—or at least indulged in some degree of speculation, but in Shichika Yasuri's case, even this variety of thinking was a pain.

Speculation was not among his special moves.

If only he had run home and sought help from his sister, who despite her identical island upbringing was prone to speculation, he would never have been embrangled in the pain-in-the-butt adventure that was to come—but alas, it wasn't in the cards.

Whatever will be will be.

Things will happen as they will.

Such is the way of the world.

From the way the branches had been bent back from the path, Shichika was able to discern the height of whoever left the footprints. Whoever this was, they weren't very tall, but no kid either. Small footprints, on their own, could be a kid, but factoring in the disturbance of the branches, Shichika was certain they had been left by a woman.

A woman.

But he didn't think anything of it.

Well, there was one other thing.

One thing his dull mind couldn't shake—the way the footprints pressed into the ground. The soil wasn't squishy, like fresh mud, but while he couldn't say for sure, it seemed as if the footprints on the left were deeper than the footprints on the right.

Something she was carrying made her favor her left side.

Something heavy.

"Hmm."

But *hmm* was as far as he got.

Nevertheless, in short time he discovered that his guess was on the mark—thin as Shichika may have been, he was a big guy with a big stride. And a woman left these footprints. Carrying something heavy. She didn't know her way. It would have been far stranger if he never found her.

But there she was.

Slim silhouette.

Long white hair—no strand of black.

The hair had made it hard at first to tell how old she was—but she was young. Like his sister Nanami, she left her hair undone, flowing down over her shoulders, but she wore a voluminous kimono in gold brocade. However elegant and brilliant, her outfit was the worse for wearing on a mountain pass, and its hem sprayed thread where it had caught so many pesky branches. Yet her sloppy[17] way of dressing made the fraying seem like a fashion statement.[18] Each of her appurtenances glimmered with luxuriance. No detail, taken singly, could be rightly called offensive—but as a whole, at least by normal standards, she came across as showy, enough to make you want to take a step back.

Then again.

To Shichika, ignorant of any norm, she somehow made no overstrong impression. Not even her curious hair—but again, there was one thing that caught his eye.

The katana dangling from her left hip.

The heavy thing was a katana.

"Hey, it's not like you're not welcome here. People can visit if they like."

Shichika addressed the woman without hesitation.

Fear didn't register.

Though perhaps a little fear would have been normal.

"So yeah, just letting you know, now that you're here, there's one big rule—no blades allowed. On the entire island."

"..."

She heard this sudden greeting from behind—

But it did nothing to discomfit her.

Taking her time, the woman turned.

Her countenance was no pushover's. Eyes perked up at the corners.[19] No grandeur left unaired.

Those perky eyes scrutinized Shichika before glancing at the thing slung from her hip.

"Then I apologize." The woman did bow her head. "I didn't know, so forgive me."

"...Hey, I didn't make the rules."

His father had.

And thanks to him, he and his sister had to do everything, including cook, without so much as a knife. After twenty years, he couldn't care less—but truth be told, this was the first time Shichika had seen a real katana.

It was possible that he had seen a sword before coming to the island—but his four-year-old mind had retained no record of it, and besides, seeing something after two decades is just the same as seeing it anew.

Look at that.

17 着崩す KIKUZUSU dressing down a formal outfit by loosening or shortening the fit
18 粋 IKI "cool" as an antonym of "obsessed"
19 つり目 TSURIME vs. たれ目 TAREME, eyes which lower at the corners

A real—katana.

It sure looked heavy.

"How'd you get here, anyway?"

"A boat," she said. "How else do you get to an island?"

Obviously.

Right. How else.

The question was embarrassing enough to make you want to take it back.

But not Shichika. He went on.

"Why are you here?"

He wasn't asking to find out. He was merely keeping faith on what his father and his sister told him he should ask at times like this. Unconcerned with how the woman answered, he thought only of what to ask next, or—crap, should he have asked her for her name first?

"I came to see Mutsue[20] Yasuri, Sixth Master of the Kyotoryu. Do you know him?"

"He died," said Shichika. "Last year."

So she was here to see his father.

In which case, she had a distinct destination after all.

Betraying only a flicker of surprise, the woman caught herself.

"Is that so." She nodded. "I assumed as much—after all, it has been twenty years—but if he's no longer with us, you must be—"

"I am Shichika Yasuri. Seventh Master of the Kyotoryu."

"Ah."

She smiled.

An understanding grin.

"What was I thinking—how silly of me to ask. What with Mutsue and his family being the only ones who live here. Which makes you—"

"His son. For what it's worth."[21]

"I see. You have a nice build. You're in good shape. I'd say you pass muster."

"Past master? I'm the present master."

"...Yes, of course."

"If you came to see my father, I hate to disappoint you."

"I did indeed, but my business remains with the master of your school. Which means, young master, that my business with your father is now with you. Excuse the tardiness of my own introduction. I am Togame,[22] the Schemer."

"Togame?"

What a strange name.

20 鑢 六枝 YASURI MUTSUE "Sixth Branch of the File"
21 不肖 FUSHŌ a humble way to introduce oneself
echoes 不承島 FUSHŌJIMA, Haphazard Island
22 とがめ TOGAME an unlikely name, the word means blame or accusation

Wait—what did she say after that?

The Schemer?[23]

Shichika was on the verge of asking his first unrehearsed question, but the woman made the first move.

"Let's see this Kyotoryu of yours."

She drew the katana at her hip.

A thin sword,[24] four feet[25] long.

Its temper line[26] perfectly straight.[27]

Blade engraved with the image of a tiger.

"An early work of Kasamaro Mibu, one of the thirty-six Fugaku[28] Swordsmiths—I had feared it may be no match for Mutsue Yasuri, Hero of the Rebellion, but for a go around with his son, it may just do the trick."

"A go around? What do you mean?"

"Nothing more than its customary sense. Have at you!"

This was the first sword Shichika had ever seen—and of course the first sword anyone had pointed in his face—but he did not flinch. Although his real eyes had never witnessed a sword, his mind's eye had seen them constantly over his twenty years of training on the island; he hadn't slacked off in the year since his father's passing.

He was ready.

Shichika Yasuri feared no sword—

"Gadzooks!"

However.

The many secrets of the Kyotoryu were not to be aired on this precise occasion. Coming at him with her stalwart battle cry, her sword raised high—Togame caught her foot on an outcropping of rock and fell flat on her face.

Thus Shichika, Seventh Master of the Kyotoryu, made the acquaintance of Togame the Schemer.

It was the first moon of the new year, in an era long before *Gadzooks!* had fallen out of fashion.

■ ■

"Kyotoryu" means "Way of the Empty[29] Sword."

It was founded in the chaos of the Age of Warring States.

23 奇策士 KISAKUSHI neologism for an expert on surprise strategies
24 太刀 TACHI progenitor of the katana: meant for use on horseback
25 尺 SHAKU just under a foot
26 刃文 HAMON "blade pattern" line marking the tempered portion of the blade
27 直刃 SUGUHA straight HAMON
28 富岳 FUGAKU another name for Mt. Fuji
29 虚しい MUNASHII futile (when the word is inflected in this manner)

By Kazune Yasuri.[30]

The reputation of katana[31] as the epitome of handheld weapons is perennial—a fact destined to go unchanged. Its strengths are too numerous to tally, but if forced to offer only two, they would be that it is long, and it is heavy. Its length makes it lethal, as does its weight. This combination would give anyone the upper hand. But as with all things far and wide, these strengths double as weaknesses. The length of a katana, like its weight, make wielding it impractical.

Thus came Kazune to his philosophy.

Swordsmen, he reasoned, are the strongest creatures on earth. But to truly be the strongest, you must be void of any weakness—even if it means surrendering your strength. He took the discipline places no swordsman before him had dared to venture.

Kazune forsook the sword.

A true swordsman needs no sword—to him, this was the key. For the next ten years, he retreated to the mountains and toiled in seclusion as he shaped the Kyotoryu. And later, in the service of the House of Tetsubi, one of the six daimyos responsible for the current shogunate, his art sent tremors through the battlefield.

Not kenpo of any stripe. And not mutodori.[32]

This was swordplay—swordless and lethal.

So legend had it.

Legendary, but true? True or false aside, that much was known to those who cared to know. Yet few among the living were familiar with the workings of the Kyotoryu—the only school of swordplay with no sword at play. Its secrets were unknowable, not even rumored. To witness it at work, you had two options—train, or fight—and the former was next to impossible. Kazune decreed the school would only be passed down by bloodline. The gates of the school were more than barred: they were invisible.[33] The only viable option was to provoke one of the masters with a katana—and the moment you witnessed the Kyotoryu would be your last. Even if you somehow survived, you would think twice before bragging about losing, sword in hand, to a man without a sword.

The school was shrouded in darkness.

Its techniques had been showcased only twice before the public eye: during the Age of Warring States, by Kazune, and during the Rebellion, by Mutsue. Its powers were only to be loosed amid the chaos and confusion of the battlefield.

30 鑢 一根 YASURI KAZUNE "First Root of the File"

31 日本刀 NIHONTŌ Japanese swords in particular

32 無刀取り MUTŌDORI borrowing moves from swordplay to wield other objects, or even fight barehanded, against an armed opponent

33 門外不出 MONGAI FUSHUTSU "must not pass through the gates" hermetic secret

And after nineteen years of training under Mutsue, his son Shichika became the newest Master of the Kyotoryu.

"Miss Togame—was it?" Nanami asked in a calm tone, sounding completely at ease.

To recap.

The woman, Togame, who had banged her head against the ground so hard to go unconscious, wound up in Shichika's water bucket and rode back to the hut strapped to his back. Nanami, changed into a short-sleeved robe, raised an eyebrow when her brother returned laden not with water but a woman—his failure to return with water obviously not being the reason for the gesture—but simply couldn't leave the fainted woman outside. It took the two of them to carry her in, whereupon they dispossessed her of the glimmering thing slung from her hip. The sword was trouble—though in her hands, not exactly big trouble, judging from her last display.

Nanami had spent more time on the mainland than her brother, but she too had gone these twenty years without seeing a stranger. Nevertheless, she regarded the woman before them with equanimity. Not simply because she did not share her brother's aversion to thought—Nanami had readied herself daily to meet a situation such as this. She exuded prudence. Should the sky crumble and fall, she would be there to catch the pieces.

Their hut had a dirt floor and a step-up into a single room.

The brother and sister took their breakfast together, discussing what to do next. Just as they finished eating, Togame woke from where she lay at the edge of the room. Nanami stood and offered her a cup of water heated by the fire.[34] Let us take it from there.

"You're the first visitor we've ever had—please forgive us for being so ill prepared to entertain you."

"Please, I owe you the apology. I showed up unannounced."

Togame accepted the sayu. It seemed that she had known Mutsue had a son, but had she known about a daughter? From the way she had approached him when they met, she seemed to have arrived at Haphazard Island with some intelligence. She must have known—but Shichika could not be bothered to take the thought this far. He assumed that if she hadn't known, she had put two and two together, which meant that there was nothing left to say.

His virtuous sister knew better than to wait idly for her not-so-virtuous little brother to introduce her.

"I'm Nanami. Daughter of Mutsue Yasuri." She paused to look Togame in the eye. "I hear you came to see our father—would you mind me asking what your connection was to him?"

To the point.

"We never met," Togame said. "I wouldn't call it a connection."

[34] 白湯 SAYU plain hot water

"No?"

"No," Togame confirmed. "Let's just say I didn't have a standing invitation, Nanami."

Behind the polite welcome Nanami had extended was a detectable backdrop of nervousness and caution—but Togame repaid her courtesy with brusque arrogance. The Schemer's bearing suggested not even the slightest shame at arriving unannounced. As towards Shichika, she addressed Nanami without formality.[35] But for someone who had eaten dirt and earned herself a fat bump on her forehead, such airs were nothing if not comical. Or were they? Up until she took her fall, the woman had been searching in vain for this very hut—her destination—and lost her way...for her to maintain such composure after such a misstep was perhaps less comical than admirable. But regardless of whether Nanami saw the humor in it, she didn't let it hurt her feelings.

She had approached this situation from the first without concern for how Togame held herself. Her sole interest was why Togame had arrived. Shichika may have been the Seventh Master of the Kyotoryu, but with their father gone, Nanami was head of the house.

"Your sword is in safekeeping—I believe my brother has already informed you, but on this island, carrying or using any kind of blade is not allowed."

"I suppose I have the Kyotoryu to thank for that."

"Yes...but why attack my brother?"

"I merely hoped to spur him to reveal the school's secrets. But I'm afraid my skills are not so sharp as his. I'm the Schemer—not a swordsman."

"Still," Shichika inserted himself into the exchange, "you sure know how to draw a sword."

Too bad she couldn't do more.

"Hah." Togame laughed defiantly. "That much I've practiced."

"..."

Why not go all the way?

Shichika did not approve.

"Your method was crude—I cannot say I'm much impressed."

"Far be it from me to try to convince you otherwise, but I had my reasons. I knew Mutsue Yasuri of the Kyotoryu by name, but not by face. I'd hate to go after the wrong guy. What better way of confirming his identity than to force his hand and make him show[36] the power of the Kyotoryu?"

"In which case," deduced Nanami, "either Mutsue or Shichika would do." She nodded comprehendingly.

But what was there to comprehend?

"How about you have another go?" Nanami glanced at the doorway, where leaned the blade. "Though I can't say that I recommend it—the Kyotoryu

35 呼び捨て YOBISUTE speech omitting honorifics like さん SAN or さま SAMA
36 名札代わり NAFUDAGAWARI "as a nametag"

may make him look unarmed, but Shichika is a sword, meant for killing.[37] Not halfway. All the way. Consider yourself lucky for tripping on that rock. If your sword had so much as grazed him, you would have more than a bump on the forehead."

Nanami's words were keen enough to chill the room.

While her face said otherwise—she was angry that a blade had been turned against her brother.

Togame swallowed her breath, but not before Shichika could swallow his. He wanted to counter that he could in fact control his strength—how else could he train?—but his swallowed breath blocked any protest.

"I'll take that as sufficient evidence I've come to the right place. I need this life of mine. Today is not my day to die."

"Well, then."

We are ready to hear you out, invited Nanami.

She was clearly holding court, and Togame was her subject. Between them, Shichika felt vaguely excluded, but he was not sensitive enough to interpret their exclusion as offensive. He merely figured it was best to let his sister handle things from here.

Togame tried to pique his interest.[38]

"Seventh Master of the Kyotoryu. Don't you desire the world?"

"Nah."

"Indeed. Who doesn't? To be born into this world is to vie for its dominion. Don't shy from your ambition. The Rebellion is fresh in our memories, but who could deny the determination of the rebels? Even the current shogunate had to seize their power first. No one has any reason to hold back in desiring such an office—wait, did you say 'Nah'?!"

Fool me once.

Shame on you.

"Yeah. I mean, not 'Nah' as in 'No'..."

Shichika searched for the right words.

Suddenly put on the spot, he had refuted her by reflex, without so much as understanding her question. Try as he might to take heed now, he couldn't see what he was supposed to take. That was it—he should tell her that he didn't get it. What was he to think when she came at him asking about the world? The only one he knew was Haphazard Island. How could he desire what was his?

This confounding, unenthused reaction made Togame roll her eyes. Nanami felt the need to intervene.[39]

"Please remember. This island is the only world we know. If you start

[37] 殺人剣 SATSUJINNKEN "the sword that takes life" concept in martial arts philosophy vs. 活人剣 KATSUJINKEN "the sword that gives life"

[38] 水を向ける MIZU WO MUKERU "to offer water" from the custom of doing so to summon spirits

[39] 助け舟を出す TASUKEBUNE WO DASU "send a lifeboat"

from the end and explain things backwards or beat around the bush, you may as well assume you've lost him."

"Thanks for clarifying." Togame nodded. "Now, if it's all the same, I hope you won't mind if I ask for you to leave. I don't want any little birds—"

"That's out of the question," Shichika cut her off before she could finish, and not by reflex. "Two reasons. First, the Kyotoryu is shared across our bloodline. If our father was alive, he would have both of us here beside him. Second...I'm not so good at thinking. I can't understand difficult things. If you have something important that you want to say, it's in your best interest for sis to be here."

"Understood."

Faced with Shichika's response, Togame retreated, her arrogance intact. The first part was well and good, but the second was just embarrassing.

"Right you are—well then, so long as you can keep this strictly confidential, I'll get started."

"As simply as you can, please."

"Have you ever heard of Kiki Shikizaki?[40] The swordsmith."[41]

"Nope."

"Indeed. Even out here on this godforsaken island, anyone who calls himself a swordsman would know that name—no, for the Swordless Swordsmen of the Kyotoryu in particular, Kiki Shikizaki is a natural enemy. The same goes for you as for your ancestor Kazune. I'm sure he would agree that—wait, did you say 'Nope'?!"

Fool me twice.

Shame on me.

"Come on, Shichika. You know who she's talking about. Dad taught us about this. Kiki Shikizaki...the famous swordsmith from the war. Right, Miss Togame?"

"Huh? Is that really all you know?"

Togame wasn't razzing Nanami. She was really asking. She didn't even bother asking Shichika—and rightfully so. It sounded like their father had told them about the swordsmith, but Shichika, who skipped over any words that were too hard, seemed to have remembered nothing. It was his special move, and wholly unrelated to the Kyotoryu.

"What are you talking about? Is this Shikizaki, uh—what you said before...oh right, one of the guys from Mt. Fuji?"

"Not exactly—that's hardly it... Nanami, how much did your father tell you about Kiki Shikizaki?"

40 四季崎記紀 SHIKIZAKI KIKI
SHIKIZAKI "Cape Four Seasons" KIKI shorthand for the two oldest Japanese chronicles: 古事記 KOJIKI "Record of Ancient Matters" and 日本書紀 NIHONSHOKI "The Chronicles of Japan"

41 刀鍛冶 KATANAKAJI blacksmith specializing in swords

"Just what you mentioned—that he's the ultimate rival of the Kyotoryu, and that he had some deep connection[42] to the founder of our school."

"Anything else?"

"I'm afraid that's all. I don't even know what the connection was."

Togame was silent, her face fixed in thought. These two knew almost nothing of the celebrated swordsmith. She could see if only Shichika was in the dark, but since Nanami didn't know much either, Togame could safely guess that Mutsue had been stingy with the details. Why might that have been, she might have pondered.

Shichika, however, could not care less[43]—if Togame was going to tell them about the swordsmith, she could just get down off her high horse.

Not like it mattered to him if she told them.

"In the Age of Warring States, more than any other era in this country's history, swordsmen were supreme—the power brokers of the battlefield were not the lords or the captains, but the swordsmen."

Thus Togame began her story from the first—no, from zero.

"Kazune Yasuri was one among them—but the light of glory was cast forth by the swordsmiths. The forges.[44] The craftsmen.[45] If the swordsmen were the players, the smithies were the crew—nay, the stage directors. Needless to say, without a sword, the swordplay would be curtains. Kyotoryu being the exception."

"Obviously."

Shichika was onboard. This level of discussion was well within his grasp. He almost wished that she would stop right there, but she was only getting started.

"Those thirty-six great swordsmiths represented one camp, but the most heretical of heretics was Kiki Shikizaki. He pledged allegiance to no school, and manned his forge alone, aloof to the world, and yet his swords reigned over the warring states like none before or since."

"Reigned how?" asked Nanami. "Over the warring states?"

"Quite literally. Unlike the Kyotoryu, who as you know swore its allegiance to the Tetsubi, Kiki Shikizaki swore fealty to no state or house. He allowed his swords to infiltrate the various powers. All told, they landed in twenty-five different states—a thousand swords."

"Wait, a thousand?" asked Shichika.

"Just a thousand?" questioned Nanami.

The siblings clashed heads. They looked each other in the eye.

"I guess it's not that many," Shichika gave in.

Their dynamic was clear.

[42] 因縁 IN'NEN a fated bond
[43] 露とも TSUYU TOMO "not a dewdrop"
[44] 刀工 TŌKŌ swordsmith (emphasis on production, manufacturing)
[45] 刀匠 TŌSHŌ swordsmith (emphasis on skill, mastery)

"A thousand swords across twenty-five states," Nanami said. "Did each have forty?"

"No, each had a different number. In fact, that was the problem. Trust me, if I showed you a map, you would see how brutal the imbalance was—*the states with the swords were the states with the power. The more Shikizaki blades a state possessed, the greater their dominance in battle.*"

"Isn't it the opposite?" asked Nanami, somewhat tentatively. "As in, *The better the state fought its battles, the greater it became,* the more Shikizaki blades they were able to collect?"

"No doubt, that's the historical reality," Togame agreed, "but the illusion I described was no less a reality. *Those who possessed Shikizaki's swords held the power.* The only ones free from this illusion were the Tetsubi, who retained the Kyotoryu. Maybe that was why your father never told you about Kiki Shikizaki—"

Out of his pride for the Kyotoryu.

Could that be?

Shichika wanted to interrupt and say his father wasn't like that, but kept quiet. Not because it was a pain, but because he was starting to get just a little curious about this Kiki Shikizaki character. He didn't want to change the subject.

This swordsmith truly was the opposite of the Kyotoryu.

The swordsman who forsook his sword.

Against.

The thousand blades that reigned over the warring states.

"There is an emblematic episode. Were you aware that, at the close of the war, well before today's Owari[46] Bakufu was established, one man unified the nation, albeit only for a short time?"

"Yep."

"Ha, even you know that much—wait, you do?!"

"Yeah."

"Unreal."

Togame didn't like this.

Fool me three times?

She was pissed.

"Where was it," muttered Shichika. "Oh yeah. Tosa in Shikoku. They joined forces with the other domains on the island—Awa, Sanuki, and Iyo—and planned to reign over the nation from Shikoku. They called him the Old Shogun, right?"

He couldn't claim to know much more. Their father had tried to provide them with a proper education, a part of which was history, but Shichika remembered only isolated facts.

[46] 尾張 OWARI homophone with 終わり OWARI "The End"
a genuine historical domain headquartered in present-day Nagoya

The Old Shogun.

The daimyo responsible for putting an end to two hundred and fifty years of war. But by the time he had seized power and unified the nation, he was old, without an heir, and unable to control what would happen to the nation he had unified. Though he may have been shogun, he had no family to succeed him. Nevertheless, the Old Shogun was a mighty force, and the Owari Bakufu had merely picked up where he left off—or that's what Mutsue had taught.

"Did the Old Shogun have swords from Shikizaki too?" asked Nanami. "Based on what you've said, he must have owned more Shikizaki swords than anyone."

"True," affirmed Togame. "When he overtook the nation, the Old Shogun possessed five hundred and seven Shikizaki blades—a majority of them. With that many, it would have been stranger if he had failed to rule the land. Given the...illusion we discussed."

"A majority—sounds obsessed with collecting. Like some kid."

"He was insatiable. But this is how he seized the throne so swiftly. Listen—I had planned to touch upon this later, but now is actually perfect. In the short time the Old Shogun was in power, his government barely had a chance to govern—with one important exception. And I don't mean important to me. Important to history. Do you know what it was?"

"Nope."

"Oh, um..."

Togame was wary of a fourth back and forth with Shichika. Now she didn't know what to say. Things were not proceeding as planned.

"From what you've said so far, you must mean the Sword Hunt," Nanami chimed in, more than accustomed to her brother's curtness.

"The Great Sword Hunt,"[47] she elaborated. "Among the most ignoble acts of legislation in our nation's history—some say, it was the reason that the Old Shogun's bloodline did not rule after him."

"Oh yeah," said Shichika. "I remember now."

He wasn't simply faking after having heard the answer. He actually did remember. He must have learned about it from his father. The Great Sword Hunt—a stupid law requiring every person in Japan, without exception, to hand over their blades, supposedly to amass enough metal to cast a giant buddha.

"But that was just a front, right? Weren't they really hunting swordsmen? The way I remember it, the Old Shogun was trying to smoke out all the warriors and rid their kind from Japan. They may as well have called it what it was: a swordsman hunt."

"That motive was there, to be sure," said Togame. "The Old Shogun start-

[47] 刀狩令 KATANAGARI REI federal seizure of civilian swords for governmental use occurred several times in Japanese history; this simulacrum represents Sword Hunt at its worst

ed from the bottom as a foot soldier, brandishing a single sword, but he made it to the top. He knew as well as anyone how far and fast a swordsman could climb. He must have deemed *the world had room for no swordsman but himself.* But what you termed a front was no lie, either. On Mt. Sayabashiri in Tosa, on the grounds of Seiryoin Gokenji Temple, a statue of Gautama, known affectionately as Katana Buddha, was cast from melted swords collected in the hunt. Today, Mt. Sayabashiri is renowned as a tourist destination, especially among swordsmen, who view it as a holy site and journey there as pilgrims."

Togame shot Nanami a sidelong glance, no doubt to see if the sister guessed what was coming. It seemed that she had caught the gist.

"But *neither the surface nor the underlying reason was the truth of the story,* right?" Nanami picked up the thread. *"He just wanted to collect all of the Shikizaki swords."*

"Precisely!" Togame slapped her knee with the satisfaction of a storyteller. "The Old Shogun was trying to collect all thousand Shikizaki swords. After relieving the daimyos of their portions, he scoured the land for every sword that had landed in private hands—this was the true purpose of the hunt. He was convinced the Shikizaki blades were the reason he'd been able to claim power—an illusion? Perhaps. A delusion? Maybe so. But he was a believer. Those swords were his *true purpose,* and their truth was sacrosanct. Which was all the more reason for him to seek out the remaining four hundred and ninety-three. To clad his regime in steel."

"Stupid law." Shichika was fed up. "Some guys can handle power, and some guys can't. It would've made more sense if he were actually trying to hunt swordsmen."

"In a sense," Togame said. "But in the three years before the hunt was curtailed, the Old Shogun came nowhere near eradicating all the warriors,[48] although he did deliver on his buddha, and amass well over a hundred thousand swords."

"Hundred thousand—that's all?"

"Hundred thousand—that's a lot!"

Here we go again.

Shichika and Nanami locked horns.

You know who gave in.

"I'll admit that hoarding a hundred thousand swords to find five hundred may have been overkill," Togame agreed, "but by and large, what they found was nothing special. Run of the mill. Nevertheless, they managed to collect the vast majority of the Shikizaki blades. Most were already in the hands of the daimyos, who by then were sitting ducks, but it took no small amount of strategy to track down the hermit swordsmen who held the others."

48 武士 BUSHI samurai

"Vast majority? You mean they didn't get them all?"

"Not all of them. They found another four hundred and eighty-one. In the end, the Old Shogun possessed a grand total of nine hundred and eighty-eight Shikizaki blades."

"Wait, what? How come they ended the Great Sword Hunt after three years, before they found them all? Oh, I get it. The rest must have been busted in the war."

"Wrong—the Old Shogun gave up."

"Why?"

What would make the ruler of a country give up?

"Flawed as the Great Sword Hunt may have been, it was the law of the land. They managed to trace the whereabouts of all one thousand swords. But for some, only the whereabouts."

"But if they knew where they were, they should have grabbed them. We call him the Old Shogun now, but back then, he was the Shogun. So what was he afraid of? Even if the swords had rightful owners, he had the power, and might was right—right?"

"If he were only so lucky.[49] Remember, Shikizaki didn't create normal weapons—frankly, I'm not even sure it's accurate to call *those things* katana. They were forged under the premise that ***people don't use swords—swords make them who they are***. Some call his swords the Mutant Blades,[50] which I think is closer to the point."

"The most heretical of heretics," said Nanami.

"Exactly. And the twelve remaining swords were the most peculiar of the lot. Some today maintain that the nine hundred and eighty-eight swords the Old Shogun managed to collect were ***merely prototypes for the remaining twelve***."

"Made a thousand...just for twelve?"

"Even loopier than hoarding a hundred thousand for five hundred," sneered Togame.

She pulled a folded piece of paper from her kimono.

It bore the following markings in red ink:

Zetto the Leveler
Zanto the Razor
Sento the Legion
Hakuto the Whisper
Zokuto the Armor
Soto the Twin
Akuto the Eel

49 問屋が卸さない TONYA GA OROSANAI "can't buy that wholesale" no such luck
50 変体刀 HENTAITŌ "Odd Body Katana" vs. 変態 HENTAI pervert

Bito the Sundial
Oto the Cured
Seito the Garland
Dokuto the Basilisk
Ento the Bead

Nanami was the first to offer her opinion.

"That's a funny bunch of names. Are these swords famous?"

"Less so than you might think. But their power is more awful than the most legendary enchanted blade.[51] Allow me to put things in perspective. Take, for example, this fifth one on the list."

Zokuto the Armor.

"This sword was located shortly after the Old Shogun launched the Great Sword Hunt—at the time, it was being held by the captain of a band of pirates marauding the Inland Sea. When the pirates proved resistant to negotiation and unprepared to bow to his authority, the Shogun issued a new law dubbed the Pirate Ban.[52] Ostensibly intent on maintaining the peace, the handy pretext aimed to help them seize the Shikizaki blades and drub the pirates in one go."

"A lot of work for a single sword."

"Indeed. And that was only the beginning. The Pirate Ban was one of the more orthodox decrees. Nevertheless—it was a failure. That one sword managed to defeat every last bruiser in the Shogun's army."

"You mean it beat them?"

"Creamed them. But don't expect to read that in any history book—that was the Old Shogun's first encounter with the horrors of the Twelve Possessed, Shikizaki's masterpieces. And over the ensuing three years, *he met the same fate twelve times over.*"

"..."

Silence reigned over the scene. The madness[53] that Togame told of wasn't lost on the two siblings, however sheltered and unworldly they were—and yet.

"Being so powerful may have allowed them to collect so many Shikizaki blades—and yet, from the sound of it, that might be a blithe interpretation."

"I'm not sure if the same goes for Kyotoryu, but most schools have a saying: 'A sword will choose its owner.' The sense is usually positive, though not always. It may sound close to Shikizaki's line about how 'People don't use swords—swords make them who they are,' but it's a world apart... We know each sword was brandished by an individual of uncommon skill. Turning this around, we could say these individuals *only came to possess the swords*

51 名刀妖刀 MEITŌ YŌTŌ swords renowned for magical abilities
52 海賊取締令 KAIZOKU TORISHIMARI REI real law enacted in 1588 by Hideyoshi Toyotomi
53 荒唐無稽 KŌTŌMUKEI absurdity and nonsense

because their skill was so exemplary. That goes for the pirate, too. But I'm afraid that leaves much unexplained."

Togame paused. "There's that illusion again. No—more than an illusion."

"And more than a delusion?"

"I'm not saying every word of this is true."

"So that's why they're legendary, enchanted swords..."

"That is why they are more—Nanami, you said the reason for the Old Shogun losing power was the fallout of the Great Sword Hunt, but the deciding factor was unquestionably these twelve defeats, lost as they may be to history. The Old Shogun was in no position to appoint a successor from outside his bloodline. In the end, his fiefdom was worth no more than fifty thousand koku[54] of rice."

"I had no idea. That's nothing like what I've heard."

"Reality is not for civilians, and history is writ by the victorious. Why would the winning side sully their journal with details they'd rather forget?"

With an air of finality, Togame folded up the piece of paper and drank the cup of steaming water Nanami had offered her. Instead of stowing the piece of paper at her breast, however, she passed it to Shichika.

"Which brings us back to why I am here today on your island, Shichika Yasuri, Master of the Kyotoryu. I need your help retrieving the Twelve Possessed of Kiki Shikizaki—I have come here to enlist you."

"..."

Silence. Thick enough to slice.

Shichika was not so socially inept to refuse her outright—though Togame, after so many surprises, had likely braced herself for such a disappointment—in actuality, he was slow to answer half because Togame's words had captured his imagination, and half because her account was too grand for his brains to comprehend.

He turned to Nanami for help. *When in doubt, ask sis.* But Nanami—had closed her eyes. It appeared that she was brooding over Togame's words. Heavily—she sighed.

"Is this what you meant by desire the world?"

She opened her eyes. Glaring at Togame, who appeared to wince. The Schemer caught herself, but before she could respond, Nanami continued.

"Maybe things were different during the Age of Warring States, but at this point, those twelve swords would never be enough to take over the country. It doesn't matter whether your story is a fantasy, or a delusion, or the truth—or anything else. The current bakufu is secure. Even during the Rebellion, they had enough power to—"

"Enough power—exactly." Togame welcomed the assist. "The nine hundred and eighty-eight swords reclaimed by the Old Shogun are now in the

[54] 石 KOKU one koku = ten cubic shaku, enough rice for one person to eat for one year. Fifty thousand koku is barely high enough to qualify its owner as a daimyo.

possession of the present bakufu. Supposing the illusion is a reality, it may be *precisely why* the bakufu is secure."

"But in that case, what made the Old Shogun fall from grace?"

"Fall is a strong word. He simply lacked a successor—though a shogun without one sounds like some fairy tale. Anyway, Nanami, you're basically correct. In these times of peace and order,[55] discovering the twelve lost swords would matter little. When I asked if Shichika desired the world, that was a rhetorical question and merely a way of launching my explanation of the Shikizaki blades. It's not like the world's mine to offer."

"Okay."

Okay—but was it?

Shichika saw no use keeping up if even simple questions had no answer.

And yet.

"While I can't believe you'd never heard about the Shikizaki blades, that's not what I came here to say—"

"Wait a second, do you work for the bakufu?"

Bullseye. The way he said it cut through the conversation.

"I guess you could be working for one of their enemies—if they weren't wiped out in the Rebellion. Not likely, huh?"

"I would have preferred not to tell you just yet."

Togame was flustered. Shichika had ruined her story. And still she sat there, looking silly, holding out the folded piece of paper, playbill of the Twelve Possessed—for him to take.

"You're right—but how'd you figure me out?"

"I didn't. It's not like I gave it any real thought. But you seem to know things, inside out—like about what's his face the swordsmith, and even the Kyotoryu. That line about enlisting me didn't help. I got to wondering if you wanted these twelve swords *to give the bakufu an even thousand*."

"You didn't think a whitehaired lady in a crazy outfit couldn't possibly be working for the government?"

"Huh? No. Why?"

"..."

There's no running from stray fire.

Togame should have known, but she glared unpleasantly at Shichika.

"No matter... For your information, this is not a costume...but I guess the truth is out. Allow me to introduce myself formally. I am Togame the Schemer, Grand Commander of Arms of the Yanari Shogunate Military Directorate, Owari Bakufu."

"Grand Commander of Arms, you say."

Having gathered that Togame was not some nobody, Nanami must have been waiting for the other boot to drop. Perhaps she even guessed a moment

[55] 天下泰平 TENKA TAIHEI halcyon days

before her brother that Togame was affiliated with the shogunate. But their guest's official title was far longer than she could have imagined. She was stunned. Nanami wasn't one to show it, but the waver in her voice was hard to miss.

Meanwhile, Shichika was unfazed. He knew the shogunate was called by that name, but nothing about its structure, and had no idea how high up a Grand Commander was. It sounded important, to be sure, but he didn't know why. The concept of rank was beyond him.

Nanami would know.

"Hey, sis. So she doesn't command his legs?"

"Arms as in an army, Shichika. It's a directorate consisting entirely of strategists. Thanks to lessons learned during the Age of Warring States, it came into being concurrently with the current bakufu. In fact, during the Rebellion, Dad wielded the Kyotoryu under them."

"So...my dad worked for your dad, Togame?"

"..."

She was at a loss to answer. Better put, she was about to lose it.

"What'd I say?"

"Nothing. You're just so innocent, I could kill you. Let's make this clear. I didn't inherit my title from my father. The office of Grand Commander is nothing like the Kyotoryu. It isn't passed down.[56] Where I come from, ability is all that counts. If you have what it takes, the world can be yours—even if you're a woman or a child."

"Even if you can't swing a sword?"

"I use my head. As a Schemer, I take pride in my eschewal of armaments. My inability to wield a sword makes me a perfect arbiter of swordplay."

She spoke down to Shichika, not expecting a blockhead martial artist to understand, but what really puzzled him was her suggestion that any world where ability didn't count existed. Maybe he'd implied that she was some princess sitting on her daddy's fortune, but it wasn't worth getting riled up about. She was wrong to spout, "nothing like the Kyotoryu." And if she shooed armaments, why did she end up swinging a sword, he wanted to nitpick.

Parley as Shichika might with Togame, they seemed to be talking past each other.

"Much of our work happens behind the scenes, alongside the Onmitsu.[57] Though by now 'alongside' may be a bit misleading. Our organization probably won't be in future history textbooks. And it's not like we carry badges. You'll just have to trust that I'm not an imposter."

"I trust you," Shichika answered readily. "Your high-fluting attitude is proof enough."

Togame took an overly deep breath, trying to push through this affrontery,

56 世襲 SESHŪ to succeed the previous generation
57 隠密 ONMITSU ninja operatives active in Japan from the Nanboku era

but she seemed to reconsider and acknowledge that his trust was the best thing she could ask for.

She turned away from Shichika, toward his sister.

"And you, Nanami?"

"You've asked the Master of the Kyotoryu. If Shichika trusts you, I trust you. Now that I understand your affiliation and who you really are, most of what had been confusing me makes sense."

"I can see how that would clear things up. But I'm afraid from where I sit this is not the most advantageous of developments. If knowing that I work for the government causes you to hold back, I should not be so transparent."

"Why would we hold back?" asked Shichika.

The frankness of the question baffled Togame. "Because—"

"If it's about our father, don't worry," Nanami interjected. Her words were candid and unvarnished. "Our father taught us to come to terms with—his banishment. We harbor no ill will for the bakufu."

"That's reassuring."

"But really, go on. If you're working for the bakufu, they must have ordered you to find the twelve remaining swords—but why now? Other than allowing them to gloat over amassing all thousand of the Shikizaki blades, what good does it do? The Owari Bakufu has been in power over a hundred and fifty years—and in all that time, the only threat to their regime was the Rebellion. And it's over."

"The Rebellion isn't over. Not exactly. Yes, the Owari Bakufu has lasted for a hundred and fifty years—long enough for anyone who understood the meaning of the Age of Warring States to die away. These Shikizaki blades have become little more than talismans—but we'd do well to take another look. What if the ringleaders of the Rebellion had all been *wielders of the Possessed*?"

Nine hundred and eighty-eight swords—versus twelve. It was no match in numerical terms. But if it took nine hundred and eighty-eight experiments to attain the twelve—

"In retrospect, it would be an open question whether they could have been crushed by force. The Old Shogun was powerless against the Twelve Possessed—and remember, he was on the offense. His foes did nothing more than respond in kind. Imagine what would have happened, how far he would have fallen, if they paid him back and then some."

"We're talking a hundred fifty years ago. The swords must have changed hands by now."

"Certainly, but the owners are none of our concern. These swords, as Kiki Shikizaki made them, do the owning. And if the Possessed have found new homes, that's not exactly bad news for the bakufu. We live in a peaceful world. There's no way the dozen who have them now could be as tough as those stalwarts."

"Are you saying the bakufu is scared of another Rebellion?" asked Shichika. He was thinking—indisposed to thinking as his brains may be.

It seemed to him the bakufu, or at least its upper ranks, had taken the Rebellion as a cue to round up the remaining Shikizaki blades before someone beat them to it. If the Old Shogun really had failed twelve times standing, he could see where they were coming from. What if the twelve swords, each so menacing alone, were used in concert, in the spirit of the late Rebellion? That would terrorize the bakufu. Which made collecting the last swords a matter of national security.

But this reasoning left much to be desired. Their strategy must have another side. What if they ended up aggravating whoever owned the swords?

"That's where the Schemer comes in." Having read his mind, Togame spoke decisively. "Someone like me, who works behind the scenes."

"Um, I've been meaning to ask..." Nanami said. "What exactly does a Schemer...do? Is it some new rank the bakufu created in the last twenty years?"

"No. I made it up."[58]

Not a whiff of shame. Made up? She made it up?

"The Great Sword Hunt is history. At this point we need to proceed with the utmost caution. While I have my own opinions on the matter, I'm in no position to quibble over the particulars of an order from on high. If my liege charges me with gathering the Shikizaki blades, I'll set to work hatching a scheme."

"Hatch—"

"Just as a tactician deals in tactics, the Schemer deals in schemes—to the extreme. The most exceptional tasks are reserved for my most exceptional office." Togame struck a pose[59]—like she was on stage. "Which brings me to you, Master of the Kyotoryu. Let's join forces. As a Swordless Swordsman, you must be curious about how the other half lives—and about these Shikizaki blades and the ultimate dozen."

"I won't say no...but why me? Why the Kyotoryu? Earlier, I wondered if you might be an enemy of the bakufu because *who else would bother coming here*—right? So why are you here? You originally came for my father."

"Not necessarily. I knew, by now, your father would be at least two decades past his prime—too far along to head off on a wild sword chase. My plan, should he refuse, was to ask for his permission to borrow the son he raised here, on this island. Just for a while."

"Borrow..." growled Nanami. She wasn't happy.

Shichika could tell. This could be bad.

If this Togame lady was rubbing Shichika the wrong way, she might feel

58 自称 JISHŌ self-ordained
59 大見得 ŌMIE "big pose" moment in Kabuki when an actor postures for the audience

downright abrasive to Nanami. Perhaps the dynamic between the women only seemed different because they were both smart.

"If this son of his proved capable, that is."

"First of all," Shichika took the wheel before Togame could continue with her provocations. A rare moment of engagement from someone so averse to action. "You don't need any help—not from me or from my father's school—not if you're working for the bakufu. The Kyotoryu may be unrivaled in its strength, but it's also the school of a banished criminal. The bakufu has money. You can hire proper help."

"No. My help can't work for money. I tried that already, thank you very much. Or should I say, I followed standard policy, which is to contract work to ninjas."

"Ninjas?"[60]

"The Maniwa Clan, to be precise. But I suppose you haven't heard of them, either. For future reference, theirs is among the oldest orders, up there with the Iga and the Koga.[61] We've hired them for countless other jobs. Worked with them for years. But suddenly *they stab us in the back*."

What was Togame saying? Stabbed in the back—by ninjas? This was not the world Shichika knew. The clans were known for their unflagging allegiance. You would sooner find the sea gone dry than suffer their betrayal.

"Why did they do it?"

"Why wouldn't they? A single Shikizaki blade is worth more than the finest piece of art. Enough to buy a country.[62] Anyone who works for money will stab your back for money." Togame cast her eyes upon the piece of paper sitting on the floor. "Once they had Zetto the Leveler[63] in their grasp, they made off like bandits. And I don't mean the ninja that we hired. I mean the whole Maniwa Clan."

"The whole..."

"*The entire clan went rogue*. And thanks to them, all ninjas have lost the better graces of the bakufu. Almost makes me sorry for their brethren, the Onmitsu, humiliated by association."

"Oh, those guys. Right... But if the ninjas betrayed you, the unthinkable came true. That sucks. You have a point about money, though. Makes sense. How about honor? You need someone who works for pride, whom money can't buy. Honor makes a swordsman. That's what my dad always said."

"Swordsmen are useless to me. The Shikizaki blades—poison them."

"Really?"

"Trust me, samurai were the obvious next choice. I found some good ones, too. And from the strongest and most loyal warriors, I cherry-picked

60 忍者 NINJA "those who hide/endure"

61 伊賀 甲賀 IGA KŌGA two legendary ninja enclaves, based in present-day Mie and Shiga, respectively

62 国 KUNI either province or nation, like the English word "state"

63 絶刀 鉋 ZETTŌ KANNA "The Absolute Katana: Plane" (as in the carpentry tool)

one swordsman. A fine young buck of barely twenty named Hakuhei Sabi."

"Sabi?[64] Sounds weak to me. And twenty? That's even younger than me."

"I take your point. But his skill was genuine. He was an incomparable artist with a sword. By now, a hundred fifty years after the Great Sword Hunt, there are only six swords, including the Leveler, whose whereabouts and owner are both known. But on his first day, Sabi tracked down the most evasive sword among them, Hakuto the Whisper."

"Go, Sabi, go."

"But once he had it in his grasp, he disappeared."

"Whoa, Sabi."

"Like I said. It poisoned him. To a man who works for honor, the honor of possessing a Shikizaki sword was irresistible. Since most of the bakufu's upper ranks got their start as swordsmen, however, the profession didn't lose credibility as a whole. Nay, it is I, Togame, who lost their trust."

Which made perfect sense. Her lofty bearing made it hard to see, but she had failed outright, and twice. Adding insult to injury, both times her hired hands absconded with the swords. To put it cynically, she had done nothing but place the swords in stronger hands.

It only takes three strikes.[65] The third time's the charm, they also say.

In other words—it was the Schemer's last chance.

"And now you want the Kyotoryu to save you," Nanami said. "You need *a swordsman who isn't after money—a swordsman with no use for a sword.* And no one else is qualified."

"Precisely. The blades will not poison the Master of the Kyotoryu. And honestly, I don't have time to wait—for all we know, the Maniwa and Sabi have set their sights on the remainder of the Twelve Possessed. That is the kind of men they are. Having turned traitor, they are now formidable foes, and they must be defeated. Shichika Yasuri, Master of the Kyotoryu—only you boast the skills to allow the Owari Bakufu to last a millennium. Will you fight for me?"

As if to try again—she picked up and offered him the folded piece of paper. Looked him in the eye. Nothing left to say.

"I get it."

But Shichika would not accept the piece of paper.

Much as it seemed he had no other option.

"Listen. You've made it clear why you need the Kyotoryu, but that doesn't explain why I need to find these swords for you. You're right that I don't care about money, and I need a sword like I need a thorn in my side, but frankly I couldn't give a crap about the bakufu. I ain't no samurai. I don't consider it an honor to take orders from the government."

"..."

64 錆 SABI rust

65 仏の顔も三度 HOTOKE NO KAO MO SANDO "to test the patience of a buddha"

"Like sis said, we're not sore about what happened to Dad. Twenty years ago, when we were little kids, we blamed noble folk like you, but now it's just a pain, nothing more—because here's the thing. I've come to like living on the island. I'm not in any mood to sail over to the mainland and play[66] samurai."

"You're scared."

"Sure I'm scared..." Togame had tried to strike a nerve, but Shichika was not about to disagree. "Mostly, though, it's a pain in the butt."

"Shichika—"

"Come on, Nanami. You feel the same."

Her interruption cut off, Nanami fell silent. Seeing this, Shichika faced back toward Togame and went on.

"I'm curious about this Shikizaki character. Making all these fancy swords. From what you say, it's the complete opposite of my school. But I'm not curious enough to hop into a boat. And if he was born around the same time as our founder, he must have died ages ago. Sorry you had to come all the way out here. But don't worry. You'll find someone. Thanks for the story. Would have been even better as a bedtime story. Too bad it's so early."

"You're unbelievable."

Faced with Shichika Yasuri's curt refusal, Togame couldn't help but smile. She had him. In the palm of her hand. They may have strayed off-topic, even zigged and zagged, but she had led him down the route, as planned, and had him where she wanted him. Her smile said it all.

"You think that's all I got? Please. I knew you'd say that. Word for word. After being burned twice, by those ninjas and that samurai, can you seriously see me—the Schemer—coming all the way out to this island without a surefire way of winning you over?"

Her voice was sticky with insinuation. Shichika looked puzzled.

"You think you have something? To make me move. Some reason I should help collect those twelve swords..."

"Yep." You bet she did. "I can't trust people who work for money, and I can't trust people who work for honor. Beyond that, there's only one thing anyone would work for—love."

"L-Love?"

"I can trust a man who works for love."

He had a decent body.

Handsome enough.

Maybe not so bright, but he would do.

"Shichika Yasuri. Go ahead and fall for me."

[66] ちゃんばら CHANBARA sound of clashing swords

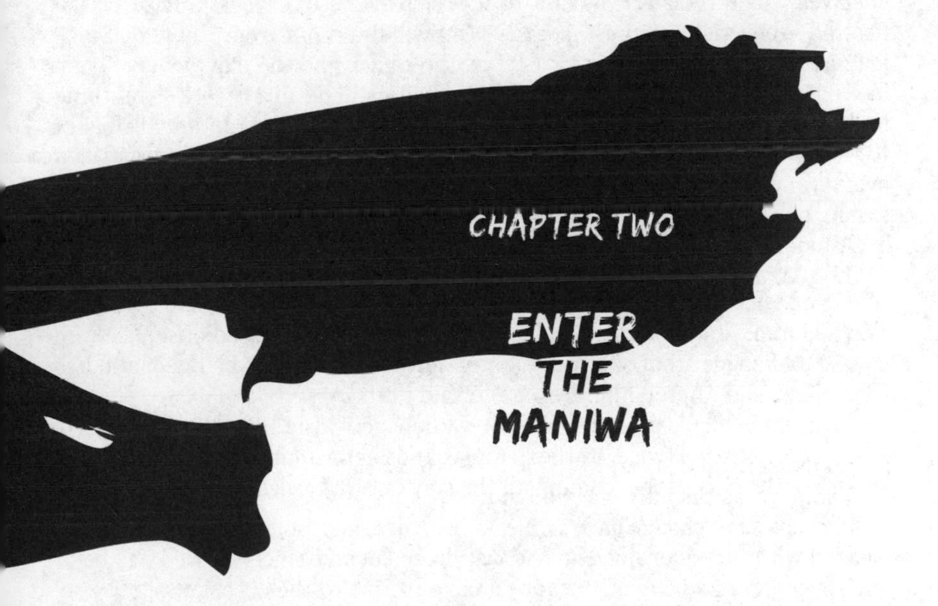

CHAPTER TWO

ENTER THE MANIWA

■ ■

Who were the Maniwa[1] Ninjas?

Unlike with all the schools of swordplay, it would behoove us, from the get-go, to let off trying to enumerate the exact number of "official" ninja enclaves, since their art, by dint of its reclusiveness, evades precise classification—but make no mistake, the Maniwa stand out from the rest. Since long before the Age of Warring States, the ninjas and the daimyo have been inextricable—not only in battle, but in politics. The dirty work—anything too vile for the public eye—was left to ninjas. While the Mutant Blades of Kiki Shikizaki reigned over the Age of Warring States, the ninja stars rained over every era. The operatives played a multitude of roles, from spy to assassin, but the Maniwa, *matchless murderers*, were the most gruesome clan.

A hidden enclave[2] specializing in assassinations.

The Maniwa Ninjas.

■ ■

It happened in an instant.

Nanami was the only one who moved.

Perhaps this should have come as no surprise. Togame, so thoroughly pleased with the killer line she had just dropped, and Shichika, who had been left speechless and stupefied, were unable to rise to the occasion.

Rising to her knees without warning, Nanami thrust her flattened hands at the shoulder of each. Though it was a light strike, Togame and Shichika, who had been facing each other, tipped sideways, losing their balance—or rather tucked their legs to catch it.

That very moment, the wall, or perhaps more aptly the boards, the wooden slats that gave the hut its shape—in any case thick enough to ward off the heat and the cold.

It *went flying*.

Inward.

As if imploding.

"Wh...aat?!"

Reacting a heartbeat later than his sister—the young and battle-ready

[1] 真庭 MANIWA "True Garden" actual city in Okayama
[2] 里 SATO small town; ninja settlement

Master of the Kyotoryu screamed and grabbed Togame in all her finery around the waist—and swept her across the room. Nanami flew behind them, as if sucked into the action—

All this, in an instant.

Splinters from the blasted wood stabbed into the wall across the room—shredded wood mixed up with metal—and not scraps of iron, but a gale of blades! Spinning shuriken[3] and soaring kunai[4]—all told, forty-five.

All forty-five projectiles blew through the wood at once—as if the boards were only paper doors—and planted deep into the other wall! Though none shot all the way through it too, each blade had sunken to the tang. If Nanami had not poked their shoulders, Shichika and Togame would have been honeycombed by this fusillade of cutlery.

This was no target practice.

Nor sniping.

It was a surprise—bombardment.

"...ard."

Shichika sprang up.

His face anything but carefree.

"You bastard! You screwed with the house my dad built!"

Roaring at the artillery strike, Shichika dashed out of the hut, or what was left of it, jumping straight through the blown-out wall rather than the door.

"Shichika!"

By the time Nanami called his name, he was already out of sight, out of the hut and up the mountainside. Chasing the knave[5] who had showered them with knives. She knew what he was thinking—*mess with me and you get messed!*—that simple. She let out a heavy sigh.

"Sometimes he doesn't get it..."

"No, he's got it right," Togame said. Shichika had shielded her but also flung her into the entryway when he bolted. She rubbed her shoulder. "If we held our ground, there's high chance he'd only strike again. In that case we'd be worse off than the wall. There's only one way to answer to a missile[6]: fast. I'm impressed... Seems your brother has a sense for battle."

"He's just acting instinctively..."

"Seems that way. No strategy in that. Running off without his sandals was not the brightest move."

"I'm not so sure. To him, sandals[7] and arm guards[8] are like sheaths. He has no use for them in battle... Uh, I suppose this breeze feels nice."

3 手裏剣 SHURIKEN "palm-of-the-hand swords"
4 苦無 KUNAI metal dibbers weaponized as throwing knives
5 曲者 KUSE MONO ruffian
6 飛び道具 TOBIDŌGU projectile weapons
7 草鞋 WARAJI handmade straw sandals
8 手っ甲 TEKKŌ cloth armoring the wrists and the backs of the hands

"It was the Maniwa. I'm sure of it."

Pensively uttering the name of the ninja clan, Togame tugged free one of the shuriken embedded in the wall and perused its features. Sure enough, the star was of the very shape the Maniwa preferred. This flagrant indiscretion suggested they weren't trying to hide—and maybe even wanted to be seen.

"Ah."

Nanami nodded. She didn't seem particularly rattled.

After all, when shuriken start flying, ninjas aren't much of a surprise. And they had only just discussed the Maniwa. The thought of them was fresh.

"How many of them?"

"One, I suspect."

Togame's reply was all the more ludicrous for its casual delivery. What's more, her tone was certain. *One?* Nanami had not seen this coming. She was baffled.

"The Maniwa stay out of each other's way—*those guys work better alone*."

"But how—"

Nanami turned from the shuriken lodged into the wall to the gaping hole where the other wall had been. No point in even asking. A squad of forty-five ninjas, each throwing their own star, would have been infinitely preferable to *one ninja throwing forty-five in unison*.

"How could they know I was here, though? They couldn't have followed[9] me. I didn't tell a soul where I was going..."

"Miss Togame," Nanami caught her mid-thought. "About what you asked Shichika. You have my blessing."

Her voice was weak, and her bearing weaker still, but her eyes bespoke conviction.

After the embarrassment of weaponry, Togame was perplexed to hear Nanami revive the conversation. What surprised her even more was what Nanami said.

"I was certain you would be against it."

"I can see why...but frankly, I couldn't care less about your story. Like my brother, I don't care about money, or about honor, or the government, or Shikizaki's swords. Not to brag,[10] since I can hardly claim to have taken vows,[11] but at this stage of my life, I have no interest in the world outside. Shichika sees something in the Shikizaki challenge—and he's the master of the school."

"..."

"I want him to go out into the world, whatever the reason. He and I have spent the last two decades on this island. After watching him train for so

[9] 尾行 BIKŌ "to chase somebody's tail"
[10] 口幅ったい KUCHI HABATTAI "wide-mouthed"
[11] 出家 SHUKKE "leave home" become a monk/nun vs. 在家 ZAIKE lay believer

long, perfecting one move after another, I can't bear the thought of his skill going to waste."

"Forgive me, but wasn't it your father, Mutsue—the previous master—who was exiled? Now that Mutsue has passed away—"

"My body isn't strong enough to last outside. When I told you that I had no interest in the world—I meant it, but there's more to it. I fear the air on the mainland would be too rich for me. And my brother—worries about me."

By now Nanami's weak constitution must have been apparent to Togame. The sister was fragile—even brittle.

"It's none of his business," Nanami asserted. "I'm done being coddled by my little brother—and have no interest in chaining him in place. What matters most to me, Togame, is for the Kyotoryu to go back into the world, where it belongs. With your rank in the bakufu, surely you can handle that?"

She wasn't so much asking as confirming.

Togame nodded urgently.

"Of course I can—I never thought it sensible for a Hero of the Rebellion to be shut up in a place like this. If your father were alive, and amenable... I would see to it that his honor was restored."

"I see," Nanami responded with some nuance to the claim. "Then how can I stand in your way?"

She stood up straight and bowed. "He managed to silence me earlier, but I'll speak to him. Take good care of him, Miss Togame."

"Let me warn you, the road will not be easy. No matter who takes care of him, he may never come home. I almost wish you'd not make such a request of me. He would be taking on the Maniwa Clan, needless to say, and also Hakuhei Sabi—and who knows whose grubby hands have made it to the six swords we don't have any lead on. Could be monsters. Demons. Serpents..."

Nanami lifted her face again and spoke.

"If you're unsure about the true power of the Kyotoryu, why not go see it in action?" For Nanami, always so marmoreal[12] in her speech, this was uncharacteristically bold. "Assuming you're correct and there is just one ninja, I'm sure Shichika has *guided* him down to the beach below. Go see for yourself—*if you can make it there before he's through*."

"Are you sure? Up against the Maniwa?"

"The Kyotoryu would never succumb to a mere ninja."

She sounded certain.

When Nanami had spurred the conversation, Togame felt puzzled—but now she saw Nanami's great faith in the power of her brother and his school.

The sister smiled.

It was—an evil smile.

"Bless your heart, Miss Togame. I can tell you're really looking out for

12 冷然 REIZEN frigid echoes 霊前 REIZEN, the space before a tombstone

Shichika. With you, he'll be in good hands, request or no."

"What?"

Togame went red.

It seemed as though she couldn't take a compliment.

Though it was not so much a compliment as a jab.

"W-W-W-W-W-Wait. We need to focus. Why is this ninja here?!"

"Sure..." Nanami giggled. "I'm focusing."

She sounded pretty evil.

Maybe she was evil.

"Miss Togame, are you sure that no one followed you? We're dealing with ninjas here. Stalking[13] is what they do."

"Thanks for the insight. I'll have you know I factored ninjas into my scheme, taking the utmost precautions to hide my tracks. That's why I told nobody where I was heading. We face numerous adversaries apart from the Maniwa and Sabi. I am perplexed as to how—"

"Miss Togame? Just one thing. Did you come to our island alone?"

"Huh?" Togame shook her head. "What do you think? The Maniwa aren't the only ones who fly solo—so do the strategists of the Directorate, and the Grand Commander is no exception. In any case, we'd want as few mouths flapping about this mission as possible."

"Okay. So how'd you get here?"

"How else do you get to an island? A boat," Togame gave the same answer she'd given Shichika—though with a moment's hesitation.

Of course. A boat.

How could she even ask? The rube.

But Nanami saw no reason to be flustered. She wasn't finished.

"Did you paddle here yourself?"

"Myself? Don't be silly. I'm a thinker. Cogitation is my forte. Do I look like I could scull over from—wait."

"By any chance—did a boatman bring you?"

"Uh, yes...no, but—"

That was it.

The boatman.

Just one more soul, turning the oars, ferrying Togame from the Shinso coast to this island—she'd told the man to sit tight, at the spot where they made ground, to keep the boat from drifting off.

"The boatman! But if it's the boatman..." With a gasp, Togame's hot face lost its blood. "He has a Shikizaki sword!"

13 忍ぶ者 SHINOBU MONO alternate reading emphasizes the literal sense of 忍者 NINJA

■ ■

For Shichika Yasuri, Haphazard Island was his backyard—though such a domesticated turn of phrase falls short of the truth. He could envision every precipice and dell, every leaf on every tree within its ten-mile circumference. He instantly intuited where the shuriken-spamming knave had fled and could pursue him with his eyes shut. Though it was really Togame who was blind.

Ninja or otherwise, no one could outmaneuver Shichika on this terrain. Amidst the chase, his quarry seemed to accept this.

Jumping from tree to tree.

Descending the mountain.

To the sandy beach—and the rote of the waves.

It was just as Nanami had predicted—although Shichika hadn't quite guided the ninja.

In the teachings of the Kyotoryu, a shuriken was not a sword. When Shichika saw the cross-shaped stars and kunai that had blown apart their hut, he hadn't the slightest clue who was behind it. He had never heard of shuriken and barely knew the first thing about ninjas. His father had once told him about the faithful soldiers who had your back no matter what, but Togame had upended that definition. The Maniwa didn't so much as cross his mind.

Which is why—

Down on the beach, watching this clown step from the shadows of the mountain[14] and out into the sun, he didn't recognize his ninja garb for what it was.

But that wasn't Shichika's fault. This ninja had a style all his own. Sleeves shredded at the shoulders, body bedizened with chains. Far from a stalker—he made you look.

He didn't even wear a mask.

Spiked hair pointed to the sky.

Seeing Shichika leap from the woods, the ninja welcomed him with a grin that threatened to tear his cheeks from ear to ear.

"Hey, tell me, Kyotoryu. Did you chase me here? Or was it the other way around?"

"..."

Zum, Shichika landed face to face with his foe—and realized he hadn't considered his next move. He'd come this far coaxed by his anger at seeing his home violated, but—

What now?

It was sad. Apart from his father and his sister, and Togame whom he had just met, Shichika knew no other human beings. He was unsure of the right

[14] 山林 SANRIN montane forest

way to behave when you run into one.

The right way.

As if there were such a thing.

His home wasn't flattened; its posts were intact. The house had been made by hand, and with a little work, it could be fixed by hand. *Why did I lose my mind like that,* Shichika even began to wonder.

But that was it.

His father built that house—that was enough.

To make him yell.

His father.

Boy, he'd lost it.

What did sis think hearing me yell like that?

Needless to say, the ninja paid Shichika's disposition little mind. He struck a pose and gave his name.

A grand pose—especially for a ninja.

"I am Komori[15] Maniwa, one of the Twelve Bosses of the Maniwa Ninja. Take heed, Kyotoryu. I bear no grudge against you, but I need to take your life."

His voice was shrill enough to turn your insides out.

A voice that couldn't possibly be issuing from a mouth.

"Maniwa? Oh, right. I heard about you."

"That was an error you will pay for with your life. If you hadn't, I might have let you go. I came, originally, to hear that woman's story."

The knave—the ninja—had more to say.

"Not much of a story. Barely worth my time, though I was surprised to hear she called on Hakuhei Sabi after we parted ways. She must have told him the same story she told you, which puts him next in line. For me to kill."

"Were you eavesdropping?"

"Yeah."

"That's in bad taste."

"You mean good. Kyahah!"

Komori's laugh was as shrill as his voice.

"Did you follow Togame here?"

"Why be so sneaky? We came together, in the same slow boat. I paddled, pumping like a seesaw the whole way—it was no joke. She sat on her derriere watching the sea and didn't lift a finger. I'm telling you, there's something wrong with her."

"Well, I'm being swamped by visitors[16] today."

Two didn't make a swamp, but Shichika said so anyway.

He'd always wanted to try out the expression.

"Kyahah, here's some more advice, Kyotoryu. Stop wasting your time

15 蝙蝠 KŌMORI "The Bat" as in the flying mammal

16 千客万来 SENKYAKU BANRAI "a thousand guests, ten thousand arrivals"

wondering how I got here. I'm here, baby. And there's something that you need to do."

"What would that be?"

"Don't be cute. Start begging for your life," Komori instructed with a callous grin. "How about, *I'll give you anything so please don't kill me!* I love that one. So much. Wow. And I reply, *I'll take your life and nothing else.*"

"..."

Were people this weird in general?

Shichika wasn't sure.

But one thing was clear: this man was scum.

He knew that much—instinctively.

"Hmm... How am I supposed to fight a ninja, though?" he wondered out loud. "As far as I can see, you carry no ninjato[17] either."

Huh?

Shichika had noticed something.

Not only did Komori Maniwa lack a ninja sword, he was totally unarmed. He could be packing weapons in his clothing, but it didn't look like it. What about the shuriken? Had he blown through his supply? No, the ninja must have more tricks up his sleeve—sleeveless as he was.

"Ninjato? Oh, right. You're the Swordless Swordsman. And for proper swordplay, I suppose there needs to be at least one sword. Kyahah, you're *that* kind of a swordsman."

"No—the Kyotoryu doesn't only work on swords. It isn't mutodori. I just never saw a ninja before."

"Don't talk back. Obedience is a virtue. Or perhaps your master skipped that lesson. But don't fret. I may not be a swordsman—*but that doesn't mean I can't use a sword.*" Komori let this sink in. "I hate to keep you waiting... I know I left that *precious sword* around here somewhere."

The ninja raised one of his chain-wrapped arms and *stuffed it in his mouth*. In any generation, there will always be some kid ready to show off how he can fit his whole fist in his mouth, but it would be mistaken to compare what Komori was doing with such shenanigans.[18] Down his throat went his *hand*, and after it his *wrist* and his *elbow*, even his *bicep*...his jawbone dislocated entirely. He was like a snake eating its own tail.

"What the hell? People can do that? I had no idea."

Shichika was stunned. They can't, of course.

Don't try this at home, kids.

"Geg gahfu hah fahra kago gah fuhrah, ge googoo ga gehgeh ga rah gongfah fugerah ga geh."

Komori felt the need to go on speaking, but it didn't amount to anything intelligible. He had reached down his throat as far as his shoulder—and now

[17] 忍者刀 NINJATŌ ninja sword

[18] 座興 ZAKYŌ parlor trick

he was backing the arm out, inch by inch.

Inch by slimy[19] inch.

At last his fist appeared—closed tight around the handle of a sword.

The grip of a katana.

Stymied by this grotesque carnival display, Shichika could only watch as the ninja pulled the handle from his throat, until finally the blade met air.

It was long. So long.

Far too long to fit in his torso.

Shichika had no idea how Komori had stuffed it in his body, but at least this solved one mystery.

This ninja didn't hide the tools of his trade on his person but—*in his body!*

He was a monster. No other word sufficed.

"Khak..."

The tip of the blade cleared Komori's lips.

He wielded the weapon, smugly.

The blade was slick with gastric juices and saliva, but there was no trace of blood. Fearsomely, he'd drawn the blade out of his body without so much as nicking himself. No rookie ninja move.

"Behold! Beware! Bear witness to Zetto the Leveler, one of the Twelve Possessed, the masterworks of Kiki Shikizaki."

For real?

What Shichiki needed to beware of was the guy's stomach.

"Care for a taste of hell? Kyahah! Coming right up. My friends call me Komori the Hell-Made because I'm so ready to dish it out. Now be entertained."

"Your nickname is Hell Maid?[20] It's not cool or scary. More like, I dunno. Cute, for some reason."

But why?

The reason would not be clear for centuries.

"Hey, Kyotoryu. Try making sense for once. And while you're at it, tell me what you think." He brandished the sword. "Look who has one of those Shikizaki blades the woman was blabbing on about."

"Hm..."

Despite being more interested in the ninja's stomach trick, Shichika eyed the blade.

It was altogether different from the sword Togame drew on the mountain.

First off, it had no curve.

Unlike most katana,[21] the blade was straight, forged in the kiriha zukuri[22] style.

It also lacked a handguard between the blade and grip.

19 ずるずる ZURU ZURU onomatopoeia for a sloppy mess

20 冥土の蝙蝠 MEIDO NO KŌMORI the synonym for hell is homophonous with "maid" (as in cosplay)

21 彎刀 WANTŌ curved blades in general

22 切刃造 KIRIHA ZUKURI straight blades with a chisel tip

Almost five feet[23] long.

Twin blood gutters[24] were engraved into the whorled face[25] of the blade.

This was one big sword.

"..."

"Come on, nothing? Speak up!"

"No, it's just—more like a sword than I expected. Like you were saying, Togame kept going on about these legendary enchanted swords. I thought it would be, you know, weirder. Not like I was expecting it to be covered in spit and mucus. Can't you keep that thing in a sheath?"

"This sucker is way too long to carry on the hip—and it doesn't need a sheath."

"Why not?"

"Kyahah! Shall I make an example out of you? But first, some good news—I've never killed somebody with this sword—but only because I just laid hands on it. Use that to your advantage, and you may beat me yet. Kyahah! Oh, how I love to entertain."

"Isn't that thing supposed to be valuable? You sure it's okay to walk around with it? I mean, shouldn't you keep it somewhere safe?"

"Other way around! I wouldn't let go of something this valuable. It stays inside me, wherever I go. Really, what place under the sun is safer than my belly?"

He had a point.

"This sword is something special. That woman spoke of poison, but no, it's the best medicine.[26] *Just having it makes me want to kill!*"

There was no more time for talking.

Without a running start, Komori leapt into the air, held the long sword high, and executed a swing aided by gravity.

"Side Splitter!"[27]

Komori was in the game.

Shichika didn't know much about how to interact with others, but this he understood.

In fact—it was the moment he'd been waiting for.

His first sparring partner in a year.

Except this wasn't sparring.

For the first time, Shichika Yasuri, Master of the Kyotoryu, was tasting battle.[28]

"Hmph!"

[23] 五尺 GOSHAKU five shaku = approx. five feet

[24] 二筋樋 NISUJIHI long grooves that lighten the mass of the blade

[25] 綾杉肌 AYASUGIHADA 綾杉 AYASUGI Japanese cedar 肌 HADA skin (bark)

[26] 百薬の長 HYAKUYAKU NO CHŌ "the leader among a hundred medicines"

[27] 報復絶刀 HŌFUKU ZETTŌ "payback from the Zetto"
pun on 抱腹絶倒 HŌFUKU ZETTŌ, to laugh so hard it hurts

[28] 実戦 JISSEN real fighting (vs. training)

He jumped backwards on his tiptoes and dodged Komori's opener. It mattered none that they were on the beach. There wasn't a single place on Haphazard Island that was unusual for Shichika. On the beach or in the mountains, there was no good or bad terrain.

The tip of the sword passed before his eyes.

A real sword.

If it cuts, you bleed.

After landing, Shichika ran backwards, putting five long strides between him and Komori before stopping and assuming a stance.

Legs saddled wide, hips low.

Left foot forward, toes pointed ahead.

Right foot back, toes pointed to the right.

Palms open, right hand high, left hand low.

Becoming a wall for his opponent.

"Kyotoryu Form One: the Suzuran."[29]

For a split second, Shichika had debated which move to use for his debut, but he settled for his most basic. He had maneuvers specifically for long swords, and for straight swords too, and from that garish opening attack, he gathered that Komori was no expert swordsman (he was a ninja, after all)—but picking the right move required thinking, and that was a pain in the butt.

Even in the heat of battle, everything was a pain to Shichika.

This also meant that he was calm.

The rattled nerves of his earlier outburst and frantic pursuit down the mountain were gone. In that sense, Komori's sideshow act of pulling a katana from his mouth worked in Shichika's favor—at least in that regard.

Kyotoryu Form One—the Suzuran.

Outside of the Kyotoryu, the world is not without its other ways of taking on a sword barehanded. If you adopt the proper method, you stand a chance. The most surefire method of all is "running away" (since the heavy sword slows down your enemy), but when that's not an option, "fighting while running" is the next best thing.

A katana is long.

That is its advantage.

It could reach him from a distance—all Shichika's attacks would fall short, but the Leveler was long enough to cut him where he stood. This was an immovable fact. If a fact couldn't be minimized, maximizing it was one way to go.

In other words, Shichika might *fight at a distance*. Evading the katana, he could nettle his enemy, trick him into leaping forward, and proceed to counterattack. A simple tactic, but simplicity truly is a virtue.

Except the Suzuran made this impossible. Legs firmly planted, all foot-

[29] 鈴蘭 SUZURAN "The Lily of the Valley" an erect, poisonous flower

work was out of the question. The stance permitted next to zero movement. It seemed to dare the enemy to move in for a hit.

"...Hmm."

In practice, it served only to encourage Komori's wariness. Standing where he landed after making his first move, he puzzled at Shichika's rigid pose. There had to be a reason to opt for such a stance against an armed opponent.

However callous this ninja seemed, he was a Maniwa—and no foil offered up on page one of the story[30] just to demonstrate the protagonist's prowess.

"How about this, Kyotoryu?"

Komori kicked the sand at his feet into a kind of smokescreen—but no, a smokescreen is for hiding. This was a sandstorm, blowing all the way to Shichika, to swarm his vision. Komori rushed through the cloud of sand—

And delivered one thrust after another.

"There! Side Splitter!"

A head-on assault.

Throwing all his weight.

While no swordsman, Komori knew this much—straight swords stab better than they slice.

But not this time.

"Kyotoryu—Kiku!"[31]

The tip of the blade never found Shichika. The smokescreen obstructed Komori's own vision, and he did not catch Shichika swiping his hand and clearing the air before his eyes. The Master of the Kyotoryu hadn't even blinked. Dodging a thrust bound for his abdomen, he swung his right foot in an arc and turned his left toes so that his left side faced his opponent.

The blade of the Leveler missed his bare back by a skin. He caught the sword near its grip in the crook of his left arm and, as if executing a pincer strike, shot out his right elbow against the tip—naturally, aiming for the flat of the blade in both instances.

Then, using his spine for a fulcrum.

He stilled the Leveler in midair.

"Gah—y-you!"

No matter how Komori thrusted or tugged, the Leveler wouldn't budge. His sneering face was finally betraying signs of panic. This ninja had only just learned of the Kyotoryu; and though he had granted Shichika some chance of winning, the power of this seizure throttled him.

Now would be the time for Shichika to strike back—if this were a different story. Komori seemed to think as much, until he saw the absurd look on his opponent's face.

As if he'd forgotten that he was in the middle of a battle, Shichika's eyes

[30] 物語 MONOGATARI tale, e.g. 源氏物語 The Tale of Genji

[31] 菊 KIKU "The Chrysanthemum" dense, uniformly colored blossom

were wide with fascination. His eyes darted from Komori to the steel of the Leveler. This simply stunned the ninja for a moment.

At almost the same time, both of them remembered they were fighting. Shichika released his grip on the Leveler and spun to face his enemy, who was within reach. Unbending the elbow he had whammed into the sword, he chopped with the blade of his hand.[32]

And when the ninja dodged his hand—Shichika answered with the blade of his foot.[33]

His heel just grazed the ninja's throat, but this, too, he evaded—yet clearly unaccustomed to handling the ponderous Leveler, Komori could only dodge the blows. He had barely room to squirm. Up this close, no sword was at its best, even one created by the legendary swordsmith Kiki Shikizaki.

The endless flurry of chops and kicks drove Komori mad.

"Mother of hell!" he groaned, dropping almost to the sand. Turning the katana sideways so he could hug it close and tumble backwards, he rolled a safe distance away from Shichika. A retreat he only could have managed on a beach—but the real surprise was seeing the side with a sword fleeing from the side without one.

Shichika neglected to close in.

If there was a time for closing in, this was it—but not for him.

Komori sprang up and raised the Leveler—but not for battle. He rested the flat of the blade on his shoulder as if it were a piece of luggage. No student of swordplay would ever be caught dead holding a sword this way.

The ninja was running out of breath.

He must have meant it about not having had the chance to feed the mythic sword a human life—the Leveler was not under his complete control.

Was the illusion just an illusion, after all?

Was an illusion not reality?

It was ludicrous to think that mere possession of a Shikizaki blade would make you stronger—

"I gotta hand it to you, Kyotoryu. I haven't seen a show like this in ages. First time since I became a Boss. I had my doubts about this swordless swordplay, but you wield your hands and feet as well as any blade. I can see why you would call yourself a swordsman. I'm impressed."

"That was nothing. You're the one who pulled a sword out of your mouth," Shichika put the fight on hold to offer his rejoinder.

Lest he let his guard down, he resumed the Suzuran.

"That Leveler's a bastard, too."

"Ah." Shichika's choice of words prickled Komori. "What did you see, boy?"

"See? Look, that last move—the Kiku—where I caught the sword against my back—*is not supposed to work that way.* It's used for catching a long

[32] 手刀 SHUTŌ "hand katana"
[33] 足刀 SOKUTŌ "foot katana"

sword, but the idea is to work your arms and elbows against your back to harness leverage—*and snap the blade in half.*"

Shichika acted out the strange ballet.

"But it didn't even bend. Did my training fail me?"

"..."

"That sword—is totally weird."

Komori sabered the air, as if showing off his favorite toy.

"Of course it is—as one of the mutant dozen. It would be far weirder if it weren't weird, although I can't claim to know anything beyond what that woman said. It wasn't long ago that I learned of this crazy old coot Shikizaki. But Zetto the Leveler was *made to be the hardest sword imaginable*. People love to talk about how katana never bend or break or lose their edge, but as a rule, swords are expendable. To use them is to abuse them. But not so with the Leveler. *It truly cannot break or bend, and thus can never lose its hard edge.*"

"No way..."

Could such a sword—exist?

"People say the curved blade is what makes a katana resist breakage, but check this puppy out—no curve, but no nicks, down the entire blade. An elephant[34] could step on it and it would look brand new. This thing's worth millions! Kyahah!"

Komori reeked of greed. Money was his everything—or perhaps, more aptly, it was his mantra, a notion he used to insulate himself from the venom of the Shikizaki blade.

"That's impossible. It's like perpetual motion.[35] If this sword is so hard, how could you ever make it?"

"Hell if I know. And if you don't know, it's not your place to ask. There's only such a thing as stupid questions. That woman might know more, but my hunch is that this Shikizaki gramps wasn't exclusively a swordsmith. He must have dabbled in the occult,[36] and in alchemy. I bet he knew some scary tricks."

Komori did not seem to care one bit.

He had no interest in developing a theory.

He was simply rational, as any ninja worth his stars should be.

"Scary tricks! I'd say pulling a sword out of your mouth is twelve times scarier. I can see now why it wouldn't need a sheath, but that doesn't explain why you would keep it in your stomach. Why can't you carry it like a normal person?"

"Simpleton. Sticking this sword in a sheath would be boorish.[37] Gotta have

[34] 象 ZŌ elephant
[35] 永久機関 EIKYŪ KIKAN an "eternal engine" defying the laws of physics
[36] 陰陽道 ONMYŌDŌ "the ying yang way" of divination vs. 道教 DŌKYŌ Taoism
[37] 無粋 BUSUI not "cool" (粋 IKI)

style."

Komori laughed expansively.

"But hold on. Have we not already proven that the Kyotoryu is no match for a Shikizaki blade? *Your sword-snapping move wasn't much to snap at.*"

"Mrg."

"That did surprise me too, though, when I heard about it. Barehanded up against a weapon, most people would try to dodge it—their most aggressive move would still only catch it midair.[38] But with you, Kyotoryu, you're bent on snapping it in two. A most laudable achievement, I must say—if you could pull it off."

"...Just watch."

Accepting Komori's challenge, Shichika shifted his stance.

One leg behind the other, unlike the open Suzuran.

Spear hands,[39] staggered, but held at the same height.

"Kyotoryu Form Two—Suisen!"[40]

"I can see your stance is different from before, but what am I supposed to watch? You bleeding to death?"

"Wait and see. Once I snap that Leveler in half—"

"Idiot!!"

Another voice.

Shichika meant business, but his brazen declaration was riven by it. He turned to see where it had come from, and sure enough, he saw the Schemer.

Incandescent finery in disarray.

Soaked in sweat and out of breath.

No wonder, after rushing here in those cumbersome adornments and hollering at the top of her lungs—nevertheless, Togame managed to catch Shichika in a rigid stare.

Not Komori, who was so obviously the enemy, but Shichika.

"Snap it in half? We're trying to collect them, not break them! If I gave the bakufu a broken sword, they'd have me spill my guts![41] Do you listen to a word that people say to you?"

"I was..."

She was right. Breaking swords was not the point.

The point was to amass all thousand of the Shikizaki blades—ideally, without damaging any.

The ninja had pushed his buttons, talking daggers about his school.

Ridiculing the Kyotoryu—meant ridiculing his father.

Is that...what did it?

38 真剣白羽取り SHINKEN SHIRAHA DORI catching a real sword with bare hands

39 貫手 NUKITE straight fingers, closed and rigid

40 水仙 SUISEN "The Narcissus"
homophone with 垂線 SUISEN "perpendicular," suggestive of the stance

41 腹を切らされる HARA WO KIRASARERU forced to commit 切腹 SEPPUKU self-disembowelment

Shichika didn't know.

He had never thought or had to think about it—or rather.

He did have to think about it, but had never.

"I don't remember agreeing to join you," Shichika said.

"That's not the issue! Do you have no sense of value?" Togame was enraged—her voice more ragged than her kimono. "No person with their head screwed on would dream of damaging a Shikizaki blade."

"You got that right!" It was Komori who agreed. "I'd never harm something so valuable. And I know a thing or two about the market."

Togame had much more to say to Shichika, but the ninja's voice—so void of feeling—made her pause. She turned his way.

"Kyahah! We had a lovely boat ride, and from my perspective, we only just parted. But I'll assume yours. Long time no see, Pussycat."[42]

Mind you.

This was long before calling women "pussycat" fell out of favor.

"Komori Maniwa! You—"

"What's gotten into you? You've been nothing but angry since you screamed your way in, you ball of energy. Upset your devoted ninja stabbed you in the back? Well, guess what. Ninjas stab. Dirty deeds[43] are how we make a living."

But then Komori took back what he said.

"Wait, maybe you do need to be upset here—no, you gotta be. If you weren't—things wouldn't add up. The story wouldn't hang together."

"Huh? What are you—"

"Nothing. Your timing really was impeccable, but forgive me, my dear Schemer, if I beg you to allow me to explain things later—let's do lunch, once I demolish Kyotoryu."

Komori trained his eyes on Shichika, who hadn't broken the Suisen, despite the sudden visit from Togame.

"Nothing gets in the way of a match between two men. Wouldn't you say, Kyotoryu? Come on. Tell her for me."

"Togame, I can't promise you I'll head off on this journey, but one thing's for sure—you'll have this Leveler in no time. Just watch. You wanted to see the Kyotoryu in action, right? Here's your chance."

Those were Shichika's words.

It wasn't that he concurred with Komori's about a match between two men.

The Leveler—the strange Shikizaki blade that not even the Kiku could destroy—had simply caught his interest.

"The sword must not be broken, or—"

"I know, I know, I won't break it. Any other requests? I'll do my best."

"Well, let's see..."

[42] 子猫ちゃん KONEKOCHAN "little kitty"
[43] 卑怯卑劣 HIKYŌ HIRETSU "unfair and foul"

Togame gave this some thought.

"Something spectacular," she said.

"Spectacular?"[44]

"Put on a good show. When we're done collecting all twelve swords, I'll need to write up a report detailing how things happened—give us something dashing. Something to make the readers keep on reading."

"..."

"Look. You break this sword—even by mistake—and the story's over. Before we're even done with Book One."

"Book One... You're writing a whole book about this?"

"Not yet, but think of the sales."

"Who would read this?"

Seriously.

What a pain to think about.

"Alright, I'll show you the most[45] spectacular move I've got—sorry to keep you waiting, Komori... Hey!"

While Shichika and Togame exchanged their pointless repartee, Komori had taken more than half the lengthy Leveler in his mouth—and down his guts.

"Ah."

"Ah!"

It was too late. Komori coaxed the long sword deep inside him, up to the grip. Arresting as it had been to watch him stick his whole arm down and pull it out, it was even more alarming to watch him swallow the thing. No matter the angle, it didn't physically add up. Unless his throat[46] stretched all the way down to his ankles, there was no way he could stuff the entire sword into his body. But stuff the sword he did.

"Ahem. No, no. I should be the one apologizing. Shall we continue, Kyotoryu?"

"Continue what? You just swallowed the whole sword. How are we supposed to battle now? What's the matter? Scared that I might break it this time?"

"You can't break it—don't even bother with that second stance. Sadly, our katana's too much for me. I can't keep up with it. I'm no swordsman, and dying on its account—now, that'd be too hard to swallow.[47] Get the joke? Kyahah!"

Komori was quite pleased with himself.

"Your Kyotoryu's all well and good against a sword, but if you'll permit

[44] 派手 HADE garish
[45] いっとう ITTŌ "the most" echoes 一刀 ITTŌ "a single slash"
[46] 食道 SHOKUDŌ "food path" esophagus
[47] 忍びねえ SHINOBINEH unendurable (in the original, the joke is a pun on 忍者 NINJA)

me to use my ninjutsu,[48] I'm afraid that you can never win. It's a matter of experience. I have it—you don't."

"Maybe so."

Shichika could hardly argue with that.

This being his first battle.

"That swordplay was just my way of humoring you," Komori added. "Consider it a present from your buddy the Hell-Made."

"Quit screwing around!"

Once again, it was Togame doing the yelling.

She might have been even louder than before.

She was losing her temper.

"That's not some toy for you to suck on. It's one of Shikizaki's Possessed! Spit it out. Now!"

"Spit it out? You're one meddlesome Pussycat, aren't you? Aren't you too old to be caterwauling like that? Alright, alright. If you say so, I'll spit it out..."

His pliancy was odd—even bizarre. Komori inhaled deeply, filling both his lungs and then some, until his back began to arch. His chest and stomach and entire upper body filled with air, like a balloon. He was the definition of bizarre.

Quite the sight to see.

Neither Shichika nor Togame could look away.

Which is to say.

They missed a beat.

"*BLAAAAAAAAAAAGH!*"

Komori spat out *all his air.*

Not the Leveler. Air.

But this wasn't air alone. *The air that he released was full of shuriken.* A gale akin to that which slammed the hut where they'd left Nanami.

He was a cannon. Shooting stars.

This went beyond the gag of stuffing things in his body—his body was an arsenal, and ready, on command, to free a swarm of shuriken.

No matter how you looked at it.

Way stranger than the Kyotoryu or the Possessed.

"Nraaaagh!"

This menace was nothing like that screen of kicked-up sand, which Shichika had cleared with a swift wave of the palm. This menace had a precedent. And at this range, he wasn't going to be gouged. He would be shredded.

Yet Shichika held his ground.

Try to escape, and he would perish.

It was lucky that he had maintained the Suisen—if it were the open Suzuran, he may have perished all the same. Reducing his exposed area to

[48] 忍術 NINJUTSU ninja techniques

a minimum, he shielded his torso with his arm and leg. Those limbs would suffer many wounds—but his vital organs would remain intact.

Whooosh!

A mighty wind blew past his body.

Mighty enough to all but knock him over—but he persevered. Persevered—not even twitching as pain bloomed through his limbs.

"Owww..."

Though he couldn't help but groan.

When he opened his eyes, four shuriken had bit into his arm and two into his leg, but none so very deep, since he had flexed his muscles in defense. Considering the number of stars thrown (up) in the assault, this was a precious bit of good luck among bad.[49] No, this wasn't about luck, good or otherwise. Shichika had put his training into practice. And it had worked.

"I could have sworn my arm and leg were blown off!"

This was no time to wallow in the pain. Shichika raised his head—embodying his inexperience. In battle, the dust rarely settles with a single blast. You can't just catch your breath and have a look around.

Which is why—

"Oops."

Even when Shichika looked—there was no one there.

No Komori.

No Togame.

"Oops."

[49] 不幸中の幸い FUKŌCHŪ NO SAIWAI silver lining

CHAPTER THREE

THE SCHEMER

■ ■

The textbook[1] approach here would be to divulge the backstory of the white-haired young lady named Togame—the Schemer, and Grand Commander of Arms of the Yanari Shogunate Military Directorate, Owari Bakufu—but those details can be filled in later. For one thing, this is hardly time for a digression, and for another, and far more critically, no small number of you must prefer her past to be a mystery just a little longer. To offer one small secret about her, however, she was not by any measure a loyal servant to the bakufu.

Her quest to capture the Twelve Possessed of Kiki Shikizaki.

Her journey to Haphazard Island.

These were not for the benefit of the shogunate.

She, more than anyone else in the world, was neither money-hungry ninja nor honor-hungry swordsman.

What, then, did she seek?

Shedding light on the matter happens to be one goal of the present tale.

■ ■

She made a mistake.

Togame knew it.

But what the mistake was, she wasn't sure. Maybe it was coming to this godforsaken island[2] in the first place, or maybe it was trying to *use* the Kyotoryu to do her bidding—why had she chosen them?

Out of all the other schools.

Shichika Yasuri. Seventh Master of the Kyotoryu.

She had learned enough from their exchanges to know that he was not so bright, but she had not expected him to be this much of an idiot. How could he be so absorbed in battle that he'd forget his employer? Granted, there could have been no other way for him to evade Komori's Star Cannon—which is why he also missed Komori snatching her off her feet and fleeing in the blink of an eye—and maybe she ought to go a little easier on him. After all, she wasn't officially his employer yet, and from the sound of it, this was his first real battle. Comparing the Kyotoryu to normal schools

[1] 教科書 KYŌKASHO textbook
[2] 無人島 MUJINTŌ uninhabited island

of swordsmanship may be absurd to begin with, but who ever trained for situations where the opponent cut and run?

Why would he?

But his opponent was a ninja.

Making a living out of dirty deeds.

If you'll permit me to use my ninjutsu.

Komori had done just that.

After bombarding Shichika with shuriken, Komori launched from the sand and landed in a single bound beside Togame, who like Shichika was so mystified by the ballooning ninja that she lost her chance to run away.

But no.

Truth be told, Togame, who lacked any martial arts skills, could never have evaded Komori Maniwa, one of the twelve bosses of a ninja clan.

Proud as she was of going unarmed.

A Schemer—an eschewer of armaments.

"Holy crap, that guy is crazy! Look at those reflexes. He braced himself before I'd even puked out all the shuriken. Anybody else would have turned and ran. Good going, kyahah! But I should have seen it coming, from any man of yours. Right, Pussycat?"

Snickering, Komori finished tying Togame to the trunk of a tree. The thick straw rope was soppy with saliva—naturally having been stowed in his stomach.

With Togame slung over his shoulder, Komori had run into the forest, sprinting left and right in random zigzags all over the mountain. Unlike Togame on her morning trek, he had taken great pains to leave no footprints and jumped from tree to tree—until, judging that he'd gone far enough, he'd stopped. When he pinned her up against the tree, she had no way of resisting him. He tied her hands around her back, and wound the rope around her body, lashing her ribs tight against the bark.

"That boy is so naive.[3] Ready for battle, but not the battlefield. Suppose that's what you get if you grow up on an island in the middle of nowhere."

"You...coward!" Togame cursed her captor. Tied up as she was, words were her only weapon. "What's the matter, chicken? Too scared to face the Kyotoryu?"

"Whoa, whoa. Easy, tiger. I'm no swordsman, nor a warrior, and never claimed to be. Put up a fair fight, as a ninja, and I'd be the laughing stock of the village. Only meatheads rely on muscle. I take a wiser approach—you might even call it tactics. Isn't that right, Schemer?"

"Don't compare us, you scumbag," spat Togame. "You're just a bully. All you do is take the easy path—I'm the opposite. I stake my life and soul on devising ways for the weak to take on the strong—"

[3] 甘い AMAI literally, sweet; soft and optimistic

"That sounds so brave. Reminds me of some of the less brave things I know about you."

"What?"

"In any case, I'm a ninja, not a swordsman. Don't confuse me with Hakuhei Sabi." Komori laughed condescendingly, his cheeks threatening to tear up to the ears. "I overheard your conversation with Kyotoryu. What do you expect from a ninja? I must say I was surprised that Sabi was okay with sloppy seconds. I suppose someone had to try and fill my shoes. But then he went and stabbed you in the back—yeah?"

"If you heard me, why are you asking?"

"Don't look so sour, Pussycat. It's not as if I peeped in on two lovers making out.[4] But you could have been a bit more careful. You may be smart, but you're wide open."

What was there to say?

The possibility of the boatman being anyone but himself—much less this ninja—had failed to cross her mind. She should have known—after all, *she knew what powers he could muster.* Even if the Star Cannon was a surprise. And here she thought she *knew his tricks* more than she cared to.

"You might not have caught me snooping, but there's no excuse for that pickup line of yours. 'Go ahead and fall for me.' Whew! Laying it on thick. I wish you'd used that one on me."

"Only to have you double-cross me? Don't waste your breath. What's your plan? You think that you can hold me hostage?"

"Hey! There's an idea." Komori gave an exaggerated shrug. "But you only just met Kyotoryu and might not serve as one. Personally," he said, grinning, "I would have picked his sister."

So he knew about Nanami. How couldn't he, if he'd been listening; but this proved it.

"Then again, maybe not—that sister of his is more than meets the eye. My Star Cannon was supposed to wipe out you and Kyotoryu—but that girl somehow saw the whole thing coming."

He was right.

Only now did the Schemer realize that Nanami had saved them from the gale of ninja stars that blew through the wall of the hut. Throwing herself into the line of fire and pushing Togame and Shichika—*before the shuriken came through the wall!*

Nanami Yasuri.

Was she another master of the Kyotoryu?

"Where's she gonna hide? She's on an island. Soon it'll be her turn to taste what the Hell-Made is serving up—after I kill you and her brother."

"So go ahead and kill me."

[4] 逢瀬 ŌSE rendezvous

"Don't act so noble, Pussycat—I know you inside out. You're brimming with schemes of how to finish me off. Your guts are far more hazardous than mine."

Komori got up in her face, so close their breath mixed.

"Don't fret. I'm not gonna kill you—we have so many things to talk about. Even when I came at you with the Star Cannon, I wasn't trying to kill you off, much less the Kyotoryu. That line about wiping you out was just my way of speaking.[5] I merely hoped to whip you to a pulp—kyahah!"

"If that was the idea, you could have exercised a little self-control—I can't speak for the Kyotoryu, but it's a miracle I didn't die. I'm feebler than you know."

"Don't sound proud about it. Kyotoru would have partially shielded you if it had gone according to plan... So, what I'd like us to discuss, of course, are these Shikizaki blades, the masterpiece Mutant Blades. I know where the Leveler is—safe inside my belly. Tell me where I can find the other eleven, along with who has them and what each blade can do."

"..."

"You said you only knew what was up with six of them, but you can't be absolutely in the dark about the other six. The Old Shogun had his finger on the whole lot. If you put your precious directorate to work, you'd at least have a place to start from."

"..."

"Trust me, I've done my best to find out all I can. I know all about this Hakuto the Whisper sword that Hakuhei Sabi ran away with. Sounds like a wild weapon. As thin and light as the name implies. From overhead, it's practically invisible. *Fit only for the hands of a true master*—right? Designed to be light as the Leveler is sturdy—or so I hear. But that's what makes it delicate; unless it's in the hands of someone who can swing it perfectly, it's bound to shatter. Kyahah! I can see why you ordered Sabi to go after it first. He's probably the only living swordsman in Japan who could handle it."

"..."

"Wasn't there another one that Shikizaki designed around the principle of strength in numbers? I believe it's called Sento the Legion. A sinister mirage—*a thousand swords in one*. Anyway. That's all I managed to discover. I'm dying to know what else you have to share with me. That's why I followed you to this landfill of an island. But in the end, you tell Kyotoryu nothing that you didn't tell me."

"..."

"Cat got your tongue?"

Komori clucked[6] at her with disgust before giving her a little breathing room.

[5] 言葉の綾 KOTOBA NO AYA "the weave of words"
[6] 舌打ち SHITAUCHI click the tongue

"I'm only gonna ask you once, so listen up. Why don't you just backstab the bakufu and team up with us? You'll get a fair cut. No funny business."

"Eat me." Her reaction was instant. "I can't trust anyone who works for money."

"You still mad about what happened? We've been over this. You messed up when you put your trust in a pack of ninjas. But I know why you need to get mad—"

"Need to? What are you—"

"Never mind." Komori steered the conversation in a new direction. "Me and the other Maniwa Bosses, we've decided to have ourselves a competition—to see who can snatch up most of the twelve swords. Once we've sold them, we'll divvy up the spoils, but the more swords you found, the bigger your piece of the pie. I'm one step ahead of the game, but the other guys aren't far behind. Especially that prick Kawauso.[7] He knows how to sniff these suckers out. If you and I had teamed up, it would have been lucky for both of us."

"Guess your luck's run out."

"I'll show you how lucky I am—I can torture you to my heart's content. What's the matter? You look a little pale. Kyahah! They say that any punishment beats being tortured by a ninja. Isn't that a horrible thing to say? I wouldn't say we do anything horrible. Per se."

"Creep."

"Don't fret. We won't get started yet. I don't have any of my toys. With that last Star Cannon I blew through most of my stash, except for the Leveler. It's not the sort of move I ordinarily pull twice in a day. You'll have to wait until we return to the mainland for the ***physical interrogations*** to begin—first, let me take care of Kyotoryu."

Seventh Master of the Kyotoryu—Shichika Yasuri.

"This game of swords is crazy enough with just us Maniwa Bosses. I'll have to take care of Hakuhei Sabi, too, as soon as I have the chance... Kyahah, last thing I want is to be sword-handed from behind while I'm torturing you."

"Then why didn't you stay and fight? You didn't look so cornered that you had to start anew."

"Remember? Only meatheads rely on muscle. The moment for that sort of thing has come and gone. Nothing's more passé than a bona fide swordfight. And where's the sport in a ninja—who regurgitates far better than he ripostes—battling a swordsman who doesn't even use a sword? It'd be like trying to cuddle with a cuttlefish[8]—not that cuttlefish aren't cuddly. Did that pun suck? No bones about it. I know I'm preaching to the choir,[9] my dear

[7] 川獺 KAWAUSO "The Otter"
[8] 烏骨鶏くらい滑稽 UKOKKEI KURAI KOKKEI as ridiculous as a silkie
[9] 釈迦に説法 SHAKA NI SEPPŌ "sermonizing the Buddha"

Schemer, but the best way to stay alive is to avoid fighting anyone stronger than you. To play it safe, I'd personally avoid anyone who's half as strong. But after that sermon of yours on the glories of weakness, I get the sense I'm not so much preaching to the choir as casting pearls before swine."[10]

"Stuff your nonsense[11] down your star hole. I have no interest in battling anyone weaker than me."

"Well, I guess you and I have different tastes after all."

"So you think highly of Shichika." In essence, that was the Maniwa Boss's assessment of that untested youth.

"Head to head, he would be hard to take. If I were a swordsman, I may even have lost. He had a chance. But I'm a ninja—and I know how to eliminate that chance."

"Lofty remarks, from a man relying on a hostage to lure his enemy into the mountains for a sneak attack."

"Tsk tsk tsk. To be a hostage, you need to be desirable. And these mountains are hardly the place to try and snare that Kyotoryu. This is his turf. Were he to show up now, the disadvantage would be mine. And if he comes for me, he's taking you down, too."

"Take me down?"

Could that happen?

Togame doubted the efficacy of a hostage scenario, but she had no way of predicting how that simple man would react to a situation like this.

When you're smart, you can't imagine being stupid.

And what if—

If the Kyotoryu...is that kind of school...

"So I'm not going to ambush him. We'll square off. I'll be a good sport."

"..."

"Don't look so skeptical. You know what I can do. You've seen my ninja skills."

Komori Maniwa. One of the Twelve Bosses of the Maniwa.

Defying physics and anatomy to stuff a plethora of exceedingly long or sharp or useful things, like rope, inside his body—*was not the main attraction.*

This was just a taste of him—merely the first sip. Komori had mentioned how Kawauso could sniff them out, but Togame had originally hired the clan because it was Komori whose powers were best suited to the task at hand.

His face was melting.

It transformed as she watched.

As if it were clay, he thumbed the skin and muscle of his face—but didn't stop there. He tugged and squeezed at his entire body until—

"How's this look? Think I'll pass?"

[10] 馬の耳に念仏 UMA NO MIMI NI NEMBUTSU Buddhist chants for a horse's ears

[11] 戯言 ZAREGOTO "frivolous words" the title of another series by NISIOISIN

Before the count of ten—*Komori had molded his head into hers.* From the neck up, he was Togame.

This was no mere disguise.

His bones and very flesh had changed.

He had her long hair—white of course.

And had even copied the bump on her forehead.

"Yuck!"

To repeat, Togame already knew about this move—but it never failed to disturb her. Komori's ninpo[12] allowed him to modify his body, on command, to have a different figure, a different feel, a different skin.

This is how he had transformed into the boatman.

The boatman she had vetted so severely—and that was why, when Nanami raised the possibility, Togame saw instantly that it was Komori who had bombarded the hut.

She'd been so careful about being followed.

And never dreamed she'd be accompanied instead.

The actual boatman—was surely no longer of this world.

"Behold, the Body Melt[13]—kyahah! Whoops, don't want to forget the rest of my body. And what a fine body it is—"

He yanked and pinched and tugged and squeezed.

Stretching flesh and bone into shape.

Transforming from a muscly man into a skinny woman—yes, with Komori's Body Melt, body type was no concern, and even gender distinctions[14] were meaningless.

Perhaps it's a cliché to describe ninjas as masters of disguise, but in Komori's case, his powers were absolute. Nobody knew his true identity—whether he was a he or a she, or old or young. Even the figure we saw on the beach might have been artificial. In all likelihood, Komori Maniwa had forgotten his original form.

The Softeninja.[15]

His ability to load that bare sword and those prickly shuriken into his body without a drop of blood was owing to this fearsome elasticity.

The owner of the supplest body in existence claiming the hardest and firmest katana was ironic, perhaps—but maybe this was necessity.

After all, it was why Togame had enlisted him to seize the Leveler, just as she had tasked Sabi with capturing the Whisper.

Pinching and squeezing to make the last few touches, Komori completed his transformation into Togame. It may have taken slightly longer than ten seconds by now, but far less time than you might expect. Forced to watch

[12] 忍法 NINPŌ ninja method, i.e. ninja art

[13] 骨肉細工 KOTSUNIKU SAIKU "flesh-and-bone crafting"

[14] 男女差 DANJOSA "gap between man and woman"

[15] 柔忍者 JŪNINJA "freeform ninja" vs. 柔道 JŪDŌ, the martial art of flexibility

herself take form before her very eyes, Togame was hardly at ease.

"That just about does it."

Even the voice was Togame's.

"Kyahah!" he laughed—in her voice. "You think that doesn't sound like you? People never hear their own voice as others hear it. But that's what you sound like to everybody else. Doesn't it make you squeamish?"

This was no impression. It was far more sinister than mimicking her voice—Komori had her vocal cords. He probably even had the same lungs and other vital organs—which is why.

It was exactly her voice.

Indeed, she felt squeamish—

Not at the sound of her own voice.

At the thought of her insides being replicated.

"Is this how you're going to fool Shichika?"

"You know it. And if you think I'm playing dirty, keep it to yourself. I'm only doing what I did for you when I seized the Leveler."

"..."

He was right.

She had utilized his transformative powers to the utmost.

"Actually—you need to keep it to yourself all the time."

With that suggestive declaration, Komori plunged his hand into his mouth. This topped the list of feats Togame hoped he would not execute as her, but lashed to the tree, she was powerless to stop him. Perhaps he was making her watch simply to force her to savor her powerlessness.

The hand he eventually pulled out of his throat was gripping a bindle[16]—packed with carefully folded clothes, from the looks of it. Of course. Togame put it all together. Komori hadn't worn his wacky ninja garb as the boatman—

"Even with your skin and bones, I'd never pass for you in clothes this baggy. If I had time to strip you bare—I would enjoy every minute of it, trust me—but I thought ahead and packed accordingly. The same kimono."

He had wrapped the clothes to prevent them from being drenched in spit. He had to have another outfit, for the boatman, packed somewhere else in his body—was his stomach connected to a fourth dimension? It was a mystery that could not be explained in terms of flexibility alone. That said, it would be futile to attempt an understanding of ninjutsu based on logic—

"Kyahah! Don't forget to write in your report to your superiors how I brought a change of clothes. Make sure you say exactly what I'm wearing. Lots of guys go crazy for those details. But I digress—the only thing you'll be submitting to your superiors—is your resignation."

"...I'd rather not have to explain how a maniac ninja like you showed up."

[16] 風呂敷 FUROSHIKI squarish cloth used to carry things...generally outside of the body

"I bet. Man, these are some fancy duds. By the way, I got a receipt. Can I expense this? That price tag made me sick to my stomach. But I guess it's nothing compared to what I'll get for a Shikizaki sword—no, not even close."

"Aren't you ashamed for being such a money-grubber?"

"Of course not. Like I said, that age is over. These days, shrewdness is a virtue. It's proof of your intelligence, your cleverness. Though I suppose the Schemer would have to disagree."

Komori sloughed his ninja clothes and changed into the outfit wrapped up in the bindle. Donning[17] a kimono is an art, and he made it look easy. A little too easy—at times, he moved his arms in ways a normal human skeleton should not allow, like when he was adjusting the position of the obi at his lower back. He slipped on a pair of the same sandals as Togame and finished off by wrapping up his ninja garb, throwing open his mouth, and swallowing the whole package in one gulp.

"Now I just need to tear apart the hem a bit...like so. Hey! Look at that. Twinsies! Kyahah! Imagine if I showed up like this at Owari Castle instead of you? That'd be a laugh. If I caused enough of a scene, you would become a wanted woman, and you'd have to help me, like it or not."

"Fool... You won't get very far. Bump into enough people, and someone will catch on."

"Don't act so serious. I'm kidding. You're so uptight. It'd be great if I could replicate your brains, but I'll need some more practice to get there. By the way, where's your weapon? When you left the boat, you had a big sword—too big for you—dangling from your hip. Did you leave it at the hut after they confiscated it?"

"I must have..."

Yep.

Unaccustomed to carrying a katana, Togame didn't think to reach for the sword when she ran off to chase after the two men. Even if it had crossed her mind, Nanami would hardly have given it back. Besides, Togame could barely swing the thing.

"Oh well. Looks like I'll have to finish this with the Leveler. I can't exactly fight him hand to hand, not with a body like this...and I'm all out of shuriken."

"Think you can pull it off?"

"Sure. He'll never see it coming. You've seen my bag of tricks, but Kyotoryu thinks I'm just some ninja who pulls swords out of his stomach. He's too gentle for his own good. Doesn't seem to have the temperament to ambush me or anything. But what do you expect from an island monkey?"

"I thought you said you'd be a good sport."

"I said we'd square off—not that I'd fight fair and square. It would have been much better if I'd turned into his sister, but sadly, I don't know her

[17] 着付け KITSUKE formal rules for donning a kimono

face well enough to make it work. Maybe I should have peeped while I was eavesdropping. I wonder what happened to her. Think she's still sitting up in that hut?"

Togame wouldn't say.

But that is where Nanami had to be.

You go and watch—I'm sure my brother will take care of things—go see the Kyotoryu in action—was what she'd told Togame.

Nanami trusted Shichika with her life.

That trust had gotten Togame into this mess...but it was no reason to inform Komori of her whereabouts.

Togame held her tongue. She wouldn't answer.

But it didn't seem like he was waiting for an answer.

"Who cares," Komori said. "Once I've thoroughly[18] squashed Kyotoryu, I'll take his shape and kill his sister. On this small island, she can run, but she can't hide. Sorry, but you'll have to wait here till I'm done."

"No! Wait."

First the Maniwa double-crossed her.

Then Hakuhei Sabi double-crossed her.

And now she had to wait here while Komori killed the Kyotoryu?

She would run out of options.

She would have no hope of rounding up the Shikizaki blades—it was that simple.

Whether or not it had been a mistake, at this point, relying on the Kyotoryu was the only strategy[19] available to her—her only scheme.

I've come this far.

How could I possibly give up now!

"What do you care anyway?"

Komori laughed, with Togame's face, narrowing its eyes.

"Whether I kill him or not, that kid isn't going to cooperate with you. What was that hot line of yours? 'Go ahead and fall for me'? Man, do I wish you'd used it on me. My comeback would've been 'No one in this world would ever fall for you.'"

"..."

"Sure, I stabbed your back for money, but if I had known what kind of person you are, I never would have signed up in the first place. And know what? I only asked you to team up with me just now so I could stab you in the back again."

Then he said it again.

His comeback line.

"No one in this world would ever fall for you."

[18] 首尾よく SHUBI YOKU "head to tail"completely
[19] 策 SAKU plan vs. 奇策 "odd plan" scheme

■ ■

Komori Maniwa has no backstory[20] worth mentioning.

Given his awesome power, now come to light, pronouns are an unresolvable dilemma, but for the sake of continuity, he—a ninja upon being born in the Maniwa enclave, was raised as a ninja of the ninjas, by the ninjas, for the ninjas.[21]

No values or ideas of his own.

When his turn came, he became a Maniwa Boss.

That was all there was to it.

A nonpartisan unit with allegiances to no country, the Maniwa Clan was, in a certain sense, a perfect portrait[22] of the ninjas. It was organized around a principle of free agency,[23] but this was not because they didn't get along. It developed organically: each ninja was a true army of one, and when they tried to work together, they couldn't help getting in each other's way. Komori fit right in, distinguishing himself as among the most reliable of the Twelve Bosses. And while the unprecedented proposal that the entire village go rogue did not come from him specifically, you can bet he was behind it.

The Possessed of Kiki Shikizaki.

His twelve masterpieces.

If they sold the lot of them—

They could all give up on being ninjas.

No more slinking around in shadows.

They would no longer have to hide, and no longer have to endure.[24]

Something unresolved was how they would unload the Possessed. One sword was supposedly enough to buy a country. Who had that kind of money? With the exception of an area of Nagasaki, Japan was pursuing a policy of isolation,[25] but they would have to seek a patron overseas. While they were at it, why not move the entire clan overseas? Japan no longer had a place for them.

It never did.

"If for no other reason..." muttered Komori, in the voice of Togame the Schemer. "I need to make sure and finish off Kyotoryu."

To recap.

He couldn't have Togame crying out for Kyotoryu or his big sister to come save her. Tying her to the tree was not enough; he had gagged her (at this

[20] 半生 HANSEI (the first) half of a lifetime

[21] の[...]による[...]ための NO[...]NI YORU[...]TAME NO of[...]by[...]for
the exact phrasing from Lincoln's renowned address in translation

[22] 鑑 KAGAMI exemplar (homophones with 鏡 KAGAMI mirror)

[23] 単独行動 TANDOKU KŌDŌ independent action

[24] 忍ばずともよい SHINOBAZU TOMO YOI the original repeats the same phrase

[25] 鎖国 SAKOKU "chaining the country"

point, you don't need to be told where he pulled the gag[26] from) and sprang off—zipping into action.

He had already laid his trap.

Repairing into the mountains with Togame in his clutches, Komori had made frantic zigzags up and down as a cover lest Shichika follow his tracks—but had left discernible traces here and there. Not pointing toward Togame, they'd lead Shichika somewhere completely different.

Tracks he would follow—without fail—precisely because of his comprehensive knowledge of the island and the mountains. A ruse, intent on laying bare the poor interpersonal skills of a youth who'd barely met a soul. Because he had never been the victim of malice, the possibility would never occur to him.

It was a matter of experience.

Plain and simple.

According to plan, Shichika followed the false tracks until he was right where Komori wanted him—the site of the natural spring, which Shichika had meant to visit earlier that day with a bucket on his back. That detail was not known to Komori, who had only picked the place because it was a clearing. Which made sense—after all, the Yasuri family had been drawing water here and tending to the spring for twenty years.

From up in the branches of a tree, Komori watched a nonplussed Shichika find himself at the end of the trail.

Kyotoryu was tall and muscular, but far from oafish.

Lengthy arms and legs.

The shuriken were gone, the bleeding stopped.

His heart and his lungs in tiptop shape.

A perfect man, one hundred percent.

Back at the enclave, Komori had trained day in day out to reach this level of skill—but it was becoming clear that Shichika Yasuri had trained at least as hard. Komori was observing Shichika in order to assume his form and slay his sister back at the hut—but his body was so fine it almost put the ninja in a trance.

Komori could shapeshift into any kind of body—but he needed a model.[27] *The humanly impossible*—like becoming a giant ten times taller and infinitely stronger than any man—was beyond him. If he continued training and honing his ninjutsu, perhaps someday he could accomplish such a feat, but it was just like in the fine arts—imitation was easy, but creating something new was challenging. At present, his Body Melt was limited to imitation, falling short of true creation.

Hence.

Komori found Shichika's toned body, in the flesh, so beautiful.

[26] 猿轡 SARUGUTSUWA "monkey's bit"
[27] 手本 TEHON "hand book" example

It's a shame I have to do this—

The uncharacteristic thought did cross his mind.

From a business perspective, that body was a hot commodity, so maybe the thought wasn't so uncharacteristic after all.

Still, it was a shame.

You could say it wasn't in the stars.

In his first true match, Kyotoryu, a swordsman who never used a sword, was up against a ninja, rather than a swordsman, who moreover came brandishing the unbreakable Leveler, forged by Kiki Shikizaki to be the hardest sword imaginable.

These were no terms for swordplay, nor could the sword be snapped.

Too bad for the youth.

No—his bad luck began when Togame chose him. If the two hadn't met, Kyotoryu would not be embroiled with the Shikizaki swords, much less the Maniwa Clan.

Nevertheless.

Something told Komori that this kid was too big a fish—or monkey—for this tiny island. There was something about him.

Just a hunch.

What if Komori could get him to be an ally instead?

As a Boss, he could invite Kyotoryu to be part of the New Maniwa.

No. No way.

Maybe under different circumstances, but not now. This job was supposed to be the last hurrah for the Maniwa. Galvanized by their fraternal competition to collect the Twelve Possessed, Komori already had a lead on several of the swords. If he asked around—posing as Togame—back on the mainland, he could no doubt locate several more. This was not the time to add an unknown quantity to the mix.

It was nowhere in the stars.

Komori felt bad for the youth.

Thinking like this was truly out of character.

"Weird," Shichika muttered to himself, pacing around the spring. "What happened to the tracks? Where'd everybody go?"

"..."

Komori's eyes were darting, but his body was motionless. He would not be discovered. Then again, he thought, this man was not like other men. Komori had opted for this plan of action because he doubted that Togame would be effective as a hostage, but it was still a gamble as to whether she'd even serve as bait[28]...and yet Shichika had swallowed it right up.

Judging from his use of the word "everybody," which lumped Komori with Togame, Shichika, wild animal that he was, had chased them simply because

[28] 撒き餌 MAKIE scattering scraps of food to lure prey

the ninja had run. In that sense, Komori had been correct in opting not to use Togame as a hostage—but as bait she wasn't much good either. As far as the gamble was concerned, Komori had lost, but things were working in his favor.

He had him good.

Absolutely. Without a doubt.

Komori checked for the Leveler in his stomach. He had flipped its orientation—no longer hilt side up, it was ensconced with the point at the top of his throat. He would probably have to catch Shichika off-guard once they were close. He wouldn't have a chance to reach down into his mouth and extract the blade. If he did that as Togame, it would be a miracle for him not to blow his cover.

Then he would launch it.

Not the Star Cannon but a Sword Cannon.

The straight sword was a perfect missile.

Since he could hardly get away with blowing up like a balloon, it would not have the same unfettered strength, but one breath in was enough to fire the Leveler through the organs of whoever stood before him. Though of course this was a move he could never execute with any other sword, not even the other Shikizaki blades. Only the Leveler could withstand such abuse.

"That'll do it."

He had memorized *the shape of Shichika*—and was thus prepared to pay a lethal visit to his sister. Shichika was confused, but the ninja would do well not to spook him; if Komori was forced to leave the clearing, his plan was ruined. His Cannon attack—whether it flung ninja stars or a sword—would not be possible in a confined environment.

Since it would be absurd for the real Togame to hop from a tree, Komori made a different entrance. As if merely walking down a staircase, he footed his way down the perpendicular tree trunk without a sound.

And pranced his way over to the spring.

He figured why not go all out.

What was it she had called Kyotoryu? Yasuri? Shichika-dono?[29] No, Togame had certainly skipped over those courtesies even in second person.

If they talked too much, the truth would come out.

He only needed one line: *He abducted me, but I fought for my life and managed to break free.* The Togame that Komori knew would not attempt such a thing, but it didn't matter. He would run straight, with arms outstretched—

And lance Kyotoryu through the guts.

"—Shichika!"

"Ah."

When Togame, or rather Komori, called to him—

[29] どの DONO "lord" appended like SAN, but in formal address

Shichika Yasuri turned around.

■ ■

As Komori Maniwa had predicted, Shichika Yasuri had given chase merely because the ninja had run—and not suspecting Komori to have left false tracks, he'd been guided all the way up to the spring.

Which is where the trail broke off.

Shichika had not the slightest inkling of having fallen for a trap. Unlike his father Mutsue and his sister Nanami, he was clueless about such maneuvers. Outside the context of a battle, he was quite vulnerable. His level gaze around the clearing for a continuation of the tracks was less humorous than it was piteous.

Dad.

What would he do now?

How would Mutsue Yasuri have combated the Star Cannon? Or would his father's Kiku have already snapped the Leveler in half? Komori said that it could never break or bend, but maybe at the hands of Mutsue Yasuri—

Or maybe not.

Shichika wasn't sure.

But his father—Sixth Master of the Kyotoryu and Hero of the Rebellion—

"..."

Ninjas.

Kiki Shikizaki. The Possessed.

This was unknown territory for Shichika.

An unknown world.

For nineteen years, he had trained under Mutsue, whom they even called a Hero of the Rebellion... That hadn't given him a big head, he hoped, but he wasn't prepared for the ninjutsu of Komori or the nature of a Shikizaki sword. He felt like a frog in a well[30] that had been sucked out into the ocean.

...The ocean.

Across the sea.

Were *such things* fairly common on the mainland? Komori had called himself one of the Twelve Bosses of the Maniwa Clan...in other words, there were eleven more of these guys, each probably capable of *that sort of thing*. And of the twelve Shikizaki blades, eleven more remained, each *peculiar like that*.

If he crossed over.

[30] 井戸の底の蛙 IDO NO SOKO NO KAWAZU Japanese counterpart for "big fish in a small pond"

"..."

What would happen to his sister?

With his father gone, he couldn't leave his feeble sister on the island by herself—but this line of reasoning failed to settle in his heart of hearts.[31]

His sister was the head of the house.

Nanami needed to be protected, but he was overprotective to a fault—that much he knew. Self-reliant in spirit, she wanted to help with the chores and would certainly hold it together without him around.

He was the one who couldn't separate himself from her.

No, that wasn't it, either.

It was worse than that.

At the end of the day, it was a pain—leaving this island for the mainland would be a colossal pain in the butt. What he had told his sister, by way of making an excuse, had been far closer to the truth.

I've been on this island as long as I can remember—

I can't just up and go over to the mainland—

I don't know anything about the outside world—

And I don't care to learn—

"..."

She said she came here in a boat.

Which meant there was a boat on Haphazard Island.

In which case—

All he needed was a reason.

A good enough reason to leave the island.

He wouldn't work for money.

He didn't care about honor.

What would make him move?

—Go ahead and fall for me.

Remembering Togame's line made him chuckle.[32] There was no way that was going to be his reason—but...

Hm.

About that boat. The ninja said he had masqueraded[33] as the boatman for the ride here... But according to Komori and Togame's exchange, they'd met before—that is to say, even before she hired the ninjas to track down the Leveler. In fact, as Grand Commander, she had hired them for countless other jobs.

In that case, how on earth had the ninja traveled with her in the boat without Togame wising up? She called herself the Schemer or whatever, but for all her insistent emphasis on her brains, the woman...

What disguise?

[31] 芯 SHIN core
[32] 失笑 SHISSHŌ "slip a laugh"
[33] 化ける BAKERU change into, transform

Could a disguise work so well?

"Hrrm."

Had Shichika been capable of redirecting his suspicion, he could have seen the light—perhaps. But guessing that Komori, no mere masquerader, could mold his body into any shape he chose would have been a tall order for anyone.

There was a chance—and yet.

Shichika stopped there.

Thinking was such a pain.

Putting that aside—and also putting aside why he might leave the island, he had to find those two.

Maybe he should head back to see his sister.

She was probably at the hut, sipping sayu.

And so on.

That was where his mind was, when from behind—

"Shichika!"

Togame rushed toward him through the underbrush.

Togame, who he was certain had been captured.

She ran towards him, nearly tripping over.

Not, of course, the real Togame, but Komori as Togame. All the same, Komori played Togame so well, right down to the way she walked, you would never notice—even if you knew.

"Ah."

Hence Shichika, not fathoming the extent of the ninja's powers, hardly stood a chance...

"Kyotoryu—Botan!"[34]

...and yet.

Playing off the turn of his hips, Shichika displayed the Botan, a spinning rear kick of Kyotoryu's own. In rapid-fire, he aimed the left blade of his foot at Togame's—at Komori's belly.

The ninja ran straight into the attack.

And doubled over in midair.

"Bwah!"

The point of the Leveler slipped out of Komori's body.

Leaving himself wide open—naturally, since pulling off a believable Togame meant leaving himself wide open—he took Shichika's foot at the center of his spleen meridian.[35] It was a brutal blow. He fell on his stomach—and puked up a mess.

A hot and slimy mess.

Which happened to include the Leveler.

The air he had sucked in was gone, blown into the sky upon impact.

[34] 牡丹 BOTAN "The Peony" the "King of Flowers"

[35] 水月 SUIGETSU "water moon" one of the zàng-fǔ organs

His raid[36] was an utter failure.

The Leveler was out of him, handle and all—Komori shot Shichika a rueful glare.

Togame's face...Togame's eyes...

Had the disguise not worked on Shichika, then?

A minute before, right before he quit thinking about Komori masquerading as the boatman, had he arrived at the truth of the matter? Unlikely. That very expression, *the truth of the matter,*[37] and Shichika Yasuri were strangers to each other.

So had he seen any difference between Togame and Komori posing as Togame? Surely not even Komori, one of the Twelve Bosses of the Maniwa, could perfectly imitate another person. There had to be some tiny difference—had Shichika not overlooked it? Unlikely. Komori's Body Melt was no stingy sleight of hand.

What of the palpable blood lust? When Komori took a deep breath preparing to deploy the Leveler at close range from his cannon belly, to send it piercing through his enemy's heart, did Shichika, raised in the wilds of this island, feel a tremor in his skin? Had he leapt before he looked, reacting faster than his mind? Unlikely. Komori, who could hold himself utterly still, could surely suppress any cues to his attack.

After all...

"Hey, Togame is that you?"

This was Shichika Yasuri—

He hadn't suspected that the person rushing at him from behind *was even Togame,* much less Komori Maniwa.

"Hm? But you just puked out a sword. Can everybody from the mainland do that, after all? Wait a sec, isn't this the Leveler?"

"...nkk."

Consider this.

Shichika knew every tree on the island, down to the last leaf. Which meant he could tell every tree from every other tree, tell every leaf apart. And why not? He saw them every day. *He knew them intimately.*

In contrast, when most people see an animal, whether dog or cat, fish or fowl, unless they see the creatures regularly, *they all look the same*—but why limit our example? Even among fellow humans, foreigners can look the same, and few could pick somebody they just met from a crowd. *Our brain is incapable of distinguishing between unfamiliar objects on command.*

Herein lies the problem.

Since before he was a conscious being, Shichika Yasuri had been living on Haphazard Island, *nary another human in his life but his father and his sister*—the real question we should be asking is: *between Togame and Komori,*

[36] 奇襲 KISHŪ sneak attack
[37] 真相 SHINSŌ true aspect

did any difference register?

For example, size.

Were they as different as, say, *a dog and a puppy?*

Gender, you say?

How many people can tell if a fish is male or female?

Their voices?

When a bird sings, can you tell whether it is male or female?

Their clothes? Their hairstyles? The color of their hair?

That brash kimono and transparently white hair—

How would he ever have memorized all of that?

The only people Shichika Yasuri could recognize on sight were his family; and since his father died, that meant only himself and his sister—which is another way of saying that Komori needn't have transformed himself to dupe Shichika. If he had only done what he told Togame he would do and squared off against Shichika instead of rushing him from behind—

Shichika would never have launched a kick, *his instinctual reaction to an attack from the rear.*

"G-Ghak..."

"Ah, okay, I get it. You're a shapeshifter. I heard that kitsune and tanuki[38] can transform, but I had no idea people could too. Crazy. So wait, though. Are you...the ninja?"

"Dammit."

Komori couldn't stand up.

Sure, he had been caught off-guard—but he had no idea Kyotoryu could kick with such terrible strength. A direct hit could knock an opponent out of commission! Komori's plan to shoot the Leveler from his belly may have sputtered, but it was perhaps providential[39] for him that he had swallowed the adamantine sword before battle. For had he not, the spinning rear kick Shichika had called the Botan might have cracked his spine. The Leveler had played a surprise role as a buttress—but it had also transferred the blow and sent it radiating through his whole body.

Komori was not moving anytime soon.

As done as a prey frozen by a snake's stare.[40]

"I guess this means I've captured the Leveler?" Shichika asked himself.

He looked back and forth between Komori, in the aforementioned state, and the Leveler, which had rattled to the ground.

"Togame requested something spectacular...but the Botan is a pretty boring move. Oh well. I made short change of a shapeshifting weirdo, so she better thank me. This is what she wanted for her report. If the cast of

[38] 狐 狸 KITSUNE TANUKI foxes and tanuki: in Japanese folklore, both are shapeshifters
[39] 僥倖 GYŌKŌ good fortune
[40] まな板の上の鯉 MANAITA NO UE NO KOI "a carp on a cutting board" unable to resist and resigned

characters includes a guy who can disguise himself as other people, you won't ever know who's really speaking. It'd be hard to—"

"Hey...you," Komori whimpered. "Why are you...so happy to help...*this woman*?"

"What?"

"I'm asking...why you'd want to let her use you. Listening to the likes of her will do you no good..."

"Huh? I'm not trying to be useful, or not useful—"

Use[41] him?

Is that what he just said?

"I didn't mean it that way. I'm just glad she's going to have the Leveler back."

"Didn't you find something fishy about *this one*'s story?" Komori continued, still on the ground. "At this point, why would the bakufu bother with the Shikizaki blades?"

"Uhh—they're scared of an uprising, right? Like, if someone with all twelve of the Possessed started an uprising on the scale of the last Rebellion..."

"That makes sense as a reason. It's reasonable. But it sounds a little too pat. Don't you think?"

"..."

Hmm.

Maybe?

Was there...another side to it?

"Today's bakufu isn't as entranced by the Shikizaki blades as the Old Shogun. They're far more...realistic. This is about *all about her.* This little Sword Hunt[42] of hers is *no more than a career move.* It's only happening because Togame the Schemer, Grand Commander of Arms, wants the bragging rights."

Komori spoke in a voice thick with spite.

"Collecting the last twelve swords wasn't some idea that came down from on high at the bakufu. *It was this woman's idea*. Even if the shogun made the proclamation, she's the one who lit the fire, just so she could put it out. And now you hear her spouting, 'It's not as if I don't have my own opinions on the matter,' and 'I'm in no position to quibble over the particulars of an order.' But the Sword Hunt is happening on *her* terms. Every bit of it is for the good of her career."

"Career?" Shichika wasn't sure what the word meant. "Isn't the Grand Commander already a pretty high position? Sounds like it anyway."

"It is. She's up there. But is *up there* enough for *this woman*? Hell no. She's heading for the summit—you're gullible, kid. You don't know to doubt, do

[41] 利用 RIYŌ utilize; take advantage of

[42] 刀集 KATANA ATSUME "gathering swords" as opposed to the historical Sword Hunts

you? No way a woman this young isn't going to play dirty on her way to the top. *A world where only ability counts* is almost impossible to find."

"..."

"When I first met her, I was stunned—by her smoldering ambition, by *that eye*. I could tell that she would sacrifice anything—or anyone—to get her way. She certainly had no qualms about using the Maniwa Clan. We're talking an entire band of ninja assassins. She's out of control. And you too," Komori said. "Now she wants to use you, too. Can't you see, Kyotoryu? You're being exploited. No good will come from teaming up with *this woman*."

"...So you betrayed her before she had the chance?"

"Yeah. But the stuff about money aside, I couldn't hope to keep up with her. I told you she wasn't satisfied with being *up there*. What do you think she has in mind? *The very top*, at the side[43] of the next shogun."

"What?"

"Kyahah," Komori laughed wheezily—but also like he was enjoying himself. "No matter how cooped up and simpleminded a life you've led here on this island, I hope you can understand how outrageous an idea that is. The shogun is getting on in years. It won't be long before he steps down—and when he does, she'll be there, beside the new shogun, who is at present still a child. And you know what that means."

"The world—"

There it was.

Don't you desire the world? she had asked him.

Right at the beginning, and not just as a way of launching into her tale of the Shikizaki blades—*she was saying that she, herself, did!*

That was some serious ambition, if true.

She hoped to bring to life the illusion about the Shikizaki blades...in pursuit of her goal?

"Still," Shichika got out, flummoxed though he was, "you can't blame her. Working your way up is a natural part of working for an organization—or so my dad taught me. But I can see why you guys might not feel so good after being used and all..."

"We could care less. I use you, you use me, that's what makes the world go round. The problem is *what she used us for*. Working your way up makes sense, most of the time, but this lady is aiming too high. Taking over the nation all by herself, not by waging war, but through sheer politicking!"[44]

"..."

It sounded like she was living in the past.[45]

The Age of Warring States was over.

No one was interested in superfluous conflict—well, almost no one.

[43] 御側人 OSOBANIN personal counselor to the shogun

[44] 政争 SEISŌ political struggle vs. 戦争 SENSŌ war

[45] 時代錯誤 JIDAI SAKUGO an anachronism

"I did some research of my own about this Sword Hunt. Just because the Maniwa are known for being assassins doesn't mean we can't do our due diligence.[46] My ninpo is especially well suited for *that line of work*. And since we have this competition going among the Bosses, I went all out—a passion project, if you will—and I hit pay dirt. Found some fun facts. Or not so fun facts."

"Stop beating around the bush. You need to understand I'm not big on thinking about stuff. I can't understand you when you talk like that. Let's back up. What you found, when you were digging. Was it that stuff about Togame working her way up? About positioning herself beside the next shogun?"

"Yeah, but I didn't stop there—I knew there was something else. There had to be some other reason being Grand Commander wasn't good enough—some reason she would stop at nothing, even suffer the betrayals of the Maniwa and Sabi, if it meant collecting all the Shikizaki blades."

Komori hacked through a cough.

It must have hurt to speak—and yet.

He was regaining his strength, which Shichika failed to notice, too focused on the conversation.

"*This woman*," Komori said, pointing his finger at himself, "is the daughter of Takahito Hida[47]—the Mastermind of the Rebellion."

The words chilled Shichika to his core.

The Rebellion is fresh in our memories—

But who could deny the determination of the rebels?

Togame had described the spirit of the uprising thus, to Shichika.

"In a different world, she would have been a princess, with a castle of her own. The bakufu branded the Hida family enemies of the state and annihilated every last one of them—yet somehow, a child was spared. I've yet to figure out where that little girl grew into a woman and how she snuck her way into the bakufu—but I can tell you this much, she's shameless about clawing her way up. She won't stop until she's at the side of the next shogun. Is it not clear *what she is plotting*?"

"What is she?"

"It should be obvious by now why being Grand Commander will never satisfy her. While by no means a low rank, it stops short of direct audience with His Excellency."[48]

Komori was melting.[49]

His bones shifted.

The flesh of his body changed by degrees.

46 調査下調べ CHŌSA SHITASHIRABE preliminary research
47 飛騨 鷹比等 HIDA TAKAHITO Hida: also an old name for northern Gifu 鷹 TAKA hawk
48 大御所 ŌGOSHO the imperial inner sanctum; by extension, "his royal highness"
49 ぐにゅり GUNYURI onomatopoeia for puttylike transformation

But Shichika completely failed to notice.

That was the last thing on his mind.

Takahito Hida—Shichika knew the name.

He had heard it from his father, Mutsue Yasuri.

The name of the Mastermind of the Rebellion.

Uttered by the Hero of the Rebellion—Sixth Master of the Kyotoryu, Mutsue Yasuri.

"This is revenge. Plain and simple."

Komori's voice was clear.

"Either vengeance for the obliteration[50] of her family line—or a reboot of the Rebellion to bring her father's vision to fruition. In my opinion—kya-hah!—it's the former. Apparently, *that woman* watched her entire family get murdered one by one. I hear that's when *that hair of hers* turned white—with terror!"

Meanwhile, Komori's hair was no longer white.

It was changing into black—*black tousled hair.* Which is why he said *that hair of hers*—instead of *this hair of hers.*

Not *this woman*—but *that woman.*

"..."

But Shichika did not react to this grotesque display.

He was distraught.

In a state of confusion.

Takahito Hida. Kaoyaku[51] of Oshu.[52]

The Traitor.[53]

Their father, Mutsue Yasuri, Sixth Master of the Kyotoryu, had always talked about it—even bragged. How magnificently, using nothing but his own two hands, the blades of his hands, he had beaten off the leader of the rebel army. A glorious tale of heroism if there ever was one!

But not necessarily common knowledge.

Shichika was sure that after the Rebellion, all mention of the Kyotoryu and Mutsue Yasuri, who had been banished to this island, was taboo for the House of Tetsubi. Apparently, Komori had not even known the Kyotoryu existed until visiting the island, in which case he couldn't possibly have known it was Mutsue who had vanquished Hida. Perhaps he hadn't dug that far, but this was not a story you would ever figure out by digging.

Still...

Togame must have known.

It involved her, after all.

I knew Mutsue Yasuri of the Kyotoryu by name—

50 根絶やし NEDAYASHI uprooting
51 顔役 KAOYAKU highly connected and influential person
52 奥州 ŌSHŪ an old northern province
53 大逆人 TAIGYAKUNIN committer of high treason

But not by face—

That was a lie.

Having seen her father slain before her eyes, she must have known.

Known the face of Mutsue Yasuri.

And that was why.

She had arrived on Haphazard Island knowing everything—*having witnessed, like no one else, the fearsomeness of the Kyotoryu—so thoroughly it turned her hair white.*

What if his father—

If Mutsue were still alive—would she have entrusted *her father's enemy*[54] with rounding up the Shikizaki blades?

I'm the son of that enemy.

And yet.

Why did she—

Not see it as a mistake?

No, she must—at least, she must by now. Nobody could overlook the error of someone with her past coming to this island.

But she was out of options.

Betrayed by the Maniwa Clan—and by Hakuhei Sabi.

Betrayed!

"That dirty little scion of an insurrectionist[55]—and no innocent herself, the wormy traitor—dares call me a backstabber and a coward? Kyahah! But look. I'm an assassin. I know exactly what she's plotting—what I saw in that eye wasn't ambition after all. It was a burning desire for revenge. Madness—no other word suffices. Me? I work for money—she's trying to pull off the unthinkable, and it's not even for the money. I can't go for that. And you, Kyotoryu. Don't you think it's foolish, after all the years you've spent honing[56] your skills, to let her use you as a tool?"

Let's make this clear—

I didn't inherit my title from my father—

She'd said that too.

After Shichika, who couldn't have known better, asked Togame his superlatively insensitive and distorted question about whether his dad had—of all things—worked for her dad.

It was just as Komori said—Shichika had been too soft in the head to see what might have driven Togame to follow the path of a Schemer.

Right, she hadn't followed in her father's footsteps.

She had become Togame the Schemer.

To inherit her father's cause.

"If you did the research on your own," Shichika whispered, "does that

[54] 仇 KATAKI overtone of being a target of revenge
[55] 賊軍 ZOKUGUN rebel army
[56] 切磋琢磨 SESSA TAKUMA incessant training

mean you're the only one, for now, who knows all this?"

"Huh? Oh, yeah, I guess so. What about it?"

"In that case—"

Shichika assumed a stance.

Spear hands.

Kyotoryu Form Two—the Suisen.

"If I defeat you for good—you'll take that information to your grave,[57] *where it can't hurt Togame."*

"Whaaat?"

Komori couldn't believe his ears. Was he being challenged to battle?[58]

"What the hell are you saying? You should be mad at her, not me—how did that boost your morale?"

Komori would never understand.

Who could have understood where Shichika was coming from, raised as he had been on this tiny island, only ten miles around? He had truly believed that his father, Mutsue Yasuri, was a hero, *from the bottom of his heart.*

He had swallowed whole[59] the title of "Hero of the Rebellion."

A sense of inferiority—is no more than a love turned inside out. While Shichika was not about to step up and declare his affection for his father, he revered the late Master of the Kyotoryu enough to lose his temper when the hut Mutsue built was reduced to splinters—enough for his sister to tease him that he always thought of Daddy. Even banished to this island, Mutsue Yasuri was, in Shichika's reckoning, a champion of justice.

Which is why, until now.

He had never even given it a thought.

People had fallen victim to the Hero of the Rebellion.

Shichika Yasuri—so face-blind he was unable to tell men from women—was recognizing for perhaps the first time the existence of the *other.*

"I am Shichika Yasuri, Seventh Master of the Kyotoryu. Prepare to die."

"Alright...fine!"

Airing the details of Togame's plot to deaden Shichika's fighting spirit was a miscalculation—it had only flared up—but Komori seemed to have fulfilled his foremost objectives.

Recovering from his wounds.

And buying time[60] for a transformation.

"I, too, am Shichika Yasuri, Seventh Master of the Kyotoryu!"

He took to his feet to face Shichika—as Shichika.

The robust build, the fit body—and the tousled hair.

From every angle, it was Shichika. A flawless replica.

57 隠蔽 INPEI bury; conceal
58 宣戦布告 SENSEN FUKOKU proclamation of war
59 鵜呑み UNOMI "gulp down like a cormorant"
60 時間稼ぎ JIKAN KASEGI "earning time"

Lying on the ground, holding Shichika's attention with Togame's story, Komori had slowly remade his body from the inside. The disclosure may have failed to discourage Shichika but had bought the ninja more time than he had bargained for. The replication process was complete.

He was still wearing Togame's luxurious kimono, which helped to tell them apart—but his voice, too, was Shichika Yasuri's.

"You don't sound like me at all..."

Komori didn't bother to recapitulate for Shichika what he had told Togame.

The air was already heating up.

Hot enough to boil.

"Kyahah! To tell you the truth, being an assassin, my ninpo isn't suited for direct attacks. My only real move is the Star Cannon, which you saw. And you already beat that move, Kyotoryu. Honestly, if I fought you head to head *when I was me*, you'd probably win."

Shichika didn't flinch at the words issuing from his own figure.

"But what's this? Now we're square![61] Same biceps, same forearms, same thighs. Same strength. Actually, one each of your arms and legs got cut up by my shuriken, so I guess I have a little edge?"

"Hmph." Shichika kept his cool. "If you're gonna bother doing that, why not make yourself into someone even stronger? Like that swordsman Hakuhei Sabi. Or maybe you guys never met? But you have lots of experience, I'm sure you've met all kinds of guys who are stronger than me. Right?"

"I'm almost jealous of how you could be so clueless. No, *those guys* wouldn't necessarily be stronger than you. A fight is all about the matchup. It's like how rock beats scissors, but is weaker than paper, which loses to scissors. So what's the best scenario? *Two rocks,*[62] *one stronger than the other.*"

"I hate to break it to you, but my cuts are basically fine. They may have bugged me if we'd done this right away, but now they barely even hurt."

"Okay. Great. So we're even then. Rock versus rock."

Komori as Shichika—

Looked at the Leveler lying at his feet.

Zetto the Leveler, which he had spit out of his body.

One of the Twelve Possessed, the masterworks of Kiki Shikizaki.

A sword that would never bend or break or lose its edge.

For the Kyotoryu, it was the worst match possible.

"*This* ought to make me the stronger rock."

"..."

"Kyotoryu—the Swordless Swordsman. But really. *If the Swordless Swordsman wielded this,* he would be stronger than the same without it. No contest."

61 互角 GOKAKU "same corners"
62 ぐー GŪ fist

Komori made it sound like he had already won.

The Leveler had fallen right by where he stood. He would have no difficulty grabbing it. Even if Shichika tried, he'd never get there first: *they had the same legs*. In this fight, distance was the only variable.

"Only meatheads rely on muscle—when there's an easier way, I say take it. If you want to call me out for fighting dirty, go ahead. As long as it's not *her* who says it, I could care less. I might even like it."

"Are you sure you aren't making a mistake?"

Shichika answered Komori's gloating with a frigid stare.

"The Kyotoryu is strong because it *doesn't use a sword*."

"Come on. We both know that's a front.[63] Assuming each side has the same potential, there's no way a guy without a weapon can be stronger than a guy with one. Or are you telling me the blades of your hand and your foot cut better than the real deal?"[64]

"Like I said, you have it all wrong. It's not because the Kyotoryu uses hands and feet as blades that I'm a swordsman even though I don't wield a sword—I am already a katana, on my own, in swordsman form. My school using a sword would be like a dog walking another dog. So listen up. I'm not losing to *me* with a sword. It'd be like—"

"I get it. No need to pile on excuses. If you keep yapping, the sun's bound to go down. Go have your pity party somewhere else—hell, for instance. Alright, *me*, let's go."

"After you, *me*. I'm gonna slam you with a spectacular knockout move. The last-but-not-the-least, held-in-reserve, ultimate secret of the Kyotoryu!"

In a blink.

Komori jumped first.

But Shichika didn't move at all—and kept up a defensive posture.

Without even trying to stop Komori from grabbing the Leveler, he stood with spear hands—waiting for his doppelganger to come and try to chop down the real him. Like Form One (the Suzuran), Form Two (the Suisen) was a countermove. Because the fingers point, it has a slightly greater range than the Suzuran, but not enough to matter against a long sword—

"*Tadaaaaaaaaaaaaaaaaaaaaaaaaaaaaaaaaaaaaaaaaaaaaaaaaaaaaaaaaaaaaaaaaaaaaaaaaaaaaaaaaaaaaaaaaaaaaaaaaaaaaaaaaaaaaaaaah! Side Splitter!*"

Gripping the handle of the Leveler with both hands, Komori leapt high into the air—vastly higher than when he jumped on the beach. The forest floor around the spring was much easier to leap from than sand, but upgraded to Shichika Yasuri's mighty legs, *a poor footing would have made no difference*.

A strike from on high—

[63] 建前 TATEMAE posturing; formality

[64] 真剣 SHINKEN "real sword" by extension, "serious business"

Made the heavier by gravity, swung—

"Uh... Ack."

—Did not swing down, or swing at all.

Komori's hands, as he started falling from the sky—did not grip the Leveler. The sword danced in the air, spinning in circles, above him.

Like it had lost its owner.

It danced.

Spinning.[65]

"Wh-Why?"

"You should learn to hear people out—even if the sun starts going down."

From the ground, Shichika spoke to Komori as he fell.

"Know what, though? You were right about me making excuses. The truth is that out of all the masters of the Kyotoryu, *not one of us could swing a sword to save his life. It's not that we don't use swords—we can't!*"

Thus it was for Shichika Yasuri.

And for Mutsue Yasuri.

And, needless to say, for the founding master Kazune Yasuri—too.

That was why Kazune forsook the sword despite being a swordsman. He took the discipline to places nobody had dared to venture—but what able swordsman would willingly forsake the vehicle of his skill?

"The same applies to me, born into this family. Today I saw my first katana... It was fine to copy my arms and legs, but my ability with weapons won't do anything for you, *me*."

"Ahh... Nkk, *me*...bastard!"

Komori fell, empty-handed.

Gravity now his enemy.

There was no use rushing now.

In the end, there was only one reason for Komori's defeat. Nanami's confidence in her brother notwithstanding, no one would normally expect a veteran Maniwa to lose to a novice Yasuri.

But lost he had.

And Zetto the Leveler was to blame.[66]

He just could not resist—using the katana.

Maybe the Hell-Made was simply being serviceable the first time—and so could maintain self-control. Still, even if his Star Cannon was depleted, Komori—a ninja, not a swordsman—reached again and again for the Leveler: proof that the sword's poison was coursing through his veins...as wary of this as he had been.

The venom of the Possessed.

Owning one made you want to kill—

"It's a good thing you let go of the sword. The ultimate secret is so insane

65 くるくる KURU KURU onomatopoeia for rotation

66 敗因 HAI'IN cause of defeat

I'm sure it would have snapped the Leveler in half. By the way, I keep calling it that[67] because I only came up with it yesterday."

As Komori continued to fall helplessly to the ground, Shichika spelled it out for the ninja.

Exceedingly politely, in simple terms.

All told, the Kyotoryu had seven secret moves.

Fatal Orchid One: Kyoka Suigetsu

Fatal Orchid Two: Kacho Fugetsu

Fatal Orchid Three: Hyakka Ryoran

Fatal Orchid Four: Ryuryoku Kako

Fatal Orchid Five: Hika Rakuyo

Fatal Orchid Six: Kinjo Tenka

Fatal Orchid Seven: Rakka Rozeki

"Too bad you won't be around to see each move on its own—but the Last Fatal Orchid is when I hit you *with all of them at the same time*. To put it your way, it's like an unstoppable[68] combination of rock, paper, and scissors. Every one of them is lethal, but when I hit you with all seven simultaneously, you're going to explode. See for yourself."

Then Shichika pulled it off—spectacularly.

Just like Togame requested.

"Kyotoryu—Shichika Hachiretsu!"

■ ■

It wouldn't come undone.

It wouldn't come loose.

Writhe as she may, the straw rope held fast to her body—not your normal knot. This was a ninja knot. If only she hadn't been gagged, she might have chewed through the twisted straw—Togame thought, chagrinned.[69]

Could things really end this way?

Could things really end up here?

Had she given up her name, her lineage, her everything—passing through mountains of corpses and rivers of blood[70]—only to breathe her last stuck on this nameless island? To think she had been poised to seize the Shikizaki swords that had eluded even the Old Shogun. Delivering the remainder of the thousand to the shogunate—would have advanced her *plan* to the final stage.

[67] 最終奥義 SAISHŪ ŌGI ultimate secret (move)
[68] 無敵 MUTEKI unrivaled
[69] 歯がゆく HAGAYUKU "itchy toothed" vexed
[70] 屍山血河 SHIZAN KETSUGA less directly translated, a hellish warzone

Her scheme, to which she devoted her entire life.

Close enough to see.

Close enough to touch.

...Oh, Father.

I was so close to avenging you!

My thoughts go out to you.

My heart goes out to you!

"...nkk!"

Calling on the Kyotoryu was my undoing.

I must have been out of my mind.

As out of options as I may have been...relying on the man who murdered my father...or even his son... Telling myself the real enemy is the bakufu, the shogun...what a convenient excuse! Did I really vow to restore the honor of Mutsue once the job was finished? Even if I had to at that moment, how could I offer to vindicate the man who killed my father?

Was this her lot?

A perfect disgrace.[71]

Was she not the daughter—of a warrior family?

"..."

Taken to the mainland by Komori as his hostage and subjected to torture, she would eventually divulge all she knew of the Possessed. She prided herself on the tightness of her lips, but she had never been trained to withstand torture. Left to a ninja's devices, she would not last an hour. There were a myriad ways to extract information out of someone, and Togame could name a few—a ninja would know thousands more.

But no.

Before any more disgrace.

She would act.

"...Hmh."

Togame laughed.

With her gagged cheeks.

Fearlessly, invincibly.

"Hmhmhmhmh!"

How could I be so foolish!

What will never come undone or come loose? Not the rope.

My determination.

What will never bend or break or lose its edge?

My schemes.

I am the Schemer. I'll scheme my way out of this mess. That's how I made it this far!

If I must rely upon the Kyotoryu, my father's nemesis, to avenge him—so

[71] 恥さらし HAJI SARASHI "shame exposing"

be it. Let my soul, my life, get whittled away, I could not care less at this point!

Most who heard the story of Togame's early years accepted that her hair turned white from terror, at the sight of her family being slaughtered.

But no.

Her hair had been blanched by an outpouring of rage.

I have sworn upon this hair of white.

No matter how often I'm betrayed!

No matter who grows to hate me!

Even if it means living a life starved of love—I will fulfill the responsibility that is mine to undertake!

"Huh..."

Someone was approaching through the underbrush. Was it Komori? How had he returned so soon? Then again, if he had settled things with the Sword Cannon, the battle would have ended instantly. In which case, what had taken him so long?

Togame braced herself—defenseless as she was.

She could only glare in the direction of the sound.

With that eye of hers...

"I see," the man said, appearing from the bushes. "I see, I see, that's what he meant by *that eye*. But he was wrong about it smoldering. Can't trust a ninja, I suppose. I like the way it sparkles. Pretty cool if you ask me."

"...? ...!"

It was Shichika Yasuri.

How had he—no! Komori had it all planned out. After he bagged Shichika, he would transform into Shichika and kill Nanami. This must be Komori, on his way...no, on his way back! What had taken him so long was *killing off the sister.* But why hadn't he changed back? Maybe he was posing as Shichika to milk more information out of her—he had a lot of nerve. How the Schemer had fallen, if he believed such a charade[72] would do.

But then she noticed something.

What Shichika Yasuri was carrying.

Zetto the Leveler. One of the Twelve Possessed, the masterworks of Kiki Shikizaki. As if unaccustomed to holding a sword, he loosely clasped the butt of the handle and dragged the long blade rattling over the ground.

Komori would have stuffed it in his belly.

So this must be the real Shichika.

"Got me thinking, though. Maybe that ninja had parents or siblings, or maybe even kids. He had to have some kind of a family. I bet they'll hate my guts for this."

"..."

[72] 三文芝居 SANMON SHIBAI "three-penny acting"

"For starters—"

Shichika thrust the Leveler upright into the earth by the tree where Togame was tied up.

The Leveler seemed like it could take it.

But yikes, she'd told him to be careful...

"Here's the first one, Togame."

"..."

For starters?

The first one?

What did he mean—

Talking like this was only the beginning—

Like he was promising to do good by her—

"Don't get me wrong—I did it for you. I don't have my eyes set on money, I haven't been dosed with the Shikizaki venom, and I have no interest in serving the bakufu—I just felt like doing it, for you."

Shichika looked at her and laughed.

At his partner[73] for the yearlong journey ahead.

"I'm going ahead and falling for you."

[73] 相棒 AIBŌ "companion stick" buddy

EPILOGUE

■ ■

—And back to where we began.

From Haphazard Island, across the water to the Capital...and the Hisho Dojo.

To that training hall—where Shichika Yasuri was no longer surrounded by the six men. They had risen to action, only to fall to the floor, where they lay prostrate on the planks. Out cold, eyes rolled back in their skulls. Not one could climb back to his feet.

Their wooden swords had not even grazed Shichika.

They had dropped to the floor, just like the six men.

"Nice work..."

Togame, leaning against the wall, clapped her hands in satisfaction and called out to Shichika from behind.

"Not that I caught all of that. Was it the move that beat Komori? I'll admit that being able to take down six, or even seven men at once is nothing to sneeze at—but how would you cope if an eighth man were to appear?"

"You mean an eighth sword—but would that ever actually happen?"

"Any day," Togame said. "The Possessed have eleven other owners."

"Eleven," repeated Shichika. "What a pain."

"That's not the half of it. The Maniwa Clan has eleven other bosses. And don't forget the Strongest Swordsman—or should I say the Fallen Swordsman,[1] Hakuhei Sabi. And after them all manner of strange and awful characters, too many to count... Anyway, I'm relieved to see you can control your strength. These men have only fainted—and you didn't break a single sword, which matters a great deal."

"Does it, though?"

"Yes. Things were only hunky-dory[2] this time because the Leveler, as a rule, cannot be broken. But that won't be the case again. And another thing, at the risk of belaboring the point: don't think you outperformed Komori. He drowned in his own tactics, and as a result, you won. You were lucky things turned out that way."

"Can't argue[3] with that. I may have acted big and strong when we were talking trash, but I'll probably lose at some point."

"My job is to make sure that you never do. While a tactician can drown in his own tactics, the Schemer ever swims in her schemes. Which is why, from

[1] 堕剣士 DAKENSHI plays on 堕天使 DATENSHI fallen angel

[2] 上首尾 JŌSHUBI "up from head to tail" satisfactory

[3] 否定 HITEI deny, negate

this day forward, you play by my rules, in battle as in life."

"You can trust me," Shichika responded without pause.

A hearty reply.

"So I guess this means I've passed the tests and proved myself worthy to serve you. Alright, Togame. Tell me these rules you want me to start following."

"There are...only four at the moment."

"Four. Let's hear them."

"First, as stated earlier, never break a sword—but the rule goes beyond that. I forbid you to attack the swords in any way. You may only counter them. Need I repeat, the only unbreakable sword is the Leveler; the remaining eleven will be nowhere near as strong. Retrieve each sword in pristine condition. Not a scratch. In a word—protect the swords, whosoever may be holding them."

"Got it.[4] I protect the swords. What's number two?"

"Protect me. Our mission is to round up all the Shikizaki blades, but it's pointless if I die in the process. I cannot have you letting me be kidnapped again, or worse. I must never be hurt. Not a scratch."

"Got it. I protect you. What's rule three?"

"Protect yourself," Togame said. "And I'm not saying this for your sake—until we take possession of all twelve Shikizaki swords, I forbid you to die. Capturing a sword is no excuse for suffering a mortal blow. Without you, the hunt is over. Which is why I forbid you to be injured—not a scratch."

"Got it. I protect myself. What's number four?"

"Protect yourself," Togame repeated—and stood. Whisking the hem of her kimono across the floor, she spun around; with her back turned to Shichika, she started heading for the exit. He couldn't see her expression. "This time, I am saying it for your sake."

"..."

"Don't die—the journey will be taxing, but you mustn't die. Can you promise that? I won't have you saying otherwise. Quick, say you got it."

"Got it. Absolutely. I'll protect everything."

Then Shichika got moving too.

In seconds, he was right behind Togame.

"So what's next? You said we'd want to get at least the first few swords before we visited Owari."

"The Kyotoryu may be notorious, but you're a nobody. If I'm showing up with you, one sword is not nearly good enough a souvenir.[5] Especially not the Leveler, which we haven't seized so much as recovered. Our next sword will be Zanto the Razor. It was forged to slice like no other. There is no substance

[4] 了解 RYŌKAI acknowledged

[5] 手土産 TEMIYAGE a gift presented to a host

in this world it cannot cut. Its owner is one Ginkaku Uneri of Inaba. I'll tell you more about him on the way—and while we're at it, let's get you some new clothes. Come."

"Sounds great. I love you, Togame."

"Good. Love me all you like."

■ ■

And thus they set off on their journey.

A wild sword chase, with no ending—or even any road in sight.

Yet this tale is heading steadily toward a conclusion: all thousand of the swords of legendary swordsmith Kiki Shikizaki, *including his masterpieces the Twelve Possessed*, were merely foils for the creation of the Kyotoryu...a single katana, Kyoto the Diamond[6]—though at present no one comprehended this, not even Togame the Schemer.

Zetto the Leveler: Check
End of Book One
To Be Continued

[6] 虚刀・鑢 KYOTŌ YASURI "The Absent Katana: File"

CHARACTER INDEX 1

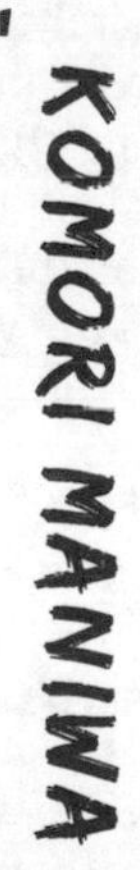

AGE	Unknown
OCCUPATION	Ninja
AFFILIATION	Maniwa Clan
STATUS	Boss
POSSESSED	Zetto the Leveler
HEIGHT	5' 10"
WEIGHT	130 lbs.
HOBBY	Ceramics

LIST OF SPECIAL MOVES

SIDE SPLITTER (SLASH)	⇦⇧⇧⇨ **SLASH SLASH**
SIDE SPLITTER (THRUST)	⇦⇧⇧⇨ **THRUST THRUST**
STAR CANNON	⇩ **(INHALE)** ⇧ **THRUST**
SWORD CANNON	⇩ **(INHALE)** ⇧ **SLASH**
BODY MELT	⇩⇩⇨⇨⇧⇧ **SLASH + THRUST + KICK**

AFTER(S)WORD

Lately, in listening to people's stories and considering their examples, I have often been struck by the importance of not being talented. How can I put this, humans are basically lazy, so when they have even half-baked talent, they skimp on the hard work that should by rights accompany it, and there's a good chance that things will get no farther than half-baked. In the worst case, because they're somewhat talented, they won't be able to discern when to fold. Not putting in the work, but not giving up either...a pretty wretched state of affairs. To put it in extreme terms, it's actually better not to have some partial talent—in order to work hard. The have-nots' desire to have is dozens of times stronger than that of the haves, so in the end, they'll end up getting much more than the haves—maybe. Surprisingly, the harder the initial conditions of a game, the more it fires you up. Same principle. If you don't have talent, you'll be able to do the work to get your hands on something rivalling talent, and that's a wonderful advantage, something that will surely bring a rich, fulfilling life. But that being said, obviously people will be happier with talent than without, and what could be better than getting all kinds of freebies without having to work for it? We're only human, after all. You may be better off without mediocre talent, but if we're talking about killer talent, well, who wouldn't want that? Though all of this is starting to sound like an excuse on the part of a fellow who isn't talented. Some would argue that "talent" is the fruit of hard work, which is maybe something we should bear in mind, but in the end, most of the time, what determines the outcome of a human life, and puts our ducks in a row, is probably not "what we can do" but "what we can't do." That's what I've been thinking lately, anyway.

Now then, what to say about this book? Not much at the moment, except that it's the story of a swordsman and twelve swords. The first of a twelve-book series. Eleven more to go.* One sword per book... That's the plan, but depending on how things go, we might launch everybody into outer space partway through, so no predictions here. It's my intention to power through as if this were my debut, though, so please bear with me. The characters and swords appearing in the story have been visually rendered by someone who needs no introduction, your friend and mine: *take*. I can safely say that my prime motivation for writing this series is to see what wonderful illustrations will arrive with future books. I have no idea what the future holds, either within the story or without, and in that spirit, this has been *Sword Tale—Book One: Zetto the Leveler.*

I offer my deepest thanks to you all for accompanying me on this reckless adventure that brooks no predictions.

* The original series was published in twelve monthly installments. This English edition features three more volumes.

NISIOISIN

BOOK TWO

ZANTO
THE RAZOR

第二話
斬刀（ザントウ）・鈍（ナマクラ）

画：竹
筆：平田弘史
本及ビ箱装幀：ヴェイア
版面構成：紺野慎一（凸版印刷）
本文使用書体：FOT-筑紫明朝 Pro L

The original Book Two Table of Contents spread

PROLOGUE

■ ■

The fusuma[1] clacked open.

By no means was this room spacious—frankly, it was cramped. Devoid of furniture, much less any decorations, it was floored with tatami[2] and bare.[3] One person, on his own, would take up almost all of the room.

In it sat a man.

He was lanky, with long hair like a girl.

A simple black kimono.

Eyes closed, he sat cross-legged in the center.

He almost seemed asleep—no.

In fact he was.

Given the hour, it was not the strangest thing—and sure, some people could probably sleep cross-legged, right?

Nevertheless.

A man asleep with a katana at his waist was rare no matter what. He slumbered with the sword, in its black scabbard,[4] slipped between his obi and left hip, and as if leaning on it.

Or perhaps—

Safeguarding it.

As if it were more important than his life.

"..."

Hearing the fusuma slide open, the man in black slowly opened his eyes.

"Hek hek hek hek."

To the sound of an utterly unnatural and bizarre laugh.

From the doorway another figure slithered into the tiny room. He was attired like a ninja—but this was not the standard ninja outfit you might be imagining. It had no sleeves, and in their place, fat chains were strung around his body.

"Od annog ahctahw tub. Ni thgir egrab dna nepo rood eht worht ajnin a evah ot gnissarrabme dat," the ninja said.

But he was totally incomprehensible.

Incomprehensible—and yet this was precisely his astonishing special trait.

An unnatural, bizarre—trait.

"Nalc Awinam eht fo sessob evlewt eht fo eno, Awinam Igasarihs em llac

[1] 襖 FUSUMA thick sliding doors that block out light
[2] たたみ TATAMI straw mats
[3] 殺風景 SAPPŪKEI barren
[4] 鞘 SAYA sheath of a katana

nac uoy tub, [5]Igasarihs Sdrowkcab em llac elpoep tsom."

"..."

To that.

The man in black only narrowed his eyes in annoyance. The hour was a factor, and after this rude awakening, perhaps he wasn't thinking straight—but even in broad daylight, a ninja who spoke thus would be hard to welcome. Perversely, having entered through the doorway like a normal person began to seem wrong in the case of this absurd shinobi.[6]

"Hek hek hek," snickered Shirasagi "Backwords" Maniwa.

In reverse.

"Gniws elgnis a htiw evlah tonnac ti gnihton si ereht taht yas yeht. Edalb emosraef a. Ikazikihs Ikik yb degrof dnasuoht eht gnoma seceipretsam, Dessessop Evlewt eht fo eno. Rozar[7] eht Otnaz? Rozar yradnegel eht pih ruoy ta anatak suoicerp taht si, ym ho?"

He added:

"Em ot ti evig."

"..."

"Dnatsrednu uoy, yrlavir yldneirf a. Kcen dna kcen eb lliw I dna eh, drows ruoy emmig uoy fi tub, em fo daeha pets a si Iromok knup taht."

"..."

"Sdnah daed ruoy morf ti yrp I dna, on yas."

Shirasagi gave a nasty look, as if to hint that he preferred the latter.

The Maniwa.

Known only to those in the know, a band of expert assassins—and the ninpo used by Shirasagi Maniwa, especially, was dangerous enough to keep the other bosses cautious.[8] Nearly every one of them had thanked their lucky stars for not having Shirasagi as an enemy. His bizarre backwards way of talking was a function of his ninpo, the absolute horror of which was only known to those who opposed him—like this man in black, for instance, sword at his hip and still sitting.

Still not moving.

Far from handing over the katana, he had not so much as twitched—unresponsive to the point that he might have been sleeping with his eyes open.

Had he failed to decipher Backwords Shirasagi's speech?

Quite possibly.

"Yako, yadyreve ees ot teg uoy gnihtemos ton s'ti? Dab taht opnin ym ees ot tnaw uoy? Sgnileef ym struh ti, em gnirongi tiuq, aohw."

Shing!

[5] 鷺白のり喋さ逆　GISARASHI NO RIBEYASHIKASA　"Reverse-Talking Shirasagi"
白鷺　SHIRASAGI　"The Egret"

[6] しのび　SHINOBI　alternative reading of 忍 NIN in phonetic characters, another word for "ninja"

[7] 斬刀 鈍　ZANTŌ NAMAKURA　"The Slicing Katana: Dullblade"

[8] 一目置く　ICHIMOKU OKU　"place an eye"to recognize (a strength)

As Shirasagi paraded his reverse speech as if he were readying himself, laying the groundwork, for *something*—the man in black, without warning, without any tell, suddenly moved.

But *moved* might be an overstatement.

A slight motion.

No more than his right hand grasping the katana's hilt—to all appearances.

"Hmm?"

When his foe took hold of the weapon, Shirasagi's expression changed—but not his easy attitude. It was the attitude of someone with absolute confidence in his own abilities.

"Kcats ruoy wolb I elihw hctaw. Skcajpalf ruoy pilf ot em tnaw uoy snaem tuo drows ruoy gnillup, egaugnal ym ni. Tsal ruoy eb lliw od uoy dnoces eht, denrawerof eb tub. Ekil uoy revenehw tuo ti pihw. Tuo ti pihw annog, tahw?"

"If you don't mind my asking."

The man in black finally spoke.

Responding to Shirasagi Maniwa.

But his next words—

"This flapjack-flipping[9] ninpo—it allows you to talk even after you've been sliced in two?"

—were a farewell.

"Huh?"

Not that holding still would have kept the gash together—but at those words, Shirasagi leaned forward, for the last time.

His torso, unstuck from his waist, tipped over onto the tatami. Because his head landed upside down, his death throes—

"Gaaah! Wh-Whennn?"

—came out forwards, but at this point, how he sounded mattered little.

"*...Hiken Zerosen,*"[10] intoned the man in black.

Not having taken a single step, still sitting.

"Ugh, he's ruining the tatami—I'll have to swap it with a mat from one of the other rooms... As for his corpse...I may as well hold off until the gore dries."

Although he had just killed, the man in black was unperturbed, as if nothing exceptional had happened, and he set his mind to planning how to clean the room.

He let go of the hilt—and rubbed his eyes.

So he did feel a little sleepy after all.

[9] 逆鱗探し GEKIRIN SAGASHI looking for a touchy spot 逆鱗 GEKIRIN flipped scale (as in snakes')

[10] 秘剣 零閃 HIKEN ZEROSEN "Hidden Sword, Zero Flash" sword too swift to catch the light homophone with ゼロ戦 ZEROSEN, infamous Japanese fighter planes of World War II

■ ■

Of course, if this were a piece of contemporary popular fiction, you may very well presume that Shirasagi Maniwa, one of the Twelve Bosses of the Maniwa Clan, was killed off after the author cried, "I don't want to deal anymore with a character who talks in such an annoying way! What sort of ninpo requires speaking in reverse, anyway?"—however, this is no piece of popular fiction, but a historical novel. In other words, the man in black was indeed that formidable.

Of the thousand Mutant Blades forged by Kiki Shikizaki.

One of his masterpieces, the Twelve Possessed.

Zanto the Razor.

Owned by Ginkaku Uneri.[11]

Undoubtedly the toughest foe to grace these pages so far—okay, out of just two!

We'll say the tougher.

Behold this unholy history[12] full of holes![13]

A skittish, scatterbrained sketch!

Tale of the Sword: Book Two ♪

[11] 宇練銀閣 UNERI GINKAKU "Surging Silver Tower"

[12] 黒歴史 KUROREKISHI a past one would like to forget

[13] 嘘歴史 USOREKISHI (neologism) "a lie history"

CHAPTER ONE

INABA DESERT

■ ■

"It's about time we came up with a catchphrase,"[1] she said abruptly.

A petite woman, but the seemingly dozen layers[2] of grandiose silk with which she bedizened herself made her look far bigger than she really was. Big as in giant. She wasn't so much dressed in these clothes as riding in them, strapped in for a stroll. Her jewelry was chunky enough to function as fortified armor. But none of this stood out more starkly than her long white hair—not a strand of black.

Our Schemer, Togame.

"Catchphrase?"

The man responsible for this response, if you could call it that, was as big as she was petite—and as minimally clad as Togame was overdressed. Wearing only the bare necessities, to the point where any less would have been scandalous. Stripped to the waist, and beyond his arm guards and his leg guards,[3] wearing only a hakama.[4] On his back he toted a massive bundle, full to bursting, but showed no sign of hardship.

Shichika Yasuri.

Seventh Master of the Kyotoryu.

"What the heck's a catchphrase?"

"What am I going to do with you? A catchphrase is a thing you say almost without realizing, whenever things get crazy. It just pops out."

"Oh. Okay. But whose catchphrase are we talking?"

"Yours."

"..."

Shichika nodded obediently.

As appropriate a response as he could offer.

"But wait a second. If I have to say it without realizing, should I be thinking about it?"

"Focus, Shichika."

Very funny. She disregarded him with gusto.

Togame launched her explanation.

"I tried writing down last month's events, on Haphazard Island."

"Huh? Oh, right. Your report."

Grand Commander of Arms of the Yanari Shogunate Military Directorate, Owari Bakufu.

1 口癖 KUCHIGUSE "mouth habit" a word or words that one is given to uttering
2 十二単衣 JŪNIHITOE twelve-layered kimono
3 脚絆 KYAHAN cloth wrapped around the shins
4 袴 HAKAMA loose pleated trousers tied at the waist

That was Togame the Schemer's full title.[5]

The report Shichika alluded to would be submitted to the upper ranks of the bakufu. A handwritten account of what Togame, sent off by shogunate decree, had witnessed in her travels.

Dispatched—on a Sword Hunt.

In pursuit of the Twelve Possessed, the masterworks of Kiki Shikizaki.

"Right, your report. I did exactly what you asked me to. You said you wanted a spectacle. I gave that scummy ninja what he had coming to him."

"I'm sure it was spectacular, but whatever you did to Komori Maniwa, I wasn't there to witness it. Ergo, it cannot be included in my report."

"Why not?" *Why make me do it then?* "I did exactly what you asked."

"Sorry to say, but I can only record what I see with my own eyes. Don't worry—we'll have other chances. But listen, Shichika. In explaining how I seized Zetto the Leveler, I came to a crucial realization."

"What was that?"

"You have no personality."[6]

Certainly one way to put it.

This brutal dig would be enough to put most people in a funk;[7] and Shichika, raised on a remote island, the embodiment of unsophistication, was no exception. He grimaced and stopped midstride.

"I-I don't?"

"In my first draft, that ninja stood out as a more compelling character. I attempted several revisions, but it was useless. No amount of reworking changed the equation. Try as I might, there was no way I could make you more compelling than Komori. When I read over my final draft, you struck me as no more than a half-naked baboon."

"Whoa, Miss Togame. Wait a second."

He was so flustered he added the formality.[8]

"When you're fighting a guy who can pull swords out of his throat, personality is not how you win. He may have had more personality, but I'm the one who won the battle."

"Sure. I don't want you losing battles. But I can't have you losing any popularity contests, either. Let's just say—you aren't florid enough."[9]

"Have some consideration!"

Apparently, *no personality* and *half-naked baboon* stung far less than the accusation of being insufficiently florid.

Which makes sense, considering his name.[10]

"Look," Togame said. "The Maniwa is like a ninja circus. Komori was only

5 正式な身分 SEISHIKI NA MIBUN formal status
6 個性が弱い KOSEI GA YOWAI his "individuality is weak"
7 鬱 UTSU depression
8 さん付け SANZUKE attaching the honorific さん SAN
9 花がない HANA GA NAI "to be flowerless," despite his moves all having floral names
10 七花 SHICHIKA "seven flowers"

the beginning. They have this one guy, Shirasagi, who talks backwards."

"What do you mean?"

Shichika could not imagine.

Much less fathom the implications.

And would there be any point to it, anyway?

"Actually, could you just stop comparing me with those Maniwacs?[11] Not just my personality, but in general."

The Maniwacs.

Catchy name for a band, too much so for a band of assassins.

Needless to say, that was lost on Shichika, and given the era, on Togame as well. "Maniwacs, that has a nice ring to it," she adopted it happily.

Poor ninjas.

"I realize I can't ask you to start acting like them overnight. They're nothing but personality. It wouldn't even be fair for me to point to them as models or goals. But Shichika, I need you to at least put in an effort."

"E-Effort..."

"Tireless effort is character-building."

"I'm not sure that's how it works..."

"For now, back to your catchphrase."

It was evidently useless to resist. "Uh huh..."

"It's like picking the title before you write the book. If you leave out your cup, it fills itself. Don't underestimate the power of a catchphrase. It can define a character. Nothing works quicker, not even close. It's your best bet, and it could be your greatest asset. I say catchphrase, but you could call it a motto, or a slogan, or a signature line. Point being, it characterizes how you speak. Take that ninja, Shirasagi Maniwa. For him, talking backwards is like a catchphrase, broadly speaking."

"Huh." Not that Shichika had the slightest idea what talking backwards meant.

"Here's a more concrete example. Remember the weird way Komori laughed? 'Kyahah!' What an excellent way of conveying his immaturity, and the madness and the cruelty it spawned. When you hear it, you say to yourself, 'This is not a normal guy.'"

"I wouldn't mind being seen as normal."

"That's well and good, but not good enough for me. I don't want my report to put my audience to sleep. What if they quit reading halfway through?"

"Aren't these reports normally pretty lame? Not like I've ever read one."

No one was expecting a romping, rollicking[12] account.

Or so Shichika believed.

"And that is precisely why mine cannot be normal. You know, that swordsman Hakuhei Sabi, who I was working with before, he had a pretty good one,

[11] まにわに MANIWA NI cutesy, derisive pun on やにわに YANIWA NI out of the blue
[12] 愉快痛快 YUKAI TSŪKAI entertaining and thrilling

too. It makes me sick[13] to compliment a traitor...but sometimes you need to give someone his due."

"Hakuhei Sabi, huh."

The mightiest swordsman in all the land—they said. Despite being a kid of barely twenty.

"For future reference, what was it?"

"He often interrupts himself to say, 'Hear that? Made your heart beat!'"

"..."

Sabi was in possession of Hakuto the Whisper, one of the Twelve Possessed, the masterworks of Kiki Shikizaki. At this rate, they were bound to face off somewhere down the line—but Shichika rapidly lost any desire to have anything to do with the man.

And yet Togame seemed to think his catchphrase was fairly dashing...

Shichika had better brace himself.

"When I was working with Komori and with Sabi, I never had to worry about their catchphrases, but in your case, I'd be remiss if I didn't do you the favor. I don't want a repeat of that last report."

"Oh..."

Some favor.

"Clueless as you are, it's my responsibility, as your employer, to take care of you. After all, I promised Nanami."

"I highly doubt my sister was worried about catchphrases."

"How about a couple more examples? Let's see, I know a guy who says 'Wipe that smile off your face!' every time you speak to him, whether or not you are smiling. Another guy cries "Ooowhoo!"[14] like a dog whenever anything big happens. Some people tilt their sentences a certain way. And then there's local accents. Those are great for personality. They announce where you're from."

"Great examples."

Shichika nodded thankfully. He had half a mind to just give in.

Arguing and debating was such a pain...

"Hey, Togame, I think I got it."

"What?"

"Not sure if you can call it a catchphrase, but there's one that I'm always thinking, or saying."

"Ah."

"It's, well, 'what a pain'—"

"*Cheerio!*"[15]

She suckerpunched him.

A fist right to the ribs.

[13] 癪に障る SHAKU NI SAWARU aggravating
[14] きゃうーん KYAUUN yelping sound
[15] ちぇりおー CHERIŌ an expression unfamiliar to most Japanese readers

But between Shichika's toned muscle and Togame's shrimpy arms, the blow—surprise or not—didn't make much of an impact. He would sooner notice a mosquito land on his skin.

"You dolt. How are you supposed to showcase your personality with such tired words? A report where the main subject is always complaining about how much of a pain everything is will make whoever reads it feel the same. Try to put yourself in my position. I'm the one who has to write you into being. What if I start wanting to quit?"

"O-Okay..."

Totally rejected.

His sole claim to personality, totally rejected.

"Think for a second. If I depict you as seeing our Sword Hunt as a pain in the butt, it's going to look like I'm forcing you to do this."

"I need to be loving it?"

"Exactly. Any impression of coercion is one that I would hope to avoid."

She was going to be evaluated.

Ah, the sorrows of serving the court.

Thing is, Shichika didn't really hate his job.

"Alright, got it," he said. "I won't call anything a pain ever again. Sound good? But Togame, I was kind of wondering, when you jabbed me a minute ago, what was that you screamed? 'Cheerio'?"

"Oh, that?" Shaking her hand (her punch had done some damage after all, though not to Shichika), Togame smirked. She knew she had him. "It's my catchphrase."

"Huh. What does it mean? Doesn't sound like Japanese."

"As if an island monkey can judge. I'll have you know that it's a grand old saying, favored by the warriors of Satsuma in Kyushu as a battle cry—you might call it their kiai.[16] Not so much a dialect as a custom. Not like I have any strong ties to Kyushu. I simply thought that 'Cheerio' is a cute thing to yell in battle. I gather this was the first time you heard me say it, but I actually use it quite a bit."

"In Satsuma country, huh?"

"Yes." Togame spoke with pride. "It suits my personality exactly."

The battle cry she referenced, while indeed originating in Satsuma, was in fact the much-more Japanese "Chesuto,"[17] while "Cheerio" was an imported word denoting some combination of "Sayonara!" "Bye-Bye!" and "Take Care!"—but you will have to wait for Book Five, when she and Shichika venture down to Satsuma, for the white-haired Schemer to finally see her error. Look forward to ten-plus manuscript sheets'[18] worth of humiliation and burnt ego.

[16] 気合 KIAI a voice emitted to concentrate one's 気 KI energy
[17] ちぇすと CHESUTO analogous to "Yeehaw!"
[18] 原稿用紙 GENKŌ YŌSHI typically 400 squares per sheet, one character per square

Let us return to the conversation.

Irrelevant as it may be to the present volume.

"Not sure I get this catchphrase thing. Can't think a good one up, not on the spot. Whatever you call it..."

Until the previous month, Shichika had spent almost his entire life in solitude on that deserted island. Before Togame came, the only two people he had ever met were Mutsue Yasuri, Sixth Master of the Kyotoryu, his father, and Nanami Yasuri, his older sister. The three of them had no use for catchphrases or the like.

Or even for what we call personality.

Which is perhaps why he could be accused of lacking one.

Back on the island, there had been no objective[19] point of view.

Everything had been subjective.[20]

"Not to worry. I knew you'd say that, so I thought up a few."

"..."

What a busybody.

That was Shichika's honest reaction.

He didn't voice it, but it must have shown on his face since he was no master of duplicity.

"I figured you may have a preference," Togame went on, oblivious and unabashed.

Those who ignore how other people feel can dominate and steer the conversation in any era.

"You have the right to choose your favorite candidate. I don't mind which."

"That's an awfully pushy right...hope there's one I like."

"Of course there is."

Togame was confident. Too confident.

Where was she going with this?

"Here's one you can use as a rejoinder. Once in a while, go 'Tee-hee!'"

"Nope." Since he couldn't be bothered, Shichika was apt to go along with whatever people said, but this time he had to voice his blunt refusal. "If I got a report about a guy like that, I'd burn it. The world has enough garbage."

"Excuse me? Having a hulk like you titter makes for a nice contrast—"

"Nice for who? Look, all I mean is, do you want to spend all day, every day[21] with a guy who goes 'Tee-hee'? Would you really want to go on a journey with him?"

"You know what? No. Forget it."

She moved on quick. She was pretty selfish.

"This one has more to do with changing how you talk. Let's try a dialect."

"A dialect? You can't pick that sort of thing up overnight."

[19] 客観 KYAKKAN "as a visitor" objective

[20] 主観 SHUKAN "as the host" subjective

[21] 四六時中 SHIROKUJICHŪ 24/7

"Why not talk like you're from Kyoto? Having a hulk like you speak in an elegant fashion would make for a nice—"

"I'm sure Kyoto has its share of hulks...and another thing. This contrast you're so keen on is a dangerous thing. One slipup, and it's over. Those stakes are too high."

"Strong rebuttal. I'm impressed."

"Enough. Why do I actually have to say this thing? If you think it's so important, can't you just cook something up for the report?"

"I'm afraid not. It must not contain any lies."

"But aren't you already staging[22] this?"

"Lies are one thing. Staging is another."

What kind of twisted code of ethics was this?

Not like he should have been surprised. This was Togame.

"Writing lies is out of the question, but leaving out real details is an editorial decision. Take this whole conversation. Every sentence is going to be pruned. Anyway, if the first two options aren't to your taste, you'll have to settle for a signature line. Personally, I find them slightly less dynamic, but they get the job done."

"It better not make for a nice contrast."

"Fear not. No more of that. Trust me, these cut a figure. I have three options for you."

"You know, can I just laugh in a specific way? How about that ninja's 'Kyahah'? I could live with that."

"Imbecile. You don't want your personality to overlap with anyone's."

"Oh."

"In a way it's worse than having no personality."

"..."

Perhaps she had a point.

It made sense, more or less.

But more importantly, when he really thought it over, he didn't want to be overlapping a perverse ninja who pulled katanas from his mouth.

"Alright. Let's hear your suggestions."

"'Aren't I the darling of the gods?'"

Repeat after me, Togame urged.

"'Aren't I the darling of the gods?'"

"I dunno, Togame...weren't you supposed to be smart enough to make up for not knowing how to fight?"

"Excuse me? Only a smart person would hit upon such an inspired catchphrase."

"If it's supposed to be a prank, yeah, it's inspired..."

Ouch.

The second he uttered that line, it'd be all over for his personality.

22 やらせ YARASE "made to do"

"You'd be saying it mostly to taunt your enemies. It would assert your superiority and show that your confidence cannot be shaken. Express your omnipotence, and crown every victory with swagger."

"Or maybe come off as a real jerk..."

"Yeah, well, if I had my druthers, you'd be a bit of a jerk. Just think how it would boost my reputation if I trained a naughty, cheeky, saucy island monkey to do my bidding. You're too nice."

"..."

What a selfish view.

There was such a thing as being too egotistic.[23]

Togame had to be plotting to portray him as a nasty fellow in order to make herself look good by comparison.

"Let's try number two. Ready? 'Time for a permanent island vacation.' There."

"There?"

Too close to home.

After spending twenty years stranded on an island, how could he smugly wish the same fate on someone else?

"You dodo. That's what gives it bite."

It somehow got even more awkward.

How did you ever become Grand Commander?

The words almost left his lips.

He had to end this conversation now.

Things had dragged on long enough, less banter than open sore.

"Hey Togame, have any more...practical ideas?"

"What? Everything so far was plenty practical... You're just much pickier than I reckoned. I thought you would go with the flow."

"Yeah, well, I'm as surprised as you we're still discussing this... I'm willing to compromise, I really am. Let's hear your third pick."

"Okay. This idea was inspired by Shichika Hachiretsu, your super killer move."[24]

"Don't call it that."

His Last Fatal Orchid, she meant.

Whatever. Close enough.

"When your opponent threatens you, just say: 'Not if you're torn to smithereens.'"

"..."

He would have liked to turn it down.

He came so close to telling her.

What made her think his Last Fatal Orchid needed a hokey[25] slogan?

23 自己中 JIKOCHŪ colloquial abbreviation of 自己中心的 JIKOCHŪSHINTEKI self-centered
24 超必殺技 CHŌ HISSATSU WAZA "ultra lethal technique"
25 不要な味付け FUYŌ NA AJITSUKE needlessly flavored

Shichika Hachiretsu was a move he had devised on his own, and he was quite attached to it.

Then again, Togame must have a slew of bogus catchphrases that hadn't made the cut; he had better settle or risk being dealt something far worse. Even if the lot of them were bogus, she had clearly labored over every one. The thought tugged not imperceptibly at his heartstrings...yet any more of this might confirm a disturbing suspicion that had arisen in him: *Could Togame be dumber than me?*

Shichika knew that he was dumb.

He was okay with it.

He was not okay, however, with Togame being dumb.

There was only room for one idiot on this adventure.

"Sounds good."

"Huh?"

"I like it. 'Not if you're torn to smithereens.' Nice feel. Honestly, I can't believe how much it fits me."

"Oh, you're picking that one? It's a little unexpected—I hadn't meant to recommend it out of all the candidates. But hey, it was good enough for me. If it's your favorite, I won't argue."

"Yeah... Do you think we could stop talking about this now?"

"Sure. Once you thank me."

"Thanks a million."[26]

"Welcome."

Togame nodded happily.

She looked altogether satisfied.

And thus Shichika Yasuri acquired his catchphrase.

"Well, I didn't think you would be so choosy, but that's finally settled. We aren't too pressed for time, all told. If we keep up the pace, I should have us there by evening."

"Not if you're torn to smithereens."

"Cheerio!"

She punched him, rather unfairly.

But that was their rapport.

It had been about a month since they first met on Haphazard Island, and by now, they had begun to let their guards down. There was nothing strictly wrong with this, but when the two of them passed the time with such inane banter on the roadways, they were bound, like it or not, to catch the eyes of whoever they passed—undesirably, considering the purpose of their journey. At the moment, however, given their location, there was no need to worry.

There was not a soul in sight, for this was no roadway.

They were in the middle of Japan's only desert landscape—

[26] 感謝感激雨あられ KANSHA KANGEKI AME ARARE it's raining thank-you's

Inaba Desert[27] as it was known in those days.

■ ■

The day before.

Shichika and Togame were staying at an inn[28] in the last town before the desert. Togame had shed layer after layer of voluminous kimono but retained an air of extravagance due to her adornments.

"Tomorrow, we'll be arriving in Inaba."

They had finished dinner and were sitting face to face.

Shichika was dressed no differently from when he was outdoors. Bare-chested, as usual, there was little left for him to strip without being totally naked.[29] In a sense, he was clad more heavily indoors, relatively speaking. Facing Togame, he let her long white hair enwrap the muscles of his abdomen.

Around his chest and arms and neck, and plenty more around his head.

Togame's hair was as long as it was white—long enough to wrap all the way around Shichika, and then some. A young woman's hair stops even a mammoth[30] in its tracks, but whether or not such a saying actually exists, nobody stumbling upon the scene would fail to find it odd.

This was not some sexual fantasy[31] come true for Shichika (or Togame). While you would have no way of guessing it, this was a strategy, a course of action developed in the wake of battling against Komori Maniwa, one of the Twelve Bosses of the Maniwa Ninjas, back on the island that had been Shichika's only home.

Komori Maniwa.

His was a fearsome ninpo where he *shapeshifted into any other person in existence*—the Body Melt, incomparable to any mortal method of disguise. Morphing into Togame, he had attempted to ambush Shichika.

Purely in terms of outcome, the ninja failed.

Having never met a stranger in all his years on Haphazard Island, Shichika was not equipped to remember the details of Togame's appearance. It was absolutely fruitless for Komori to pose as her—no matter how expertly.

That time, Shichika was lucky.

But now that he had vanquished Komori Maniwa, his inability to tell one person from another was just a decisive, fatal weakness. Not being able to

27 因幡砂漠 INABA SABAKU today's 鳥取砂丘 TOTTORI SAKYŪ Tottori Sand Dunes
28 旅籠 HATAGO a lodge offering room and board to travelers
29 全裸 ZENRA "complete nudity"
30 大象 TAIZŌ "big elephant"
31 変態性欲 HENTAI SEIYOKU fetish; perversion

differentiate between Togame, his employer, and the foes he had to vanquish was unacceptable. If he lost track of who was who in a melee at some point on their quest to find the swords, the Kyotoryu would no doubt shred Togame, whose martial artistry was nil.

That simply would not do.

Other people aside—Togame had to act, and fast, to make sure Shichika could pick her from a crowd.

Therefore.

To ensure he knew her from the others, she fed his muscle memory using her most striking feature: her white hair. Thus the scene at the inn was educational in nature.

"Don't chew on it. You'll damage it."

"Can I lick it?"

"Go ahead. Lick it and remember how it tastes. But don't twist your body like that. It hurts my scalp."

"Okay, I won't."

Education is a funny thing. Shichika and Togame had been working on this almost every night since coming over to the mainland, and it was finally beginning to pay off. He could recognize her now, *to some extent*.

That aside.

The topic was the morrow.

"Right, Inaba. That's where—what was it again?"

"Gekoku Castle[32] stands," replied Togame. "We are to find Zanto the Razor. I suppose this is as good a time as any to tell you more about the sword."

"Yes, please. I wish you'd have told me earlier, but you were keeping it secret."

"Not secret. Classified."

"What's the difference?"

"It's a matter of severity. Anyhow, I've mentioned that the Razor has a keener edge than any other blade. Supposedly it can cut through any substance in a single swing."

"Wow."

Shichika did not sound like he cared.

Perhaps he wasn't taking her too seriously.

Such a claim would sow the seeds of doubt in most.

"Sounds like it's up there with the Leveler. Like how you said the Leveler was forged to be so hard it—hey, wait a second. What would happen if we tried to slice the Leveler with the Razor?"

"I wonder. Only one way to find out—though I would never allow it."

Togame chuckled.

She seemed to find his innocent question funny.

[32] 下酷城 GEKOKUJŌ "harsh-underneath castle"
pun on 下剋上 GEKOKUJŌ, a bid to bring down one's ruler/leader

"My guess is the Possessed became more powerful from one piece to the next, in a simple hierarchy. Since to the best of my knowledge the Razor was created later, if I had to guess, I'd say that it would make the cut."

"Hoot," Shichika interjected facetiously—and looked away from Togame and off to the side.

But she saw right through him.

In his battle with Komori on Haphazard Island, Shichika came out on top although the competition had been fierce. Nevertheless, it was not the Leveler that he had beaten. Which was fine, since the goal of Togame's journey was to collect the swords without a scratch.

Yet she knew it weighed on his mind.

The Kyotoryu.

Could a swordless school of swordsmanship triumph—over swords themselves?

She could tell that he was itching for the challenge.

For him, this journey was a match between the Kyotoryu swordsmen who forsook the sword and Kiki Shikizaki—the swordsmith who trusted in swords.

There was nothing wrong with being so competitive, but it was something Togame had better keep her eye on.

"So the Razor beats the Leveler..."

"It was a conjecture.[33] Don't take the question too seriously. What's more, the answer would depend on who is wielding the weapon. We know that a Possessed empowers its owner, but is at its most fearsome in the hands of an able swordsman."

"Makes sense. It's wrong to focus only on the sword. So what now? Who has the Razor? Don't tell me another ninja."

"As it happens..."

With the Leveler in their safekeeping, eleven swords remained, the whereabouts of only five of which were known at the moment. Among these, Togame had picked Zanto the Razor as their first target. This was partially due to geographic considerations, but there was *a far simpler reason* at play.

"Your opponent is a swordsman."

"Right on. After all, the Kyotoryu is a form of swordplay. A swordsman will be easier to face than a ninja."

"Ginkaku Uneri...a ronin[34] or...the lord of a castle, after all?"

"What?" Shichika was baffled. "How do you mean, Togame? How can you be both?"

"Usually you can't. But I keep forgetting how little you know. Perhaps I should start over from the beginning."

Which is exactly what she did.

[33] 推測 SUISOKU estimate
[34] 浪人 RŌNIN a samurai who has no master

"Once upon a time, when the Old Shogun launched the Great Sword Hunt, the owner of the Razor, Kinkaku Uneri[35] by name, was a samurai in the service of the daimyo of Tottori."

"So, like, the grandpa of the other guy?"

"Basically. To be precise, he lived ten generations before Ginkaku, current owner of the sword. A contemporary of your forefather Kazune, founder of the Kyotoryu."

"Okay...so this guy would have been around during the Age of Warring States—and out there on the battlefield wielding one of the Possessed. In the heyday of the Shikizaki swords."

"I wouldn't compare him with Kazune," cautioned Togame, "who was always on the frontlines fighting for the Tetsubi—but you could say he had a modest reputation as a warrior. Just not at the level that goes down in history."

"Really?"

"I gather Mutsue never mentioned the Uneri?"

"Nope, he didn't. So they couldn't have been too outstanding."

"Like I said. Kinkaku had a modest reputation. It's like this. No matter how strong you are, if you only have one person to fight, you can only win a single battle. This area had no shortage of battles, but comparatively speaking, things were peaceful."

"Got it. You're saying it's because our founder fought at the forefront on the toughest territory[36] that he became so legendary. Huh."

Upon saying this, Shichika appeared to delve into his thoughts.

Thinking did not exactly suit him.

Nor was it like him.

It gave Togame pause, but she went on.

"Then, when the Old Shogun unified the nation, he launched the Great Sword Hunt. This was when the Shikizaki blades in the possession of the daimyos were snatched up, all at once, by the shogunate."

The Great Sword Hunt.

Perhaps the most ignoble law in Japanese history. Ostensibly enacted to amass enough material for a giant buddha statue, it grabbed the swords from every hand across Japan. Its hidden motive was to end the cult of the katana and to rid the domain of any kind of swordsman—but the true motive was the Old Shogun's maniacal obsession with collecting all thousand of Kiki Shikizaki's Mutant Blades.

Charming how only the outward objective, erecting a giant buddha, was met. Ironically, Seiryoin Gokenji Temple, on Mt. Sayabashiri in Tosa, and home to the Katana Buddha, became a favorite pilgrimage for swordsmen—whom the shogun failed to quash.

35 宇練金閣 UNERI KINKAKU "Surging Golden Tower"

36 激戦区 GEKISENKU severely contested district

The underlying project to collect all thousand of the Shikizaki blades fell short as well.

"But the shogunate got all the other swords, except for the Possessed, right? Wait...if Kinkaku was working for Tottori, wouldn't that mean the Razor wasn't his to—"

"He strayed from the way of the samurai," Togame passed swift judgment on the man. "Kinkaku Uneri refused to hand over Zanto the Razor, saying it was no possession of the daimyo, but his alone to keep." Of all the Mutant Blades whose exact whereabouts were known from before the Great Sword Hunt, one sword, and only one, could not be captured: Zanto the Razor.

"So he was working for a daimyo but wouldn't surrender it? Listen to that! But there must be more to the story. I bet it hurt the reputation of the daimyo of Tottori, his lord."

"Exactly. Kinkaku, labeled a traitor, was wanted—dead—but he managed to counter every attempt on his life. With the Razor."

"Sounds about right."

"All told, between the forces sent by the daimyo of Tottori and the Old Shogun, he fended off ten thousand strong—ow!"

Strongow.[37]

No, ten thousand strong—and ouch.

When Shichika, wrapped in Togame's hair, heard what she said, he fell backwards—an oddly exaggerated reaction for the era—and as a consequence, tugged hard on Togame's scalp.

"What the hell!" she screamed.

"That's crazy though! Ten thousand?" Shichika raised himself and yelled back. "You're saying he fended off ten thousand guys alone? No way a guy like that exists! I'd be amazed to hear someone had chopped apart ten thousand daikon,[38] but men? How could that be? And if he actually exists, why not save him for last? Why take him on second, as basically my first real opponent!"

"Hold on, this is history we're talking—Kinkaku, not Ginkaku."

She petted him to calm him down. He was usually gentle and kind, but when you got him worked up, there was no stopping him—Togame was finally beginning to grasp Shichika for who he was.

Unlike some swords, the boy snapped easily.[39]

That said, he was a man now, turning twenty-four this year... His island upbringing had taken a toll and stunted his emotional growth. Or rather—Togame had no way of knowing what kind of a father Mutsue had been, but his older sister, Nanami, who acted like his mother, seemed to have spoiled him.

"I'm fine. You can stop now," Shichika said after a while. "Still, ten thou-

[37] 超えいた KOEITA [not a word]
[38] 大根 DAIKON root vegetable often rivaling the size of a human limb
[39] 切れやすい KIREYASUI quick to lose his temper

sand. How could one guy put such a dent in humanity's headcount? Why try to stave off a population explosion[40] in our era? Plus, I can't see how one sword could stand up to that much abuse. Unless it was the Leveler..."

"Well, this is over a hundred and fifty years ago. That number may not be credible, but we must assume that the Razor had been swung at least often enough for such rumors to be whispered with credulity. Shichika, even if the Kyotoryu is swordplay, you don't use swords yourself, so I can see why you would be skeptical. But a blade doesn't need to be as hard as the Leveler to last. Theoretically, a masterpiece sword[41] can be used indefinitely."

"You serious?"

"Indefinitely might be a bit of a stretch. In the hands of a third-rate swordsman, its edge will be lost after ten kills from all the fat and muscle. A first-rate swordsman knows how to take a life without hurting his sword. You could even say that killing without harming your sword is what makes a first-rate swordsman."

"..."

"Otherwise, how could all thousand of the Mutant Blades of Shikizaki still exist? The nine hundred and ninety-nine that aren't the Leveler would long ago have snapped or corroded. But that is not the case."

Of course, she conceded, there was no way to guarantee the safety of the six precious[42] whose whereabouts were lost. For her to reach her goal, they better be safe, but she had to face the facts. There was a difference between a wish and wishful thinking.

"Taking a life without hurting his sword, huh. Sounds like Kiki Shikizaki didn't think of his swords as expendable, and the Leveler was just the most extreme example..."

"True, but the deciding factor is who wields them. In that sense, perhaps the Razor was in the best hands possible. The daimyo of Tottori and the Old Shogun failed to capture it, but life went on. The Great Sword Hunt was rescinded, and the Old Shogun..."

"Met his ruin?"

"Not exactly ruin," Togame took issue with Shichika's word choice. "He lived a long life and died peacefully. But having clashed with him, Kinkaku Uneri was dismissed from Tottori and became an unaffiliated[43] ronin."

"Unaffiliated. That's one way to put it."

Shichika burst out laughing.

His father, a swordsman (Master of the Kyotoryu Mutsue Yasuri hadn't wielded a katana but was a swordsman all the same), dubbed the Hero of the Rebellion in the only bona fide war to take place under the Yanari, had to pay

[40] 人口爆発 JINKŌ BAKUHATSU no less of a deliberate anachronism in the original
[41] 業物 WAZA MONO a top-notch katana, durable and sharp
[42] 真打 SHIN'UCHI "true forged" the best swords in a production run
[43] 無所属 MUSHOZOKU usually describes independent politicians who belong to no party

for a crime he committed shortly afterwards. Banished to an island along with his family, for nineteen years he never left the island, until his spirit left this world the year before.

Togame felt like Shichika may be seeing his father in Kinkaku Uneri, but she dismissed the thought.

What did she care.

In the first place, she would rather spend as little time as possible thinking about Shichika's father—even though she originally ventured to Haphazard Island intending to ask him, not Shichika, to help with gathering the swords.

After all—Mutsue Yasuri had been among her most hated foes.

"But even upon being expelled, Kinkaku Uneri refused to leave Inaba. He did not take service with another master but dared to make his home within its borders, where he lived out the rest of his days. It seems the land claimed a soft place in his heart. Over the years, the Razor stayed in his family and was passed down as an heirloom—"

"And now it's in the hands of Ginkaku, the current head of the Uneri. Does that mean that tomorrow, we'll be dropping in on Uneri's mansion in the town of Inaba, Tottori?"

"No," Togame shot him down. "The Uneri mansion is gone."

"Gone?"

"I should say, Inaba is gone."

"The entire city?"

"More than that. Tottori, as a territory, has ceased to exist."

"What could make it stop existing?"

"Ever hear of Inaba Desert?" asked Togame, seeing how surprised Shichika was.

This was turning out to be a lengthy introduction.

"Yeah...my dad told me about it. Tottori is famous for it, the only desert in Japan. He said he visited once just for fun. Supposed to be awesome. Everywhere you look is sand. I was actually hoping we would go there."

"Don't worry. Before long, you'll have had enough." Togame was getting sarcastic. "About five years ago, Inaba Desert began steadily increasing in size. What once covered a fraction of the coastline has swallowed Tottori whole."

The entire territory.

"Inaba has become a wasteland, unfit for living."

The desert had *grown*.[44]

The rapid environmental development could be described no other way. The local authorities, longstanding stewards of the desert, and the Yanari, who boasted absolute unparalleled authority, were powerless against this natural disaster. Its scope was formidable, but it was the pace that made

[44] 成長 SEICHŌ grow (organically)

controlling it impossible.

The end of Tottori, and of Inaba—though Shichika could not have known, stranded on that island for the past twenty years.

"No swordsman or sword is any match for nature."

To judge from the fatalism in his voice, this meant something to him, too. When the desert started spreading, Togame was already working for the bakufu, and despite it being outside her wheelhouse[45] she drew up all kinds of countermeasures; they were only a drop in the bucket and had almost no effect. Thus she intimately understood what Shichika was feeling.

Helplessness.

That's what you call it.

"Still," Togame said. "Perhaps it's too soon to conclude that no swordsman—or sword—can master nature. That wasteland is no place for human life, but out there, Shichika, one swordsman has made himself at home."

"...?"

"Or to speak your language, one sword, Ginkaku Uneri, lives—alone in Gekoku Castle, the only structure left standing in Inaba—with Zanto the Razor at his hip."

■ ■

The following day—

Togame the Schemer and Shichika Yasuri, Seventh Master of the Kyoto-ryu, set off side by side into the desert, leaving their footprints in the sand. They were heading for Inaba—or, in its place, Gekoku Castle, though no road stretched before them.

"Good thing it's cold out," said Shichika, gazing up at the sky. "If this was the middle of summer, you would be dead, wearing so many layers."

"Nonsense. In summer I take some off. About three layers."

"Big difference. You make me carry all the luggage, saying you're not strong enough to help, but I bet the whole lot of it weighs less than your accessories."

"More nonsense. Women have a special set of muscles just for fashion."

"Special muscles? You have extra body parts?" Shichika sounded appalled. "I can't see clothes as anything but in the way."

"I've given up on making you wear a shirt, but do me a favor and please don't take your pants off. I don't want to travel with a perv."

"Don't worry. I'm starting to like this hakama you bought me. It's good for moving, and good for fighting."

[45] 他部署 TABUSHO "different department"

"How is moving different from fighting?"

"Just is."

"Interesting."

Crunch, crunch, crunch.[46]

The two walked on, leaving footprints in the sand.

They estimated that the walk would take them the whole day.

Leaving aside the joke about special muscles, Togame's ability to travel on foot for such a distance was revealing. Even if she was not skilled in the martial arts, she was in no way without stamina. Needless to say, for Shichika, walking for a whole day cost him barely more energy than spending the day in bed.[47]

"If the desert swallowed the city, does that mean if we dug around we might find houses and stuff?"

"We've been walking quite a while. This area was sand before the desert grew. But who knows. If you dug enough you might find something. From five or six hundred years ago."

"Wow. So wait. Then Tottori's Gekoku Castle was built in the middle of the desert."

"The lay of the land has shifted over time, so not in the middle as it stands today. Once upon a time, it stood on the edge. The castle is literally a natural fortress. Since no general trains his troops for a desert assault, it was hard to attack and easy to defend. Still, it was quite the undertaking to build on sand. What could be harder?"

"And that's why it's the only building standing in Inaba—but hey, Togame. There's something I've been wanting to ask you since last night."

"Yes?"

"You originally hired that maniac Komori to capture the Leveler because he was the most flexible ninja around, which made him a perfect fit for the most rigid sword. After that, you asked Hakuhei Sabi to capture the Whisper because it was the most difficult to handle, and no one in all of Japan can wield a sword better than him."

"Precisely."

"Okay. So how come you're asking me to get the Razor? Is there some reason you think it's a good fit, or a good match[48] for me? Since I don't use a sword, I can't see how any of that would matter."

"There were geographic considerations. From what I know, Zanto the Razor is the closest of the Possessed to your home on Haphazard Island."

"So it was the most practical."

"Sure, but more importantly, as Master of the Kyotoryu, you never use a sword, and thus no sword would ever be a good match or a good fit. That is

46 ざくざくざく ZAKU ZAKU ZAKU onomatopoeia for sand/gravel
47 布団 FUTON sleeping mat
48 組み合わせ KUMIAWASE combination

what makes your school what it is. That is why I picked you to help me round up the Possessed, and why your situation is different from Komori or Sabi—but Shichika, there is one exception[49] among the swords."

"You mean out of the Twelve Possessed?"

"I mean all thousand of the Mutant Blades. That sword is Zanto the Razor," Togame declared.

"What do you mean?"

"Don't you get it? A sword that is *merely* sharp is of no concern for you. Cheerio!"

She nailed him in the ribs.

Hers was a fearsome catchphrase that would embarrass her later, the more frequently she uttered it—but we'll get to this curse in due course.

"Why do you keep hitting me in the same spot?"

"Don't tell me I hurt you."

"Hurt me? No."

"Of course not," Togame said. "Your body is so finely tempered that I'm almost entranced[50] by it. I have a hard time keeping my hands away from your amazing muscles. But Shichika. Not even a body like yours can stop a blade."

"Right."

"You can train all night and day, but your flesh can only get so hard. Any razor—small 'r'[51]—will cut skin if you touch the blade. Therefore, it matters none how sharp Zanto the Razor is. It's not like you will be crossing blades, yes? It should be no different than your average katana."

"Makes sense."

Shichika could see her point.

This Possessed was the one exception.

The Mutant Blades each had their special powers, but only one was comparable, at least for Shichika, to a *normal sword*. And that was Zanto the Razor.

"Okay," said Shichika, "I'm relieved that you aren't an idiot."

"First time I've had to convince anyone of that. Whatever. Anyway, capturing this sword from Ginkaku Uneri will simply be a matter of your swordplay versus his. As long as he isn't any stronger than he would be with another sword, this should be a relatively easy one for you to capture."

"You told me all about his ancestor Kinkaku yesterday, but not what to expect from this guy. Can he cut down ten thousand guys too?"

"Not sure. But I know he's good. I hear he's a master of iainuki."[52]

"Iainuki..."

[49] 例外 REIGAI "outlier"
[50] ほれぼれする HOREBORE SURU marvel; plays off 惚れる HORERU fall (in love)
[51] ただの名詞 TADA NO MEISHI the common noun
[52] 居合抜き IAINUKI drawing a sword at spectacular speed, often for performance

"They say it's the trademark of the Uneri family—Kinkaku included. It would be fair to label him a specialist... But in terms of personality, he is an eccentric.[53] While everyone else in Inaba abandoned the land where they were born and raised, he stayed."

"Is the desert still expanding?"

"Not anymore... Last year, it suddenly stopped. By then the whole of Inaba was buried, but the damage to neighboring territories has been slight."

"I see."

"It was four years of hell. But Shichika, I meant to ask you. Does the Kyotoryu have any special moves for countering iainuki?"

"Huh? Oh, well, I'm not sure for iainuki specifically—my dad called it an *extreme* form of swordplay—hold on, though. While we're on the topic, I have some things I want to ask you too."

"Such as?"

"Between Ginkaku Uneri and Hakuhei Sabi, who's stronger?"

"Having never met Uneri in person, that's hard for me to say...but I would put my money on Sabi. His skill is unfathomable.[54] His ability to fight without damaging a sword is nonpareil—no other swordsman could handle the Whisper. For him, a stunt like cutting down a hundred men is easy-peasy."

"In your opinion. If that's the case, who would you bet on between me and Sabi?"

"..."

For a moment, Togame was at a loss to answer.

"I'm amazed how hard it is for you to lie," laughed Shichika. "I think I understand why you can't lie in your report."

"That's not it, Shichika. Sabi may be unrivaled as a swordsman, but based on fighting style, I think your chance of beating him is—"

"That's not what I'm getting at, Togame."

Shichika's tone was bold, almost arrogant.

"What I'm saying is you've only had *a taste* of what the Kyotoryu is made of—if you really understood the school, you would never think to ask a stupid thing like if I had a special move for iainuki."

"So not even Sabi poses a threat."

"Well. I'm not sure about that."

And I'm not sure I ever want to meet him, he added, his voice returning to normal—to the easy, carefree, unenthused Shichika.

"Whatever happens, Togame, you have nothing to worry about."

"Hmh... *Ch-Cheerio!*"

This time she stomped his toes with her seta.[55]

And it did hurt.

[53] 変人 HENJIN "odd person"

[54] 底が知れぬ SOKO GA SHIRENU "can't see the bottom"

[55] 雪駄 SETTA flat-soled Japanese sandals

"Wah, what the?"

"M-Make no mistake! No one cares about you. My sole concern is our safe recovery of the Razor! I could not be less worried about what happens to you. I could replace you in a heartbeat!"

"..."

This brand of humor—what can I say.

A Japanese tradition, though as yet it had no name.

"R-Really? You could replacc me? M-My mistake."

Shichika was a piece of work, too, for feeling genuinely wounded.

But that aside, this travel scene met a juncture.

The two stopped.

Straight ahead, directly in their path, they espied something lying on the sand. A dead man, sliced into two clean halves.[56]

[56] 一刀両断 ITTŌ RYŌDAN a single unstoppable swing

CHAPTER TWO

GINKAKU UNERI

■ ■

The "Maniwacs"—the cutesy nickname fast becoming standard between Shichika and Togame, although that band of expert assassins, demented as they were, would surely have resented nothing more than to be branded thus—had, by now, gone rogue[1] en masse. Until the Mutant Blades of Kiki Shikizaki made things complicated, the enclave had worked with the Owari Bakufu on what could be called intimate terms—or at least in close cooperation. It would be exaggerating to say the Maniwa answered directly to the shogunate, but relative to the Onmitsu, who did, the ninjas had certainly been held in higher esteem for their ninpo.

The Directorate for which Togame was Grand Commander was often responsible for backroom operations that never saw the light of day. It would be fair to say she knew more about the Maniwa than any other personage of the shogunate. But even her knowledge had limits: her intelligence on the Twelve Bosses was spotty and she understood the ninpo of only a few of them, one of whom had been Komori—and yet.

The dead man, slashed in two and left to rot, had a face she recognized.

Yes.

It was Shirasagi Maniwa. One of the Twelve Bosses of the Maniwa Clan.

■ ■

It was like a nightmare, thought Shichika.

It had not been there before—the only thing in sight had been the two halves of the abandoned corpse. But when he and Togame rushed to see the body, the wind picked up.

The next instant, *a castle[2] towered over them.*

Without warning.

No gate or moat or ramparts or embankments—only the keep,[3] rising from the sand.

"What the..." Shichika was sure the castle *hadn't been there*. Or at the very least, they hadn't *seen* it.

"I told you it was a natural fortress." In stark contrast to his bafflement, Togame reacted with total nonchalance as if she had expected nothing less.

[1] 抜け忍 NUKENIN to abandon a ninja group (or the expectations of ninja identity)
[2] 平城 HIRAJIRO a castle built on flat ground
[3] 天守閣 TENSHUKAKU tall fortification usually surrounded by castle walls

"Do you know about mirages? They're a natural phenomenon, where a difference in temperature causes light to refract, making faraway things appear close, or things on the ground appear to float, or flip. They can even make things you know are there invisible... We are in a desert, with the sea nearby. The conditions are perfect. One might call it atmospheric camouflage."

Togame casually explained that the castle had no gate or moat or ramparts or embankments so as not to disrupt the mirage.

"*Unless you come this close, you'll never notice it*—that's what makes Gekoku Castle hard to attack and easy to defend. Unknown to most—but legendary, to a select few."

"What? So you knew it was going to do this? You should've warned me. That scared the crap out of me. Stop keeping secrets. Did this really need to be classified?"

"Oops. I thought it would be funny."

"..."

It was a prank.[4]

At the worst possible time.

It bombed,[5] more or less.

"Look at this guy..."

Not like she was changing the subject, but Togame crouched beside the corpse and looked it over. The body had started to decay, but remained recognizable. While Shichika did not exactly crouch, he mimicked Togame and peered down at the body over her shoulder.

Sleeveless ninja garb.

Chains wrapped around him.

But this ninja, while a denizen of the shadows, wore no mask—combined, these features should have been enough to jog his memory of Komori Maniwa, whom Shichika had fought the month before, but the only living people he could recognize were his sister, Nanami, and Togame the Schemer, after considerable practice. Nothing about the dead man struck him as familiar, but the expression on Togame's face made him wonder.

"Someone you know?" he asked.

"Shirasagi Maniwa, one of the Twelve Bosses of the Maniwa Clan."

Togame's voice was neutral.[6]

"I know of him... Unlike Komori, we never worked together, and I know little of his ninpo. But we've crossed paths several times. I mentioned him when we were talking about catchphrases. He's the one who talked backwards."

"Oh," Shichika nodded. "So I'll never find out what that was like...for better or for worse. But for starters, what's a Maniwac Boss doing all the way

[4] 茶目っ気 CHAMEKKE being playful

[5] 外した HAZUSHITA missed

[6] 無感情 MUKANJŌ void of feeling

out here, in two pieces?"

Growing up on Haphazard Island, Shichika wasn't used to corpses. He was also never taught to find dead bodies scary, and thus, the pitiable sight of what was left of Shirasagi Maniwa wasn't particularly unnerving—but having witnessed firsthand the skill of Komori, another of the Twelve Bosses of the Maniwa Clan, he was unable to take this situation lightly.

"This guy must have packed at least as hard of a punch as Komori."

"Komori was tough, but his ninpo wasn't meant for battle. His Star Cannon and Body Melt were perfect for assassination, but not ideal for fighting face to face. While I can't say for sure what style of ninpo Shirasagi favored... rumor has it that his skills were well-suited to combat. In which case, at least in terms of fighting prowess, he would outrank Komori."

"Yet somehow—he got chopped in half."

Shichika examined the cross-sections of Shirasagi's body. What a smooth cut—the blade had not even remotely strayed. It almost felt like if you pressed the halves together, they would stick. The cut went clean through flesh and bone, like it was all the same—but even more foreboding was the way that it had razored through the fat chains the ninja wore over his costume. After finishing off Komori, Shichika had learned from Togame that these chains were a variety of chain mail[7]—the Maniwa wore them as a kind of armor. If his armor had been slashed, Shirasagi Maniwa must have been felled by a blow so powerful that nothing could stop it.

"As you may recall, the Twelve Bosses of the Maniwa are competing to see who can snatch up the most of the Twelve Possessed. Shirasagi must have caught wind of Zanto the Razor being at Gekoku Castle, in the hands of Ginkaku Uneri, and come out to investigate, only to be slain."

"By who?"

"By Ginkaku Uneri, obviously." Togame raised her head—gazing at Gekoku Castle, which (apparently) had materialized out of nowhere. "If he could do this to a Maniwa Boss, perhaps I underestimated his abilities. I had thought the Razor would be one of the easier swords—evidently, I was wrong."

"Yeah, well, I already beat one Maniwa Boss..."

"Indeed, but luck was on your side."

Shichika couldn't argue with that. He had been more than lucky—his opponent had practically fallen at his feet. All the same, Shichika was confident he could have beat the ninja anyway, no matter what the circumstances, but knew enough not to say so. It was pointless.

"Let's look on the bright side..." Togame shook her head and stood. Her expression told Shichika nothing, but he had never been good at reading other people, especially when they were silent. "The Maniwa may have beat

[7] 鎖かたびら KUSARI KATABIRA "shroud of chain"

us here," Togame elaborated, "but their attempt to seize the Razor was in vain. From a certain angle, this is a boon for us. If Shirasagi had won himself the Shikizaki blade, we would have trudged into the middle of Inaba Desert for nothing."

"Got it, bright side." Shichika nodded, but he wasn't so soft as to miss the message behind what she was saying. "Still, Togame, if the ninja failed to catch Ginkaku Uneri off guard, he must be on the lookout. There's no way he doesn't know how valuable the Shikizaki blades are—well, who knows what this guy said to him. Backwards or whatever. Worst-case scenario, Ginkaku Uneri could have fled Gekoku Castle. And brought the Razor with him. Not like that gives us any clue about where it is."

"I don't think that will be a problem. Even after the whole of Inaba was consumed by desert, this man refused to leave. A couple of ninjas would hardly be able to push him over the edge. What's more, from the looks of Shirasagi, Uneri has the utmost confidence in his abilities. This is no two-bit samurai who cuts and runs."[8]

"What, then?" asked Shichika. "Maybe we should come back another time."

"Out of the question," Togame replied straightaway. "Look, at the pace the Maniwa are moving, we have no time for setbacks.[9] In fact, I'm feeling good about where we are. Thanks to this plot twist from Shirasagi, my report to my superiors just got a lot more interesting. Collecting one of the Possessed from a foe who defended it from the treacherous Maniwa makes for a great story. But the real triumph here is that I no longer need to worry about writing dialogue for that obstreperous ninja. To be frank, I was dreading his arrival because conveying his speech would be such a hassle. He also overlapped with my brand—Shirasagi and shiraga[10] were a little too close for comfort. But that's no longer a concern."

She was beating a dead horse. A bit cruel given that the guy wasn't in one piece.

"This setup is simply too good, Shichika. I can't have you suggesting that we head back with our tails between our legs. Am I to write that we did?"

"The bright side, huh?"

The hot air[11] behind her last line was not lost on Shichika—but he had no reason to protest when his employer was right.

"That's why I fell for you."

8 敵前逃亡 TEKIZEN TŌBŌ flee under fire
9 たたらを踏む TATARA WO FUMU stumbling forward
10 白髪 SHIRAGA alternative reading of 白髪 HAKUHATSU white hair
11 強がり TSUYOGARI bluster

■ ■

While Shichika had certainly been stunned by the sudden appearance of Gekoku Castle, the effect wore off with time. Once he had collected himself, he looked up to find a devastated building— a ruin, by no exaggeration. Since leaving Haphazard Island, he had been tutored by Togame in the ways of the world and had seen a fair number of castles on the road from the Capital to Inaba, but Gekoku Castle was by far the most distressed.[12]

And why would it be otherwise?

Five years prior, when Inaba Desert had begun to spread, this castle lost every one of its caretakers. Once in disrepair, any building, be it castle or mansion, falls apart—and all the sooner in a desert. The fact that this edifice was still standing, most of its masonry in place, its shape more or less intact, was miraculous. While surely built to withstand dryness and the sandstorms, a building of this scale would be impossible for Ginkaku Uneri, the sole inhabitant of Inaba, to maintain on his own. The castle was rundown enough to doubt its structural integrity, but having no choice but to enter, Shichika followed Togame into the lonely tower.

A natural fortress.

But once they were inside, it was a normal castle. Except ruined, with sand granules blowing through the hallways and the walls.

It never would have been permitted in better days, but since no one could scold them, they had stepped right in, dumping their luggage at the entrance, without taking off their sandals—Togame in her flat ones, and Shichika in his straw sandals.

They walked the halls. Togame ahead, and Shichika behind her.

That was their marching order upon entering the castle.

"Hold back, Shichika," Togame had told him by the entrance. "Let me go first."

"...?"

Noticing Shichika's puzzlement, she had rephrased herself slightly. "I'll take point."

"Point? Why? When we fight, that's my job, not yours. Or do you want to fight Ginkaku first?"

"Fool. You know what I'm like in battle. He'd tear through me quicker than a shoji."[13]

"You don't have to brag about it."

But why go first?

A paper screen wouldn't even serve as a shield.

[12] みすぼらしい MISUBORASHII shabby
[13] 障子 SHŌJI paper door

Moreover, he would never use his employer as one.

"Shichika, since you seem a bit confused, allow me to spell things out." About to step into the castle, Togame turned around, but because of the substantial difference in height, even facing him, it barely felt like they were face to face.

"This is no burglary."

"Huh? What?"

"Our mission is to secure the Twelve Possessed. By order of the shogun. His will must be obeyed. That notwithstanding, we can't just barge in and clash swords—so to speak—and snatch the Razor. We must follow procedure. Before battle, we must attempt diplomacy."[14]

"Then what do you need me for? Diplomacy is your game."

"Which is why I need to go first. But I still need you. This is not the Old Shogun's Great Sword Hunt, dare I even mention that debacle—a pox on history. It must not be repeated. If we must resort to battle, we need a just cause."[15]

"I don't get it. Is this, like, bureaucratic?"[16]

"...Let's go with that for now. If what I hear is true, Ginkaku Uneri is a friend to none. Not only a ronin, but a villainous rake, who would kill anyone for a price. His family legacy aside, he has made himself a wanted man for ignoring our repeated warnings and insisting on occupying Gekoku Castle."

"Well, that makes sense."

"It would be fair to say that every one of the five swords whose whereabouts are known, including the Razor, is in the hands of this caliber of individual. I wouldn't expect much better from the next four. As a rule, you would need to be insane to intentionally partake[17] in the Shikizaki blades' venom. As for Hakuhei Sabi, regardless of his reputation as a swordsman, he was hardly known for his decency even before obtaining the Whisper. But nevertheless, Shichika—we must entertain the *possibility*."

"Entertain it?"

"It's like this. What would you do if a good guy had one of these swords?"

Togame was less addressing Shichika than asking herself.

"We aren't burglars—but neither are we on the side of justice. Backed by the shogunate, we can kill without being punished,[18] but we can't just go around hacking people into pieces. This may be an order from on high, but we are not rounding up the Twelve Possessed out of pure necessity. Bear that in mind."

Togame spoke as if he had no choice in the matter and turned back

[14] 交渉 KŌSHŌ negotiations
[15] 大義名分 TAIGI MEIBUN defensible reason
[16] お役所的 OYAKUSHO TEKI government office-y
[17] 摂取 SESSHU imbibe
[18] 咎め TOGAME blame Togame cannot be Togamed

toward the castle.

If he was honest, Shichika had not understood half of Togame's lecture. It went in one ear and out the other. You could argue that concepts like good guy or bad guy or madman were still opaque to him due to his inexperience, but in actuality, his brain simply couldn't do the work.

Indeed, it might be best not to invoke his lack of experience.

Being, for the Kyotoryu, meant being a katana.

The sword chooses its owner—but does not choose who to kill.

That was the way.

No matter how simple and innocent Shichika may act, or by virtue of these very qualities—he lacked any logic or ethics. Honed, literally, as a katana, Shichika had not been taught how to be human.

The same went for his father who raised him.

Able to kill anyone without flinching.

Good or bad, woman or child—it had been irrelevant.

Consequently—Mutsue Yasuri became Hero of the Rebellion.

It will be a little longer before Shichika finds himself caught between the rock of his assignment and the hard place of compassion,[19] in confronting a genuinely good person with one of the Possessed.

"Hey," he said.

"What is it?"

"There's a stain on that tatami."

On the lookout, searching through the castle, Shichika had noticed a black splotch on a mat along the edge of one of the larger rooms. Both of them instantly knew what the stain was.

Blood.

"I guess this is where he killed Shirasagi?"

"Wrong," Togame shot him down. "The color of the straw is unlike any other in the room. If the mat had been here all along, you would expect it to have faded the same way as all the others. The original mat must be in the room where this mat was stained with blood."

"Makes sense. I can see that. But why would anyone go to all the trouble?"

"There must be a den[20] where he spends most of his time. Shirasagi barged in, and they fought. He won, but messed up his tatami. And who wants to wake up on tatami stained with blood? That's why, so far as I can tell, he swapped it with one of these mats."

Shichika looked solemnly at the ceiling. Tall as he was, it was too high for him to reach, even on tiptoes. A castle was a castle, no matter how dilapidated.

"What's wrong? Is something still unclear to you?"

"No...well, it's just that Ginkaku Uneri has to be nearby. With blood you

[19] 人情 NINJŌ human feelings

[20] 居室 KYOSHITSU living room

have to worry about the smell, so I can't see him switching it with the tatami in the room next door to him, but I doubt he would bother going far."

"Perceptive. Well then, let's have a closer look."

"Gotcha."

Then.

The two of them arrived before the fusuma.

They were deep in the recesses of the castle—but there was nothing special about the doors they stood before, nor any sign of life. Only, ever since entering Gekoku Castle, *this was the only room whose fusuma were closed.*

In every other room, the fusuma and shoji had been opened up entirely.

This had to be it.

"..."

"..."

They looked each other in the eye.

Shichika motioned to touch the fusuma, but Togame signaled for him to stop. While she didn't come out and say so, she conveyed that it was her intention to go first. Shichika obediently withdrew his hand, of no mind to upset her. In their dynamic, he recognized he was the servant. When she told him to go ahead, he went ahead; and if she said to stay behind, he stayed behind.

It must have been for want of care the door stuck in its jamb, but when Togame put her back into it—

The fusuma clacked open.

By no means was this room spacious—frankly, it was cramped. Devoid of furniture, much less any decorations, it was floored with tatami and bare. One person, on his own, would take up almost all of the room.

In it sat a man.

He was lanky, with long hair like a girl.

A simple black kimono.

Eyes closed, he sat cross-legged in the center.

He almost seemed asleep—no.

In fact he was.

"..."

"..."

Again, they looked each other in the eye.

Then they turned back to the man at the same time.

The man in black—was asleep with a katana at his hip.

In a black scabbard.

Black handle, black tsuba.[21]

A sword—so hidden[22] by the black of its surroundings as to be almost invisible.

[21] 鍔 TSUBA the elliptical and often ornate handguard of a katana

[22] 保護色 HOGOSHOKU protective coloring

Shichika felt a strange sensation. Different from the month before, when Komori pulled a sword out of his body—on that occasion, before he had a chance to ask, the ninja declared the sword to be Zetto the Leveler, one of the Twelve Possessed, among the masterpieces forged by Kiki Shikizaki.

This was different.

No one had said this was Zanto the Razor.

Not Togame, and not Ginkaku Uneri. Strictly speaking, he had no proof the man sleeping before him was in fact Ginkaku Uneri.

But Shichika's intuition[23] made it clear. He knew.

That sword—was Zanto the Razor.

"Um...excuse me?"

Of course, Shichika lacked any reason or explanation as to why he knew... *the idea popped into his head, it could easily be wrong, he had better relax...* his feelings swirled, but the strange sensation only lasted for an instant.

And then—

"Are you Ginkaku Uneri?"

On hearing Togame's supple voice, the fleeting experience vanished from his mind, nearly disappearing from his memory.

In her usual supercilious tone, Togame addressed the man, whose eyes had yet to open. "I am Togame the Schemer, Grand Commander of Arms of the Yanari Shogunate Military Directorate, Owari Bakufu."

Her standard introduction.

If this were a more conventional story, now would be the time to reveal an item bearing the insignia of the shogunate, but Togame belonged to an office so shrouded in secrecy,[24] so buried in the background, that she carried nothing that could prove her identity, which could only be announced verbally.

"That sword you have—Zanto the Razor, is it not?"

"Pipe down," the man muttered. In polar contrast with Togame's piercing voice, his murmur seemed to fade away. "Yes, I am Ginkaku Uneri...and who are you? Miss Togame from somewhere...and this sword is indeed Zanto the Razor...but quit hooting and hollering.[25] I just woke up. Your voice goes straight through my skull."

"...My apologies."

Togame lowered her voice somewhat—and smiled. She must have been relieved, having uncovered the man she wanted, and by his side the sword.

The man—Uneri—was awake now, but remained seated on the floor. Eyes heavy, barely even open, he acknowledged the presence of Togame and, a step behind her, Shichika.

He kept the katana at his hip. Even when he was asleep.

Shichika doubted it was the best way to protect the sword. Did he keep

23 直感 CHOKKAN "direct sense"

24 影 KAGE shadows

25 ぴーちくぱーちく PIICHIKU PAACHIKU onomatopoeia for ceaseless yammering

it by his side, slung at his hip at all times, afraid that someone might steal it at any moment? If so, the man was pretty insecure. Then again, a stunt like carrying the Leveler inside you was probably unique to Komori Maniwa, and the other owners of the Twelve Possessed had to be beating their brains to think up ways to keep them safe...

"And? What brings a bigshot[26] from the bakufu to the middle of the desert? Wait, you called my name. Another eviction notice... No, you want the Razor."

"Yes, the Razor. How about giving it to me?" Togame came right out and asked him.

Straight talk. Perhaps a little too straight, thought Shichika, a step behind her. She had said they would attempt diplomacy, but now that he thought about it, could a highhanded woman like her actually negotiate? She had been just as direct the month before, on Haphazard Island, in offering Shichika a job (he wasn't sure how she saw it, but on its own, her "diplomacy" had all but failed back then)...

"By give, of course, I don't mean give away. The bakufu will find a way to make it worth your while. I can tell you one thing, though. No good will come from being so possessive. It's just a sword."

"The other day..."

Uneri spoke in the same sleepy voice, declining to engage Togame.

"Some poser[27] ninja came to give the same kind of speech... Was that guy a friend of yours?"

"My friend? As if," denied Togame.

The Maniwa had stabbed the Schemer in the back, and in her position, who wouldn't be dismissive? But if she was already correcting him, she might also take issue with "poser ninja"—that's what Shichika thought, anyway, which made him a pretty decent guy.

"Don't compare me—or us—to that lowlife ninja. We have come with a proper[28] deal. It may only be a sword, but I am well aware of its value. One of the Twelve Possessed forged by legendary swordsmith Kiki Shikizaki... I know full well that it is irreplaceable. But Uneri, I need you to cooperate, for the sake of the bakufu, nay, the sake of the nation, and do your part."

"...No one who speaks on behalf 'of the nation' is up to any good," Uneri answered drowsily. "Even that poser ninja was a little more convincing... although he spoke in such a weird way I'm not sure I actually understood him...*hwa*."

Uneri let out a big yawn.

His mood and tone made Togame purse her lips.

Not only highhanded, she was impatient...Shichika would be amazed if

26 お偉いさん OERAISAN very important person
27 偽物 NISE MONO fake
28 正当 SEITŌ legitimate

this attempt at diplomacy was a success, but he kept his mouth shut. No matter how ill-disposed Togame was to diplomacy, he could not do much better—no.

It was her job. Shichika, the katana, had no right[29] to speak.

In the confines of his heart, he found Togame adorable[30] for her brazen willingness to tackle a situation she was unfit to undertake—but that was classified.

"Don't tell me you never plan to leave this castle, out here in the middle of the desert. If there is anything you desire, I have ways to help you—out in the open, and behind the scenes."

"You'll saddle yourself with a ronin like me? How thoughtful—but I'll have you know, there's a price on my head."

"I could clear that up for you. Your wish is my command."

Fwaa.

Another massive yawn. He seemed unwilling to entertain Togame's offer. She was getting nowhere.

The sword's poison—had it gotten the better of him? Shichika had to wonder. Its effects might be less potent on ninjas like Komori and Shirasagi, but Uneri was a swordsman, and the venom might have found an ideal host.

"Listen, Uneri—"

"I appreciate that you've stopped shouting, but now you're so quiet I can barely hear you. Come a little closer?" requested Uneri, bleary-eyed. "It's disrespectful[31] to address a swordsman from the doorway. I don't care how important you are. That's no way to ask someone a favor."

"..."

Togame snarled her lips in displeasure, but she had to admit he had a point, at least in that respect, and so stepped through the doorway into the cramped room where Uneri sat. Shichika was unsure whether to follow her, but the room was crowded enough with just Uneri, and fitting another person might have been impossible anyway. He decided not to move, but to stay put where he was. Togame stepped her right foot, then her left into the room—when Shichika realized the tatami by the doorway was of a different color than the mats around it. This must be where, he thought. The mat that had been swapped out, in the other room—

But then.

Ever so subtly, Uneri moved his right hand.

So subtly that it hadn't really. The slightest twitch.

So that his right hand seemed to grip the handle of the katana.

That instant.

Shing!

29 領分ではない RYŌBUN DEWA NAI not his domain
30 萌え MOE geek slang for kindly affection and attachment
31 失礼 SHITSUREI "breach of manners"

A sound.

But ahead of the sound, a fraction of an instant earlier—Shichika had reacted. Deciding not to move, to stay where he was, he noticed the color of the tatami—and instantly leapt before he looked. Pretty much by reflex. Working every muscle of his body, he spun his waist for a backspin spinning kick—

"Kyotoryu—Yuri!"[32]

Trouble is, from where he stood outside the doorway, he could spin all he wanted—once or a hundred times—and the blade of his foot would never reach Uneri. Lengthy as his legs may be, the Yuri could hardly make them any longer. What his foot could reach, however barely—what it contacted midair, instead of Ginkaku Uneri—was Togame.

The move was imperfect, executed not from the proper stance, but completely upright. Yet if his heel, gyring with all his weight behind it, were to slam into Togame, whose frame bore comparison to shoji paper, the explosive[33] force could end her life. He made sure not only his heel but his entire sole made contact, so that he would be less kicking than thrusting, or better, hooking—

It slammed into her chest.

With zero training in the martial arts, she was unequipped to deal with this surprise attack, a frontal strike from behind, and her body was shot backward in a grand arc. Out of the room where Uneri sat and into the room with Shichika, whose foot, in turn, spun away from Uneri. Unable to kill his momentum, Shichika made another small turn in place. Togame, caught off guard, planted her butt on the tatami.

Then the sound.

Shing!

"You piece of—" yelled Togame, sitting up on her elbows. Her voice did pierce your skull.

"Calm down, Togame."

"Who kicks you out of nowhere and says calm down? You ass. When I felt myself being sucked back from behind, I thought aliens[34] were abducting me."

"What an imagination, but...see?"

Figuring there was no time to explain, Shichika pointed at the spot where her obi[35] passed over her stomach. The layers were prodigious, but there, the fabric had been slashed. Cutting through at least half the countless layers of kimono. The gash was clean—summoning the corpse of Shirasagi Maniwa, who had been dumped in two parts outside the castle.

A close shave. Since no person can move faster than his sheer reflexes

32 百合 YURI lily
33 炸裂 SAKURETSU ripping
34 宇宙人 UCHŪJIN "space people"
35 帯 OBI wide sash tied around the waist of a kimono

allow, it was the closest shave possible...or the Razor's lightest cut.

"Wha...wha..." Togame had lost her words. And any color in her face. "I-If I didn't wear so many layers, my body would be..."

"Um, if you were wearing fewer layers, none would have been sliced, more like."

She was a little confused.

But the Schemer had seen her share of tight fixes and quickly bounced back from it. Though yet to stand from where she planted her behind, she faced Uneri—through the doorway.

"Hey you!" she raised her voice. "What—was that?!"

"Wow. I guess that was that..." For someone who had swung his sword at an agent of the bakufu, Uneri was oddly calm, and oddly sleepy. "In all the time I've held the Razor, none have dodged my Zerosen but you...or was it both of you? Or was it *you*?" he asked impudently.

Glaring at Shichika.

Although the man's eyes looked tired—it was a fierce glare.

"You think you're surprised?" Shichika asked in turn. "I've heard iainuki was extreme, but I had no idea it was so fast."

Then he realized.

The sound he heard when Uneri clasped the handle of the sword—*shing!*—was *the tsuba contacting the sheath. He was so blisteringly fast that you heard the note almost at the same time that he touched the handle.*

No sooner had he drawn the sword than it was in its scabbard.

The flash of a katana in iainuki is customarily called issen.[36] But in the hands of Uneri, the Razor caught no light. Nothing to see, nothing to hear—all you saw was your own body, sliced in half, and all you heard was the click of the tsuba.

Which is why he called it Zerosen—no flash.

This was iainuki to the extreme, an Uneri family tradition.

"Sounds like your scare and my scare cancel out."

Somehow both on and off the mark—not that it matters which—Uneri softly drew his fingers from the handle of the sword.

But this hardly put them at ease.

Shichika corrected his rash impression of the man. He was anything but insecure; for someone so phenomenally skilled in iainuki, keeping the katana at his hip was simply the *most efficient way* of safeguarding the Razor.

"Uneri—do you realize what you've done?!"

"I told you, young lady, stop shouting... Who's that hunk of meat, your older brother? Think you're gonna strongarm[37] me into a deal? In that case, let's jump straight to the point. You're quite persuasive...but I'm just a simple swordsman, who settles my deals with the sword."

[36] 一閃 ISSEN one flash

[37] 腕っぷし UDEPPUSHI brawn

"My older brother?! Do I look like his little sister to you? How am I a 'little sister'?"

Her reaction, clouded by ire, was somewhat odd. Perhaps her confusion had yet to abate.

"My forefather turned on his lord and even the Old Shogun, refusing to relinquish this sword. If I say 'oops, sorry, by all means' and hand it over now, my entire lineage will be laughing in their graves. They'll laugh so hard I'll never sleep again."

"You're scared of letting go of that katana?" Judging that their diplomacy was in shambles, Shichika interrupted the bickering at last. "This move of yours, the Zerosen—without Shikizaki's Razor, you can't whip it out as fast, right? You're scared of losing that?"

"And if I'm scared—what of it?"

"Just saying. That's the trouble with being *a swordsman who uses a sword.*"

After a pause, Uneri chuckled. "What do you know about being a swordsman? Far as I can see, you carry no blade."

"I am a swordsman. Make no mistake."

"If you were, you would know better. A swordsman has no use for words. He acts. If you want the sword, shut up and try to take it—and I'll shut up and fight."

"That stubborn, huh?"

"It's a matter of dignity," Uneri said without a shred of doubt. "Sure, I am scared. I don't have to have the Razor to perform the Zerosen, but having tasted its speed and power, I could never go back. What scares me isn't someone trying to take it, but *my own speed*. You must have felt pretty good about yourself just now saving the young lady's life. But that was nothing. At peak speed, the Zerosen moves faster than light."

Try me, Uneri beckoned unto Shichika with his fingers.

"Togame—"

But Shichika turned down the invitation. Better put, he completely ignored Uneri. Instead, he turned and addressed Togame, who was still sitting on the floor.

"There's a few things I want to check. You good?"

"Pardon me?"

Togame seemed taken aback by Shichika's obtuse remark, but he remained unfazed.

"Hey." Now he was speaking to Uneri. "We're gonna have a strategy meeting.[38] Take a nap or something. We'll come right back."

"..."

"Get ready to show off—I want to see the Zerosen, at peak speed."

[38] 作戦会議 SAKUSEN KAIGI time-out for brainstorming

"...Shut the fusuma behind you."

Unlike Togame, Uneri didn't seem to think it rude—though he might have become warier of Shichika. He spoke again a few moments later in a voice that was impenetrable.

"I'm sensitive. If light gets in, I won't be able to sleep."

"Is that so. Gotcha. Later."

Shichika shut the fusuma, taking an extra couple of seconds thanks to the poor fit. If it was Togame's job to open the fusuma, how symbolic, thought Shichika uncharacteristically, for it to be his job to close it.

"Shichika, what do you think you're doing—"

"Wait, Togame, I'm not taking back[39] what I said, but the speed of this guy's iainuki is no joke—I'll be ready to go back in, after a quick break."

Shichika offered his hand to Togame. She looked incredibly uneasy, but after a time, she took it. While he had taken pains to go as easy on her as possible, once the blade of his foot had whammed her in the breadbox, she was not about to stand back up. She was shoji paper. If she hadn't worn so many layers—she was right in a sense—the Yuri might have shattered her sternum.

"Oh....one more thing." The voice came from beyond the fusuma. It sounded tired—Shichika had not been serious in recommending a nap, but evidently Uneri was perpetually about to sleep. "The white-haired young lady told me her name—but you, young man, what's yours?"

"..."

Shichika looked to Togame. She nodded softly.

Since she was acting as an agent of the bakufu, Shichika wasn't sure if his school's involvement could be made public and had held off on announcing himself to Uneri, but she seemed to have no problem with it.

Then there was no reason to hesitate.

Shichika was proud of who he was.[40]

A pride handed down from his father.

"Seventh Master of the Kyotoryu—Shichika Yashurri."

...

It wasn't on purpose.[41]

[39] 撤回 TEKKAI undo

[40] 身分 MIBUN status/station

[41] 噛んじゃった KANJATTA "ended up biting (one's tongue)" i.e. stumbling over a line

CHAPTER THREE

RAKKA ROZEKI

■ ■

No one who speaks on behalf "of the nation" is up to any good—or so claimed Ginkaku Uneri, but toward what end remains to be seen. From a man like him, perhaps a comment like this was to be expected, no more than a captious[1] remark meant to perturb the Schemer. What was certain, however, was that Togame, on the receiving end of this opinion, was no true servant of the nation.

They were not burglars—

But neither were they champions of justice.

Their orders may have come down from on high, but they weren't rounding up the Twelve Possessed out of necessity—but in that case, why had Togame the Schemer resigned herself to such a journey?

To put it simply, she sought revenge.

One might say she had a vested interest.[2]

Her father was the Mastermind of the Rebellion—Takahito Hida, Kaoyaku of Oshu.

If the Great Sword Hunt was among the most ignoble laws in Japanese history—then Takahito Hida was surely among the most ignoble of men. But history is no more than a record written by the victors, a journal tweaked to cast them in a favorable light.

Togame had *her own* opinions, however.

She acknowledged that her father was a failure.

How else could you describe defeat in battle?

Nevertheless—ignoble was not the way she saw him.

The slaughter of every member of her family made a lone wolf[3] of Togame—destroyed her lineage, with not an intimate relation left alive—and so she could never abandon the memory.

She proceeded to abandon everything else.

Her name.

Her history.

Her sympathies.

Her loyalties.

Her word.

Her heart.

Then—she infiltrated the bakufu. All to carry out the unrealized ambition, the cherished dream of Takahito Hida—but she still had a long, long

[1] 揚げ足を取る AGEASHI WO TORU finding fault

[2] 私利私欲 SHIRI SHIYOKU "private gains and desires"

[3] 天涯孤独 TENGAI KODOKU alone in the whole world

way to go. Her investment of time and energy had won her a high rank, Grand Commander of Arms of the Yanari Shogunate Military Directorate, Owari Bakufu—but Grand Commander wasn't good enough. For the sake of her father, for the sake of revenge, she had no choice but to rise higher, to a much higher rank.

At bare minimum, a position where she could speak directly to the shogun.

Within earshot.

Close enough, should she desire, she could have his neck—a rank that high.

Otherwise—she had no hope of changing the history books of tomorrow.

The defeated cannot tell their story.

And dead men[4] tell no tales.

Come what may, Togame must survive—and be victorious.

For her, when all was said and done, collecting the Twelve Possessed of Kiki Shikizaki was no more than a means to an end—it was not for the bakufu or the shogun, and certainly not for the nation.

Not a matter of necessity or circumstance, it was strictly personal.

In which case, what of her companion, Shichika Yasuri?

What gave him a reason to fight?

Having lived as long as he could remember on Haphazard Island, raised out of contact with the world, the concept of nation could not have been more foreign[5] to him. The Master of the Kyotoryu, who forsook swords, would never seek out the Twelve Possessed simply because they were his opposite. His curiosity did not amount to motivation. His lack of motivation, and lack of affection for swords in general, may have been what drove Togame to enlist the Kyotoryu—but neither was a factor for Shichika.

Why, then?

The answer was characteristically plain and simple.

He was fighting for Togame.

A woman, and until recently, a stranger.

He had been stuck on Haphazard Island, forever refining his skill, not with purpose or significance, nor by necessity or circumstance. Now, at the age of twenty-four, he finally had a reason to exist.

Swords do not choose who to kill.

Yet—a sword will choose its owner.

Shichika had chosen her.

Komori Maniwa, the first partner Togame had enlisted on her quest to round up all the swords, had given Shichika the dirty details as to why she was hunting down the Twelve Possessed—her acts of valor, her distinguished exploits, were all performed not out of loyalty, but a deep thirst for

[4] 死者 SHISHA the deceased
[5] 一番縁遠い ICHIBAN ENDŌI "the number-one distant in ties"

vengeance. That could never move Shichika. The affairs of an institution with no bearing on an island monkey like himself were dismissible. He did not care to consider or cope with any delicate balance of interests. But there was one thing he could not ignore: the name of Togame's father, Takahito Hida—Mastermind of the Rebellion.

Takahito Hida.

The name of the man whom Shichika's father—Hero of the Rebellion, Mutsue Yasuri, Sixth Master of the Kyotoryu—had killed with his own hands, the blade of his school—indeed, the very man whose death had earned Mutsue his title.

Shichika's father had killed Togame's father.

Before her eyes.

Which was when her hair turned white.

...Shichika did not go so far as to see it as a way to make amends[6] for the misdeeds of his father—in fact, he was unsure whether killing enemies in battle was truly criminal. Swords don't pick who to kill. He was more than simply unsure, however—he hated himself for never having given it a thought, felt a terrible self-loathing for having swallowed whole the notion that his father was a hero. More than anything else—this woman had seen her own father murdered and devoted herself to avenging him, yet felt compelled to call upon the Kyotoryu for help, as the only means—and Shichika had been unable to imagine how she must have felt.

That was all there was to it.

The reason he was fighting.

For Togame.

■ ■

"Stop looking so bent out of shape, Togame."

"I'm so not bent out of shape!"

"'So not'?"

"Oh, uh... I'm not so bent out of shape!"

Slight difference.

The gusto behind her swift correction made her initial phrasing even cuter.

But this was no time to be feeling disarmed.

To recap—they had called for a break and left Uneri's den. Another room in Gekoku Castle would have served as far as Shichika knew, but Togame insisted that strategy meeting or not, they had to go the whole length, where-

6 罪滅ぼし TSUMI HOROBOSHI "sin exterminating"

upon the pair exited the castle.

Out into Inaba Desert.

Night had fallen, but the starry sky was too spectacular to describe it as pitch dark.

Sitting on the sand, they faced each other—even in a setting such as this, it was crucial that they maintain their evening imprinting[7] routine, and Togame's white hair enwrapped Shichika's torso. A tower rising behind them in the desert, a woman dressed in elegance, and a beefy man her white hair enshrouded made for quite the avant-garde[8] tableau.

Furthermore, Togame's kimono was coming undone. Partly the mark of Uneri's Zerosen—but she favored a casual styling to begin with, and this degree of sartorial distress seemed to fall within the scope of fashion for her.

"You sure sound childish sometimes... How old are you anyway?" asked Shichika. "You're older than me, right?"

"That's none of your concern. Who are you to be making my age an issue? In any case, I am not bent out of shape."

"Seems like you have a lot on your mind."

"Even if I did, I wouldn't share. Telling you would be like the pearls thing."

"...Aren't you abbreviating that a little too much?"

Like casting pearls.

No matter how upset she was, she could have kept in another word at least.

"Well, Shichika, what was it you wanted to check? Uneri's iainuki far exceeded our expectations...but I saw no reason to put the battle on hold."

"No, I didn't mean to put it on hold—or if I did, it was only to check if he'd be fine with it beforehand."

"...Fine with it?"

"To see if he would follow us out. But he didn't."

"That's true..."

"The moment you stepped over the threshold and entered that room, he drew his sword on you. Flipping that around, *as long as we don't go into the room*, he won't come after us."

This, Shichika said, was the first thing he wanted to check.

"No...I see your point. But why does that matter?"

"One difference between normal swordplay and iainuki...well, since I don't use a normal sword, I don't mean from the sword-user's point of view, but his opponent's..."

Since arriving on the mainland, Shichika had been carted to a number of schools of swordplay exemplified by the Hisho Dojo. The first reason for these visits was to gain a firmer grasp of what the Kyotoryu could do, the better to plan out their campaign for tracking down the Twelve Possessed.

[7] 刷り込み SURIKOMI the precise term for the biological phenomenon

[8] 前衛的 ZEN'EITEKI the Japanese term is a fairly direct translation of the French word

The second reason was to give Shichika more experience in battle, even if these exercises were not exactly live. They never left the realm of training—the swordsmen Shichika confronted didn't use real blades, only wooden replicas.

As a result, the quickdraw intrinsic to iainuki was absent from those practice sessions. Until today, Shichika's only knowledge had come secondhand, from his father, but having witnessed it in action, he now understood a thing or two about iainuki.

"When they come at me like that...real, wooden, doesn't matter—it bugs me out."[9]

"Huh? Obviously. Who doesn't when there's a weapon in your face?"

"That's not what I'm getting at..."

Shichika searched for the right words. It was hard to verbalize his impressions.

"A sword is more than just a weapon. It's also a pretty effective piece of armor.[10] I don't mean just parrying, but you know, if I did this..."

Shichika thrust out an arm, still wrapped in the tendrils of Togame's white hair. She reacted with an ambiguous grunt.

"In my case, it's a hand—but when I do this, it's hard to approach me, and hard to strike at me."

"Only a stick—yet a wall."

"Hey, that's a good way to put it. Simple."

Shichika smiled, glad to see that he was making sense. Of course, his choice of words being awkward at best, his point had come across mostly thanks to Togame's acuity.

Put your sword between you and your opponent.

The teaching has survived into present-day kendo.[11] The wall that your opponent makes is quite challenging to penetrate, as anyone who tries will quickly realize. There are several ways around this, and unless you are the Kyotoryu, you have a sword and your own wall at your disposal, whereby strategy comes into play.

"That Kiku move I've shown you is a great example. In the Kyotoryu, as a general rule, you treat the katana as part of the body and attack it—you turn their unity[12] against them and break down the wall first—except in our case, you've forbidden it."

Mutodori, or fighting without any katana, sounded well and good, but any blade subjected to a Kyotoryu move usually sundered. Since they were on a mission to gather the weapons, the aforementioned general rule was out of play. "Protect the swords"—that was Togame's strict directive. In practice,

[9] 鬱陶しい UTTŌSHII annoying
[10] 防具 BŌGU protective gear
[11] 剣道 KENDŌ the martial art of swordsmanship
[12] 物我一体 MOTSUGA ITTAI others and self are one

the shackle mooted the larger part of Kyotoryu's techniques. But given the mission objective, Shichika had no choice.

"Still, even if I'm not going to *break down* the wall made by the sword, I at least need to *bring down* that wall—but with iainuki, there's no *wall* in the first place."

"Ah...I see," Togame said. "If the sword must be drawn, then it is in its sheath for the stance[13]...although 'stance' may not be the best word when Uneri merely sits cross-legged on the floor...then again, I've heard iainuki called za-ai,[14] so I guess it works."

"Yeah, but how's he move that fast? If that wasn't peak speed, I can't imagine what would be. Not that I believe he'd be faster than light."

"I wonder. It might not be a bluff. If we can't see it, he might already be faster than light."

"The Zerosen."

Shichika cast a sidelong glance at Gekoku Castle. *Can't see it*—just like the castle. They hadn't seen it until the last moment, and had yet to see the blade—only Uneri.

"So because iainuki has no wall, it's easier to attack him?"

"Wrong, Togame—no wall means it's harder. If you can see it, you can counter it—and if you can't see it, you can avoid it. But you can't counter or avoid something that *isn't there*."

"..."

"Keeping your katana in its scabbard is like not showing your hand—that's what Dad always said. I mean, the fact of the matter is, you never know when the first strike will come. He has it locked down, so you need to be cautious. Just when you think you have the upper hand, you'll lose it. The moment you come within this guy's range, he draws, just like he did with you—so simple, nothing to it. I need to be cautious, while he only needs to wait. Ceding the first move and settling for a counterstrike[15]—but at the same time no style is more aggressive."

"So he intentionally leaves himself open—inviting you to attack."

"Right. But all that aside, any quickdraw is a handful. Though I knew that from the beginning—"

"A handful? Why? A sword is still a sword."

"Yeah...um..."

Togame the Schemer.

The head of a big-picture organization that directed military engagements with all manner of ingenuity and intrigue—lacked any proficiency, as bears repeating, in the martial arts.

She could not fight if her life depended on it.

13 構え KAMAE opening form of a move
14 座合 ZA'AI iainuki, only seated
15 邀撃 YŌGEKI interception

When she visited Haphazard Island, she did wear a katana under the pretext of challenging the Kyotoryu to a duel, but that weapon was already on its way back to Owari. As a schemer, this was a point of pride—or perhaps more like a point of caution. The "sword" had killed her father and wiped out her entire family. She would get the job done *without laying a finger of her own* upon a sword of any kind—and thus.

She had a tenuous understanding of what swordplay actually involved.

Ultimately, her job was to oversee the big picture.

Shichika, himself, had virtually no combat experience and was not in a position to enlighten her. The dicey[16] conversation was holding together only thanks to the Schemer's sagacity.

"It has to do with the 'wall' I mentioned—say someone swings their sword at you." Shichika chopped his hand before her eyes. "How would you dodge it?"

"I would fail to, of that I am certain."

"Do you need to sound so proud about it?"

"We're not blocking it? Okay, then I guess to the right..."

"The correct answer would be: ahead and to the right. I'm not sure if this is just the Kyotoryu, or a general rule, but you 'dodge forward' against an attack that forms a vertical arc."

"I can see why it would be alarming for someone to rush up at you in a lethal contest. Especially if you are supposed to be doing the attacking."

"Same principle when they stab, but..."

Thrusting a spear hand at Togame and stopping just before her throat, Shichika followed up with a wide horizontal swipe—to trace the path[17] you could expect from iainuki.

"This way, you can't dodge forward. Or to the right."

"If I tried, the sword would catch me."

"If you can't block it, you have to back away. Like you did," he told Togame. To be precise, she hadn't backed up so much as been yanked back—but she knew this was the wrong time to resent it or split hairs.

"Then what," she egged him on. "Is that all?"

"When you can block, you block—but not against Zanto the Razor. If I caught it the wrong way, he'd slice all the way through me, like he did those chains on the Maniwac. In the Kyotoryu, just like we have the Kiku for when somebody takes a stab at you, a move called the Sakura counters sideway swipes, iainuki or not—but it would definitely snap the Razor."

"Which defeats the purpose."[18]

"Right, defeats the purpose. But this Zerosen, it's not like I can see it coming. Evading it is the best I can hope for. I can't see the path it makes and

16 際どい KIWADOI precarious
17 軌道 KIDŌ trajectory
18 本末転倒 HONMATSU TENTŌ wagging the dog

only hear it clicking back into the scabbard. The beginning and the ending come at basically the same time. I'm sorry, but on the spot, there's no blocking such a move."

"So you're toast.[19] Despite all your bragging."

You've only had a taste of what the Kyotoryu is made of—well, that certainly was bragging. The Sakura might work against iainuki, but that meant nothing if he couldn't use it. In which case, he just sounded like a sore loser.

"Hey, Togame. Don't jump to conclusions. I'm not saying I can't handle this—but he...Ginkaku Uneri, seems to know just iainuki and nothing else, doesn't he? That's unbalanced for a swordsman, but you could also say he has absolute confidence in his specialty. Um, that last Maniwac—what was his name again?"

"Shirasagi Maniwa."

"Right. Shirasagi."

The corpse of Shirasagi. Two clean halves. Before they entered Gekoku Castle, Shichika buried his body in the sand, and it was gone without a trace. Togame had said there was no need to give a ninja such a funeral,[20] but Shichika had persisted. The man deserved the courtesy as much as anybody.

"Why do you think he lost to Uneri?"

"Why? A weird thing to ask," Togame said. "We both know why. He fell prey to the Zerosen. That wound permits no other reading."

"Sure. But how could Shirasagi lose to the Zerosen *so easily*? Don't you think that's strange? According to what Komori told me, dirty deeds are how a ninja makes a living—what would make a ninja challenge Uneri to a proper fight?"

"..."

Togame nodded. He had a point.

"It is—strange. The body didn't look so old. Uneri and Shirasagi must have fought fairly recently—yet Uneri, for his part, showed no signs of injury... A Maniwa Boss, cut down without even dealing a parting shot?"

"Komori liked to entertain,[21] but I gather that's rare for a ninja."

"Yes...but what of it? Do you have some kind of an idea?"

"Nothing as solid as an idea—but I was thinking, maybe *Shirasagi had no choice but to fight fair and square.*"

"No choice..."

"I knew something weird was going on. Remember that bloodstained mat we saw before we got to Uneri's room? It was a different color from the tatami around it, and worn differently too. We thought it must have been a mat from somewhere else."

"True, but what's so weird about that? You were right. We found Uneri in

19 絶体絶命 ZETTAI ZETSUMEI "sure death"
20 弔い TOMURAI simple ceremony for the dead
21 接待好き SETTAI ZUKI enjoys playing the host

a room not far from there."

"It might not be as big as some of the ones I've seen on our journey, but at the end of the day, Gekoku Castle is still a castle—and this guy has the whole thing to himself. He has plenty of rooms, to use however he likes. If one gets bloody, he can just switch. I don't see why he would bother switching out a mat."

"...I can see why you would think that—it stands to reason. But everyone is different, and people pick favorites... What if Uneri simply likes that room the best?"

"That's exactly what I mean," Shichika said. "But *why* does he like it?"

"..."

It certainly wasn't luxuriant[22] or comfortable[23]—cramped, and out of the way, it was a manifestly inconvenient living room. So why had Uneri chosen it as his den?

"Probably *because* it's cramped and out of the way."

"Are you saying that *he likes it that way*?"

"I bet he does, *for repelling his enemies*. It makes sense, if you look at how it's built. To enter, you have to use the fusuma from the next room since it's not connected to any other space. No windows either—if you replaced the fusuma with bars, you could use it as a jail cell. And so—to get to Uneri, you have to enter through the fusuma, and step in through that doorway, taking him head-on."

"Head-on—ah, I see. Only from the front."

"Exactly. In iainuki, the sword sweeps—it works great in front of you, but not so great behind you. Well, even if you're swinging up or thrusting, it'd be the same. But in a room that small, people can't get behind you. The sweeping arc gets in their way whether they're trying to flank you on your left or your right."

"Of course."

No choice but to fight fair and square.

Not even a Maniwa Boss.

No room—for dirty deeds.

"So you're saying that he didn't chase us when we left—because his strategy depends on being in that tiny room. Of course—why would he let us go otherwise, after we already crossed swords."

"In battle, you want to be on favorable terrain, right? Like when I fought Komori, on Haphazard Island, we were in my domain. But in that room—Uneri has the edge, no doubt about it."

Every inch of the room fell within the range of the Zerosen.

And its speed defied imagination.

"In which case—we would be without any measures after all. Being so

[22] 豪華 GŌKA extravagant

[23] 暮らしやすい KURASHI YASUI "easy to live in"

circumspect[24] is unlike you."

"I told you, don't jump to conclusions. I'm thinking as hard as I can."

And he was.

Shichika Yasuri was thinking.

But not because his natural tendency to call everything a pain had been suppressed—he may not have been saying so out loud, but in his heart, he chanted the words over and over. What a pain—even carrying on with Togame like this. He would rather run back into Gekoku Castle and get to it with Uneri.

But Shichika controlled himself.

For Togame's sake—he could not lose.

As her katana, he could not allow defeat.

By any means necessary—they would take possession of the Razor.

Using all that he had learned from his father, and from his sister, and from Togame thus far on their journey—Shichika was doing his best to strategize.

He was not a thinker—but he was thinking.

"So, my first idea is to drag him out of the room."

"Makes sense," Togame agreed. "Just getting him into the next room would expand your options—you would enjoy considerably greater freedom of movement than in that cramped space where neither side can maneuver. But good luck with that. The man just sat there absolutely still and watched us go, as if roots were holding him in place. Uneri will never leave that room. Unless, that is, you have a way of luring him out."

"Well, he's holed up in his fort—weird as that is, when he's already inside a castle. But if we turned this into a siege,[25] he'd have no choice but to come out of that room sometime."

"Don't start thinking about lighting the castle on fire. It could cost us the Razor. Remember our foremost objective."

"Hmm. We don't have any missiles, and even if we did, they must be no match for the Zerosen. If that's out, I guess we have no other choice."

"Than?"

In other words, there was a way.

Togame could not contain herself.

"Come on, spit it out."

"You sure?"

"What's the holdup."

"Okay. So the first part is you go in the room."

"Right. I go into the room."

"And then you let the Zerosen cut you in half."

"Naturally. The Zerosen cuts me in half. Good thinking, Shichika. What next?"

[24] 回りくどい MAWARI KUDOI roundabout
[25] 持久戦 JIKYŪSEN a protracted war

"If Uneri doesn't like bloodstains on his floor, there's no way he likes dead bodies. He'll carry it outside, just like he did with Shirasagi Maniwa. He'll leave not just that room, but also the castle itself. He'll have nowhere to run, and nowhere to hide, in the desert."

"Then? Then?"

"That's when I get him."

"Cheerio!"

Contending with less of a height difference than if they were standing, Togame's sandal caught Shichika right in the chin. The force, however scanty, was enough to make him lose his balance—and tug at the white hair wrapped around his body, hurting Togame herself. To use a metaphor imperfect for the era, she felt like the kind of person who steps on her own shoelaces and takes a digger.

"But I'll have been cut in half, won't I!" she hollered as if they were a comedy act.

Way to be, Togame.

"I told you: 'Protect the swords' and 'Protect me'! What kind of a bodyguard uses his employer as a decoy?"

"Yeah, so I guess we can't use that one."

"I guess not! What a plan to even consider!"

"So I give up on luring him out of the room, but—I still have this other idea."

"..."

Togame's glare warned that this plan better not involve her being sliced in half, but as if to wave away her apprehensive gaze, Shichika assured, "*If fighting him fair and square is my only choice—I'll fight him fair and square.*" His voice was dead serious.

Nevertheless.

"...Shichika, if that's the whole plan,[26] I'm going to get angry."

"Uh, haven't you been angry all this time?"

"Don't mock me! If we honestly have no choice but to fight him fair and square, why back out like we—"

"For one thing, I wanted to check with you about my reasoning. Not counting the time with Komori, where it just sort of happened, this is my first real battle ever. But—it won't be my last. For this to contribute to my next fight, I need *to be learning* as I fight—because a win today is not enough to guarantee a win tomorrow. If I only win out of sheer luck, like with Komori, it's no good."

"Urk..." Togame wasn't expecting her biting rhetorical question to provoke a sincere explanation and missed a beat. "You said that was the first thing. Aside from wanting to check whether Uneri would follow us, is there another reason why we took this time out?"

[26] 結論 KETSURON conclusion

"The second one is more concrete. You were in the wrong position. On Haphazard Island, Komori abducted you while I was focused on fighting him, right? I didn't want a repeat[27] of that—and decided to regroup."

"Oh."

Yanked back by the Yuri, Togame had landed on her butt in the adjacent room. Not that she'd been scared stiff, but reeling from the impact, she couldn't even stand up on her own—

"'Protect the swords'—and 'Protect Togame,' right?"

"...If you know that, don't dare come up with a plan where I get cut in half."

The words themselves were snide, but it was not by chance that her voice betrayed embarrassment. Maybe Shichika noticed, and maybe he didn't, but it had no effect on his own tone.

"That's why you need to stay behind me," he said. "Go behind me this time, like I did last time. We switch positions, like a changing of the guard. That way, I can protect you—and you can be my backup[28] plan."

"Backup?"

"Just in case. If I go at him, fair and square, and that doesn't settle things—having you behind me is sure to *come in handy*. It might even bring down the domain he's created for himself—"

"I think you already know, but I have to remind you... Trusting your back to my martial prowess may not be wise," a dubious Togame counseled.

But Shichika laughed this off.

"I'm not sure I can explain this well...but *I want you there*. If it was just about keeping you safe, you could wait outside the castle while I went in, alone, to fight Uneri. But instead, I'm asking you to brave the danger because I need you there."

"..."

"I guess you could say *strength comes from having something to protect*."

■ ■

Apart from the geographic considerations, Togame the Schemer had charged Shichika with capturing Zanto the Razor out of aptitude, as she had tasked Komori Maniwa with Zetto the Leveler, and Hakuhei Sabi with Hakuto the Whisper. Up against the Kyotoryu, a sword with an edge like no other was no different from a rusty razor—but even from a different angle, you could still say Togame had been right. Ginkaku Uneri was the natural choice for Shichika Yasuri to compete against in his first real battle.

Reason being.

27 二の舞 NI NO MAI "second dance"

28 保険 HOKEN insurance

Despite having owned one of the Possessed for quite some time and being a swordsman—Ginkaku Uneri had a strangely high tolerance for the katana's poison.

The venom of Kiki Shikizaki's blades.

A merciless venom that drove swordsmen mad.

That the Great Sword Hunt was the superlative expression of this insanity is no longer a subject of debate—and further to the point, Hakuhei Sabi, extolled as the greatest swordsman in Japan during his day, fell victim to the venom and betrayed Togame and thereby the Owari Bakufu. And as we saw in Book One of this saga, even Komori Maniwa—a ninja, not a swordsman—had not been totally immune to the Leveler's toxicity.

But Ginkaku Uneri was different.

To be sure, the venom was gnawing at his body, potent as could be—but in terms of personality, there was no perceptible difference between who he was before inheriting the Razor from his father, and who he became thereafter. Mere possession of a Shikizaki blade will drive you to murder—but since Uneri *felt the same drive* before the Razor fell into his hands, and was already killing like it was his job, the sword could not be held accountable. No change transpired when he became the owner—which, for a swordsman of his caliber, was inconceivable. The venom of the Twelve Possessed was that intense.

After all—these were the swords that reigned over the warring states.

In sooth, ten generations back, in the Age of Warring States, the sword's poison had overmastered Uneri's forebear[29] Kinkaku Uneri, permeating every nook and cranny of his body—how else could he have been so insubordinate, in his refusal to hand over the sword, as to make an enemy of the daimyo of Tottori and the Old Shogun, unifier of the nation? Even Ginkaku Uneri, at a remove of so many generations, suspected the account of the ten thousand slain was hogwash,[30] but the madness had not stopped with Kinkaku: for henceforth, every son of the Uneri who came into possession of the Razor, all the way down to Ginkaku's own father, was incontrovertibly deranged.

Crazed from the venom of the Razor.

There was no way around it—the Zerosen of the iainuki style passed down through the Uneri family matched the Razor so perfectly that the katana seemed custom-made to that end.

Swords don't choose who to kill.

But—a sword will choose its owner.

And the Razor had chosen the Uneri.

As the lineage deemed fit for its insanity.

"..."

[29] 先祖 SENZO ancestor

[30] 眉唾物 MAYUTSUBA MONO "eyebrow spit" thus called from a superstition that saliva rubbed into the eyebrows would discourage the antics of shapeshifting tanuki and foxes

Notwithstanding.

Ginkaku Uneri himself, the current master, neither saw himself as crazy or not crazy—in other words, whomever the venom had possessed had no capacity for gauging the extent of its possession.

Yet it was from a place altogether separate from madness that Uneri safeguarded the Razor.

Ironically, it was just as Shichika asserted to Togame outside the castle—*strength comes from having something to protect.* Uneri derived his strength from protecting Zanto the Razor—and Gekoku Castle.

Five years ago—

Inaba Desert, hitherto a tourist destination that aided the local economy, suddenly turned against the people of Tottori.

At incredible speed, it grew before their eyes—swallowing the fiefdom whole.

Homes. Fields. Mountains. Rivers.

Life as they knew it disappeared.

Buried by the desert—without a trace.

But for one structure, Gekoku Castle, originally built upon the sand—since its occupants had vanished, it may as well have vanished too.

Indeed.

Down to the last living soul—they had fled the desert.

Abandoning Tottori.

For Hoki, Mimasaka, Harima, Tajima—anywhere but here.

Heading for the hills. Like bats out of hell, into thin air. They all left Inaba behind. However much a pariah,[31] Uneri had not been without close friends in the town—but they were no exception to the exodus.

And so.

When the spread of Inaba Desert began to falter—all that remained of Inaba were Gekoku Castle and Ginkaku Uneri, on his own.

That is to say, he remained not by choice, but because he had no choice. Or by his own estimation, he felt that he had missed his final chance to leave.

If only he were not the last—had he been, for example, the second to last, he would have been uncertain, and would have had his reservations, and may have racked his brains, but likely would have absconded in the end.

But as the last man standing, he had no choice.

Even reservations were not his to have.

...During the Great Sword Hunt, Kinkaku Uneri had turned against Tottori, nay, the entire nation, to guard the Razor—holding his ground in Inaba. The city claimed a soft place in his heart—that is, if you believed the legends, but his descendent, Ginkaku, who for reasons beyond his control had been forced to dwell indefinitely in Gekoku Castle, understood that the emotions

[31] 鼻摘み者 HANATSUMAMI MONO "someone who makes you pinch your nose"

of his ancestor had not been so warm and fuzzy.

More like—a fixation.[32]

Or call it—a delusion.[33]

Perhaps, dignity.

For Kinkaku Uneri, protecting the Razor and remaining in Inaba had been two sides of the same coin—and this remained the case down through the family line, as each new generation of Uneri met the venom of the sword.

But its current owner saw himself differently. He understood where Kinkaku Uneri had been coming from, but it was only by being fundamentally different from the rest of the Uneri men. Ginkaku, being different, could see through to the essence of the situation. And just as he had missed his chance to leave Inaba—so too had he lost his chance to lose his mind.

He alone was different.

And yet—they called for his protection all the same.

I need them... he thought, quite calmly. *I need something to protect.*

Otherwise—I'll lose the will to fight.

He was sure of it.

What did she call herself—the Schemer?

While he had forgotten the details, the white-haired woman, Togame, against whom he had drawn his sword (not as a warning, nor as a bluff, but intent on slicing her in two), had some connection to the bakufu. He had not attacked her thinking she was lying, but rather—presuming what she said to be true.

In this regard, I am just like my ancestors.

Different he may be.

But what they had protected—he protected.

Another Sword Hunt?

Apparently.

For quite some time, Uneri had been living in Gekoku Castle as the only resident of Inaba, but the visit from that "poser ninja" Shirasagi Maniwa was not his first—comers were in no short supply, and ran the gamut from common thieves to respectable merchants—

And down the gamut, to the last man, he had drubbed them out.

Most of his killings since hunkering down at Gekoku Castle had been emissaries from neighboring territories, dispatched to advise him to vacate his stronghold, but Uneri saw no issue: he was protecting what he needed to protect.

But it had been so long.

So long—since anyone had sought the Mutant Blade. But neither ninja nor agent of the bakufu—would make it more than three steps into his space.

Confined to his den, with his back to the wall, Uneri was able to execute

32 偏執 HENSHŪ nuance of 偏執病 HENSHŪBYŌ paranoid disorder

33 妄執 MŌSHŪ possessed by an idea

his iainuki to its maximum offensive and defensive potential—holed up in his fort, indeed. No matter the size of the intruding party, no more than two people could step through the doorway at a time—

Felling ten thousand.

Perhaps here, Uneri mused, in this particular domain, it was a possibility.

However.

The trouble was—that lurch[34] had noticed something notable about his domain. When he used his spinning kick to hook the unassuming Schemer through the doorway—had he realized?

I thought I saw him looking at the new tatami—or was it a coincidence?

Nevertheless, given the way he paused their dealings, and left the floor—and perhaps even the castle—that inkling had no doubt by now become a certainty. Lurch had seemed carefree—but could not possibly have been so dumb[35] as to find nothing suspicious about Uneri declining to chase them. *Unable to.* And even if it had been a coincidence, and the lurch had noticed nothing, the white-haired woman would have when Uneri had not followed them. While he had managed to cut down the ninja, Shirasagi Maniwa, in one fell swoop—

Say they did notice—if that were all, I needn't worry.

It would be a problem, but only a trivial one.

Far more serious, however, was what the lurch did next—dodge the Zerosen. Even if he had dodged first and noticed the tatami after—a dodge was a dodge.

What was it he said?

Right, Kyotoryu.

Master of the Kyotoryu, Shichika Yasuri (he had corrected[36] his slip of the tongue).

Uneri knew of Kazune Yasuri—and Mutsue Yasuri.

One battled in the Age of Warring States, and the other was the Hero of the Rebellion. While Uneri did not know of the particulars, as rumor had it, the Kyotoryu was a style of swordplay that forsook the sword. When first he heard of it, he wondered if it was not an art of the fist rather than the sword, but evidently[37] it was something else entirely. Having never heard from someone who had seen the Kyotoryu firsthand, its mysteries remained a mystery to him—

Until the man himself showed up.

Seventh Master, he said.

His given name seemed to contain the character for "seven," which suggested that he was indeed Mutsue's son. A big guy, but practically a kid...

34 のっぽ NOPPO tall (but not necessarily imposing)
35 ぼんくら BONKURA dimwitted
36 言い直した IINAOSHITA restated
37 目に明らか ME NI AKIRAKA clear to the eye

Swordless, alright.

That move with his foot, when he guarded Togame from the Zerosen—if that was any indication of the Kyotoryu—

From what I can recall, it was not so far from iainuki...in which case, was that...a form of kenpo modeled after swordplay?

Under normal circumstances, a swordsman would have no reason to give up his sword—but if he did give up his sword, he would surely have a reason. And the school centering around that reason was the Kyotoryu.

So much for that.

No use dwelling on it.

What kind of swordplay the Kyotoryu entailed was absolutely immaterial—Uneri saw no need to brood over the schools and skills of his adversaries.

Because.

Enter his space, and they were dead—

That summed up the Zerosen. What could be simpler.

"—Hm."

From the shaft of light—Uneri perceived that the fusuma had opened.

He had been reflecting, he believed, on his circumstances—but when he came to his senses, he realized that he must have fallen asleep. Now, to ensure that he would wake up whenever he had "guests," Uneri had sabotaged the fusuma, to make it stick (this being yet another of his domain's chief quirks[38]). He was such a restless sleeper, woken up by almost anything, it would be fair to call his sensitivity a condition, and a grave one at that.

He slowly opened his eyes, which had shut unbeknownst to him.

Beyond the doorway was Shichika Yasuri.

"...Hey."

Since Togame was nowhere to be seen, for a second Uneri assumed that the woman (who seemed unfit for battle anyway) had stayed outside the castle, but that was not the case. Hidden by Shichika's enormous body, her petite figure[39] was merely out of view—but right behind him. Uneri could see her gaudy kimono through the gap between Shichika's feet.

He's hiding her—no.

Protecting her?

Could his request to start anew have been motivated by a hunch that she'd been in danger? True, Uneri had aimed to kill her with his Zerosen—but if that was a concern, why wasn't she left outside as Uneri had presumed?

Was he choosing to have his back against the wall[40]—or rather, a woman? Was he cornering himself, steeled by a determination never to withdraw or retreat? In any case, Uneri saw no good reason for it—why go so far? Instead one might simply—

[38] 特徴 TOKUCHŌ characterizing feature
[39] 矮躯 WAIKU small body
[40] 背水の陣 HAISUI NO JIN "water-to-the-back formation" that disallows desertions

No.

Rooted with the Razor on his hip, Uneri was in no position to judge. To keep something safe, you kept it by your side—if that was what Shichika was thinking, then Uneri could understand.

But understand was all.

"Sorry that took so long," Shichika said.

His expression was all too cheerful, too lax for someone about to engage in combat. Thus far in life, Uneri had met all kinds—and anyone who showed up for a fight wearing a face like this was either reckless or fearless, or terrifyingly good.

Possibly all of the above.

"Ah... And?" answered Uneri.

He felt a little sleepy.

No matter, the Zerosen will dull none from a little drowsiness—nor will the Razor.

"Young man, have you come up with a strategy to best my Zerosen?"

"More or less," Shichika met Uneri's provocation with a casual reply. "I'm nine-tenths sure it's gonna work, but it's my first time using the move against an actual practitioner of iainuki—I haven't had a chance to practice.[41] That would be my one concern."

"Are you telling me the Kyotoryu has specific measures against iainuki?"

"It has recommended ways of battling iainuki, nothing like an overarching strategy—but up against someone as skilled as you, I think I'll succeed."

Shichika's carefree tone made him sound almost too dauntless.

"With this move, the faster your sword goes—the more surefire my hit will be."

"..."

The faster it goes.

Letting these words sink in, Uneri caught wind of a change in Shichika's appearance. Like the first time he showed up, he was bare to the waist—but now he had shed his arm and leg guards and stepped out of his sandals. With sand drifting in from every opening, the castle was in such a state that keeping your shoes[42] required no apology—(even Uneri slipped on sandals when he left his domain)—and yet.

He's drawn his sword.

If the Kyotoryu used no blade that was not the foot and the hand, it made perfect sense for arm and leg guards to play the role of sheaths. In which case, Shichika was pointing his bared sword at Ginkaku Uneri—or so it appeared.

"By the way, Mister Uneri, I have a request," Shichika said. "Just once, could you pull out the Razor—Zanto the Razor, and show me the blade?

[41] ぶっつけ本番 BUTTSUKE HONBAN "opening night with no rehearsal"
[42] 土足 DOSOKU "dirty feet"

When you do iainuki, or the Zerosen or whatever, it's way too fast for me to see. I know it's odd for the Kyotoryu master to be saying this, since I don't use swords myself, but I'd be lying if I told you my interest isn't piqued by the idea of a katana that cuts through anything."

"...Hmph."

If he were to unsheathe the sword and bare its steel, it would take a split second to return the Razor to its scabbard and unleash the Zerosen—was this some cheap ploy to create a chance to strike? It was too half-baked[43] even to be termed a measure... Still, Shichika's delivery all but vouched that it was no strategy or the like, but his sincere wish to see the blade... After all, the young man had removed his arm and leg guards and bared his own weapon, as if to say, *I'll show you mine, you show me yours.*

Either way.

Sincere or not, the answer was the same.

"Not happening."

"Whaaat."

"In our iainuki, concealing the blade from the opponent is essential. Sorry...okay, I'm not, really...but if you want to see it so bad, why not just defeat my Zerosen and knock me down and take the sword as yours? Then you can look it over all you want."

"Sword hog."[44] The request was made to be denied, but Shichika's puffed cheeks seemed to indicate that he was genuinely upset—however. "Fine," he said. "I'll try it your way."

Thus ended the preliminaries.

Shichika—assumed a stance.

"Kyotoryu Form Seven—Kakitsubata!"[45]

He straddled his feet, parallel, but one ahead of the other, sinking into his knees and bending at the hips, to make his upper body lean slightly forward—his hands pointed like spears, his elbows at right angles, parallel again and offset, like his feet. His weight on the front leg, as if to tumble forward, and facing straight ahead—eyes trained upon the seated figure of Ginkaku Uneri.

Poised like a runner, ready to dash.

Well now.

For all his playful nonchalance, Kyotoryu seemed mighty orthodox in his approach to battle. Was he of a mind to sprint from that room into this—to settle the score once and for all?

He said the faster your sword, the more surefire the hit...but those words seemed either a foolhardy diversion or a bluff—he was aiming, simply, to land the blade of his hand or foot before Uneri had a chance to draw—

43 不完全 FUKANZEN incomplete

44 けちだな KECHI DANA "what a miser"

45 杜若 KAKITSUBATA "The Iris"

But that would never breach this domain.

Resolved to fighting face-to-face, he looked poised to barrel straight into the thick of it, but such a stunt only meant he thought too lightly of the Zerosen, where the sword leaves and meets the scabbard in an instant.

Not that I was looking forward to this—but how disappointing.

"Kyotoryu—a foe that gives no satisfaction."

"Wow...it's an honor to be recognized by someone as strong as—wait, 'no satisfaction'? Was that a putdown?"

Playing the fool so late in the game, Shichika got the silent treatment from Uneri.

Either way.

The second Shichika passed through the doorway, the fight would be over. In a space this cramped, none could evade the sweeping path of iainuki—and if he blocked it, more fodder[46] for the Razor.

Behold, Ginkaku Uneri's—Danger Zone![47]

"Alright. In that case. On your mark..."

Shichika—sank deeper into his knees—

"Get set... GO!"

And mounted a frontal assault.

Springing off his rear foot, throwing his momentum ahead—clearing the threshold in one bound.

Onto his second step—and third...

No third step!

"Zerosen!"

Uneri's right hand clasped the handle of the Razor. The moment he did, the move was already over, and the sound of his tsuba reaching the sheath—*shing!*—rang through the air of the cramped room—

Yet.

"—...?!"

There was a reason Uneri failed to notice right away. Zanto the Razor was of such astounding sharpness that whatever it cut—be it animal, vegetable, mineral, or scoundrel[48]—the blade met almost no resistance. In fact, it would be no exaggeration to say it met with no resistance whatsoever. Every substance—sliced like tofu. The blade could even slice the air—and as such, it was all the same. Moreover, the Razor belonged to Ginkaku Uneri, and he had unleashed the Zerosen, an iainuki move unique to his family—thus there was sufficient reason for *his failure to cut Shichika Yasuri asunder* to take an extra instant to reach his brain.

That mere instant was fatal.

[46] 餌食 EJIKI prey

[47] 絶対領域 ZETTAI RYŌIKI "absolute realm" sliver of thigh visible on a girl wearing a skirt and high socks vs. 絶対零度 ZETTAI REIDO "absolute zero," the coldest temperature

[48] 森羅万象有象無象 SHINRA BANSHŌ UZŌ MUZŌ all manner of creation

"Kyotoryu—Bara!"[49]

■ ■

"Did we do it?!" Togame cried out from behind.

Done it, Shichika had—but what he had done was hardly unusual, as pedestrian as it got in the world of swordplay. The only difference was that the move was executed with incomparable dexterity, so high it was off the charts.

He had feinted[50]—faked him out.

Kyotoryu Form Seven—the Kakitsubata.

In contrast to Form One, the Suzuran, and Form Two, the Suisen—the static and defensive stances he had employed against Komori Maniwa the month before, back on Haphazard Island—Form Seven, the Kakitsubata, was a dynamic move, deployed offensively.

Even somebody oblivious to the martial arts would comprehend this at first glance—which is why Uneri thought that Shichika was charging full speed at him to beat out the Zerosen even if it meant being mowed down.

But that was not the case.

Despite being an attack move—the Kakitsubata was no simple battle charge.

Shichika had not delved into details with Togame during their strategy meeting because it would have gotten too complicated, but just as his school taught him to run through an overhead slash, Kyotoryu had a response to horizontal swipes: *Attack either before the swing, or after.* If a lateral strike could not be blocked or evaded, there was no other choice. It was a basic teaching in any case, as basic as it could get—

Uneri had expected him to attack before the swing.

But Shichika had opted for after—as obvious a strategy as this may seem up against the Zerosen, a move so fast that it could not be seen, Shichika did more than opt for it. He made Uneri *think the opposite*—that he would attempt to strike first.

Feinting, with the Kakitsubata.

When Shichika crossed through the doorway, intruding upon Uneri's domain, between his first step and his second step—and his zeroth step when he was immobile, to be precise—he altered his *movement speed*.

From his zeroth step into his first—in other words, as his rear foot sprung from the tatami, he was soaring, as far as Uneri was concerned. But from the first step into the second, as the front foot sprang to action—Shichika threw the brakes.

[49] 薔薇 BARA "The Rose"
[50] 陽動 YŌDŌ diversionary measure

The difference between his opening speed and closing speed was unbelievable. Seeing him accelerate, you never expected the coming drop—he slowed down twice as fast in that sense. The effect was marvelous—Uneri, skilled as he was, misjudged the timing of his iainuki.

His opponent hadn't taken a second step—much less a third.

He motioned for it—but didn't follow through.

Or he did follow through—but only afterwards.

All of it a single move.

Uneri was sure he had seen Shichika pass through the doorway and all the way in—a misjudgment.

Iainuki has a shortcoming, in that once the blade is drawn, it cannot be stalled midway—unlike the kaleidoscopic[51] footwork displayed by Shichika in his Kakitsubata, its speed cannot be adjusted freely, and can only mount ad infinitum.

The Danger Zone had also worked against Uneri—in being so determined that mere passage through the doorway guaranteed a kill, he effectively claimed to kill by reflex.

A wall.

What was absent, then, could be envisioned—to the extent that Uneri might as well have foolishly announced to the world when he would strike. He could not but draw against a charging foe, regardless of his velocity—

And the clincher:[52] the Zerosen was simply too fast.

The Razor returned to its sheath with a *shing!*—and a frame later, Shichika's front kick, the Bara, exploded toward Uneri's left shoulder.

Uneri shot backward—slamming his back against the wall behind him. He groaned as if the air were purging from his body.

"...nkk!"

And yet.

When Togame asked her question—"Did we do it?"—Shichika could not respond with a forthright, *We did it!* Far from it. He clicked his tongue in disgust and leapt back—through the door into the other room, where she was standing—

And suddenly resumed Form Seven.

"Shi-Shichika?"

"Crap. I barely even hit him... How could that bastard *spring back* and dodge me like that..."

Shichika was not complimenting Uneri for nimbly springing from his preferred position, so much as blaming himself for flinching, *at the last second, and turning the Bara's full-bore charge into a hit and run.*[53]

The strategy, at least, had been successful—as hoped, the Zerosen had

[51] 変幻自在 HENGEN JIZAI protean, changing and seeming at will

[52] 極めつき KIWAMETSUKI ultimate

[53] 引き技 HIKIWAZA in kendo, a quick strike before springing away

only grazed the skin of Shichika's chest and whiffed. Nevertheless, its force was intimidating enough[54] to usher a minute change of heart.

Simply put:

"I chickened out."

The faster the sword goes, the more surefire the move—too true. If the Zerosen had launched a split second later, Shichika would likely be in two clean pieces—and in the corner of his mind, he had pictured this. The picture had the necessary mass, all the more due to its position in the corner, to throw his heart off-balance.

Thus his own reflexes came into play, and kept him from catching his speed again after he slowed down—it was this failure on his part that permitted Uneri to dodge the Bara.

Shichika's lack of combat experience—was to blame.

Togame probably should have made him practice against actual swords rather than wooden replicas on their journey, even if a training session with iainuki was asking for too much. Shichika did not know real swords, outside of his battle with Komori, which had not lasted long.

It wasn't the swords the young man feared, but their moves.[55]

A fear of swordplay that used swords.

To Shichika, who had been raised, by order of the Kyotoryu, apart from blades of almost every kind, this fear would prove, without a doubt, to be an issue of extreme urgency.

"Shichika! You—"

"Don't move, Togame. Don't step out from behind my back."

They could not attend to the issue now—nor was it the one to be tackled here. What mattered was Ginkaku Uneri, who had yet to receive a decisive blow.

Just like that—he was getting up.

Yes.

At long last—Uneri stood from his seated position.

"A nice surprise," he muttered as if to himself. "I thought it was a fluke, the first time—but it can't be, after the second... I'm wide awake now, Kyotoryu. I haven't felt so alive since they spanked me the day I was born."

"...My pleasure."

Good morning, Shichika greeted.

Good morning, Uneri returned.

"And goodnight[56]—I suppose."

He stood with a pronounced sag in his left shoulder. It seemed that the Bara—hadn't been ineffectual, hadn't been dodged entirely. But with Uneri's mastery of iainuki, he needed only his right hand to draw a katana; an injury

54 あまりの剣圧 AMARI NO KEN'ATSU so great a "sword pressure"
55 剣技 KENGI "sword performance"
56 おやすみなさい OYASUMI NASAI "do rest"

to his left shoulder was not a serious concern. In fact, the adrenaline[57] put Shichika at a disadvantage.

Now Uneri was for real.

"My iainuki is all about waiting—no fancy footwork for me. But I can tell what kind of state[58] you've achieved from what you just did."

"You think? Nah. That was the Kyotoryu at its most basic. True, it's the seventh of the stances."

"Is that so. I'm impressed."

"Don't flatter me. I can't handle praise."

"Nonsense. Now that you've knocked me off my high horse, how else do I nurse my wounded pride? Take it like a man—but that footwork. Your hakama must've blocked my view."

"I bet."

Easy to move in. Easy to fight in.

This is what that meant.

When Shichika sped from his stance and slowed back down, the movement of his feet and muscles was obfuscated by the garment Togame bought for him—hence, easy to fight in. Uneri might have guessed what Shichika was up to, were his legs exposed. In this sense, the hakama was Shichika's armor.

"Even so—don't expect it to work twice."

Having complimented his foe, Uneri reached for the katana on his hip.

Shichika instantly went tense, but this far from the doorway, fully beyond Uneri's domain, it was perfectly safe, wasn't it—

Shing shing shing shing shing!

In rapid fire[59]—Uneri's tsuba chimed.

Ringing like a round of voices in his room.

"Zerosen Hentai[60]—Flight of Five."

In rapid fire—Uneri had unleashed *five Zerosen*.

Of course, Shichika could not see the blade's path.

Not even one out of the five arcs. The tsuba clanged away, but as far as he could tell, Uneri's hand never left the handle of the katana—

From quickdraw to scabbard, five times over, in a row!

"This way, you can speed up and slow down all you want—to no effect. The Razor will slash through the margin of error."

"Urk..."

He was right.

Against a swipe, attack after the swipe—but the teaching did not account for this rapid fire. Two or three, perhaps, but five...and that may not even be

57 手負い TEOI being wounded (but not dead)
58 境地 KYŌCHI figurative land/place
59 連撃 RENGEKI a series of attacks
60 編隊 HENTAI formation (of fighter planes)

the limit—

In the Uneri school of iainuki, not showing the blade to the opponent was essential—still, when you think about it, if the hype is true about iainuki, and the first swing is always fatal, drawing is one thing, but there ought to be no need to rush the sword into its scabbard—even in the way of remaining alert[61] just in case, it was excessive. Shichika must have only hit and run with his Bara because he intuited this.

Indeed.

The quicksheath after the quickdraw allowed for a series of strikes.

"That was your secret move[62]..."

"Secret move? This? No..."

Uneri grinned.

But when he did.

Shing!—the tsuba clanged again, and the shoulder of Uneri's black kimono, where Shichika had grazed him with the Bara—burst open, spilling vast quantities of blood.

"Whoa!"

"Bloodlust[63]—a Zanto the Razor exclusive!"

Uneri winced with pain—but the grin had yet to leave his face, and he only looked emboldened. His blood began to drench his kimono and his feet—he must have severed a main artery.

"Yikes...did you just go and cut yourself? What for?"

With the horizontal swing of iainuki, it should have been impossible to cut himself—he must have done it after the quickdraw, while the blade was on its way back—so fast this, too, had been impossible to see. Commendable, and yet...

Why would he ever cut himself?!

"Don't get it, huh?" Uneri's voice was tortured. "You see, Kyotoryu, this was the secret behind Kinkaku Uneri felling ten thousand. Look."

Plip. Plip.

From the tsuba of the Razor, blood dripped into the puddle forming at Ginkaku Uneri's feet and created little ripples.

From around the tsuba—no, it was the mouth[64] of the scabbard.

Blood was leaking—*flooding*, from inside it.

Clearly the blood was Uneri's. After cutting himself, he had slipped the blade (too fast for Shichika to see) into its sheath, without shaking off the blood that clung there.

Plip. Plip.

Drops of blood—drip after drip.

[61] 残心の姿勢 ZANSHIN NO SHISEI keeping up one's guard in defense
[62] 隠しだま KAKUSHI DAMA hidden ball (trick)
[63] 斬刀狩り ZANTŌ GARI play on 残党狩り ZANTŌ GARI mopping-up operation
[64] 鯉口 KOIGUCHI "mouth of the carp" thin hole, like puckered fish lips

"L-Look at what... I still don't get it."

"Take ice, for an example. Know how it's more slippery when it begins to melt than when it's frozen solid?" asked Uneri. "Same principle. Moistening the inside of the scabbard, filling the whole thing up with blood until the cavity is sopping wet—makes the quickdraw even quicker. When you drastically reduce the friction factor between blade and sheath—the Zerosen meets the speed of light. That is the Bloodlust, a Zanto the Razor exclusive. Usually," Uneri added haughtily, "I use the blood of an opponent."

His bleeding showed no sign of stopping—and while his face was losing color, he didn't seem to care.

"*The more it cuts—the faster it gets.*"

The Zerosen's peak speed.

But it knew no limit, according to that logic. Supposing the tale of Kinkaku Uneri and the ten thousand was true—what kind of instantaneous peak velocity had the Razor clocked when it vanquished its ten-thousandth foe?

"...!"

The faster the sword, the more surefire the hit—despite having been forewarned, and suffering precisely such an attack, Uneri doggedly[65] persisted, going so far as to slice his own flesh to quicken the Zerosen.

Faster, faster, faster, faster, he seemed to coax.

As if speed alone were something to be proud of.

As if speed were his reason for being.

As if what he protected—was worth it.

Shichika had an opportunity to *stop fighting fair and square*—and the chance had not escaped him. Filling a scabbard with blood demanded quite the wound—and the gash on Uneri's shoulder was not only ugly...if left unattended, it was liable to take his life. In any case, as long as he didn't step through the doorway, stayed outside Uneri's domain...he could assume Form One, Form Two, whatever he liked—they would be at a standstill. If he only waited it out, eventually the blood inside the scabbard would begin to clot,[66] working contrary to purpose and increasing the friction. Ill-disposed to thought as Shichika may be, he didn't need to think to understand this much. The Bloodlust was a move meant for large numbers—best used on the battlefield, where an endless supply of blood can be procured, which was not the case in a duel. Against Ginkaku Uneri as he stood now, merely waiting would not only afford Shichika the upper hand, it could hand him victory—

And yet.

Taking an idle stance and waiting it out because he no longer needed to fight fair and square—was not how Shichika Yasuri had been taught.

As the Kyotoryu.

A katana incarnate.

65 厭いもせず ITOI MO SEZU tirelessly

66 凝固 GYŌKO congeal

Facing Ginkaku Uneri, who truly had cornered himself, Shichika maintained the Kakitsubata—poised for attack.

"Nice moves," Shichika said.

"Huh?"

"Seeing you—I'm ashamed I was hiding my best one." Shichika sounded genuinely embarrassed. "Enough holding back—I'll show you what the Kyotoryu is made of."

"What? You mean you had an ace up your sleeve, too?"

"I wouldn't put it—that way. But you could say I've been holding back a tad."

"Hmph..."

Uneri opted not to call his bluff, or say this was a ploy or a distraction.

He didn't think so—and in the face of the Zerosen, slick with Bloodlust, it hardly mattered anyway. Ginkaku Uneri had that much confidence.

In Zanto the Razor.

And in his Zerosen.

"I see."

But then—Uneri spoke again.

Not to Shichika, but toward Togame, standing behind him.

"Out of curiosity, young lady, if I may... You offered to grant any wish if I handed over the sword."

"...? Ah, yes," Togame replied from behind Shichika.

Her face was hidden, but her voice conveyed her thorough bafflement. Why was Uneri bringing it up this late in the game?

"The bakufu will certainly make it worth your while—effective[67] immediately, that is, if you so please."

"Then," said Uneri—his voice anything but sleepy. "If I hand over the Razor, could you restore Inaba to the way it used to be?"

"..."

They were talking through the buffer that was Shichika.

Diplomacy.

Just as Shichika could not see Togame's face behind him, Uneri could not see Togame, nor could Togame see Uneri, with Shichika between them as a wall—perhaps this was why Uneri opened up, and perhaps he meant it.

Perhaps it was also why Togame—could not bring herself to lie.

Lying now—was not who she was.

"Out of the question," she refused him outright. "In the eyes of the bakufu, Tottori is as good as lost. But that aside, there is no way, even in theory, to return a land that the dunes claimed[68] to its former state."

"Understood..." Uneri nodded, not the least bit morosely, but like a man freed of doubt. "So I wasn't making a big mistake when I tried to kill you—

[67] 有効 YŪKŌ valid

[68] 砂漠化 SABAKUKA desertification

what a relief."

"Hey, I have a question," Shichika butted in.

He couldn't help it.

"Why are you doing this?"

"...Beats me."

"Is this about the dignity you mentioned?"

"Who knows." Uneri shrugged it off.[69] "Just because I said that doesn't mean I meant it."

"..."

"I just wanted something to protect—that was all I ever wanted, but I had nothing else to protect."

"I see..."

Something to protect.

For Shichika, it meant Togame.

He had chosen to protect Togame.

Even if the Kyotoryu, and Shichika himself, were targets of her vendetta—he had decided to protect her.

She was his reason for fighting.

He fought in order to protect her.

"Alright—let's go."

"Sure. The Zerosen is ready to fly.[70] It's time for you to witness the speed of light. And if you really do have an ace up your sleeve—I'd love to see it."

"See? *Not if you're torn to smithereens.*"

The catchphrase they had picked that morning.

Such execution—that was perfect.

"On your mark, get set..."

Set for kaleidoscopic footwork.

Kyotoryu Form Seven—the Kakitsubata.

As if to tumble forward, at any moment.

"GO!"

Shichika took a step, igniting his reserves of energy.

Except this time—he did not spring off of the back foot.

He sprang off of his front foot, shooting backwards.

With a snap, he threw his forward-leaning weight into reverse—making for quite the feint, poised as he had been to sprint ahead.

Not motioning without following through—or following through, but only after a delay—this time Shichika stepped backwards.

His feint was not ineffective.

By reflex, Uneri drew the Razor.

Even though—Shichika had not set foot into his domain.

Shing!—rang the tsuba.

69 とぼける TOBOKERU act dumb

70 出撃 SHUTSUGEKI sortie

But not once.

"Zerosen Hentai—Flight of Ten."

Shing shing shing shing shing shing shing shing shing shing!

An onslaught of Zerosen, to catch him no matter how he stalled—and all the swings at speeds far outstripping[71] the same move executed seated. It was as if sword was meeting scabbard sooner with each successive strike and accelerating without reserve.

Not even the Bara of the Kyotoryu.

Could violate.

Or infiltrate.

His razor-thin *Danger Zone*—

"——nkk!"

And yet.

Shichika's next move flabbergasted Uneri. Who wouldn't read stepping back as a stall, a harbinger of springing into the fray? Yet Shichika drew what had been his hind foot in the same direction, behind, only even faster.

The kaleidoscopic footwork of Form Seven allowed him not only to boost or brake his momentum but to travel backward at will—but under the circumstances, why shoot back at full speed?

He had fallen back the length of one tatami mat.

He could charge all he liked, but the Zerosen was bound to catch him when he had to close such a distance. The feint and fake-out made no sense.

To begin with—

Behind him stood what he was trying to protect, Togame—had he not positioned her there so he could not back out when he faced Ginkaku Uneri? Steeled by a determination never to withdraw or retreat?

Wrong.

That wasn't why.

"...Huh?"

As stated elsewhere, she was not proficient in the martial arts. Or rather, prior to that issue, and not to mince words, her reflexes were impossibly dull.

Thus—when Shichika started back in her direction, *darting towards her*, the thought of dodging or evading him did not so much as cross her mind.

"Hmh?"

Not even when his sole was an inch away.

If this were a manga, set in the present day, now would be the time for a sound effect like "DGSHH!" Having leapt, Shichika Yasuri planted a backwards dropkick square in the face of Togame the Schemer, so perfectly that it was a work of art.

"Gadzooks!"

Her scream, so novel[72] in its day, filled the air.

[71] 凌駕 RYŌGA surpass, overtake

[72] 今風 IMAFŪ "now-style"

This was the last thing Uneri expected to see—but unlike the Kakitsubata footwork, Shichika had not jumped back and kicked Togame in the face as a feint. Surprising Uneri was not Shichika's intention.

He flexed the leg that hit Togame like a spring—and leapt once more.

Yes.

Togame was his *wall*—or in this case, springboard.[73]

Shichika crossed through the doorway—*but did so without entering Uneri's Danger Zone*. To be precise, he did not cross over the threshold—so much as *under the lintel of the doorframe*.[74] Feeling it graze his back, he launched into Uneri's den at a steep angle.

A cramped room, every inch within range of the Zerosen.

A cramped space, every inch within range of the Zerosen.

However—this was only if you conceived of the room *two-dimensionally*, rather than *three-dimensionally*.

Area is not the same as volume.

Small as the rooms may be—they had high ceilings.

Too high for Shichika, tall as he was, to reach even on his tiptoes—and thus, as long as he cleared the range of the Razor, he would be outside the Danger Zone.

...Shichika had asked Uneri to show him the blade as a precaution. He had wanted to know how long it was. Naturally, Uneri had not obliged, and Shichika had guessed its length by eyeballing[75] the scabbard. It seemed to him like it would be okay—and thankfully, it was.

"U-Urk..."

Uneri held the handle of the Razor—but could not move.

The tsuba did not make its sound.

He had not drawn—he could not draw.

Making a series of spins, Shichika slowed his flight off of Togame and *landed in the middle of the ceiling*, directly above Uneri.

"K-K-Kyotoryu!"

"What's the matter, in over your head?"

Uneri gripped the handle of the Razor, at a loss.

All he could do was stare and shudder.

The Danger Zone had been inverted.

Within this room—no place was safe.

Ginkaku Uneri would have done well to think more deeply about the Kyotoryu, if only in his dreams. A form of kenpo modeled after swordplay...was not a good place to stop.

If he had thought more, perhaps he would have understood.

73 三角飛び SANKAKU TOBI "triangle jump" a leap having three points of contact: start, middle, finish

74 鴨居 KAMOI the wood-framed channel overhead through which the fusuma slides

75 目測 MOKUSOKU "eye measure"

Why a swordsman might forsake the sword.

More than anything, it opened up a plethora of foot techniques[76]—having both hands free would seem to be the main advantage of letting go of a katana, but not so. The Kakitsubata, and the springboard, and the rebound up onto the ceiling shared something fundamental.

Namely.

Without a sword—the body is light.[77]

Uneri would have done well to brood over the fearsome benefits of a person as large as Shichika being light and possessing a mobility at odds with his size.

"Even if you get it now, it's too late—by the way, with a *footing* this good, *this move* will be three times as powerful—wait and see!"

Because this one actually doesn't tear you into smithereens, he made a minute correction.

Then he *bounded* from the ceiling toward the floor.

And—

Threw all of his weight into a trio of furiously spinning kicks, his ankle an adze[78]—! "Kyotoryu Fatal Orchid Seven: Rakka Rozeki!"[79]

Tottori's renowned Inaba Desert...

It was the instant that Gekoku Castle fell.

[76] 足技 ASHIWAZA moves using only the legs
[77] 身軽 MIGARU agile
[78] 斧刀 FUTŌ "axe katana"
[79] 落花狼藉 RAKKA RŌZEKI "Effrontery of the Falling Flower"

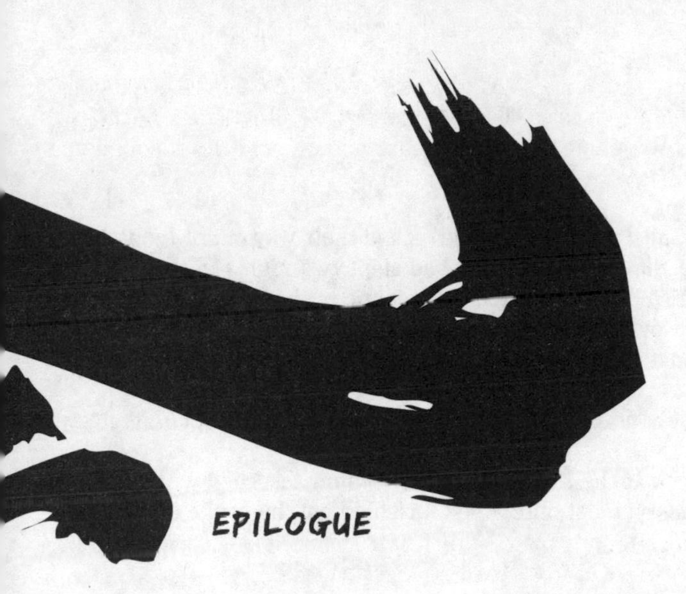

EPILOGUE

■ ■

The following evening.

Shichika Yasuri and Togame had backtracked their way out of Inaba Desert and returned to the inn where they had slept two nights earlier. Track, of course, being a turn of phrase: there were none in the desert. Heading on west, toward Hoki, would have been too trying for Togame, though perhaps not for Shichika, and it had been the plan all along to return and then bypass[1] the desert.

But Shichika knew nothing of their next destination except that it lay westward.

Which is why, back at the inn, as Togame became absorbed with packing Zanto the Razor, theirs at last, into a box for shipment, he spoke up.

"Where to next?"

"..."

Togame did not answer.

Not just now. For over a day since Shichika had kicked her in the face and used her as a springboard, she had not said a single word to him. Understandable, but Togame the Schemer, several years his senior, was acting remarkably unadult.

"Hello~o."

"..."

"Hey, Togame."

"..."

"Togame, don't ignore me. You haven't spoken since, like, yesterday. Did you get hurt or something when I kicked you? Hope not. Maybe you cut the inside of your mouth, so it hurts when you—"

"Zip it!"

But she buckled before he even apologized.

Poor form.

"Don't ramble on like nothing happened when I'm mad! Open your eyes. Act like you're sorry! You disregard my feelings, only to ask me whether I'm hurt. Unreal. How was I to know you needed me behind you—as a springboard!"

"Oh, that's what you're mad about."

"I'm not mad!"

She was all over the place.[2]

[1] 迂回 UKAI circumvent

[2] 支離滅裂 SHIRI METSURETSU incoherent an ironic callback to the Last Fatal Orchid, with which it shares the first syllable and last character

Shichika explained that he hadn't had a choice. So he did feel bad about what happened—not that he'd been showing any signs of remorse.

"If the Kakitsubata to Bara relay worked on him, that would have been it—I swear that using you was only the backup plan. Without the angle and the arc I caught, I never would have cleared him and stuck[3] to the ceiling."

In other words—Uneri was not unaware of the hole in his Danger Zone. His domain had an opening once you saw that it had a height in addition to a length and width. But he couldn't have anticipated using an ally for a springboard—

"Then say so during our strategy meeting! Why that odd tease about strength coming from having something to protect?"

"Sorry, the line just popped into my head."

"Just popped in!"

"Stop snarling, okay? I did use you as a wall, but not as a shield. I figured if I filled you in from the beginning, you would jump back reflexively, no matter how...unathletic you are. It's not like I have eyes on my back. Unless you were exactly where I needed you, behind me, I couldn't pull off the Rakka Rozeki."

"And thanks to that, I missed seeing your Fatal Orchid. Again."

"Come on. I've shown you Rakka Rozeki. In the dojos."

"I want to see it for real. Anyway, whatever."

Shouting had evidently cheered her up.

However immature, she knew how to let things go.

In any case, they had secured the Razor. With their mission accomplished, perhaps she saw this as the wrong time to complain.

Process be damned, that was her ultimate goal.[4]

"Know what though, Shichika? Whether it's the Rakka Rozeki or the footwork for the Kakitsubata, your taijutsu[5] reminds me of a ninja."

"Huh? Really? I know so little about ninjas. Hard for me to say."

Then again, mused Shichika, *that ninja we met last month, Komori Maniwa, sure knew how to jump*—

"Leaping and jumping is the bailiwick of the ninja, not the swordsman—who, as a species, keep their feet planted on the ground. Perhaps Kazune Yasuri, founder of the Kyotoryu, wove elements of ninjutsu into his concept for the school."

"Maybe." Shichika nodded. "That means the Kyotoryu can hold its own against those Maniwacs who aren't swordsmen. Minus Shirasagi—how many of those bosses do we have left, ten?"

"Correct. Yet—now might not be the time to be saying this, but if I may, Shichika, it's about the Kakitsubata. That kaleidoscopic footwork, accelerating and decelerating to whatever speed you like, is fabulous—but there has

3 張り付く HARITSUKU cling
4 至上目的 SHIJŌ MOKUTEKI "supreme purpose"
5 体術 TAIJUTSU "physical technique" comprehensive term for martial arts

to be a catch."

"Catch?"[6]

"Hiding your footwork with your hakama worked great this time. But the opposite could hold true, too. Against a lesser foe than Uneri, that kind of fake-out would be meaningless. Like for me, standing behind you. I had no idea when you were supposed to be feinting, or accelerating, or decelerating. As far as I could tell, you were just charging right in—footwork like that would be lost on an inferior opponent. And another thing. That Form Seven—it's dazzling for advancing or falling back, but no good for strafing."

"Exactly,"[7] Shichika agreed.

That weakness was evident to him as its practitioner, but Togame could tell too, just by watching him from behind, which was a bit surprising.

Well.

She did say she was a military strategist.

"No good for it, or I can't at all. The stance for strafing would be Form Six—of course, it still won't be as dazzling as charging in and out. That's not the meat of Form Six... Keep your eyes peeled for it."

"I certainly will," Togame said. Then she gave the box containing Zanto the Razor a light pat, a proprietary claim of sorts. "Good, all packed up. Once we've mailed this to Owari, we'll be on our way. Where to next? Izumo.[8] Bypassing the desert, we'll go through Mimasaka, Bicchu, and Bingo."

"Izumo, huh. That's where the gods hang out."

"An apt detail, for there, at a shrine of noble origins, whose history goes back farther than the modern bakufu or the Kyotoryu, Sento the Legion awaits us—a thousand swords, held by a thousand maidens.

"Once secured, the Legion would pose an interesting challenge in terms of shipping," Togame noted. "When already the Leveler, and even the Razor, making it safely to the bakufu requires tricky thinking... Oh, by the by, Shichika."

"Hmm?"

"Did you never actually see the Razor? I don't think you were around to watch me clean the blood from the blade and the scabbard... Did you want to take a look? It's neatly packed up, though."

"Mm..."

Hoping to gauge its precise span, and the exact extent of the Danger Zone, Shichika had asked Uneri to show the blade—and it had been no lie that he was also simply curious.

A sword that could cut anything.

Who wouldn't want to see?

Yet—

[6] 弱点 JAKUTEN weakness
[7] 当たり ATARI "hit" spot-on
[8] 出雲 IZUMO "whence clouds emerge"

"Nah, I'm good," he said.

"Oh? That would save me the trouble of packing it again—but are you sure? There's no need to be shy about that much of an imposition."

"I'm good."

"I see."

"Yep."

Shichika had made himself scarce, and not by chance, as Togame had scrubbed clean the Mutant Blade. He was of a mind to move on without beholding the naked Razor.

When all was said and done, he had glimpsed none of the Zerosen—had brought down[9] not a one. That was all there was to it, then.

"..."

Ginkaku Uneri, pilot of the Zerosen—had perished.

It was partially the doing of Shichika's Rakka Rozeki, but the self-inflicted wound from the preceding Bloodlust had been deep. Uneri would not live to see the bleeding stop—and expired on the tatami, its two dimensions dyed one shade of red.

A fitting end for a warrior, perhaps it was not.

A fitting end for a swordsman—it was not.

Yet it may have suited the man.

"What's going to happen to Inaba—and Gekoku Castle?"

"Nothing. That land has left the jurisdiction[10] of the bakufu, and can only wither and die. But long after you and I have departed from this world, even a thousand years hence, the ruins of Gekoku may yet remain—a castle, though, it will never be."

"So without people—there's no castle?"

"Nor town, nor country."

"Uh huh."

"No swordsman or sword can conquer nature—may be the point."

"That's the point, in the end."

"As far as I can see."

"Man."

Strength comes from having something to protect.

Shichika had said it just to convince[11] Togame—but not so for Uneri. There were those who lived by having something to protect—this battle had made that clear to Shichika.

While coveting nothing, Ginkaku Uneri had wanted to protect something. Shichika, raised on Haphazard Island without possessions to call his own, did not need or covet anything to protect, but he wondered—just maybe, would doing so for this woman make him stronger?

[9] 撃墜 GEKITSUI shoot down (an airplane)
[10] 管轄 KANKATSU administrative control
[11] 言いくるめる IIKURUMERU nuance of bamboozling

"Still, Togame."

"What now?"

"That last thing Uneri said[12] showed some serious style," Shichika shared what had been on his mind since then. "Not just style, it had a lot of personality... Would you say that was a catchphrase?"

Ahh... Suffering a direct hit to the skull from Fatal Orchid Seven, Uneri had fallen on his back, never to rise again, and with a hollow stare, though not without a kind of peace, he had intoned: *Finally...I'll catch up on my sleep.*

"Not exactly," answered Togame, her face not so forgiving, and borderline acerbic. "That was a farewell—his last words, or a parting message, if you will. Perhaps even a testament. It's the sort of thing you only get to say once in a lifetime, when you're on your way out."

"Okay."

"Don't let it bug you. Certainly, in terms of demonstrating personality, last words have a lot more impact than a catchphrase, since you only have a chance to say them once in your entire life. But Shichika, as long as I'm around, that chance will not be yours to take."

And she meant it.

"Don't waste a moment mulling over how to say goodbye."

■ ■

Thus, Shichika Yasuri finished out the month without seeing the blade of Zanto the Razor, one of the Twelve Possessed of Kiki Shikizaki. He would not first see that edge[13]—nor learn the figure of its steel, so sharp that it could cut through any substance in a single swing—until the next time it was pointed at him, in the last moon of the year.

Zanto the Razor: Check
End of Book Two
To Be Continued

[12] 台詞 SERIFU line (in a drama)
[13] 刃 YAIBA blade

CHARACTER INDEX 2

GINKAKU UNERI

AGE	Thirty-two
OCCUPATION	Swordsman
AFFILIATION	None
STATUS	Ronin
POSSESSED	Zanto the Razor
HEIGHT	5' 5"
WEIGHT	124 lbs.
HOBBY	Sleeping

LIST OF SPECIAL MOVES

DANGER ZONE	⇦ ⬃ ⇩ ⬂ ⇨ SLASH + THRUST
ZEROSEN	⇦ ⬁ ⇧ ⬀ ⇨ SLASH
ZEROSEN: FLIGHT OF FIVE	⇦ ⬁ ⇧ ⬀ ⇨ SLASH SLASH
ZEROSEN: FLIGHT OF TEN	⇦ ⬁ ⇧ ⬀ ⇨ SLASH SLASH SLASH
BLOODLUST	⇦ ⇨ ⇦ ⇨ SLASH + THRUST + KICK

AFTER(S)WORD

On the subject of whether people who have something to protect are stronger than those who don't, time and place and circumstance are all factors, but if you zoom all the way out and gain a little headroom, I think it's common for the thing you're protecting to be protecting you, without you noticing, which makes me think it might be better to have something to protect. If you don't have something to protect, I suppose that makes you free to do as you please, but freedom is no easy thing to wrangle. While it's true that having something to protect may put you on the defense, that doesn't mean not having something to protect will force you onto the offense, and thus treating the two situations as opposites is, in a certain sense, misunderstanding the issue. When you think about it, the "thing" in "something to protect" doesn't always refer to a physical thing, or a living presence, like friends and family, or a lover, but oftentimes something more like dignity, or honor, or pride. If we're including these metaphysical things under the rubric of "something to protect," I think we can say there isn't a person in the world who doesn't have something like that. It might be going a little too far afield, but apparently, whether it's a world war or a contest between individuals, when one side is on the offense, fighting to get something (to be blunt, trying to steal), and another side is on the defense, fighting to protect something (to be blunt again, trying to prevent something from being stolen), the defender wins in most cases. There's a major gap in motivation, since people worry more about losing things than they do about acquiring them. Which is perfectly natural, but if you think about it this way, the concept of protecting something is not as pretty as its language suggests.

We all live life protecting something, and even those with nothing have those empty-handed selves to protect—which brings us to *Sword Tale—Book Two*, featuring no such themes. Set in an imaginary version of Tottori, Inaba Desert is modeled after the real-life Tottori Sand Dunes. I love that place and visit frequently. Without a doubt the best part is being totally surrounded by sand. It makes me want to see an actual desert sometime before I die. Shichika Yasuri, Seventh Master of the Kyotoryu, and Togame the Schemer have barely started on their journey, but I plan to send them plenty of other places that I love, or haven't been able to visit. take's illustrations bringing those scenes into the visual realm is something I look forward to throughout the writing process. With that, I draw *Sword Tale—Book Two: Zanto the Razor* to a close. The title of Book Three is...um, what was it again? Oh yeah, Sento the Legion.

As always, I remain deeply thankful to all of you for supporting this series.

NISIOISIN

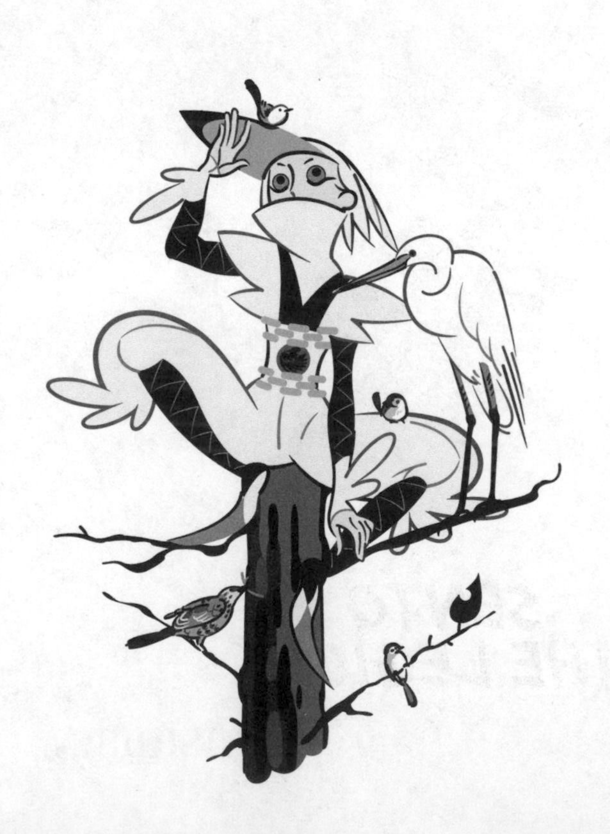

BOOK THREE

SENTO
THE LEGION

The original Book Three Table of contents spread

PROLOGUE

■ ■

"This history is all wrong."

Who said that?

Not sure.

Who was it?

When was it?

Can't find the memory.

No—there was no memory to begin with.

"It's nothing like what actually happened—it's all wrong. No part of it holds up against the facts. What a bunch of malarkey. Wrong, wrong, wrong."

It was a calm voice.

Calm[1]—but calamitous.[2]

Cool, but with the pensiveness of cool blue flame.

On and on.[3]

"Wrong—this version of history is unthinkable. Completely different from how things were meant to be—it's not right. It's just not right."

Not right.

Different.

Wrong.

However repetitive, the voice was unerring.

Unhesitating.

"■■■."

It called to me—

What did it call me?

Not sure.

The name—I threw away.

An old name, no longer mine.

A part of the discarded past that I could live without.

"Trouble is, wrong as it may be, this history has its own balance—■■■. It's balanced, to *perfection*. Fully formed, at equilibrium, like the surface of a quiet pond—so quiet you almost think that you can walk across it."

Only it's not frozen over, the voice added morosely. One step, and down you go.

Who are you?

Who the hell—are *you*?

I don't know *you*.

[1] 淡々 TANTAN evokes the placidness of fresh or shallow water

[2] 炎々 EN'EN burning bright; identical to above but for the three marks, which denote water

[3] 延々 EN'EN ad nauseum

"■■■, what do you think history is?"

You, a stranger, asking *me*.

I won't answer.

I have no interest in answering.

Not for lack of understanding—although I don't understand.

But, in a way, I understood.

This was—a memory.

Not a memory I could remember, or was mine to have—a reminiscence, nothing more. Why even answer—I was only rcmembering.

In which case—

It was something that *I* threw away.

Just like the soundless name.

My memory—painted over black.

"Good answer," the voice said.

How did—the *me* of memory answer?

That too, a memory.

A memory thrown away.

Good answer?

"Alright, here's what I think, ■■■—we point to history as proof that we lived. To prove we lived with gusto. You see—"

The voice was kind.

But I knew it had another side.

That much, *I* knew.

That *you*—were very angry.

"Things should take the shape they're meant to take."

The voice spoke forcefully.

Resolutely.

"■■■," *you* said, "I think it's time that pond experienced some waves."

Never know unless you try—*you* said.

Try?

You would stake *your* life on such a long shot,[4] on such a slim,[5] no, far[6] chance?

Right.

You must have known.

You had to know.

There would be no contest,[7] no hope.[8]

You knew it best—and yet.

"I think I'll toss a stone into that nice, quiet pond—to see what kind of

[4] いちかばちか ICHIKA BACHIKA "one or eight" originally a gambling term

[5] 十中八九 JUCCHŪ HAKKU (odds of) "eight or nine out of ten"

[6] 万が一 MAN GA ICHI "one in ten thousand"

[7] 敵う KANAU to rival

[8] 叶う KANAU to be granted

ripples I can make, and to prove that no matter how still its surface, it's only water."

And thanks to that.

How many do you think will die?

Not only foes.

Your allies—how many?

Your people—how many?

That, too—*you* knew.

But said *you* didn't.

"What will happen—is beyond me. Hard to say. Maybe nothing will happen, and nothing will change, and the struggle will be in vain. After all, I'm part of this history, so righting wrongs won't be easy. At the very least, though, I can expose them as wrongs."

Unrightable wrongs.

Can be exposed as wrongs.

Really?

"■■■."

Again—*you* call *my* name.

Then you repeat, as if to convince yourself—as if you, too, would be swallowed by some tidal wave otherwise.

"This history is all wrong."

Still, after all.

I have forgotten it.

■ ■

—Well! Enough of these teasing ruminations!

The next stop on this Sword Hunt is Izumo.

You can't have Izumo without miko,[9] and you can't have miko without Izumo!

Izumo belongs to them—exclusively, let's hope!

As in "Hack and slash![10] Their decoupage[11] hobby," thank you?

Must we begin with such vocabulary?

No blood, no tears—just laughs!

Behold this bizarre blunder of a history!

Tale of the Sword: Book Three ♪

[9] 巫女 MIKO shrine maiden(s)

[10] 切った張ったの大騒ぎ KITTA HATTA NO ŌSAWAGI "big commotion of knifing and plastering"

[11] 張り絵 HARIE "glued picture" vs. the more common spelling 貼り絵 HARIE collage

CHAPTER ONE

TRIAD SHRINE

■ ■

In present-day Japan, Izumo would fall within the eastern portion of Shimane.

From time immemorial, the gods have gathered there—so legend has it. This is the reason, so well-known it hardly deserves mention, why Kannazuki,[1] the tenth month of the lunar calendar, is known strictly within Izumo as Kamiarizuki.[2] If you were to peruse the *Record of Ancient Matters* or *The Chronicles of Japan*, you would find a slew of myths taking place in Izumo. For in this era—nay, in any era of any history, it has deserved its reputation as a sacred place. And smack dab in the middle of Izumo—stood Triad[3] Shrine, in all its grandeur.

Triad Shrine.

Overseen by one Meisai Tsuruga,[4] owner of Sento the Legion,[5] the next sword Togame the Schemer and Shichika Yasuri, Seventh Master of the Kyotoryu, were hoping to collect.

■ ■

"...Hey, Togame. I forgot to ask before—this Sento the Legion, the third of the Twelve Possessed among the thousand Mutant Blades created by Kiki Shikizaki—is it, like, actually legion?"

"Yes," Togame answered Shichika's meandering query with a forthright confirmation. "A thousand swords in one bunch. Hence the name."

"Okay, I know I might sound like a dumbass taking issue with the Shikizaki legend so far into this, but wouldn't that mean there are more of the Possessed than the nine hundred and eighty-eight swords he supposedly made for practice?"

If the Legion was a thousand swords, weren't there one thousand and eleven of the Possessed, instead of twelve? Shichika wanted to know—but Togame had another point to make.

1 神無月 KAN'NAZUKI "month when the gods are absent"
2 神有月 KAMIARIZUKI "month when the gods are present"
3 三途 SANZU "trinity" of hell's punishments: getting (1) scorched, (2) cannibalized, and (3) harried with swords and staves by hungry spirits
4 敦賀迷彩 TSURUGA MEISAI 敦賀 a major port town of old, in present-day Fukui 迷彩 camouflage
5 千刀 鎩 SENTŌ TSURUGI "The Thousand Katana: Brand"

"You do sound like a dumbass. A dumbstruck wiseass[6] to use the full[7] term."

"Um, I don't think it's short for anything."

Shichika had thought it a worthy observation, but her reaction was icy.

"A thousand swords in one—if that is its selling point, so it must be. The two swords we already collected had their own special characteristics, did they not? Shichika. Tell me you haven't forgotten."

"Well, the first one, Zetto the Leveler, was so tough it could never bend or break...*hardness*. Then there's Zanto the Razor, whose edge can cut through anything in the world in a single swing...*sharpness*."

"Correct," Togame nodded. "And the third, Sento the Legion, was forged to be overwhelmingly many...*numerousness*. Hence a thousand—but a thousand in one."

"That's some crazy bargain sale..."

And Shichika was the dumbass here?

But Togame went on unperturbed. "There's a saying—no two swords in this world are alike. There's some truth in that. Two swords can never be made in the same environment, under the same conditions, with the same factors at play—and even if the same swordsmith hammers them in the exact same way, the product will inevitably be different. Mere lookalikes. Siblings, in their own way, but by no means twins."

"Huh... Wait, then—"

"Yes. Kiki Shikizaki liked to experiment. You could say he was competitive, or that he loved to push the limits of the possible. Point being, all thousand swords making up the Legion—*are perfectly identical*."

In material. In weight.

And in their edge—in every way.

"So physically, the exact same sword."

"You may recall me telling you that Kiki Shikizaki did not design his swords to be expendable. The Legion would perhaps be the exception. If one bends or breaks, you still have nine hundred and ninety-nine left on hand. Expendable to the extreme."

"Hmm...they say a good katana takes some time to get used to. When it degrades, a swordsman is weaker until he grows familiar with a new blade," Shichika recited a bit of secondhand knowledge. "But I guess if the next sword is perfectly identical, you're already familiar with it...and don't have to spend time figuring it out."

"Precisely...that's one way to put it. You could also say that of the thousand Mutant Blades, only the Legion is—an ordinary katana."

"Ordinary... Yikes. That's what ordinary means for Kiki Shikizaki?"

"His sheer inability to do ordinary things in ordinary ways was what made

[6] 薮から棒、 YABU KARA BŌ, "(poking) a stick out of a bush" or non-sequitur...

[7] 略して野暮 RYAKUSHITE YABO "abbreviated as" 野暮 YABO boorish (antonym of 粋 IKI cool)

him so extraordinary. When a normal attempt, too, engenders the abnormal—you would be Kiki Shikizaki, the legendary swordsmith."

"So this sword is normal to the extreme... Expendability is what makes it special, and that's why its name is...Legion."

Killer metal.[8] Made to be broken.

"But expendable as they may be, follow procedure when capturing the thousand swords. Not one among the bunch shall be bent or broken. Do you hear me, Shichika?"

"Yep, loud and clear. Thanks for the warning. They'll be fine. But Togame—if that's the only special thing about the Legion, I can't see how it should be a problem. It's like the Razor—there might be tons of them, but it's just a normal sword for me. Because of the rule about not harming any, the swordsman won't be replacing them. A thousand or no, you can only use two max at a time—which gives me a chance to show you how the Kyotoryu tackles the dual wield."[9]

"I'm afraid it won't be easy," Togame said, "tackling one thousand opponents."

"Huh?!"

Shichika was so startled that he almost *dropped Togame*—but at the last second, he took a knee and caught her midair. Her face was so petrified she couldn't even scream.

"Y-You idiot!" she finally shouted. "If I fell from *all the way up here*, I would die! What are you trying to do, kill me? I would be banged up beyond all recognition by the time I arrived at the bottom of the mountain!"

"Yeah, Komori of the Maniwacs is about the only one who could survive such a fall..."

Shying from Togame's piercing voice, Shichika turned his head slightly to look behind him—at the stone steps of the staircase he was climbing. On their way up they had passed through several torii,[10] but the gate down at the trailhead was hidden in the mist.

Not like anyone was counting—but at this point in their nearly linear, precipitous ascent, Shichika had climbed around six hundred stairs. Over halfway there. The final stretch.

Their destination was Triad Shrine.

It was a thousand steps up to the building complex.

Officially, Mt. Taizan,[11] upon which the Triad Shrine was erected, fell within its limits—but its premises were generally understood to be the building complex atop the thousand steps, beyond the final torii.

At first, Togame had been so intrepid.

[8] 金偏に殺 KANE HEN NI KOROSU "the radical for 'metal' plus 'kill'" (yields 鎩 TSURUGI brand)
[9] 二刀流対策 NITŌRYŪ TAISAKU "two sword-style countermeasure"
[10] 鳥居 TORII "where the birds are"
[11] 大山 TAIZAN "big mountain"

Adamant about climbing on her own.

Her resolve had crumbled somewhere around the hundredth step. Dear readers, determine, wise as you are, whether such a number represents a failure or a victory, but after starting off with no shortage of confidence, she was considerably disappointed. Undexterous as she may be, this was the woman who had walked across Inaba Desert to Gekoku Castle. Purely in terms of stamina, she was not about to lose to anyone—but walking on flat ground and walking on a staircase work completely different muscles. And there was something ineffable about the steepness of these steps. When she gave up at the hundredth stair, she was facing the facts.

"Shichika," she had gasped. "Sorry, this is too much. Carry me."

"..."

What a weakling!

Whether or not Shichika thought so, he asked, "Um...you want a piggyback ride?"

"Ugh, how can you be so shameless?"

"Shameless?"

"You're asking me to hug a man from behind."

"Yeah, so what?"

"Our bodies would be touching. That's what."

"So what?" Shichika looked genuinely confused. "If you don't want to piggyback, you can sit on my shoulders."

"Cheerio!"

Togame punched him in the face. Soft as her fist was, any punch to the face is going to sting, at least a little—but the fact that Shichika chose not to dodge it (as unbelievably slow as it was, by his standards) perhaps proved his dedication. Or maybe he was a masochist.[12]

"Sit on your shoulders? Creep! Piggyback is one thing, but ride on your shoulders? That's no way for a grown man and woman to behave!"

"Huh? Back on the island, me and my sister always—"

"Always?"

"...Forget it."

Catching the fury in Togame's eyes, Shichika decided to stop talking. It was probably the ethical choice.

"What do you want me to do, then? If it's shameless for our bodies to be touching, how am I supposed to carry you? You'll have to climb up by yourself..."

"Fool. I am the Schemer," Togame asserted, soaked in sweat. "I have the perfect solution."

—And.

This perfect solution entailed Shichika holding out his arms and sup-

[12] 被虐趣味 HIGYAKU SHUMI taste for taking abuse

porting Togame as she lay sideways—a bridal carry[13] as it is known today, neither of them thought of it as such. Even taking Togame's noble heritage into consideration, this was a little much. No one who saw them would have guessed they were employer and employee.

Of all the ways to carry a person, this was the hardest, but Shichika walked the next five hundred steps of the staircase with astonishing[14] ease, chatting all the way. All the same, it was far from unreasonable for Togame to shout the way she had, upon nearly falling (with six hundred steps stretching below them) from such a precarious posture.

In that moment, she only refrained from socking him and yelling "Cheerio!" because it would have been dreadful, after his save, to be the cause of her own demise. In due course, every instance of the exclamation would come back to haunt her, so its omission here may be a tiny victory in its own right.

But there are still two books to go before Togame learns that she meant "Chesuto."

"Off...we go."

Shichika stood from his knee, adjusting Togame's position. Once he found one that felt comfortable for her and was easy for him to maintain, they began to climb the stairs again.

He wanted to return to their conversation but had lost its thread. While he was trying to remember, Togame helped him out.

"I'd expected you to retort, 'Tackling one thousand swords, you mean.' What shall we do with you?"

Ah yes. The opponents.

"I could have sworn I already told you there would be a thousand miko."

"Huh? You did?"

"Yes. I did."

She had. It's right there, at the end of Book Two.

"...In that case, I didn't forget, I must not have caught it when you said it."

"How many times have I told you to listen to me? Not that I could have divulged more, had you asked me at that point."

"Classified?"

"Classified."

"At that point, yeah, but what about now, Togame? Come on, seriously—a thousand opponents? When you first told me about the Twelve Possessed, I thought you said they had twelve owners."

"I did. But fear not. The setup hasn't changed midway or anything, not regarding this matter. I knew about it from the beginning."

"Not regarding this matter..."

Had anything else?

Changed midway.

13 お姫様抱っこ OHIMESAMA DAKKO "princess hug"
14 舌を巻く SHITA WO MAKU "tongue-rolling" a gesture of amazement

"The Legion has only one owner—Meisai Tsuruga, mistress of the shrine."

"Meisai Tsuruga. Never heard of her."

"It would be weird if you had, island monkey—anyway, among the owners who are known, she is an outlier, basically a nobody. Not being a swordsman."

"Not a swordsman, huh."

Shichika did not look pleased.

The Kyotoryu may be swordplay minus the sword, but in general, the opponent was presumed to be a swordsman. While it would be pointless to attempt a fair comparison, if Shichika were forced to say who had been a greater challenge between Komori Maniwa and Ginkaku Uneri, his answer would be Komori. Not because he was stronger than Ginkaku—but because he was a ninja rather than a swordsman.

"Since the stage was going to be a shrine, I suspected as much—but if there's only one owner, how can there be a thousand opponents?"

"Because Meisai is the Mistress of Triad Shrine, obviously. The size of this place puts it in another league from all the other shrines in Izumo—she can easily employ a thousand miko. And every one of them protects a piece of the Legion."

"Ah, okay. We saw a bunch of the ladies, on the way here."

"Yep," Togame admitted. "I didn't want you to get worked up, so I kept quiet—but that was them. The Kuromiko,[15] protectors of the Legion."

"..."

So it was them.

Those girls.

After entering Izumo—which was nothing without miko, just as the miko would be nothing without Izumo!—Shichika and Togame had happened upon maybe a dozen of them along the road to Mt. Taizan—and in a way befitting of their name, each Kuromiko cut a striking figure.

Caparisoned in vestments of black.

Faces veiled by white talismans, as if they were Chinese revenants.[16]

But foremost—they carried swords.

Those were it, then.

"We've seen all kinds of characters since leaving Kyoto, but they gotta be the weirdest ones...so they're who I'll be fighting this time around. But Togame, I know you didn't want me getting worked up or whatever, but shouldn't you have said something? We passed at least like ten of them—if you had spoken up, we could have snagged at least that many by now."

"This is precisely what makes you an idiot."

"Okay."

"And why you have no personality."

[15] 黒巫女 KUROMIKO "dark shrine maidens"; echoes 黒ミサ KUROMISA Black Mass
[16] 大陸の妖怪 TAIRIKU NO YŌKAI "continental monsters/spirits"

"O-Okay."

"And why you are so far from florid."

"O...O-O...Okay."

She was really digging in.

But ironically, in a bridal carry, her every utterance only came across as a flirtation.

"Use your head. What good is ten swords out of a thousand? Need I repeat, the Legion represents all thousand swords collectively. Why provoke them and make things harder on yourself?"

"I see—your point."

But there were still a thousand enemies to reckon with.

It was mind-boggling, but wouldn't they need to collect one sword at a time anyway, just as a thousand-mile journey started with a single step?

"Well, there may be a thousand enemies, but the Legion has but one owner—Meisai Tsuruga. If I engage in some diplomacy, doors will open."

"Ah...more diplomacy."

"What? Feeling confident enough to best a thousand alone?"

"Not exactly."

Legend had it that Kinkaku Uneri, ancestor of Ginkaku and owner of the Razor, cut down ten thousand men during the Great Sword Hunt enacted by the Old Shogun—but this was not the Age of Warring States, and from Shichika's standpoint in the pacific[17] climes of the Owari Bakufu, facing a thousand foes was simply inconceivable. To tell Togame whether he was confident or not, first he would need to grasp the concept.

And yet.

All this aside, Shichika had his doubts about Togame's capacity for diplomacy. When she offered Shichika a job, as when they met Ginkaku Uneri, her negotiations ended in failure. To make matters worse, the two people she had hired before Shichika—Komori Maniwa, one of the Twelve Bosses of the Maniwa Clan, and Hakuhei Sabi, the Strongest Swordsman in Japan—had both stabbed her in the back.

She was certainly clever—and since crossing over from the island, he had learned enough about the world to see how *improbable* it was for someone as young as her, and for a woman at all, to hold a rank like Grand Commander of Arms—yet her cleverness failed to gain them much traction[18] in practice.

As a military strategist, her job was to command the big picture. Perhaps she was simply unaccustomed to getting involved on a more personal level. That was Shichika's impression.

She read him like a book.

"I can tell when you are questioning my authority," she said, "but fear not. Unlike with Uneri, the odds are in our favor."

[17] 太平 TAIHEI peaceful e.g. 太平洋 TAIHEIYŌ the Pacific Ocean
[18] 空回り KARAMAWARI to spin your wheels

"You sure?"

"Third time's a charm—and now we have the Leveler and the Razor. That's why."

"That's why..."

"That's why—diplomacy might work."

Togame laughed conclusively, making it difficult for Shichika to persist. He had long decided to leave negotiations to her and was aware he lacked even enough cleverness for it to fail him. They say that big men are all brawn and no brains—and young Shichika Yasuri was the spitting image of this maxim. They also say the brains of small men are nothing special—but Togame being female, the maxim is irrelevant.

"As it is, Triad Shrine is an organization. Negotiating will be easy."

"Organization, huh. Do they have any connection to the bakufu?"

"What makes you think they would?"

"Well, I heard somewhere that someone in the bakufu was in charge of managing the shrines and temples... Was it the magistrate[19] or something?"

"Hmph. I'm impressed that you would know a thing like that."

Togame reached up and petted Shichika on the head.

She had meant the gesture to be condescending, but riding in his arms, the princess bride looked downright affectionate. Not a mood you would expect from two pilgrims heading up a sacred staircase toward a shrine.

And by the way, Shichika looked genuinely happy being petted.

He was a simple man.

"You must have mentioned it when you were talking about the Katana Buddha."

"Ah yes, that's possible."

The Katana Buddha—that holy statue found at Seiryoin Gokenji Temple, on Mt. Sayabashiri in Tosa.

The work of the Old Shogun—old, from our perspective—who just before the advent of the current bakufu had prevailed over the warring states and unified the nation. The hundred thousand swords that were seized, by his decree, over the course of the Great Sword Hunt were melted down and cast into a giant buddha. Constructing the statue was of course only a cover for the Great Sword Hunt, the real motive of which was to gather all thousand of Kiki Shikizaki's Mutant Blades, said to have reigned over the warring states from behind the scenes—

It had been well over a hundred years. Togame was attempting to round up the twelve swords even the Old Shogun could not collect.

Shichika, who had been raised in isolation, without knowledge of the world, and no faith of his own, was sufficiently fascinated by Seiryoin Gokenji Temple, and its reputation among swordsman as a holy site, to remember

19 寺社奉行 JISHA BUGYŌ Edo-era magistrate of temples and shrines

these details, and little else, from what he had been told along the journey.

"Indeed, the Magistrate of Shrines and Temples is in charge of managing them—but it is no simple chore.[20] If it was a temple, fine, but this is a shrine."

"Huh. Aren't they basically the same? I mean, they're both religion."

"You're one to think so. What's the best way to explain this—actually, it may not even be necessary..."

But Togame went on.

She thought it best to outline the fundamentals.

"You just lumped them together as religion, but... There's Buddhism. Then there's Christianity,[21] the practice of which has been banned in Japan. Then there's Islam, deemed one of the world's three major religions along with the first two. And don't forget Confucianism, on the continent... In most cases, when we say religion, we mean a set of *teachings*—yet Shinto[22] is not a teaching, but a *way*. That's worth keeping in mind."

"...?"

Teaching. Way.

Shichika did not understand the difference.

Not actually expecting him to, Togame wrapped things up without fielding any questions. "Basically, it's hard for the bakufu to order the shrines around—especially in a place like Izumo, haven of the gods. They have extraterritoriality[23]—or even autonomy."

"That so."

"That is so. If it weren't, we would have forced them, organization or not, to hand over the Legion. The fact that this was not an option is why we have stopped here, on our journey, to collect."

"Gotcha. But what about during the Old Shogun's Great Sword Hunt? Was the Mistress of Triad Shrine the owner back then, too? An ancestor of Meisai Tsuruga, just like with Uneri?"

"I'm afraid not. The exact details are unclear, but apparently Meisai Tsuruga already owned the Legion when she took over Triad Shrine... Despite its size, grand even among the shrines of Izumo, it is not mainstream[24]—but it was not until her arrival that the place became a fortress."[25]

"A fortress... You can tell from the looks of those miko that it isn't. Those black costumes make them way more striking than your average miko."

"Yes. Which brings us finally to what makes Triad Shrine unique... although honestly, since you're about to see it for yourself, I won't say much.

[20] 一筋縄 HITOSUJI NAWA a single length of rope (would not get it done)
[21] 耶蘇教 YASOKYŌ "faith in the revived" YASO is also a phonetic approximation of "Jesus" vs. キリスト教 KIRISUTOKYŌ the modern term for Christianity
[22] 神道 SHINTŌ "the gods' way" The aforementioned faiths all end in 教 KYŌ teaching; Shinto, like kendo and other martial arts, ends with 道 TŌ/DŌ way
[23] 治外法権 CHIGAI HŌKEN outside the jurisdiction
[24] 本流 HONRYŪ "main stream" 流 RYŪ flow: the same character as in e.g. Kyotoryu
[25] 武装神社 BUSŌ JINJA a militarized shrine

Once we've arrived, leave the diplomacy to me. Even with a thousand miko—I'll make sure you'll wind up fighting Meisai one on one, if worse comes to worst."

"That's the worst case?"

"Avoiding combat altogether would be ideal—but if that were possible, we wouldn't be going to all this trouble. Remember what happened with Uneri. The venom of the Shikizaki blades—is no joke."

"I know. But take it easy with your negotiations. If we could avoid fighting altogether, there'd be no reason for me to be here. I have a hard time picturing fighting a thousand people at once, but if you tell me to, I'll do it."

"..."

Togame could have interpreted these words, which came so easily to Shichika, as an expression of selfless loyalty and felt a stirring of the heart—but what they evoked in her was nothing so emotional.

If you tell me to, I'll do it.

It was no lie or bluff. In fact, in just such a manner, he had vanquished both Komori Maniwa and Ginkaku Uneri. He did whatever Togame told him to do.

Words like "vanquish" had a nice ring to them—but it was also plain murder, under the aegis of shogunate decree.

Bloodshed.

In fighting Komori, there had been at least some element of proper self-preservation—but what about Ginkaku Uneri? He was a bad man, with a bad cause, doing bad things—but did that allow them to take his life, just so they could take away his sword?

It was Togame who had ordered it.

She recognized their Sword Hunt was basically a sanctioned form of robbery, backed by the powers that be. Which is why she emphasized diplomacy—even when it was meaningless to try. She didn't need anybody telling her that not all battles could be avoided—nevertheless, she tried. Not just with the Razor. The first time she rounded up the Leveler, working together with Komori, and the time she rounded up the Whisper, with Hakuhei Sabi, things had started diplomatically.

She knew she was a hypocrite.[26]

Hopelessly apart from justice.

Nevertheless—her mission required definition.

And diplomacy gave it definition.

For reasons of ambition and revenge, Togame had no choice but to see her mission through—her position was far more desperate than it seemed from the sidelines.

She had gone as high as she could go.

26 偽善 GIZEN "fake goodness"

Her only hope of getting any higher was to hatch the ultimate scheme. She had to accomplish the impossible, and collecting Kiki Shikizaki's errant masterpieces, a feat not even the Old Shogun had been able to accomplish, fit the bill.

And so, she was ready to risk everything.

She had abandoned everything before.

And was prepared to throw it all away again.

"..."

"Togame. What's wrong? Tell me."

"No—it's nothing."

Right. It was nothing. Throwing everything away again was nothing.

Yet—what was the deal?

Shichika Yasuri had no agenda and nothing to lose—he was unencumbered by questions of righteousness and definition or ambition and revenge.

He cut down Komori and Uneri without hesitation.

A sword in and of himself.

A katana will choose its owner.

But not who to kill.

And the Kyotoryu was a katana incarnate.

What made him reliable made him terrifying.

Togame seriously had her doubts—did this sheltered island boy have what it takes to engage in burglary and savage warfare? Wouldn't his purity stop him from committing murder? You could say his fight with Ginkaku Uneri at Gekoku Castle had been a touchstone.[27] And based on the results, he passed with flying colors.

Flying perhaps too high.

His lack of hesitation smacked of the inhuman.

He needed to be that—it had been true of Komori Maniwa and Hakuhei Sabi, who preceded him. Komori and Sabi were fine with killing; they practically whistled[28] while they worked.

And yet—both men must have had their own agendas, or else abandoned something to *become who they were.*

Not so for Shichika.

Shichika was not broken—but he could kill.

If abnormality meant that a normal attempt, too, engendered the abnormal—then Shichika was not that. He was a normal guy. He laughed normally, yelled normally, cried normally—and killed normally. He could act broken normally—that was the kind of swordsman Togame had hired.

While he may have lacked a personality—he said bizarre things like they

[27] 試金石 SHIKINSEKI "gold-testing stone"

[28] 鼻歌混じりに HANAUTA MAJIRI NI "with humming mixed in"

were hunky, and did bizarre things like they were dory.[29]

For instance, after his battle with Ginkaku Uneri—on the road to Izumo, during one of their lighter chats, he had said to Togame, "Good thing Uneri had no relatives," in the sincerest of tones. "No one will be sad, now that he's dead."

She had considered responding to his remark, uttered in a genuinely kind-hearted manner, but thought the better of it.

There was a facet of truth to what he said.

But this truth—it was not anything for him to say.

Sheltered island boy.

The purity of his upbringing—perversely insulated him from ethics and morality. He was unable to tell right from wrong. He would do whatever he was told to do.

He really meant it when he said so.

Even the miko, servants to the gods[30]—he would shred them, without a thought. He may or may not beat all thousand—but needed not the slightest conviction to kill any opponent, swordsman or woman or not.

Even if she told him *the backstory*[31] *of the Kuromiko.*

He would kill them.

Could sheltered, in a single word, explain everything away?

He may have been fine for the Age of Warring States.

But in a world at peace, his presence was conspicuous.

It was fine this time.

In a pinch, *so far as the bakufu was concerned*, it was not a problem if he killed Meisai Tsuruga—and the thousand Kuromiko, while he was at it.

Their backstory—consigned them to such a fate.

And yet—it mattered none to Shichika whether or not there was a problem. They could be a person whose killing would cause problems—they could have relatives, enough to pack a funeral—but if he were told to kill somebody, he would kill.

Was this good or bad? Oh, it was good.

Was it good or evil? Evil, certainly.

But Togame had known this.

Known the Kyotoryu was such a school, from the beginning—of her life.

She knew—because *this was how* Shichika's departed father, Mutsue Yasuri, late master of the Kyotoryu—had murdered her father.

For this very reason—their kind did not betray, and would never stab her in the back like Komori or Sabi.

A katana, having chosen its owner, could not.

29 平気で…平左に HEIKI DE…HEIZA NI plays on similarity between 平気 HEIKI "carefree" and 平左衛門 HEIZAEMON, an old-fashioned male name

30 神 KAMI in Japanese, a noun on its own can be singular or plural, but Shinto is polytheistic

31 正体 SHŌTAI true identity

But in her management of Shichika, Togame the Schemer would do well never be too sure—she prided herself on being unarmed, but in hiring the Kyotoryu, she had made a big exception. For the most part, it was a good thing for Togame that Shichika was not a loose cannon, but rather the surest of swords...and yet she had to take pains not to drown in it. She would be no better then. No different from those on whom she swore to take revenge.

Which is why she could not be careless with her word.

Regardless of how it was for Shichika—regardless of how he was, for her part Togame had to go into this with the utmost conviction.

"...heh."

A gentle laugh. Laughing at the way she was, out of self-deprecation? Not quite. Shichika had adjusted his grip for the bridal carry and grazed her side in a way that tickled.

"Stop it! Creep."

"Huh? Whuh, what?"

"Ugh..."

She had lashed out, but it had been an accident.

She would bury the hatchet.[32]

Three months.

It had been that long since he and Togame had teamed up, and she had long since confirmed that when it came to things romantic, Shichika was a puritan.[33] Her clarity on this matter made burying the hatchet easy.

At this point, the keen Schemer was beginning to realize that lounging like a princess bride was not the most becoming way to travel. Riding on his shoulders was out of the question, but a piggyback ride might have been preferable... With all her layers, there was no way that he could feel her body against his back. But this arrangement had been her idea, and she could hardly renege on it now.

Meanwhile, Shichika was simply thinking how this was no easy way to carry her. Yet, since his muscles more than compensated for any difficulty, the thought barely registered.

This style of portage wasn't bringing them any closer.

"Okay, so if things work out—or as you say, if worse comes to worst, and I wind up fighting Meisai Tsuruga one on one, what then? What kind of moves does she have? She might not be a swordsman—but doesn't she at least use a sword?"

"Truth be told, I'm not so sure," Togame said. "She's basically a nobody, and none of us knows much about what happens in Izumo—but like you said earlier, apart from having strength in numbers, the Legion is nothing special, *no more than a first-rate katana*. In a faceoff, you'll have the advantage."

"Damn right."

[32] 矛先を収める HOKOSAKI WO OSAMERU stop pointing the tip of a spear or pole-arm
[33] 朴念仁 BOKU NENJIN shunning adornments or otherwise stubborn

But Shichika remained uneasy, not knowing anything about his foe—and said as much.

"What did Meisai do before taking over this shrine? That might give us a clue."

"She was a brigand."[34]

"Huh..." Shichika responded vaguely. Having grown up on an island, the word must have meant little to him.

Still, a brigand. Or a former brigand, anyway.

Which made her fine to kill—as far as the regnant bakufu was concerned.

"Since the time of the Great Sword Hunt and the Old Shogun, the Legion was held by the chieftain[35] of a certain group of brigands. Over several generations. I don't know what kind of moves the chieftains used—but whatever they were, they were enough to keep the Old Shogun from seizing the sword."

"Huh. Where are the brigands now?"

"They disbanded when Meisai took over the shrine—evidently."

"From that to working at a shrine? Why the change of heart—I'd like to know. Oh yeah, I meant to ask you—among the Twelve Possessed, there was one called Soto the Twin, right? To guess from the name, that one's paired... After tackling a thousand-in-one sword, I have to deal with some dual combo?"

"Funny. Little is known of Soto, what manner of sword the Twin is... For the sake of my report to the bakufu, I can only pray[36] for something more exciting than a mere set of two." But this was only sarcasm. You could never tell with Shichika, but Togame was not being serious. "Anyway, there's no use thinking so far ahead. It remains to be seen whether we even make it there. Even after safely capturing the Legion, we'll have our fair share of problems to solve. Foremost being how to ship the swords back to Owari—I still haven't figured that one out."

"Yeah, you were saying that."

"The Leveler and the Razor were taxing enough, but this will be another headache. What to do—hmm."

Togame looked pensive.

Pensive, and yet reclining like a princess bride.

When something around a hundred steps remained, she would concoct a compelling reason and have him let her down, to climb the stairs on her own. She could hardly arrive at Triad Shrine in the arms of her retainer.[37] When she would be engaging in diplomacy on behalf of the bakufu, it would not do to have her adversary think lightly of her—and luckily, the strength

[34] 山賊 SANZOKU "mountain bandit" vs. 海賊 KAIZOKU "sea bandit" pirate
[35] 頭目 TŌMOKU head of a group or clan
[36] 祈る INORU wish; supplicate
[37] 従者 JŪSHA follower

had mostly returned to her legs by now.

"Shichika. About how far have we come?"

"Huh? I'd say eight hundred steps or so."

His stores of energy brimming over, he answered Togame's question with the most pedestrian of expressions. He had a better complexion than before their way up the mountain, as if he had benefitted from a modest amount of exercise. There was no limit to the power of this hearty youth.

"Good. In that case."

Togame meant to express her intention to ascend the rest of the stairs on her own, but that became unnecessary.

They had not exactly lucked out.

Better to say they were out of luck.

Eight hundred, Shichika had estimated, and under the torii situated at, in fact, the eight hundred and fiftieth stair—a figure stood sweeping dead leaves with a bamboo broom.

In miko vestments of black.

And yet—unlike the shrine maidens in the world below.[38]

Only her hakama, covering her lower body, was black.

Her face was not hidden by a talisman.

She was not carrying a sword.

But what truly set her apart—was her demeanor.

Radiating, effortlessly, the singular aura of a sanctum-dweller who stood entirely apart from the Kuromiko and all the other denizens of the world below—she worked her broom. The stairs had been so steep they had not noticed her until they were this close—which made it seem as if she had appeared out of thin air.

Stunned, Shichika nearly dropped Togame for the second time—thankfully or otherwise, it was not the first, and she managed to throw her arms around his neck, almost clinging to him.

In that posture, which did not lend itself to ready explanations.

They encountered[39] Meisai Tsuruga, the third adversary on their Sword Hunt.

"How do you do?"

Her voice, coming at them from above, defied description.

In how chilly it sounded.

[38] 下界 GEKAI low with respect to the heavens, casting Mt. Taizan as an otherworldly realm

[39] 遭遇 SŌGŪ accidental meeting

CHAPTER TWO

MEISAI TSURUGA

■ ■

Meisai Tsuruga was a tall woman.

It was hard to say how old she was—she looked young, but gave off a strange air of experience. Her abundant jet-black[1] hair, allowed to grow indefinitely, was tied back into two trailing tails.

And that black miko costume.

Hers must have been a little different because she was the mistress.

"Meisai Tsuruga was the name of the priest who oversaw the shrine before me. I figured why not try it on for size. My real name? Can't remember. Or maybe I never had one. Brigands have no use for names," she said sociably.[2]

■ ■

With so much time on his hands, Shichika opted to take a seat. For his bench, he chose the stairs they had ascended, sitting on the thousandth step. This placed him directly under the Grand Torii of Triad Shrine—a huge gate carved from stone, and easily two or three times larger than those they had passed through on their ascent. Shichika favored heights, like hot air,[3] as one might expect,[4] and for an instant he thought about scaling the torii to have a seat on top (since at this point, he had yet to learn how strictly such behavior was forbidden), but plenty satisfied by the view straight down all thousand of the steps, he held off for now.

He had a look over his shoulder.

The building complex[5] was no less majestic than the thousand stairs or the enormous torii. Triad Shrine was a fastidiously kept example of gongenzukuri.[6] Togame had only just explained this was a kind of yatsumunezukuri[7] where the honden[8] is separated from the haiden[9] by a patio of stone—

1 漆黒 SHIKKOKU the color of black lacquerware
2 気さく KISAKU good-humored, in contrast with 奇策(士) KISAKU(SHI) Scheme(r)
3 煙 KEMURI smoke (also said to favor heights per a Japanese saying: cats, and fools)
4 ごたぶんに漏れず GOTABUN NI MOREZU not being an exception (see above note as to what it implies)
5 社 YASHIRO Shinto shrine proper
6 権現造 GONGEN ZUKURI style of shrine architecture incorporating stone
7 八棟造 YATSUMUNE ZUKURI style of shrine architecture involving many rooves
8 本殿 HONDEN inner chamber of a shrine, closed off to visitors
9 拝殿 HAIDEN chamber of the shrine where prayers are made

But Shichika had soon forgotten all of that. All he saw was majesty. This kind of an emotional response was not beyond him. But then again, who could take the word "majestic" as a compliment from him, when until recently, his concept of architecture was limited to that ramshackle hut on Haphazard Island.

Togame the Schemer and Meisai Tsuruga—the brigand gone miko—had gone off together, to confer in the privacy of the honden.

The time had come—for diplomacy.

"...Hrmm."

Of course.

Shichika knew his presence would have resulted in no benefit—since, as a rule, he was always in the way. At best, he would butt in with a random comment and derail the conversation. He understood why Togame had told him to "Go play over there, Shichika"—if she wanted him to amuse himself, alone, there were other ways she could have said it, but whatever.

Still, scenes from last month passed through his mind.

Ginkaku Uneri. Lord of Gekoku Castle.

Master of Iainuki, withdrawn into his Danger Zone—

He had dared to draw his sword against Togame, a servant of the bakufu, during that session of diplomacy—Shichika had swooped in to the rescue, but in his absence, Togame could have been sliced in two.

Proud as she was about being weak as shoji paper.

A schemer who had no use for weapons.

All the more reason why his presence was essential. And it was no less true during a round of diplomacy.

What about the venom of the Shikizaki blades?

Just having one will make you want to kill—

No.

That much was clear to her, too. If Shichika understood something, then so much the more Togame—after what had happened to her last month, she must have a solid strategy in mind.

Besides, she had showed up at Haphazard Island on her own—in terms of pluck, she came with a warranty.[10]

Shichika could worry all he wanted. Despite having teamed up with him for the Sword Hunt, Togame would probably never stop acting like she was going it alone. Even Shichika, dim as he was, saw this.

And he was fine with it.

He was a sword.

A katana, by the name of Yasuri—of the Kyotoryu.

It was common practice to give up your sword ahead of an important meeting—Shichika had learned this from their diplomatic chat on Haphazard

[10] 折り紙つき ORIGAMI TSUKI "folded paper attached"

Island. His sister Nanami had relieved Togame of the katana she had been carrying, out of character. Which made his presence last month, at Gekoku Castle, an exception.

Yeah, that was different.

Meisai Tsuruga and Ginkaku Uneri were nothing alike.

Uneri had been a drawn sword[11]—in perverse contrast to his style of swordplay, the man himself was like a katana whose scabbard had been lost. But Meisai was different. In the first place—

Right.

She was not wearing a sword.

So long as she was not pulling a Komori and storing one in her stomach—the Legion's owner carried not a piece of the thousand.

The poison.

In that case, the sword's poison—couldn't reach her.

As they had ascended the remainder of the stairs alongside Meisai, from the eight hundred and fiftieth step up past the thousandth step, where Shichika was sitting now, and proceeded onto the shrine grounds—Togame, resigned to the horror of being witnessed in her posture, had not ordered Shichika to put her down—the Mistress of Triad Shrine had welcomed them with the openness and congeniality one extends to friends of ten years standing.

Laughing heartily...

"Hahaha! From the bakufu? Sure you are—just kidding, I believe you. This kind of a story is much more fun when you believe it."

Togame must have been planning out her diplomatic hand all hundred and fifty of the steps. It would be going too far to say she plumbed the essence of Meisai over the duration of their climb, but the Schemer seemed ready to decide on the course of conversation.

They would wind up fighting one on one, if worse came to worst.

So Togame had predicted.

The lady doesn't look so tough.

Meisai was tall, but only for a woman—next to Shichika, her height was not an issue. It didn't look like she spent much time training. Of course, since he had met so few people, he was not equipped to judge an opponent's prowess from her appearance.

Still, she didn't carry a sword.

Did not carry one—was unarmed.

"Triad Shrine is still a shrine, but at this point, in name only," she had said on the steps. "There isn't a single priest left. No one but us miko—you'd call us a convent,[12] if we were a temple."

Shichika had tried asking Meisai about the strange outfits he had seen

[11] 抜き身 NUKIMI bare blade
[12] 尼寺 AMADERA Buddhist nunnery

the Kuromiko wearing in the world below. Swordless, and without the white talisman with which the others hid their faces, Meisei only came across as strange because her hakama, ordinarily red, was black—yet it underscored the eccentricity of the other maidens encountered en route.

"They aren't just down below. There's more up here."

It was hard to say whether it was intentional, but Meisai had dodged his question by offering the irrelevant detail.

"Maybe fifty of them. We're a fortress now—it's part of our duty to patrol the neighborhood. I have so many to take care of, the only way to make room is to scatter them around."

When Togame had explained the situation, Shichika had put two and two together and assumed the miko must be friends of Meisai from her brigand days—but evidently, he was wrong. Seven years back, when she took over the shrine—she stepped out of the game entirely.

Supposedly she never saw those friends anymore.

Then again.

There was something odd about this shrine regardless.

Not mainstream, Togame had said.

"Man..."

He had not been subjecting his brain to anything too difficult, but it had somehow filled up to capacity, and Shichika keeled over, lying flat out on his back. If the torii were a guillotine,[13] he would be the star of a beheading. And in that posture—a number of miko entered his field of vision.

Kuromiko.

Like he'd seen below.

Miko—dressed head to toe in black.

It was hard enough for Shichika to tell people apart, but when they wore the same clothes, carried swords in the same fashion, and hid their faces with the same type of veil, differentiating them was hopeless—any given one looked like the rest. You did not have to be Shichika to think so. The talismans hid their faces perfectly, and they all wore their hair in more or less the same style.

"Convenient for a screen adaptation."[14]

That was what Meisai had said.

Shichika had not caught her meaning.

Not if it's live-action, Togame had taken issue with the remark. Shichika had not understood this either. But maybe that was for the best. Maybe he wasn't supposed to.

But even if they looked basically the same, Shichika could tell that the miko working on the upper compound outranked the guards that they had seen below.

[13] 断頭台 DANTŌDAI "head-severing platform"

[14] 映像化 EIZŌKA to cinematize

Which reminded him of something.

He had his worries about his boss Togame engaging in diplomacy in a closed room with the enemy (and once diplomacy was underway, things were out of his hands)—but something else was eating him.

Sento the Legion.

All fifty of the Kuromiko who were tending to the grounds—not like he had checked them all, but from the looks of it, they were armed—had a sword slung from her hip. Here and there, he saw one with her sword on the right, instead of the left, but he guessed that only meant those miko were left-handed.[15]

Those swords—were pieces of the Legion.

That's what Togame had said, anyway.

And yet—something *felt off* to Shichika.

This, too, involved last month. The moment he beheld Zanto the Razor at the hip of drowsy Ginkaku Uneri, in Gekoku Castle—he could sense the sword was among the Twelve Possessed of Kiki Shikizaki.

He was certain.

And as it turned out—he was right.

At the time, he thought it was a hunch—knowing he could easily be wrong, he had told himself not to make a hasty judgment.

But when he brought it up with Togame, she suggested that since Shichika was a swordsman, perhaps something in him could sense the presence of a Shikizaki blade.

That would mean these things had souls,[16] or some similarly fantastical idea. Shichika acknowledged the possibility. But this time—

He felt nothing.

When he saw the swords the Kuromiko carried, he felt none of that sensation he experienced the month before—neither the ones on the guards under the mountain, nor the ones on the maidens up on the compound elicited a special reaction.

They felt like—normal swords.

That was all.

Hmm.

He must have been pretty bored to fixate on a thing like that. No doubt Togame had forgotten that exchange by now—well, with her memory, it was unlikely she had actually forgotten, but to be sure, it had not been grouped with her important memories. Barring a reminder, she would probably never think of it again. Her line about him sensing a presence? She probably hadn't meant anything by it.

But Shichika thought it had been an interesting idea.

Fantastical as it was.

[15] 左利き HIDARIKIKI "favoring the left"
[16] 魂 TAMASHII spirits

Shichika believed it was possible—in fact, he hoped that it was true.
That things had souls.
That katana could have souls—since after all.
Shichika Yasuri was a sword himself.
Still—yeah.
Togame had been absolutely sure, so the swords the Kuromiko carried must be pieces of the Legion. They had to be. Shichika decided that the lifeforce he sensed the first time he saw the Razor was a figment of his imagination, and promptly switched off his brain.
"Hey."
When one of the Kuromiko happened to come near Shichika's spot—not because she had any business with him, but simply trying to get by, so she could descend the stairway—he went ahead and greeted her. If she seemed friendly, he could ask about those talismans. With those things covering their faces, did they ever have trouble watching their step?
"...nkk!"
The Kuromiko shrank away and beelined[17] in the direction she had come from.
Shichika dropped his jaw.
No guy enjoys a girl running away from him when he says hello, but Shichika was not equipped to feel that way. Even so, he thought this odd behavior suspicious. Meisai Tsuruga may call herself a miko, but she was the shrine's mistress. In which case, it was understandable that this maiden would be scared of Shichika who was, after all, her boss's "enemy"—nevertheless, something weird was going on.
That wasn't hostility, at all—just fear.
But what was scary about Shichika?
Since he had yet to mention to Meisai that he was Master of the Kyotoryu—the Kuromiko could not possibly know who he was. What did an armed gal have to fear about an unarmed guy lounging on the ground?
This shrine's weird.
That there was no one here but miko meant that it wasn't functioning as a shrine, to begin with—Meisai had said as much herself.
Shichika lost himself in a recollection of the time Togame brought him to Yahata Shrine[18] in Kyoto. He let his eyes fall shut.
He would sleep here for a bit.
By the time he woke, the negotiations would surely be over.

[17] 一目散 ICHIMOKUSAN "leave at one look"
[18] 八幡神社 YAHATA JINJA the actual shrine is written the same but read 八幡 HACHIMAN

■ ■

She was led into a room floored with wood planking. On her way, in the hallway to the honden, she had seen several more of the Kuromiko, but it reassured Togame to find that they had the room to themselves. Meisai was sincere, and really did intend to speak with her in private, although Togame had been wary of a sneak attack—

That said.

This woman was being straight with her—something made Togame sure of that. It was fine to be wary...but she probably had nothing to worry about.

"Well then."

Meisai, who had entered the room first, sat herself down, cross-legged on the floor, without a cushion.[19] Then she asked Togame to sit in front of her. Togame did as she was told and sat, on her heels,[20] facing Meisai.

"Nice hair, young lady,"[21] Meisai commented to start things off.

Togame's hair was white down to the roots—it had not been dyed or turned white over time—*certain events* had made it that way. A young woman like her with completely white hair was unforgettable. Togame was used to hearing all about it. At this point, she thought nothing of it. However.

"I'm not young enough for you to call me young lady," Togame stated plainly.

She had already been caught comporting herself so shamefully, lounging in the arms of Shichika, and could not risk being taken any more lightly. Meisai had declared that she believed Togame was from the bakufu, but did she really? The woman was likely forming her opinion as they spoke.

"But you are a young lady. In my eyes," Meisai contended. "I recognize, young lady, that you may not be as young as you look—but neither am I as young as I appear."

"...I'm sure."

As I appear—unlike Shichika, Togame had great faith in her ability to notice personal details, but could not guess Meisai Tsuruga's age. She was certainly older than Shichika or Togame—but a precise estimate eluded the Schemer. Or any estimate.

The former brigand—looked nothing of the sort.

True, her openheartedness was in line with the free and easy roguery[22] that gave the brigands their air of romance—but there was something about her not of this world.[23]

19 座布団 ZABUTON "seat futon"
20 正座 SEIZA "formal sitting" legs folded underneath to maintain proper posture
21 お嬢ちゃん OJŌCHAN a term of endearment used when addressing younger women
22 自由闊達放蕩無頼 JIYŪ KATTATSU HŌTŌ BURAI liberated from society and prodigal with resources
23 浮世離れ UKIYO BANARE to exist at a remove from the affairs of others

And yet an island monkey—she was not.

A shrine standing atop a thousand stairs could not be further from the world.

But as the mistress of this shrine gone fortress, as the guardian of Mt. Taizan and Izumo, it would be wrong to say that she was truly separated from the world.

"Madame Meisai—"

"Take your time, dear—ah, there you are."

Meisai gently blocked her visitor from diving into the discussion. The door had opened, and a Kuromiko stepped inside, toting a sizeable carafe[24] of sake. Without a word, she proffered it to Meisai and scurried from the room.

Meisai popped the cork, held the spout to her lips, and guzzled sake with abandon. When she was through, she placed the carafe in front of Togame.

"Drink up."

"..."

"On principle, I don't discuss important matters with a person who won't drink with me."

Clearly it isn't poisoned –Meisai promised. Without comment, Togame seized the carafe in both hands and took a long, smooth draught.

A sacramental libation,[25] it seemed.

Not a single god hates sake—or so they say.

But if Triad Shrine had stores of sacred sake to offer[26] to the gods, it was still an active shrine, in some capacity. Even without priests, they were doing the bare minimum.

"You know how to drink."

"Thanks."

Meisai seemed amused. Togame placed the carafe on the planking, with a thud, before dabbing at the corner of her mouth.

"Are we good?"

Togame. Haughty as ever.

Call it diplomacy, but she had no intention of toadying or groveling.

"Certainly. Now we're friends. But why leave out the boy?[27] Doesn't this concern him, too? He is your man, I take it, young lady?"

"He is my sword," quipped Togame. "On principle, if whoever I am speaking with is not carrying a sword, I leave my sword behind."

"Your sword, huh."

Meisai laughed.

...Togame was well aware that such a declaration carried little weight

[24] とっくり TOKKURI a tall vessel, narrow just before the pouring spout
[25] お神酒 OMIKI "god sake"
[26] 供物として KUMOTSU TO SHITE as offerings
[27] 坊や BŌYA kid; male counterpart for お嬢ちゃん young lady

after that shameful first impression. There was no getting beyond a flub[28] like that.

"Well, young lady. To be frank, I know what you have come here to discuss—the Mutant Blades of Kiki Shikizaki, yes?"

Sento the Legion.

"...What makes you think that?"

"Factually speaking, the authorities have imposed upon this self-governing territory only once in history—during the Great Sword Hunt of the Old Shogun, needless to say."

"..."

"When I was a brigand, my seniors often spoke—or bragged, of the commotion of that era. As if they themselves had contended with the Old Shogun..."

Meisai let her eyes fall shut, returning to her brigand days.

"You announced yourself as the Grand Commander of Arms, did you not? The odds are good you came here for Sento the Legion." She turned to face Togame. "Have you launched another Sword Hunt? In that case, I'm not so sure an army of two is going to cut it—"

"Close, though not exactly—but you have the right idea. If my intentions are that clear to you, I can skip the preliminaries."

When they were ascending the stone steps, Togame thought she was the one feeling out her hostess, but it was mutual—if the subtle interrogations hadn't begun at the opening stage, Meisai would not have perceived their aim so accurately.

"Our objective, as you have surmised, is to gather the remaining Shikizaki blades—to round up the Twelve Possessed that even the Old Shogun could not capture."

"To what end?"

"Domestic tranquility,[29] naturally."

"Ahh."

Meisai answered the shameless claim with an equal share of shamelessness.[30]

Duplicity—deception filled the air.

Togame knew this would not proceed like her negotiations with Ginkaku Uneri—or with Shichika and Nanami Yasuri back on Haphazard Island—obviously. Meisai Tsuruga was a leader with a thousand people working under her. But Togame the Schemer expected the difference to make diplomacy more viable.

The truth is that she had not entered this meeting with any kind of ironclad plan—her strategies were not nearly as developed as Shichika trusted

[28] 失点 SHITTEN "lost score"
[29] 国家安寧のために KOKKA AN'NEI NO TAME NI for the peace of the nation
[30] 白々しい SHIRAJIRASHII bald-faced

them to be.

It would even be fair to say she had nothing in mind. On the contrary, how could she engage in diplomacy *any other way*?

Otherwise—how could she be responsive?

Meisai was the owner of a Shikizaki blade.

Like the others—she was surely broken.

Togame had to allow for any outcome.

"To date, we have obtained two of the Twelve Possessed."

"Oh?"

Finally, something that was news to Meisai—and her reaction demonstrated clear interest, exactly as Togame hoped. This teaser of information would come in handy later.

"We seized Zetto the Leveler from Rairaku Namida[31] of Mino—and Zanto the Razor from Ginkaku Uneri of Inaba," she continued. "As owner of Sento the Legion, I'm sure you must have heard of them."

"The Leveler, endowed with the absolute durability of a perpetual motion machine, and the Razor, able to sever anything in existence—of course I know them. Well done." Meisai seemed genuinely impressed. "Two swords even the Old Shogun couldn't catch—that's quite the feat."

By the way, Rairaku Namida was the original owner of the Leveler, at least during their era. In truth, Togame had obtained the Leveler from him with the help of Komori Maniwa—but she declined to mention that she had temporarily lost the sword thereafter, when Komori double-crossed her. Such information would not help her case. Then there was Hakuto the Whisper, captured from Senryo Kizuki[32] of Echigo but pinched not long after by Hakuhei Sabi, the Strongest Swordsman in Japan—in another episode she was not about to mention.

They had pursued two swords, and two swords they had captured.

Image was important.

"Your sword, the Legion, would be our third," Togame said.

"Indeed it would—but young lady. I can't imagine you and your boy picked them up legitimately. What went down during the Great Sword Hunt—"

"We would never resort to such barbarism.[33] Times have changed—and while I cannot wholly disagree with what you said, please understand that we intend, if possible, to go about our business peacefully."

"If possible."

"That's right."

Togame ignored Meisai's sardonic remark.

[31] 涙磊落 NAMIDA RAIRAKU 涙 NAMIDA tears
the characters in 磊落 RAIRAKU visually suggest many 石 ISHI stones 落 falling
also part of the stock expression 豪放磊落 GŌHŌ RAIRAKU (manly) openness

[32] 傷木浅慮 KIZUKI SENRYO 傷木 KIZUKI "wounded tree" not a real surname
homophone of 気づき KIZUKI noticing (yet, ironically 浅慮 SENRYO imprudent)

[33] 横暴 ŌBŌ sweeping violence

Her sights were set.

"I remain a servant of the bakufu—and the affairs of Izumo, regardless of its extraterritoriality, are not unfamiliar to us. That includes everything happening on Mt. Taizan and at Triad Shrine—both on the surface, and *behind the scenes*. Madame Tsuruga—if you would be so kind as to relinquish Sento the Legion, the bakufu could potentially be of service, behind the scenes."

"Ahh."

Meisai could not have sounded more dismissive.

Was she just bluffing? It was unclear.

A former brigand—ministering to the divine.[34]

Either way, she did not seem the type to respond to elementary diplomacy. Or rather—the people of Izumo, an independent territory since ancient times, had never kowtowed to authority—be it the bakufu or the shogun's clan.

Autonomous—that made it sound like a good thing.

But in actuality, the nation had essentially abandoned Izumo.

Saying it was for the best—let sleeping gods lie.[35]

Only during the Great Sword Hunt had the authorities imposed upon Izumo—the Old Shogun had been fearless, indeed.

He lived so long before Togame was ever born, but she had to wonder.

What kind of a man was he, in person?

"Not a bad deal—if you ask me."

"I'd call it a bargain," Meisai agreed. "But it's too simple—and that ruins it."

"What makes it too simple?"

"In my book, nothing is obtained in the absence of resolve—but young lady," countered Meisai, "you said earlier, *On principle, if whoever I am speaking with is not carrying a sword, I leave my sword behind.*"

"..."

"You did say that."

"And?"

"You were half correct—and half mistaken. But in being mistaken, too, you were a half part correct—which renders you totally correct at the end of the day."

"...You're not making any sense."

Meisai grabbed the carafe from where it sat before Togame and took yet another swig. "It's gobbledygook. Let me ask you."

"What about?"

"Your boy, what else? Clearly you don't have a sword yourself. You're not built for fighting—it looks like you don't have a muscle on you. But what's up with him? You called him your sword—yet from the looks of him, he's

[34] 神職 SHINSHOKU "god profession" usually, Shinto priest(ess)

[35] 触らぬ神にたたりなし SAWARANU KAMI NI TATARINASHI "no retribution from untouched gods"

unarmed... Where's this sword of his?"

"It's just in his nature."[36]

Togame felt uneasy but decided to disclose who Shichika really was.

"His name is Shichika Yasuri. Seventh Master of the Kyotoryu, Shichika Yasuri."

"Seventh Master...Kyotoryu." Meisai, who seemed to know of the school, echoed the words. "The Kyotoryu," she did so once again after a pause. "Of course—that's why you called him a sword."

"Almost too good[37] of a sword," noted Togame—as a flourish of diplomacy, but there was truth in what she said.

"And with this sword, you cut down Rairaku Namida and Ginkaku Uneri?"

"That's right."

These questions were meant to test her mettle, but Togame answered without skipping a beat. Out of the two personages, the Kyotoryu had been responsible for only Ginkaku Uneri; Rairaku Namida had been offed[38] by Komori Maniwa, but since Shichika had subsequently killed Komori, it was no great falsehood.

In terms of *sowing terror*—it was more effective.

"But make no mistake. In both cases, it was a proper duel. To be honest, I have my qualms about what transpired—but swordsmen, as a species, can speak only through the sword."

"Proper duel...that's one way to put it. Abuse of authority is another. But who knows—when you are squabbling over Kiki Shikizaki's swords, perhaps that is the most appropriate course of action."

"I want to proceed peacefully. That is the honest-to-goodness truth.[39] You have my word. I want you to believe me."

"...Hero of the Rebellion, Kyotoryu. The Swordless Swordsman," Meisai muttered. It was not clear if she had heard Togame. "I'm interested—no, I'm riled up about it. I just have to know. In a clash between your boy's Kyotoryu and my Sentoryu—who would win?"

"Huh?"

Sentoryu?

What—the heck?

"To go back to what I was saying—about you being half-right, half-wrong, half-right elsewise, and hence totally correct. Still, you are fundamentally mistaken. Which means—I'm the one who actually benefitted by it."

"...You're not making any sense."

"Because it's gobbledygook," Meisai said. "Alright, that settles it. Young lady—or, if you please, Togame the Schemer. As the Mistress of Triad

[36] 質 TACHI disposition pun on 太刀 TACHI, progenitor of the katana
[37] 斬れ過ぎる KIRESUGIRU cuts too well
[38] 屠った HOFUTTA butchered, slain
[39] 本心 HONSHIN "main heart"

Shrine, Mt. Taizan, Izumo, I would be fine with handing over Sento the Legion...as long as you'll abide *a few conditions*."

■ ■

"Mm..."

Shichika awoke to approaching footsteps.

Togame stood right by his head.

Meisai Tsuruga was behind her.

It seemed like their diplomacy was over.

"How'd it go?" he asked—and meant it.

But Togame sounded disappointed.

"Worse came to worst."

CHAPTER THREE

KUIZAME MANIWA

■ ■

The extraterritoriality of autonomous Izumo was more than a formality. Each one of the checkpoints[1] set up along the border was a veritable gauntlet. Passing through without the proper clearance would have posed a steep challenge—or in fact been flat-out impossible. Even Togame and Shichika, who came backed by the powers of the bakufu, only made it across after an elaborate inspection process.

And yet, if Togame and Shichika had arrived in Izumo slightly later, they could have sidled through the checkpoint as they pleased—it would have only taken seven more days.

The trouble started the day after they arrived at Triad Shrine.

The checkpoint they had used when entering Izumo—was destroyed.

The garrison installed there was annihilated. Dozens of lives wasted.

Destroyed—devastated.

"If slipping by is not an option, I may as well cut my way through."

Skin drenched with blood, a man with noteworthy bangs was strolling through the mass of corpses—having a ball.

"Ah, there we go, there we go, there we go—I love it when I don't need to sneak around. Good, good, good."

Dressed in ninja garb, but with the sleeves torn off.

But wearing no mask, parading his face for all to see.

Chains wrapped around his body.

There could be no clearer tell—for a Boss of the Maniwa Clan.

"Not a word from either of those guys, Komori or Shirasagi—not like either of them needs the likes of me to worry where they are—but by now, there's a chance that someone knocked them off when they were reaching for the Shikizaki blades. Not sure about Shirasagi, but I know Komori got one, Zetto the Leveler—if someone beat him, what the heck happened to the sword? Intriguing, intriguing, intriguing."

The man wore a pair of ninja swords on his waist.

One look at the destruction of the checkpoint, and it was evident these swords were to blame—oddly, rather than wear them on the same side, left or right, he wore one on each hip, with the chains wrapping his arms linked to the handles of each sword.

"I may as well follow my lead and devote myself to capturing Sento the Legion. For the sake of my friends, and for my own sake. Triad Shrine... where am I going, Mt. Taizan? Alright—here I come, here I come, here I

[1] 関所 SEKISHO barrier station

come."

Being one of the infamous Maniwa Bosses, this ninja could have easily bypassed the checkpoint, sneaking through the mountains or down the river, but he opted to destroy the border crossing. The most ruthless, flashy method of invasion possible.

"What could be better—than murder."

One of the Twelve Bosses of the Maniwa Clan, Kuizame[2] Maniwa.

The Hungry Shark.

■ ■

Shichika and Togame were accommodated at a teahouse, set at a remove from the rest of the shrine. No more than a single square chamber[3] centering on an open fire pit, the room was by no means spacious, but adequate for two people to spend the night. Shichika may have been far bigger than average, but Togame was unaveragely small, and between the two of them, they struck a balance close to normal. They were also fed; and though the portions were meager, griping about two free meals, morning and night, was one easy way to ask the gods for trouble. While it would be wrong to say that they were feted, the hospitality was beyond what any enemy should expect.

But still.

Things seemed upside-down—something was up. There had to be a downside.[4]

Shichika sprawled out on the tatami—thinking.

It wasn't like him, and didn't suit him, but he was thinking.

Togame wasn't in the room.

He was alone there.

"..."

Worse came to worst.

That was how she put it. In other words, as a result of her diplomacy, Shichika Yasuri would be fighting Meisai Tsuruga, one on one. Good thing he wouldn't have to fight a thousand enemies at once. What a relief.

But Togame had looked so glum.

She had wanted them to go about their business peacefully—that was part of it, but the main reason for that look was the set of stipulations Meisai

[2] 喰鮫 KUIZAME "eating shark"

[3] 四畳半 YOJŌHAN four rectangular mats and a square half-mat, radially arranged into a square

[4] 裏腹な、裏や腹 URAHARA NA, URA YA HARA wordplay and not an actual expression, consisting of:
裏 URA reverse 腹 HARA the flat of; stomach (figuratively "intention" as in what's in it)
裏腹 URAHARA opposite; saying one thing and doing another
a more straightforward rendition might be "tricky secrets and designs"

had tacked onto their duel.

If Meisai was defeated, dead or alive, ownership of the Legion would be granted to Togame—the shrine's mistress gave her word. But in the event of the opposite outcome, where she defeated Shichika—her request was for Togame to grant her ownership of the Leveler and the Razor, the two swords they had captured.

Blatantly unfair.

If he risked his life and won, all they got was a single sword, even if it was actually a thousand...but if Meisai won, she got two—she had a lot of nerve to ask for terms like that.

Apparently Togame saw this coming—or had even intentionally led them to this outcome. After all, she had made that suggestive comment on the stairs: *Third time's a charm—and now we have the Leveler and the Razor.* Togame must have dangled them on purpose in her negotiations. Once she agreed to Meisai's unfair terms, they sealed the deal—a good scheme, when you thought about it. Meisai had a much higher chance of taking the bait, versus a more equitable arrangement where each side had one sword on the line—though Togame would have likely still called it the worst.

Yet Meisai had the gumption to tack on yet another stipulation—something Togame had not anticipated. A task she would need to perform if Meisai were to battle Shichika. Perhaps it was not so much a stipulation as a demand. A demand concerning Sento the Legion.

"As you know, the Legion is a Mutant Blade comprising one thousand identical swords, forged in a huge batch[5] on the premise of quantity, or *numerousness*. Seen together, they're impossible to differentiate—in fact, there would be no reason to try. May as well compare the raindrops. Since they are all the same, you have no way of telling them apart."

Meisai paused.

"Or so you'd think. But Togame the Schemer. What if I told you that among the thousand swords, one sword was the original?"

The original, she emphasized.

"Think for a second. If you want to make a thousand of the same sword—you need a template, for everything to follow. A sample, if you will. Add in the nine hundred and ninety-nine swords based upon it, and you have Sento the Legion."

The first sword—among the Legion.

"Or maybe," said Meisai, "he modeled the second sword after the first, and the third sword after the second, the fourth after the third—and the thousandth after the nine hundred and ninety-ninth. Even so, one sword would have been the first... Ever since I came into possession of the Legion, as a brigand, when it was passed down from the chieftain who came before

[5] 量産 RYŌSAN mass production

me—I've had this suspicion. What would I need to do to figure out which one was first?"

However.

She had tried in vain.

For this was one of the Twelve Possessed, masterpieces of the celebrated swordsmith Kiki Shikizaki—it stands to reason that swords crafted to be indistinguishable would be just that: indistinguishable. Otherwise, the Legion would not deserve to be called a Mutant Blade.

Except.

For that reason.

For that very reason.

"There's my condition—Togame the Schemer. *If you can figure out which sword among the Legion was the first*—I agree to fight this master of the Kyotoryu."

Meisai had something else to add.

"You are free to question the Kuromiko as you please—I hereby grant you access to however many you may need to carry out your search. But hear this: your boy is not allowed to help you."

Those were the terms.

Which is why Shichika was waiting, with nothing to do, stretched out on the tatami. An idler[6] at heart, so quick to be bothered, he was in his element.

It's been—what, a week?

Shichika had a poor grasp of dates, but that seemed about right.

Togame had accepted all of Meisai's stipulations and started the investigation. First she examined the swords carried by each of the fifty Kuromiko at work around the shrine—after which, she descended the thousand steps, returning to the world below, again and again. Taking a cue from Meisai, she began by consulting five of the Kuromiko on patrol, who instructed her on where to go in her quest to inspect the remaining nine hundred and fifty swords.

In the evenings, Togame came back to the shrine—or rather, Shichika went down and picked her up. While she was able to descend all thousand steps herself, she was unable to make the climb. She must have gotten over her humiliating encounter with Meisai, since on the way back up, she would not deign to take a single step herself.

Perhaps this was her characteristic hauteur, or maybe she was only tired. The radius monitored by the guards that Triad Shrine dispatched was not exactly narrow—meeting with all nine hundred and fifty of them and examining their swords proved to be quite the project. *While I have no specific date in mind,* she said to Shichika, *I hope to bring the process to an end within the month. Until then, gather your strength.*

[6] 怠け者 NAMAKE MONO one who lazes

Thus, for the most part, Shichika had nothing to do during the day.

He wondered why he wasn't allowed to help Togame—not like he would be much of a help in finding the original sword out of all thousand, which sounded like a real pain. But it beat actually sitting around all day (as far as Shichika's mood was concerned).

That aside, he did worry about Togame. They were being treated well, but they were smack in the middle of enemy territory—if you thought about it, surrounding herself with Kuromiko, who were supposed to be the enemy, and asking to see their swords was basically a form of suicide. Shichika's job was not only to capture swords; he was Togame's bodyguard[7]—

This had occurred to him on the third day (a little late) of the investigation. He brought it up with her, but her answer was blunt.

"Ridiculous. Why would Meisai botch her chance to obtain two of the Twelve Possessed?"

Yeah.

That made sense.

By the way. When Togame was out in the field, she dressed not in her usual extravagant kimonos, but in the costume of a regular miko, which she had borrowed from Meisai, arguing that a stranger wandering around Izumo stood out too much, even if she was just conducting research. Evidently Triad Shrine had regular miko costumes in their inventory. Too bad for Shichika he didn't have a weakness for miko, or he would have been in for a real treat—but presented with this departure from her usual attire, he did not feel nothing at all, it is told.

So—a week.

About a week.

Togame had said that she was almost through with looking over all the pieces of the Legion—the real investigation had yet to begin, but he was glad, at least, for Togame to be finished up with traveling back and forth between the shrine and the world below.

Though she could use the exercise.

He still had his misgivings.

Togame was so laborious in everything she did.

What made the Legion special was its massive quantity. Unlike with Komori and Uneri, he couldn't simply topple Meisai, and unless she promised otherwise, he would likely end up fighting all thousand of the miko—still, Shichika felt like Togame was playing too much by the rules too seriously.

He sat up from the floor.

And slipped out through the tiny door.[8]

It was a beautiful day.[9]

[7] 用心棒 YŌJINBŌ "caution stick" for fending off robbers, etc.

[8] にじり口 NIJIRI GUCHI small hatch used to access a teahouse

[9] 晴天 SEITEN "clear heavens"

He had some time before venturing below to pick up Togame—but he was tired of napping and felt like taking a little walk. Togame had told him to take it easy, but there is a limit to how much a person can sit still. Waiting expends a surprising amount of energy.

He was bored.

However, there was another major reason, albeit one beyond his comprehension, for his irritated mood. Ever since Togame had shown up on Haphazard Island, they had been together constantly, not parting for a moment—never really doing their own thing. This was only because Togame felt so obligated to shepherd[10] him around, since at first he really did know nothing, but now that he was spending all this time alone, he was feeling a lot of pressure. True, it also meant that she trusted him enough to leave him alone.

But basically, he was lonely.

Lonesome.

Heading towards the honden, for no specific reason, he noticed someone coming his way—a Kuromiko with no sword, Meisai Tsuruga. Carafe in one hand.

"Hey," Meisai was the first to speak, easygoing as ever. "I was just heading to the teahouse—what's up, Kyotoryu boy? Time for a chat?"

"...Sure. I don't mind."

He was okay with that.

He wouldn't have approached her on his own, but now that they were talking, there was something he did want to ask her. She led him toward the honden, where they sat on the narrow deck[11] engirdling the building.

"Figured you were bored," she said. "I'd like to show you a good time, but as head of the shrine, I had some pressing business to attend to."

"Sure. I don't mind," he repeated his previous reply.

When it came to conversation, his moves were limited. But he went on.

"Since we're here, though, talking—there is something I want to ask...if that's okay."

"Sure."

Meisai was happy to oblige.

She was hard for him to read—no, hard to understand. Perhaps this was to be expected, for someone who had met so few people in his life, but Shichika had never met anyone like her—he had questions.

A few.

Fact is, if Togame succeeded, he was going to have to battle Meisai—so he had to ask, *What was the Sentoryu?*

Sentoryu—he had first heard about it from Togame.

It was the school that Meisai Tsuruga belonged to, she who was not a swordsman.

10 保護監督者 HOGO KANTOKU SHA guardian and supervisor
11 縁側 ENGAWA "rim side" 縁 EN also means "connection" (e.g. in Buddhism)

The moves of a woman who didn't look that tough—she wasn't carrying a sword, so he couldn't ask her to show him. Even if she was, Meisai was no dummy and would never tip her hand—but learning more about the Sento-ryu was Shichika's top priority.

At the moment, however, none of that was on his mind.

There was only one thing that he wanted to ask.

"You know how Togame's looking for the first sword in the Legion? How come I can't help?"

"What? You wanted to help?"

"Not wanted to—but because of your weird rule, I've been sitting around all day. I'm so bored I could die."

"I bet." Meisai giggled. "Well, the young lady must not have informed you of the ways of Triad Shrine—you make it sound like it's my fault that you're bored, but even if I hadn't made that stipulation, the young lady would have refused your company."

"Hunh?"

"*The investigation must proceed without a hitch.* I made the stipulation just in case—given the Schemer's smarts, there was probably no need, but I figured why not."

"The ways of Triad Shrine? What do you mean?"

Togame had not told him.

Was it—classified?

"Mm, I doubt it was classified. Certain people know—what goes on 'behind the scenes,' as the young lady put it. She'll probably tell you when the time is right. 'Behind' is in fact an apt term, and if Izumo didn't enjoy autonomy, this shrine would be crushed in no time."

"What are you saying? I can't understand you."

"Remember how I said this shrine was like a convent?" Her tone was even. "That wasn't the best metaphor. We're more like a sanctuary[12] for women."

"Sanctuary?"

"A place for women to escape[13] bad marriages."

Meisai averted her eyes from Shichika and scanned the scene before them. Perhaps she thought to point out an example, if a Kuromiko was nearby, but unfortunately, none were in sight.

No, not unfortunately.

Dim as he was, Shichika understood.

The Kuromiko were openly avoiding him.

They behaved differently toward Togame—but toward Shichika, they were openly—even morbidly distant.

"Buddhism and Shinto stem from completely different mindsets—but this is not about doctrine. It's a Triad Shrine tradition. Call it the legacy of

[12] 駆け込み寺 KAKEKOMI DERA a temple that sheltered abused wives 駆け込む KAKEKOMU dash into
[13] 縁切り寺 ENKIRI DERA same as above, but suggesting a divorce 縁切り ENKIRI "ties-cutting"

the priests of our past who stood outside the mainstream."

"I'm not sure I get it...who are all these miko? And how come you don't wear a sword—but give them swords?"

"Because for them, the swords are necessary...maybe even a necessary evil."[14]

Shichika was confused. *Maybe I've been waiting for people like you to come here all along,* Meisai muttered, only deepening his confusion.

"The Kuromiko are all—victims," she explained. "Continually abused for long periods of time, by men who broke their spirits. They run the gamut. We have women who served the finest households, girls sold off by their parents—even daughters of daimyos."

"Broke...their spirits?"

"It's a whole world that happy-go-lucky boys like you don't know of," Meisai jibed. "Not only their spirits. Their hearts and bodies were ravaged to the limit. And beyond the limit, the ravages continued. Their abusers must have felt guilty because they only beat them under lock and key—it stays hidden, until the woman falls apart in some clear manner. You want to know what happens once they fall apart? They're cast off, just like that."

"..."

"The thousand Kuromiko, working at this shrine—were rescued from those painful circumstances. Do you see now why they would be scared of you? To the Kuromiko, men are to be feared and evaded, just for being men. Which is why I cannot have the young lady, in her inspection of these thousand swords, accompanied by a man."

"Feared and evaded...men, women." Shichika had to be honest. "I don't understand."

"I see. Perhaps that's no surprise. You are a swordsman, after all. A different world."

Swordsman.

Shichika had not missed Meisai refer to him this way—Togame had said as much, but this was proof. Meisai knew about the Kyotoryu...

The true colors of the Kyotoryu.

"But—that explains why Togame kept telling me to stay inside and take it easy. Makes sense now. She didn't want me startling the Kuromiko. She was watching out for them."

"Watching out for them, as another woman."

"Huh."

"Have you also figured out, by now, why I give them pieces of the Legion? The venom of Kiki Shikizaki's swords works like medicine."

"Medicine?"

"Just as too much medicine is poisonous, this venom can serve as med-

[14] 必要悪 HITSUYŌ AKU "necessary evil": likely a modern, direct translation from Western languages

icine. Of course, the swords allow them to defend themselves as well. The miko of a fortress shrine bearing arms is to be expected. But most of all—the venom plays an important role in healing the parts of them that have been broken. Assuming that these Mutant Blades really do have powers that surpass human comprehension—"

"..."

Just having one will make you want to kill.

So a sword infused with such a poison—could rehabilitate a damaged heart in the right hands. Perhaps that dose of aggression was exactly what a wounded spirit needed—

This was a surprise.

Shichika had never imagined—the Shikizaki blades could heal. No, Meisai Tsuruga was probably the first person in history to use them for that purpose.

But she was not off the mark.

These were broken blades, forged by a broken man.

Could a broken sword undo a broken heart? It sounded possible.

Could the latent murder of the Legion vivify, too?

"And if they don't, psychology[15] has the placebo effect[16]—this is what legends do for us. In the end, it doesn't make a difference whether the power is real or a fantasy."

"...I was sure, because you were the owner of the sword—you scattered the pieces to avoid the venom."

"Sounds like you were expecting a real villain. To be honest, I think the power is mostly symbolic, but it has been fairly effective, if I may say so as an observer of the last seven years. Even forgetting the question of the venom, the power of carrying a blade allows these women to stand on an equal footing with men. And to protect themselves."

"Huh."

Togame thought—the opposite.

To an obstinate degree, she shunned the idea that being armed would make you strong. Equipping the katana known as Shichika Yasuri for the Sword Hunt had surely gone against her natural inclinations.

"So this shrine—is like an infirmary?"[17]

"In a way—you could say that."

"What about those talismans that hide their faces? Are they some kind of charm for healing their spirits?"

"No, no. They simply hide their faces. Like I said, all of these women come from trying circumstances. They need to hide their faces so they can devote themselves to anonymity. And being a shrine, blatant scare tactics

[15] 心理学 SHINRIGAKU the exact term for the modern discipline; anachronistic in the original, too
[16] 偽薬効果 GIYAKU KŌKA "fake medicine effect"; again, insouciantly anachronistic
[17] 療養所 RYŌYŌSHO place for patients to recuperate

have a place here."

"Okay."

"The talismans are only masks. What matters—are the swords."

The pieces of the Legion—one of the Twelve Possessed of Kiki Shikizaki.

They did the job alone. According to Meisai.

"I thought the Kuromiko up here ranked higher than the ones working below, but from what you're saying, I guess that isn't true."

"Actually, you've got it backwards. The fifty who stay up here are the sickest of the thousand—their hearts were marred so violently they can't sleep through the night."

"..."

"But by carrying swords, they are able to maintain a sense of self—the Legion guides their hearts. And therefore," Meisai said, arriving at her point, "I cannot give up the Legion."

Here, for the first time.

Meisai Tsuruga shifted from her easygoing mood.

"I want to help as many women as I can. By beating you, and gaining the Leveler and the Razor, two more of the Possessed—I can help another two girls. This is why—winning against you is my only option."

"Uh huh. Sounds good to me."

His mood had not changed whatsoever.

Earlier in their conversation, they had said that Togame had hitherto kept quiet on the details of Triad Shrine—hinting, but never actually telling Shichika—out of a fellow woman's consideration for the Kuromiko. However, this was perhaps not the reason. Or not the only reason. In reality, Togame, in her position, had perhaps a pair of reasons to be cautious—first, if she told Shichika, he might start sympathizing with the Kuromiko—and with Triad Shrine as a whole, in which case her katana may begin to stray. And second—if she told Shichika, *and he showed no concern whatsoever—*

Whatever Togame thought might be the case aside.

It was the second of these two that actually transpired.

"I'll fight for my own reasons. You fight hard for the girls. Sounds like this is going to be a good battle."

"So much for my plan to invite pity," Meisai said, looking rather pleased.

She hoisted the carafe and took another zealous swig before offering it to Shichika.

"Drink up! Then we can get down to business."

"Yeah." Shichika drank from the carafe as told. "Blegh! Gahak...hack... This water's gone bitter!"

"This is the good stuff." Appalled, Meisai took the carafe back from Shichika. "Bitter water... What are you, boy, a teetotaler[18] or something?"

[18] 下戸 GEKO nondrinker

"Oh, is that alcohol? I've actually never drank before."

"Why didn't you say so? I would never have made you. Forcing a drink on someone is a disgrace to drinkers[19] everywhere... Anyway, for someone so happy-go-lucky, you sure are callous. I suppose I'm the one who tried to take advantage of your sympathy, but no dice."

"It's because I'm a sword." Shichika coughed. "Nothing moves me but Togame."

"If you usurp the Legion, hearts could be torn afresh—are you fine with that?"

"Fine or not, it's just the way it is. If Togame wants the Legion, there's nothing else for me to do. You have to give up."

"I take it," Meisai asked pointedly, "you have no use for inner turmoil?"

"...?"

"Give up, you say—once you've decided, do you never have misgivings? Aren't you just being lazy about having any? And scared of making your own choices? Because it'd be such a pain?"

"Such a pain—I'll give you that."

"How many people have you killed?"

It was a sudden, stunning thing to ask. But it seemed not to faze Shichika remotely. "Two," he replied.

"Two—a low body count, for a person like you."

"I'm an island monkey. My first battle was only two months back."

"In gathering two of the Twelve Possessed, you killed twice—in other words, each of the owners."

"Yeah, exactly."

Thanks to Togame's cunning fudge,[20] these "owners" weren't identical between Shichika and Meisai, but since it was beside the point, and thereby not an obstacle, their conversation continued.

"Will you kill me too?"

"Guess so...but didn't you use to be a brigand? If this wasn't Izumo, you would've been nabbed ages ago—that's what Togame said, anyway."

"Same goes for the thousand miko. More than a few of them are wanted by the law."

"Whoa, really?"

"Just escaping can be a crime—which is why they hide their faces."

"Right—the painful circumstances. What about you, though? How many people have you killed so far?"

"Too many to count. But at least forty-three—that much is certain."

"Forty-three? How do you know?"

"I had forty-three comrades," she replied without missing a beat. "That's

[19] 酒呑み SAKE NOMI tipplers
[20] 情報操作 JŌHŌ SŌSA "information manipulation"

how many I killed to quit my life as a brigand, seven years ago—it's a number I can't possibly forget."

"..."

She never saw those friends anymore, Meisai had said.

So—that was what she'd meant.

"Although you could spin it around and say those forty-three are the only ones I remember. Some might say that makes me a savage butcher. But the same woman is unable to kill if she lacks the resolve. Or has nothing to relinquish. You, however, don't seem to have that issue."

"I—don't really...I guess."

"In that case," probed Meisai, "what are you fighting for?"

"I told you. I'm doing it for Togame," Shichika answered the provocative query without faltering—it may have surprised Meisai even if she saw it coming. "I've fallen for her. What else could it be?"

"...And so much for my plan to foster doubt," Meisai muttered with a sigh of grief.

That sigh reminded Shichika of the sister he had left behind on Haphazard Island—his sickly sister, who could sigh with the best of them. How was she doing? Was she eating and everything?

Then—he remembered. Something else.

"My mistake."

"Huh?"

"Not two—it's three. I wasn't thinking. I killed one other person."

"You did? Was it—on this Sword Hunt, like with the others?"

"No, before that. About a year ago, back on the island. *I killed my dad.*"

■ ■

To be honest, these forced authorial asides—in plain terms, the moments in each book where the basic setup of the story is regurgitated—are in need of a better system since there are only so many pages to work with, specifically three hundred sheets of manuscript paper. When the titles denote Book One, Book Two, Book Three, what reader is going to jump ahead to this installment? The dear reader who does would probably push right through, saying, "Whatever, must've been covered in the first two books." An excess of these repetitions can only bog things down and annoy. Some measure appears to be necessary, but with no practical solution in sight—

Togame the Schemer was the daughter of Takahito Hida, Kaoyaku of Oshu.

Takahito Hida, the rebel who needs no introduction. Takahito Hida—

mastermind behind the only major conflict to take place under the Owari Bakufu, the Yanari Shogunate's reign. A close call—but in the end the Rebellion was suppressed, and with so relentless a counteroffensive that the entire Hida family, excluding Togame, perished in the flames of war.

And the man who dispatched Takahito was none other than Mutsue Yasuri.

Sixth Master of the Kyotoryu—Hero of the Rebellion.

Togame escaped with her life, but only after her father was slain before her very eyes—overnight, her hair turned completely white. This was the turning point, what made her who she was today, and her traumatic first encounter with the Kyotoryu.

Thereafter, her life was pandemonium[21]—she lived only for ambition and revenge. Infiltrating the bakufu, that limitlessly hateful entity responsible for murdering her family, she climbed high, despite being a woman, by dint of her wit and ingenuity.

Commanding the military directorate was no more than a waypoint. The neck of the shogun was still out of reach.

Which brought her to—the Sword Hunt.

The idea that it was for the good of the nation was a pack of lies.

And Shichika—knew as much. Komori Maniwa, the first person he killed off in battle, had spilled the beans.

Her ambition. Her desire for revenge.

That did it for Shichika. If Togame, who saw the shogun as an enemy and could not possibly have a soft spot for the Kyotoryu, had come all the way to Haphazard Island to ask for help because she had no other choice—then quite frankly, she won his heart.

There was a part of him that sought to make amends.

For the first time he realized that his father, his hero, had left victims like Togame in his wake. The desire was real—to atone for her life in place of his father, who had been absolute for Shichika.

But more than that, as a katana incarnate—he chose her.

Her spirit[22] made him—fall for her.

"Sure, I don't see why not," his older sister Nanami, head of the household, replied when he told her he was joining Togame on her Sword Hunt—despite Nanami's languid tone and indifferent bearing, her gaze alone was severe. "But Shichika, I think you had better keep quiet about knowing her personal history..." she advised.

That sounded about right.

But right or not, Shichika always did his sister's bidding. Thus, Togame had yet to grasp the actual reason he had joined her—

"Also," Nanami said, "Mutsue Yasuri was her mortal enemy—don't tell

[21] 修羅と羅刹 SHURA TO RASETSU Asura and Rakshasa (constantly battling demons, or their world)
[22] 心意気 KOKOROIKI zest

Miss Togame *how you've killed our dad too.*"

Which is why Togame didn't know that, either.

"...Huh?"

"Hey."

Perhaps Nanami hadn't thought twice about her choice of words, but in truth, she should have warned her faithful younger brother not to tell *anybody*—a rare fumble for her. Because of this oversight, Shichika allowed the crucial piece of information, so key to the entire story, to slip out in a chat with, of all people, Meisai Tsuruga, an enemy.

Luckily, if that's the word—it was all that he was able to reveal.

For it was right when she made to respond to the crucial bit—that she and Shichika both noticed.

Rising simultaneously from the deck—they looked *way up there.*

Nurtured in the wild, Shichika trusted his eyes—and if Meisai was looking the same way, she saw it too.

Atop the Grand Torii—which even he had kept himself from climbing—a man stood tall.[23]

In sleeveless ninja garb.

Not even a mask.

Chains wrapped around his body—a man with bangs.

It hardly mattered how long the man with ninja swords on both his hips had been there—what mattered was that he was there now.

"Hey, hey. You noticed me already? You guys are quick." Despite the stares he was receiving from Shichika and Meisai, the man on the torii didn't sound the least bit apologetic. Though he was a good distance away, and not really shouting, the hum of his voice seemed to whisper in Shichika's ear. "I was hoping to hear what was coming next—tantalizing stuff. Still, I've caught the gist of it. Enough to grasp the situation. Thank you very much. Really, I should be bowing low and waiting for you to tell me it's fine."

"..."

"..."

Shichika and Meisai were speechless. They may have been absorbed in conversation—but both of them had been facing forward. Even in a psychic blind spot[24] like the top of a torii, a person standing so dramatically—

"Allow me, from on high, to announce myself—ah, feels good to be announcing myself instead of sneaking around. Good, good, good, good," sang the man. "I am Kuizame Maniwa, one of the Twelve Bosses of the Maniwa Clan. It is my pleasure to make your acquaintance."

"Oh..."

Once the man gave his name, Shichika noticed (really late)—the same weird ninja outfit, right, as Komori Maniwa, from the fight back on Haphazard

23 仁王立ち NIŌDACHI stance of the statuary Deva gods who guard a temple gate

24 精神的に盲点 SEISHINTEKI NI MŌTEN 精神 SEISHIN spirit 盲点 MŌTEN "blind point"

Island, and Shirasagi Maniwa, found dead in Inaba Desert—the chains wrapped around this one's arms seemed a little longer than the first two's, but he had to be—

"A Maniwac!"

Since coining the cute shorthand a month earlier, Shichika had called the Maniwa Clan nothing else, but this was his first time saying it to one of them.

"Mani-what...?"

The ninja stumbled on his perch atop the torii.

Catching himself just in time, he was...

"Brilliant! I don't believe it! What an angel you are for giving a clan of expert assassins such as ours a neat nickname. Under different circumstances, you and I would surely have become fast friends!"

...quite pleased.

The world was full of idiots.

"You know this guy?" Meisai, willfully disregarding the exchange, asked Shichika.

"Not him exactly," Shichika answered. "It's like he said—they're ninjas. The Maniwacs. A clan of expert assassins—with their sights set on the Shikizaki blades."

"I see..." Meisai nodded in acknowledgment. Apparently she had not heard of the Maniwa, but she could tell that Kuizame was no joke[25]—her face had turned to stone.

"You, sir, Shichika Yasuri of the Kyotoryu—possess Zetto the Leveler and Zanto the Razor. And you, ma'am, Meisai Tsuruga, Mistress of Triad Shrine—possess Sento the Legion," Kuizame noted politely. "So then, Komori—hmm. What a shame. And Shirasagi, who was reaching for the Razor—gone as well. What a shame."

"..."

"That said—If I kill both of you fine people," the ninja observed with a joyful smile, "all three swords will enter my possession."

...If he really had been listening to Shichika and Meisai, he should have gathered that things could not progress so smoothly. Even Shichika knew this—the Leveler and the Razor were not here, and the Legion, owing to its massive quantity, was not the type of sword anyone could capture just by defeating Meisai.

And yet Kuizame had spoken thus.

As though he simply wanted to fight the two—no, as though he simply wanted to kill them both.

"Ah—good, good, good, good—the rarefied air, of strife."

Kuizame soundlessly bared both his ninja swords—but not by grasping each blade's handle. To Shichika, it looked as if the swords had drawn

[25] ただもの TADA MONO a nobody (usually used with a negative: "not a —")

themselves—but upon closer examination, their handles were linked to the chains wrapped around his arms. By shooting his hands into the air,[26] Kuizame pulled on the chains, freeing both swords simultaneously. As though they were kusarigama,[27] he proceeded to spin them on either side, vertically, like high-speed propellers.

Togame had told Shichika the chains were a kind of chain mail, basically armor—of course, when it came to the Maniwa Clan and their enclave, not even the Schemer knew all there was to know. In fact, she had never even heard of Kuizame Maniwa, much less met him.

Togame was hardly to blame, but one of the bosses could use the chains *like so*—in a ferocious and vicious[28] attack.

"Behold the Dust Devil.[29] This ninpo is why they call me 'Kuizame the Sand[30] Trap.'"

"..."

Where was this guy in the last book?

His moniker begged the question.

But there were other pressing concerns.

Shichika turned toward Meisai—he had no idea what kind of moves her Sentoryu involved, but unarmed as she was, how could she show him? In which case—he would have to fight alone.

Considering the duel to follow, he couldn't let Meisai get herself killed—but he would be lying if he said he wasn't anxious. Evidently Kuizame Maniwa fought with swords, but those bonkers weapons were not the sort the Kyotoryu was designed to counter—Shichika could not treat him like a swordsman.

At this point though, he had no choice but to go all out—since he had scared away the Kuromiko, there was mercifully no risk of an imbroglio[31]—and since those ninja swords were not the work of Kiki Shikizaki, he could snap them all he wanted—

"Here I come—oh what fun."

Kuizame leapt from the torii. Normally, jumping down from a high place, not to say that doing so off the Grand Torii was normal, you bent your knees to some degree to absorb the impact, but not Kuizame. Legs straight, swords whirring on both sides—he let gravity do the work and plummeted straight down.

"Nkk—"

Shichika dashed ahead before Kuizame even landed. Come what may, he would need to fight this battle a safe distance from Meisai. But then a shadow

[26] 万歳 BANZAI "ten thousand years" i.e. "Long live"; here, the gesture that goes with the cheer
[27] 鎖鎌 KUSARI GAMA sickles swung from chains as weapons
[28] 獰猛獰悪 DŌMŌ DŌAKU relentless savagery
[29] 渦刀 UZUGATANA "whorl katana"
[30] 鎖縛 SABAKU restrain with a chain pun on 砂漠 SABAKU desert
[31] 巻き添え MAKIZOE roping others into the fray

passed him, as if cutting through his thoughts—Meisai Tsuruga, running low to the ground.

"Huh?"

That fast.

Before he knew it, she had overtaken him.

"A few days ago, I received word that a checkpoint on our border had been annihilated—and based on the harrowing report, I gather that this Dust Devil was to blame. I hate to steal your scene, but as the mistress of this fortress shrine that guards Izumo, I cannot let the ninja be," Meisai excused herself, in a single breath, as she blew past Shichika. "And our duel would not be fair if you had no clue about the Sentoryu while I knew of the Kyotoryu."

Tup.

With a firm step, she sprang off, even faster—leaving Shichika behind. This was a first for him—and came as a shock. Not in his battle against Komori Maniwa, not in his battle against Ginkaku Uneri, and not at the dojos of Kyoto, where Togame had brought him to train—had Shichika ever been surpassed in athletic ability.

Meisai zipped by—like it was nothing.

Shichika's legs halted of their own accord.

No stopping her.

But what was she planning to do?

She had no sword!

"Heh..." Seeing her rush his landing zone, Kuizame was unshaken—in fact, he chuckled like it was his idea of a good time. "Meisai Tsuruga. I heard you ask him, 'What are you fighting for?' If you don't mind me answering: Money! I pride myself on never having fought for any other reason. All the same..."

The blades spinning on either side of him—sped up, no longer a mere whirlwind but a raging tornado.[32] At that velocity, the chains that swung the ninja swords were fearsome weapons in their own right.

Maniwa Ninpo, Dust Devil.

"If you have to be asking such questions, don't even bother fighting—'What are you fighting for? What for?' Nobody has time for your philosophy! Don't be ridiculous!"

He landed—without a sound.

And where Kuizame landed—was where Meisai crossed his path.

"...nkk!"

Unarmed.

Not equipped with the Legion—no blade on her person. Shichika could tell, as Master of the Kyotoryu, as a swordsman who was his own sword.

But after they intersected—it was Kuizame Maniwa who was mangled.

[32] 竜巻 TATSUMAKI "dragon roll" whirlwind

Evading the protection of the chains, a deep cross had been slashed into his chest, whence sprayed out vast quantities of blood—and as if to dodge this fountain of gore, Meisai had followed through and charged nearly twenty feet beyond her foe.

It was only then that Kuizame fell.

Flopping down like a dead shark—clearly for good.

"*It* may be dead, but a man is a man—I can't ask the miko to clean this up. Would you mind taking care of the corpse?"

"..."

Meisai's voice was easygoing as ever, as if she had merely finished up a little chore—but Shichika had no words, nor any other reaction, at the ready.

"About your father..." Meisai reprised. "As a servant of the gods, I will ask no more of it. Sure I'm curious, but I can tell that the rest of it is not for me to hear. You should not be so careless—about who you tell."

■ ■

That night, arriving at the bottom of the thousand steps to bring Togame home, the first thing Shichika did was to inform her of the scuffle with Kuizame Maniwa. Perhaps she had anticipated this—and for that reason swapped her usual finery for a miko costume, which in Izumo helped her blend into the background.

Now that the Maniwa were involved, it didn't matter what they promised Meisai; tomorrow they would work together, Shichika insisted. As her katana, he could no longer permit their separation.

Togame dismissed him as overprotective. He thought this was bravado, but he was wrong.

She had news—brandishing a sword.

"I found the original Legion."

In any case, this much seems certain: If the next Maniwa Boss also bites the dust in an instant, their main part in this Tale of the Sword will be the pushover's.[33]

[33] かませ犬 KAMASE INU "dog for biting" foil (in dogfighting, boxing, etc.)

CHAPTER FOUR

THE SENTORYU

■ ■

Since no matter how you look at it, no matter how you read between the lines, this Tale of the Sword is no detective novel, the riddle portion of this episode must be brought to a close, swiftly and in good faith. It doesn't take much to see how incredibly difficult it must have been for Togame to find the original piece of Sento the Legion, one of the Twelve Possessed of Kiki Shikizaki—after all, each piece was perfectly identical—mass-produced, in the strictest sense of the term, by an unrivaled artisan of the sword. As mentioned elsewhere in reference to his other Mutant Blades, the means whereby he brought this katana to life is lost to history, for now—at any rate, whether you're hunting for the first sword or the last, the fact remains: differentiating *completely identical objects* is a fool's errand.

Unless Kiki Shikizaki marked the swords on purpose—explained Togame.

Not with a difference in the swords themselves, of course.

That would negate their status as the epitome of mass-produced, and the epitome of expendability.

But what about the scabbards?

While infamous as a swordsmith, Kiki Shikizaki did it all—he sharpened his blades, cast his own handguards, wrapped his own handles, carved his own carvings, and milled his own scabbards—if this legendary man, who fashioned every part of his katanas on his own, were so inclined to leave his mark, he would have done so on the scabbard. The handguards and the handles determine the exact feel of the sword—if you changed something about them, it would be a *different sword*, since it would feel different to hold. But if you changed something about the scabbard, the container for the blade—a slight or even noticeable difference would be fine...

The Schemer banked on this.

It was a baseless, crackpot theory. If she was right, it should be possible to find the first piece of the Legion—or rather, *if she was wrong, finding the first piece would be impossible*. Her reasoning was neither inductive nor deductive: it worked perforce, but perhaps this characterized her schemes. By piling theory upon theory, she dared to weave sense out of chaos. As had been the case with Komori Maniwa and Hakuhei Sabi, she made her fair share of mistakes—but when she pulled it off, the spoils were none too shabby. She had arrived at a conclusion in a week, despite giving herself a month, because she had committed to her conjecture. She stopped looking at the blades entirely, and focused only on the scabbards.

All thousand pieces of Sento the Legion.

Even the scabbards, at first glance, were identical—from mouth to tail,[1] all looked the same. Having no pattern and no carvings of any kind, they were painted a plain[2] orange.

But even identical swords would not have been handled the same way. The conditions of their ownership—or custody, would necessarily be different, from one sword to the next. Whereby the *history*—the scars marring the surface of each scabbard would take a different form and pattern.

They were different.

There was a difference.

Togame produced her trusty magnifying glass and pored over the scabbards, checking the marks on each and every one, taking notes. Of course, some dings were obviously new, the result of negligible wear and tear, and these she disregarded. She had to be extremely careful about what she deemed irrelevant, but what mattered most was that she caught the oldest marks—the deep cuts that appeared to be from the last century. Only scabbard markings of this age could have been made deliberately by Kiki Shikizaki, thus warranting her attention—

If she could discern some kind of geometric cipher[3] established through the number and position of these markings, she could discover not only the first piece of the Legion, but *the order in which all the pieces were created*—yet this was beginning to go over Shichika's head. With his limited vocabulary, the very word "cipher" was nothing but a cipher.

Anyway—Togame presented Meisai with the katana.

Since no interpretation of scabbard markings was by any means guaranteed, Togame spoke more cautiously than usual—so far as she could tell, she had found the original.

Perhaps the idiosyncratic explanation baffled not just Shichika, but Meisai—but she accepted the sword cordially.

"The scabbards were a blind spot. Thanks. I'm thrilled."

Considering how Togame had delivered—even going above and beyond their agreement to crack a code that revealed the entire order of production—the owner could not be more grateful, no doubt.

Still.

"Still, the more I think about it, the less I get it," Shichika said. "Why did Meisai ask you to find the first one, anyway? If the thousand swords have an original they were based on, I guess it's only human to want to know which one that might be, but what good will it do? She's not going to worship it as a god, is she?"

1 鞘尻 SAYAJIRI butt end of the sheath 尻 SHIRI buttocks
2 無地 MUJI "no ground" not patterned
3 暗号 ANGŌ "obscure numeral"

He was speaking his mind.

Looking over the sword before Togame proffered it to Meisai, he had felt no spark—none of the lifeforce of Zanto the Razor. He failed to see what set it apart from the other swords the Kuromiko carried—sure, it was supposed to be one among an indistinguishable thousand, first piece or not, but still.

Honestly, even the swinging swords[4] of Kuizame Maniwa made a stronger impression as katana.

If that particular piece served, wouldn't picking a random one and cooking up an appropriate explanation have worked just as well?

"True," Togame admitted. In a way, Shichika's doubts amounted to a complete negation of the work she had endured for the past week, but she did not take it personally.

"At first I thought Meisai was giving us a problem we could never solve, to keep the battle from happening..."

However—after actually speaking to her, he had realized this wasn't the case. If Meisai's story about the true nature of Triad Shrine was true, she had her heart set on the Leveler and the Razor. It was not the mania of a collector, or the venom of the Shikizaki blades doing the talking.

She was driven to obtain the Mutant Blades—out of necessity.

"If that was her plan, she could have stuck to it," observed Togame. "Just as I could have given her a made-up explanation, she could have shot down anything I said. My argument was full of holes. If she had felt so inclined, she could have stomped all over me. Everything was riding on my powers of persuasion since I didn't have a scrap of evidence."

"Yeah. In that case, maybe it's better not to think too much about it."

"She must have her own reasons. But listen, Shichika—my work here is done. The rest is up to you. While I was investigating the Legion, I tried to learn about the Sentoryu—but sadly I was unable to scrounge up any clues. Searching for the original Legion ate up all my time. In which case, you will be walking blind into this battle, against a foe whose methods are a mystery."

"Ah, about that... I think I'll be fine," assured Shichika. "I've got the Sentoryu figured out from watching Meisai slash up that Maniwac."

"Huh, is that so?"

"Yeah. If it's how I think it is, I can see why Meisai was curious about our school. As Master of the Kyotoryu, I'm curious about the Sentoryu myself. But just thinking about it like a normal person, without playing favorites—matched up against the Sentoryu, the Kyotoryu wins out..."

Be that as it may.

Shichika Yasuri of the Kyotoryu versus Meisai Tsuruga of the Sentoryu.

The long-awaited battle was set for the next day at high noon.

4 鎖刀 KUSARI GATANA "chain katana" (not a real word, unlike kusarigama)

■ ■

Which brings us, without further ado, to the next day at high noon.

Shichika and Meisai faced off before the honden of Triad Shrine—the stone patio in between them. As usual, Shichika had doffed his arm guards and straw sandals, baring his sword for battle. Meisai was caparisoned in her black miko outfit—but unlike every other time he saw her, she had a sword. One of the Legion—perhaps even the "first piece" that Togame had presented to her. All the same, to Shichika, her sword was nothing special.

The Kuromiko had cleared the premises. Not one of them was visible by the time Shichika had awoken. They would only be a hindrance to the duel—whereby, at present, there were only three people on the shrine grounds: Shichika and Meisai, along with Togame, serving as witness to the duel.

"I meant it when I said the fifty who stay up here are the sickest of the thousand—I don't intend this to take too long. Let's get started, and be done with it."

"You sound pretty relaxed for somebody whose life is on the line—that's supposed to be my thing, you know?"

Meisai was her usual easygoing self, and Shichika exuded nonchalance—indeed, neither of them acted like their lives were on the line.

But in the battle that was about to unfold, they certainly were.

Their lives, as well as their swords.

"For our arena, let's set the boundary at the thicket surrounding the shrine—Mt. Taizan is a treacherous place. If you lose your way, you may never be seen again. But otherwise, this is no dojo match. Feel free to enter the honden or the haiden, jump onto the roof or up onto the torii. Use the terrain however you please."

"Yeah, well, since I'm the challenger, and this is your turf, you get to decide—but are you cool with having Togame as our only witness? Wouldn't it be fairer if you picked one of your Kuromiko to watch, too?"

"I cannot expect them to be neutral judges—but fear not, I aim to emerge victorious in a manner that allows no room for a bad call," Meisai declared with the utmost confidence. "Whoever wins, no grudges—dead or alive. That said, I'm open to the possibility of a surrender. If you lose all hope, just say the word."

"Understood..."

Nodding, Shichika glanced at the sword slung from her hip—*the first piece*. Catching him looking, Meisai drew the blade.

Curved, about two and a half feet long, marked by a lengthwise groove.[5]

[5] 鎬造 SHINOGI ZUKURI sword having a long groove running near the ridge

With a beveled[6] spine, and delicately patterned[7] face.

A dull glint reflecting the sun—

Mass-produced or not, it was a fine specimen of a katana, hammered by none other than Kiki Shikizaki.

"Well then, Kyotoryu—show me what you got."

"Gladly—as long as you show off this Sentoryu you're so proud of."

"Proud?" In answering Shichika, Meisai narrowed her eyes somewhat. "The Sentoryu is not a source of pride for me. *This stuff*—is swordplay, and nothing more."

"..."

How come she wasn't proud?

It confused the heck out of Shichika, but he quickly brushed it off with a snort—*hmph*.

The Sentoryu.

Her clash with Kuizame Maniwa had happened like a bolt of lightning; it was over in a second, but Shichika had witnessed every frame. Which is why, the night before, he had told Togame that he had the Sentoryu figured out.

As long as you show off—but not for his sake.

Meisai had dashed full-speed ahead to meet Kuizame where he landed—and *shot her hands into* the rotations of the Dust Devil to catch the swords' handles. Redirecting their gyration onto Kuizame, she used his own two blades to slash a cross into his chest.

Double Cross[8]—is what Meisai called it later.

It happened in an instant—but an instant was enough.

The Sentoryu had a fancy name, but its fundamental premise was dattojutsu[9]—the hardly unheard-of practice of using an opponent's sword against him. And just as Ginkaku Uneri had his signature version of iainuki—the Sentoryu appeared limited to dattojutsu.

Dattojutsu—a kind of mutodori.

That would explain why Meisai Tsuruga was usually unarmed—considering the purpose the pieces of the Legion served at Triad Shrine, Meisai had no reason to keep one for herself. Even unarmed, she was perpetually ready for battle.

In which case, the essential meaning of the Sentoryu was simple—any katana, on any person, could readily be used to do her bidding. Although empty-handed, Meisai carried a thousand swords. As in the Kyotoryu, there was no reason to be armed—but in the Sentoryu, your opponent hauled around the sword for you.

[6] 三ッ棟 MITSUMUNE when the edges of the ridge are planed to form three longitudinal surfaces
[7] 小乱 KOMIDARE "minor riot"
[8] 二刀・十文字斬り NITŌ JŪMONJI GIRI
slashing 十 JŪ, the two-stroke character for "ten," using two swords
[9] 奪刀術 DATTŌJUTSU "sword-robbing technique"

Kyotoryu and Sentoryu.

So much in common—and yet.

"Alright, let's get started."

Shichika assumed a stance.

Form One—the Suzuran.

"Right—if we keep gabbing,[10] we'll never begin."

Meisai assumed a stance too—an unremarkable middle guard.[11]

Yes, *despite not needing her own sword, she was armed*—but rather than negate Shichika's reasoning, this backed it up. Up against the Kyotoryu—a Swordless Swordsman—she had no choice.

While they worked in a comparable manner, there was also a decisive difference between the Kyotoryu and the Sentoryu—although both involved a swordsman who went without a sword, the Kyotoryu persisted in it, whereas the Sentoryu obtained one in the end, from the enemy or elsewhere—in which case.

However comparable their workings, the Sentoryu did not work against the Kyotoryu.

No sword can be stolen from a foe without a sword.

Meisai had been forced to abandon the core tenet of her school and equip one.

In that regard, the Kyotoryu was more versatile.

The school may have been designed to combat swordsmen, but there was no enemy it could not face, be they ninja or miko—armed or otherwise.

Which is why, as Shichika said to Togame the night before—*thinking about it like a normal person, without playing favorites—matched up against the Sentoryu, the Kyotoryu wins out.*

Thinking about it, like a normal person.

Since joining forces with Togame, Shichika had started *thinking* fairly regularly, even if it was a pain—and perhaps he was to be commended for thinking at least that far about it, like a normal person—

But that was where he stopped thinking.

Something a normal person might think would be obvious to Meisai Tsuruga, a practitioner of the Sentoryu who knew about the Kyotoryu, in which case—*why had she agreed to the duel?*

Shichika had stopped before getting that far.

To anyone raised in a society, it was self-evident that if you're thinking over here, they're thinking over there, but Shichika had yet to understand this—or that one thought ought to lead to another.

Of course, this was not the case for our specialist in thought, Togame the Schemer, with whom Shichika might have conferred the night prior; but his suggestive comment had satisfied her, and besides, exhausted after so many

[10] 御託を並べて GOTAKU WO NARABETE spouting cant; 御託 GOTAKU originally, oracular utterances

[11] 中段 CHŪDAN sword raised to stop a body blow

days investigating pieces of the Legion, she had not been listening well. Big picture strategies were her game, and hands-on tactics his—but thinking of things on such segregated terms was perhaps not ideal. Their negligence might be attributed in part to Shichika's "thinking" having been on target one month back, at Gekoku Castle—in a stroke of beginner's luck.

Ignorant of this, Togame called for the lethal match to start.

"May the best[12] sword win—go!"

The Suzuran, with which the reader is already acquainted, is a passive stance—Shichika was basically waiting for Meisai to make the first move. Which in this case—

"Whuppah!"

—involved hurling the Legion at him.

It spun parallel to the ground.

Throwing one's sword was not a move that a swordsman would ever resort to, but Meisai was no swordsman—and next she threw the scabbard too, spinning it off her free hand in the same way, horizontally.

"Hah."

A volley of projectiles—scabbard flying after sword.

But after his experience, back on Haphazard Island, against the Star Cannon of Komori Maniwa, one of the Twelve Bosses of the Maniwa Clan—this was nothing. Shichika's palms were already extended, and he swatted both sword and scabbard to the heavens—he was certain that Meisai would be the next projectile in the series, but in fact she did the opposite.

The exact opposite.

She turned her back on Shichika—and sprinted off the other way.

"Wha...no."

Running? So soon? After whipping her sword?

Shichika's brain was abuzz with question marks—but the battle had begun. If the enemy ran, you had to chase them. He bounded over the flat stones in pursuit.

Leaving Togame, the judge, all alone.

"Ah..."

He could hear Togame's voice behind him, but there was nothing he could do—with her deplorable athletic skills, she had no hope of catching up to the two fighters.[13] Their battlefield extended to the edges of the grounds—an impossible range of terrain for Togame to monitor. All that remained for her to do was to carefully collect—without a scratch—the piece of the Legion that Shichika had thoughtlessly sent skyward.

But Shichika had his own difficulties catching up to Meisai, who stayed just ahead of him. In terms of physicality, he was overwhelmingly superior—but in a repeat of the day before, when they faced Kuizame Maniwa, run as

12 尋常に JINJŌ NI play fair
13 戦士 SENSHI warrior

he might the gap between them only grew—

Like the Kyotoryu, the Sentoryu was swordplay without a sword.

Indeed, Meisai's first move had been to throw away her sword—while dattojutsu and mutodori were not so uncommon, the benefit of specializing in them was the same as the Kyotoryu's—one need not be encumbered by a heavy, awkward sword. If your enemy carries your weapon for you, you can remain agile. The human body is basically complete on its own—even a small stone held in the palm will make a difference in your speed. It goes without saying that carrying a katana greatly impacted your maneuverability.[14]

He understood why Meisai was fast.

Yet—the same condition applied to him too.

If he had no katana either, how come he couldn't catch her?

The fact of the matter was that Meisai's legs were not as strong as Shichika assumed—he was stronger. The difference was in how each of them ran. Shichika simply dashed as fast as his legs would take him, but Meisai knew how to *outpace her opponent*, and how to *stay ahead*—you could say it was a more developed version of Kyotoryu Form Seven, the Kakitsubata, which Shichika used on Ginkaku Uneri back at Gekoku Castle.

Hollowed Ground[15]—a run peculiar to the Sentoryu.

Mind games,[16] as you might expect, were not Shichika's forte.

He was no stranger to tricky footwork, since he used it himself for the Kakitsubata, but he never imagined an enemy would use it back—the possibility hadn't so much as entered his mind. It had been the same with Komori Maniwa's transformational ninpo, the Body Melt.

But the Hollowed Ground could not be sustained. If they played this *game of tag* for long enough, Shichika would eventually catch Meisai, even with his normal run—and Meisai was thoroughly aware of this eventuality.

Aware—and prepared.

This was what distinguished her from Shichika, who automatically chased Meisai when she ran away.

When she made it to the offertory box in front of the haiden (Shichika was certain she would veer left or right), she turned to confront him.

A katana in her right hand.

And the katana—was the Legion!

"Hu...huh?!"

Shichika was running too fast to stop—as he was putting on the brakes, Meisai flashed her blade—

"One Liner—"[17]

[14] 機動力 KIDŌRYOKU mobility
[15] 地抜き JINUKI reverse display 地 JI (back)ground 抜き NUKI pulled out/pulling away
[16] 駆け引き KAKEHIKI dealing, horse trading
[17] 一刀・一文字斬り ITTŌ ICHIMONJI GIRI
slashing — ICHI, the one-stroke character for "one," using a single sword

Not as quick as Ginkaku Uneri and his Zerosen—but judging the cut far too fast to handle, Shichika gave up on slowing down and simply let his feet slide—so that his upper body leaned hard. Undeserving of the word "dodge," this was no more than a spill. Nevertheless, it did the job, and Shichika managed to avoid the flash of steel.

From this position, Shichika prepared for Meisai's next attack.[18]

He had to wonder: if she was unarmed, where had she found the katana? The answer became evident when Meisai, not about to chase Shichika over a cliff, returned the blade *into a scabbard stashed behind the offertory box.*

Before she ran away again.

This time, toward the thicket.

"Wha—"

Finding a Legion stashed behind the offertory box should have been enough for Shichika to get a read on the sort of battle Meisai had in store for him—but alas, his mind was at a standstill.

In fact, the unexpected confrontation with a blade made him lose most of his cool—while nowhere near as rapid as the Zerosen, the One Liner gave him flashbacks. The fear of swordplay, sown by the Zerosen, was festering in Shichika. It had yet to even surface as a weakness.

Which is why he thought nothing of chasing after Meisai.

The chaser and the chased—but in this game of tag, the latter, Meisai, clearly had the upper hand.

Running after her, diving into the thicket—Shichika finally realized the nature of the trap that she had lain for him. He had stepped right into it.

And now—he had no way of stepping out.

The shadows of a thicket. There was no reason to hide them—not in here.

Legions were bound—to the trunk of every tree.

Nay, not only the trees.

Buried in tufts of grass. Springing from the earth.

A bloom of steel.

The Legion bloomed—from every foot of forest.

A Legion had been hidden behind the offertory box—but it was not the only Legion hidden. Not the only one. And this thicket was not the only stash—doubtless the Possessed was scattered across the grounds. In the honden and the haiden, on top of the roof and on top of the torii—

The Legion awaited *everywhere.*

A thousand.

Blooming.[19]

Looming.[20]

[18] 二の太刀 NI NO TACHI "the second sword"
[19] あふれている AFURETE IRU to be overflowing
[20] ありふれている ARIFURETE IRU to be ubiquitous

Blooming everywhere.

Looming everywhere.

Now he grasped the reason Meisai confined their battle to the shrine premises. It was to prevent Shichika from exiting the zone covered by the Legion.

And at the same moment, he saw why she had wanted Togame to look for the first piece!

It was to buy herself time.

While Togame was absorbed in her investigation, Meisai must have been developing her plan for setting the Legion up around the grounds—which explained why she had seemed so busy. Where and how each sword was placed, and where and how to place them most effectively, required forethought. No crew could stash the swords on the fly in the space of a night. Nor anyone memorize the coordinates of each and every piece—

It made no difference to Meisai which Legion was "the original." Well, that may be an exaggeration, but if the task diverted Togame's attention from the grounds for long enough, it made all the difference.

Regardless of whether Togame had been correct, the fact that she had identified one sword as "the original" in the span of a week was perhaps more than Meisai had bargained for—but if she had time to shoot the breeze with Shichika the day before, she must have finished just in time.

And as far as barring Shichika from helping Togame was concerned—even supposing the story of the Kuromiko was no fib—it was just a way of keeping them apart.

Last night, while Shichika and Togame were slumbering in their teahouse—Meisai Tsuruga and the fifty Kuromiko on the mountaintop were stashing swords around the grounds.

Kyotoryu and Sentoryu.

So what if Shichika was unarmed.

If a thousand swords were sown across the grounds—it offered him no advantage.

Shichika had erred in thinking that he understood the Sentoryu the moment he saw Meisai clash with Kuizame—but it was too late in the game to recover from his failure to recognize anything beyond a variety of dattojutsu in the school. And the fact that he, a retainer, would hesitate to trouble Togame, exhausted from her weeklong search for the original, was perhaps exactly what Meisai had intended—

The Sentoryu was not designed for fighting one on one. Its moves depended on the presence of hundreds upon thousands of swordsmen clashing on a battlefield. Not content to seize an opponent's sword, the Sentoryu aimed to *harness the blades of an entire battleground*—the Legion of them!

Shichika had lost track of Meisai.

All he could see—was swords.

Just swords.

Sword after sword.

Nothing but swords.

Kiki Shikizaki's Mutant Blade—Sento the Legion.

Legion, Legion, Legion, Legion, Legion, Legion, Legion, Legion, Legion,
Legion, Legion, Legion, Legion, Legion, Legion, Legion, Legion, Legion,
Legion, Legion, Legion, Legion, Legion, Legion, Legion, Legion, Legion,
Legion, Legion, Legion, Legion, Legion, Legion, Legion, Legion, Legion,
Legion, Legion, Legion, Legion, Legion, Legion, Legion, Legion, Legion,
Legion, Legion, Legion, Legion, Legion, Legion, Legion, Legion, Legion,
Legion, Legion, Legion, Legion, Legion, Legion, Legion, Legion, Legion,
Legion, Legion, Legion, Legion, Legion, Legion, Legion, Legion, Legion,
Legion, Legion, Legion, Legion, Legion, Legion, Legion, Legion, Legion,
Legion, Legion, Legion, Legion, Legion, Legion, Legion, Legion, Legion,
Legion, Legion, Legion, Legion, Legion, Legion, Legion, Legion, Legion,
Legion, Legion, Legion, Legion, Legion, Legion, Legion, Legion, Legion,
Legion, Legion, Legion, Legion, Legion, Legion, Legion, Legion, Legion,
Legion, Legion, Legion, Legion, Legion, Legion, Legion, Legion, Legion,
Legion, Legion, Legion, Legion, Legion, Legion, Legion, Legion, Legion,
Legion, Legion, Legion, Legion, Legion, Legion, Legion, Legion, Legion,
Legion, Legion, Legion, Legion, Legion, Legion, Legion, Legion, Legion,
Legion, Legion, Legion, Legion, Legion, Legion, Legion, Legion, Legion,
Legion, Legion, Legion, Legion, Legion, Legion, Legion, Legion, Legion,
Legion, Legion, Legion, Legion, Legion, Legion, Legion, Legion, Legion,
Legion, Legion, Legion, Legion, Legion, Legion, Legion, Legion, Legion,
Legion, Legion, Legion, Legion, Legion, Legion, Legion, Legion, Legion,
Legion, Legion, Legion, Legion, Legion, Legion, Legion, Legion, Legion,
Legion, Legion, Legion, Legion, Legion, Legion, Legion, Legion, Legion,
Legion, Legion, Legion, Legion, Legion, Legion, Legion, Legion, Legion,
Legion, Legion, Legion, Legion, Legion, Legion, Legion, Legion, Legion,
Legion, Legion, Legion, Legion, Legion, Legion, Legion, Legion, Legion,
Legion, Legion, Legion, Legion, Legion, Legion, Legion, Legion, Legion,
Legion, Legion, Legion, Legion, Legion, Legion, Legion, Legion, Legion,
Legion, Legion, Legion, Legion, Legion, Legion, Legion, Legion, Legion,
Legion, Legion, Legion, Legion, Legion, Legion, Legion, Legion, Legion,
Legion, Legion, Legion, Legion, Legion, Legion, Legion, Legion, Legion,
Legion, Legion, Legion, Legion, Legion, Legion, Legion, Legion, Legion,
Legion, Legion, Legion, Legion, Legion, Legion, Legion, Legion, Legion,
Legion, Legion, Legion, Legion, Legion, Legion, Legion, Legion, Legion,
Legion, Legion, Legion, Legion, Legion, Legion, Legion, Legion, Legion,
Legion, Legion, Legion, Legion, Legion, Legion, Legion, Legion, Legion,

Legion, Legion, Legion, Legion, Legion, Legion, Legion, Legion, Legion,
Legion, Legion, Legion, Legion, Legion, Legion, Legion, Legion, Legion,
Legion, Legion, Legion, Legion, Legion, Legion, Legion, Legion, Legion,
Legion, Legion, Legion, Legion, Legion, Legion, Legion, Legion, Legion,
Legion, Legion, Legion, Legion, Legion, Legion, Legion, Legion, Legion,
Legion, Legion, Legion, Legion, Legion, Legion, Legion, Legion, Legion,
Legion, Legion, Legion, Legion, Legion, Legion, Legion, Legion, Legion,
Legion, Legion, Legion, Legion, Legion, Legion, Legion, Legion, Legion,
Legion, Legion, Legion, Legion, Legion, Legion, Legion, Legion, Legion,
Legion, Legion, Legion, Legion, Legion, Legion, Legion, Legion, Legion,
Legion, Legion, Legion, Legion, Legion, Legion, Legion, Legion, Legion,
Legion, Legion, Legion, Legion, Legion, Legion, Legion, Legion, Legion,
Legion, Legion, Legion, Legion, Legion, Legion, Legion, Legion, Legion,
Legion, Legion, Legion, Legion, Legion, Legion, Legion, Legion, Legion,
Legion, Legion, Legion, Legion, Legion, Legion, Legion, Legion, Legion,
Legion, Legion, Legion, Legion, Legion, Legion, Legion, Legion, Legion,
Legion, Legion, Legion, Legion, Legion, Legion, Legion, Legion, Legion,
Legion, Legion, Legion, Legion, Legion, Legion, Legion, Legion, Legion,
Legion, Legion, Legion, Legion, Legion, Legion, Legion, Legion, Legion,
Legion, Legion, Legion, Legion, Legion, Legion, Legion, Legion, Legion,
Legion, Legion, Legion, Legion, Legion, Legion, Legion, Legion, Legion,
Legion, Legion, Legion, Legion, Legion, Legion, Legion, Legion, Legion,
Legion, Legion, Legion, Legion, Legion, Legion, Legion, Legion, Legion,
Legion, Legion, Legion, Legion, Legion, Legion, Legion, Legion, Legion,
Legion, Legion, Legion, Legion, Legion, Legion, Legion, Legion, Legion,
Legion, Legion, Legion, Legion, Legion, Legion, Legion, Legion, Legion,
Legion, Legion, Legion, Legion, Legion, Legion, Legion, Legion, Legion,
Legion, Legion, Legion, Legion, Legion, Legion, Legion, Legion, Legion,
Legion, Legion, Legion, Legion, Legion, Legion, Legion, Legion, Legion,
Legion, Legion, Legion, Legion, Legion, Legion, Legion, Legion, Legion,
Legion, Legion, Legion, Legion, Legion, Legion, Legion, Legion, Legion,
Legion, Legion, Legion, Legion, Legion, Legion, Legion, Legion, Legion,
Legion, Legion, Legion, Legion, Legion, Legion, Legion, Legion, Legion,
Legion, Legion, Legion, Legion, Legion, Legion, Legion, Legion, Legion,
Legion, Legion, Legion, Legion, Legion, Legion, Legion, Legion, Legion,
Legion, Legion, Legion, Legion, Legion, Legion, Legion, Legion, Legion,
Legion, Legion, Legion, Legion, Legion, Legion, Legion, Legion, Legion,
Legion, Legion, Legion, Legion, Legion, Legion, Legion, Legion, Legion,
Legion, Legion, Legion, Legion, Legion, Legion, Legion, Legion, Legion,
Legion, Legion, Legion, Legion, Legion, Legion, Legion, Legion, Legion,
Legion, Legion, Legion, Legion, Legion, Legion, Legion, Legion, Legion,
Legion, Legion, Legion, Legion, Legion, Legion, Legion, Legion, Legion,

Legion, Legion, Legion, Legion, Legion, Legion, Legion, Legion, Legion,
Legion, Legion, Legion, Legion, Legion, Legion, Legion, Legion, Legion,
Legion, Legion, Legion, Legion, Legion, Legion, Legion, Legion, Legion,
Legion, Legion, Legion, Legion, Legion, Legion, Legion, Legion, Legion,
Legion, Legion, Legion, Legion, Legion, Legion, Legion, Legion, Legion,
Legion, Legion, Legion, Legion, Legion, Legion, Legion, Legion, Legion,
Legion, Legion, Legion, Legion, Legion, Legion, Legion, Legion, Legion,
Legion, Legion, Legion, Legion, Legion, Legion, Legion, Legion, Legion,
Legion, Legion, Legion, Legion, Legion, Legion, Legion, Legion, Legion,
Legion, Legion, Legion, Legion, Legion, Legion, Legion, Legion, Legion,
Legion, Legion, Legion, Legion, Legion, Legion, Legion, Legion, Legion,
Legion, Legion, Legion, Legion, Legion, Legion, Legion, Legion, Legion,
Legion, Legion, Legion, Legion, Legion, Legion, Legion, Legion, Legion,
Legion, Legion, Legion, Legion, Legion, Legion, Legion, Legion, Legion,
Legion, Legion, Legion, Legion, Legion, Legion, Legion, Legion, Legion,
Legion, Legion, Legion, Legion, Legion, Legion, Legion, Legion, Legion,
Legion, Legion, Legion, Legion, Legion, Legion, Legion, Legion, Legion,
Legion, Legion, Legion, Legion, Legion, Legion, Legion, Legion, Legion,
Legion, Legion, Legion, Legion, Legion, Legion, Legion, Legion, Legion,
Legion, Legion, Legion, Legion, Legion, Legion, Legion, Legion, Legion,
Legion, Legion, Legion, Legion, Legion, Legion, Legion, Legion, Legion,
Legion, Legion, Legion, Legion, Legion, Legion, Legion, Legion, Legion,
Legion, Legion, Legion, Legion, Legion, Legion, Legion, Legion, Legion,
Legion, Legion, Legion, Legion, Legion, Legion, Legion, Legion, Legion,
Legion, Legion, Legion, Legion, Legion, Legion, Legion, Legion, Legion,
Legion, Legion, Legion, Legion, Legion, Legion, Legion, Legion, Legion,
Legion, Legion, Legion, Legion, Legion, Legion, Legion, Legion, Legion,
Legion, Legion, Legion, Legion, Legion, Legion, Legion, Legion, Legion,
Legion, Legion, Legion, Legion, Legion, Legion, Legion, Legion, Legion,
Legion, Legion, Legion, Legion, Legion, Legion, Legion, Legion, Legion,
Legion, Legion, Legion, Legion, Legion, Legion, Legion, Legion, Legion,
Legion, Legion, Legion, Legion, Legion, Legion, Legion, Legion, Legion,
Legion!

An iron maiden[21] for the eyes—one thousand swords!

"Here's what happens when the Sentoryu partners with Sento the Legion," Meisai's voice, alone, sounded in the shadows of the thicket. "Terrain Effect: Thousand Sword Odyssey!"[22]

[21] 圧殺 ASSATSU being crushed to death

[22] 地形効果・千刀巡り CHIKEI KŌKA SENTŌ MEGURI
pun on 銭湯巡り SENTŌ MEGURI public-baths touring

■ ■

And now for the requisite reminiscence.[23]

This time, into the life of Meisai Tsuruga.

Her father was the commander of the second of the Three Goshin[24] Regiments, perennial protectors of the land of Izumo, and she was his only daughter. It goes without saying that at this point neither Meisai nor Tsuruga was her name—but there would be little reason to disclose what it used to be. For one thing, it all happened so long ago, and for another, her family no longer existed.

In addition to being commander of the second of the Three Goshin Regiments, her father headed a historic school of swordplay—specializing in the Sentoryu. The dojo and its signature style were so obscure that not even Togame had heard of them, but it was pedigreed, and unknown only because Izumo was autonomous.

Meisai was to be the next head of the dojo.

Which is why she had been drilled in the methods of the Sentoryu from her early years—

Swords are expendable—the school was founded on that premise. When swords are treated as expendable—there is no longer any reason to carry one yourself. Why bog yourself down with such a heavy thing when your enemies can carry your swords for you—simple. The ultimate unarmed means of self-defense,[25] and the ultimate defense of the sacred.[26] Such was the slogan of the Sentoryu.

The school had things in common with the Kyotoryu, and even with Togame's motto.

But it went further—expendable swords.

As any reader must have recognized, this was the exact premise upon which legendary swordsmith Kiki Shikizaki forged the Legion. Swords are expendable—obvious? Perhaps. But a school of swordplay and a Mutant Blade existed based on that same obvious principle, giving Meisai's ownership of the Legion a non-coincidental air, of destiny—or perhaps (though there would be no hope of proving such a thing), Kiki Shikizaki had been spurred to forge the Legion by an awareness of Izumo's tenacious school of swordplay. Sentoryu, Sento the Legion—if the overlapping names are no coincidence, the theory may very well be fact.

At any rate.

Looking backward—twenty years, to the time of the Rebellion.

[23] 場面回想 BAMEN KAISŌ to recollect scenes from the past
[24] 護神 GOSHIN guardians of the gods
[25] 護身術 GOSHIN JUTSU self-defense technique
[26] 護神術 GOSHIN JUTSU "god-guarding techniques" a pun on self-defense

During that unprecedented,[27] unmentionable[28] uprising, spearheaded by Takahito Hida, Kaoyaku of Oshu and father of Togame—not even Izumo, autonomous as it may be, was spared. Indeed, you might say that autonomy made things worse for Izumo, since they received no aid from the bakufu: not out in the open, and not behind the scenes.

All three of the Three Goshin Regiments were routed.

If it were not for independent contributions from neighboring provinces, the haven of the gods would have been wiped from the map. That they had staved things off at the proverbial water's edge had been a precious bit of good fortune among bad.

But misfortune was all Meisai knew.

Nothing that could be termed fortunate ever seemed to come her way.

Losing her family and her family name—she lived on the road, a young vagabond[29] by the time the Rebellion was suppressed. A war orphan.[30] Nobody to help her—and not about to ask for help.

Why not? Her value system had been irreparably shattered and pulverized by the Rebellion.

The Sentoryu, its dojo small enough to fly off if you blew on it, however obscure, was the ultimate form of self-defense, and the ultimate defense of the sacred—Meisai had believed this from the bottom of her heart. Surely it was the reason her father had risen to become commander of the second of the Three Goshin Regiments.

But such pride served no purpose during the Rebellion—her father perished, and every last one of his disciples died in battle.

She had stayed behind, becoming the only survivor.

Her pride and soul had not been worthy.

From there, the fall was straight down.

Waylaying pilgrims trekking pleasantly to Izumo, stripping them of all their belongings, and sometimes killing them without mercy—she became, in a word, a brigand. In these surprise highway attacks, it made no difference if her victim was a man at arms—actually, it made it better. The Sentoryu preferred an armed opponent.

Meisai had absolutely zero qualms in using the pedigreed Sentoryu for ill. After all, it had not proved itself worthy. She worked alone at first, doing as she pleased, but came to find that even the crime world had its factions and power structures. As an only daughter set to take over the family dojo, she had failed to see—or never thought to see that even the sacred land of Izumo was home to ruffians. Finding her legs in these rough waters, sometimes clashing swords, at other times colluding, Meisai eventually joined what was,

[27] 空前絶後 KŪZEN ZETSUGO never before or since
[28] 言語道断 GONGO DŌDAN not an option
[29] 放浪児 HŌRŌJI "wandering child"
[30] 戦災孤児 SENSAI KOJI a child whose parents fell victim to war

at the time, the greatest band of brigands in Izumo, where she found her place.

The fact that Sento the Legion had been passed down among the brigands, from one chieftain to the next—was not what had attracted her, but she certainly did know that they held the Mutant Blade prior to joining them.

Well. No sense going any further.

A tale Meisai, at least, wished she could forget.

No need to reminisce.

What are you fighting for? she had asked Shichika—and the answer volunteered by Kuizame Maniwa, one of the Twelve Bosses of the Maniwa Clan, was correct.

If you have to be asking such questions, don't even bother fighting—

Nobody has time for your philosophy—don't be ridiculous—

And it was—ridiculous.

Indeed, during her thirteen years as a brigand, she never stopped to think about it once. *What are you fighting for? What are you killing for?* She did not have the time for philosophy.

She simply fought.

Simply killed.

Not exactly to survive.

Not because she didn't want to die.

She just did what she did—nothing more.

It was a few years after she had found herself the chieftain, after being with the brigands thirteen years and coming into the Legion—that Meisai faced the question for the first time, in her raid on Triad Shrine.

She showed up alone, a scout scoping things out in a manner unbefitting of a chieftain, and wound up killing all the priests—including the old Meisai Tsuruga, who led the place at the time. Triad Shrine had yet to become a fortress, so the priests were unarmed—hence she did not kill them using the Sentoryu.

She strangled them. Neck by neck.

A primitive way to kill.

But she had no remorse.

The raid was not her idea, but she had known about the shrine's beginnings since she was a little girl who would someday inherit the dojo. The place was a sanitarium for suffering womankind[31]—then how come—

How come they hadn't saved her?

She had become a brigand of her own volition.

Refused to ask for help, too, of her own volition.

And yet.

Saving even hopeless people is what makes the gods the gods!

[31] 弱き女たち YOWAKI ON'NA TACHI "women, who are weak" or "women in weak positions"

"Forgive us," the head priest squeaked out while he was being strangled.

The old Meisai Tsuruga.

She thought he was begging for his life. In which case, she had heard it all before.

She had never once listened to them.

But no—she was wrong.

"Forgive us—for not being able to save you." His voice was terribly calm. "But please, find it in your heart—to spare *those girls*."

Those girls did no wrong.

Those were his last words.

Not one of her victims had ever said anything of the sort, which must be why she found herself pondering, for the first time—

What are you fighting for?

What are you killing for?

And what are you living for?

She was not feeling guilty; it was not some awakening[32]—nothing had changed. She just found herself pondering the questions.

If there was a precise moment when she became Meisai Tsuruga—this was it.

Upon returning to the brigand stronghold,[33] she killed all forty-three of her comrades. It took very little of her time. Unlike the unarmed priests, her brigand friends were always armed. And the more heavily armed and numerous the opponents, the stronger the powers exhibited by the Sentoryu—ironically, these thirteen years of living without pride, and using the Sentoryu as an instrument of the brigands, had served to polish her technique. She had been particularly effective in the last few years, as Sento the Legion's inheritor. Her brigand friends—perhaps a pleasantry like "friends" was no longer appropriate—at any rate, those guys never knew what hit them and were massacred, all forty-three, with no time to fight back. Whereupon she took up residence at Triad Shrine under the name Meisai Tsuruga, bringing with her Sento the Legion, one of the Twelve Possessed, the masterpieces of Kiki Shikizaki.

Thus Triad Shrine was reborn as a fortress.

It had been seven years.

She still thought back on it sometimes.

What was it about that handful of words that gave her such a push—to utterly reject[34] those thirteen years?

Was it sympathy? Regret?

She wasn't sure.

If she were to ask Shichika Yasuri, he would probably answer that he had

[32] 改心 KAISHIN "renewed heart"

[33] 根城 NEJIRO "root castle" base of operations

[34] 全否定 ZEN HITEI complete negation

no idea—he didn't understand what made her tick,[35] at all. Togame, on the other hand, might. She was the daughter of the Mastermind of the Rebellion who was responsible for altering the course of Meisai's life—as well as her own.

They had both abandoned their names.

Perhaps they could see eye to eye.

But Meisai had lost interest in that sort of thing—at this point, all she knew for certain was that helping the thousand Kuromiko sheltered at Triad Shrine was helping her.

She seemed to be helping them—but in fact was saving herself.

Right, the gods wouldn't save her. The gods existed to be served.

To paraphrase a politician[36] from a later era—ask not what the gods can do for you, but what you can do for the gods.

Thus—Togame's offer was just what she needed.[37] No matter how dangerous the bridge,[38] she was prepared to cross, overlooking any danger, if it meant obtaining two more Mutant Blades.

Zetto the Leveler and Zanto the Razor.

Two more of *those girls*—could be rescued.

No, the venom would not be split into a thousand portions, like with Sento the Legion. They would be more potent, saving Meisai all the more.

Which is why she had absolutely no misgivings about defeating Shichika and acquiring two more of the Possessed.

She hatched a plan.

Laid her trap.

Fought dirty.

Because I'm fighting for those girls!

Which was to say, for herself.

"What's it gonna be?"

About half an hour after Togame had signaled them to start.

Meisai Tsuruga called out to Shichika.

With his back to a great tree, he scanned the thicket—but couldn't see Meisai anywhere, while she could see him just fine.

She had the home advantage.

In her seven years as steward of these woods, these grounds, and all of Triad Shrine—she had not been steward in name only,[39] but in earnest. Seeing Shichika backed up against the tree—she knew a Legion had been stashed there.

If she shot over to where he stood and grabbed the blade—she could

[35] 行動原理 KŌDŌ GENRI behavioral principle
[36] 政治家 SEIJIKA politician; the JFK allusion that follows is the author's and not a localization
[37] 渡りに船 WATARI NI FUNE a boat at a river crossing
[38] 危ない橋 ABUNAI HASHI "dangerous bridge" common figure of speech for a risky venture
[39] 伊達に DATE NI for show

almost certainly kill him. Since invoking the Thousand Sword Odyssey, she had kept Shichika running, and he was showing signs of fatigue. Of course he was. That was her plan—in fact, for the last half hour, she had not been trying to kill him. That went for the sword she hurled at Shichika at the onset of the battle, needless to say, and so too the One Liner at the offertory box was meant to be dodged.

She was trying to tucker him out.

Clearly, she would never best a man as big as him through strength alone—which was why she had been pulling strings[40] all week. Although she hadn't been so bold as to lace his food with poison, the two meals per day she had been feeding them, while fine for someone as spritely as Togame, could not have satisfied a man like Shichika.

She had set the scene for victory, from the first detail.

And now they were arriving at the last.

It was time to finish things up.

"We agreed surrender was an option—as a servant of the gods, I will never take a life for no good reason.[41] The gap in skill is clear. If you say mercy, I am ready to oblige."

"..."

No answer from Shichika.

Try as he may to pinpoint where her voice was coming from—it was in vain. Her words were not a tease intent on laying bare her position. Taunting was a rookie move—and one she had surpassed long before becoming a brigand.

She went on.

"Resistance is futile—the Kyotoryu is no match for my Thousand Sword Odyssey. Our schools may share the practice of not carrying a sword, but in the heat of battle, the Sentoryu is a cut above."

...If Togame had been present, she would have shot down Meisai with a few choice words—the fact of the matter being that it was irrational, even now, to claim that Shichika was automatically at a flagrant disadvantage to Meisai.

He had assumed that he would have the upper hand, and if all that the Thousand Sword Odyssey accomplished was to upend that premise, they were simply even.

Losing his advantage did not place him at a disadvantage.

Shichika had not been cornered.

Unleashing her Double Cross on Kuizame Maniwa, ostensibly to offset her unfair knowledge of the Kyotoryu, had an element of deception that was far from sporting.[42]

[40] 根回し NEMAWASHI "spreading roots" often used to mean "getting people on board beforehand"
[41] 無益な殺生 MUEKI NA SESSHŌ (set phrase) killing living things when there is no benefit
[42] 武士道 BUSHIDŌ the samurai code

She had granted him a temporary sense of superiority only to snatch it back.

If Shichika won the duel, their prize[43] would be Sento the Legion, but if Meisai won, both Zetto the Leveler and Zanto the Razor would be hers—and just as Togame had used these disproportionate, overtly advantageous terms as bait, so as to lure Meisai into the duel—Meisai had granted Shichika a temporary sense of superiority to lull him into complacency.

Just so she could visit her Thousand Sword Odyssey on his lulled mind.

And now—reminding him that he could ask for mercy was more deception at a far cry from niceties like her supposed aversion to needless slaughter.

It was better to win without a fight.

Breaking his spirit, so that he saw himself at a disadvantage, as being unable to win, as having no hope of winning—was better for Meisai. Going for the kill, into the fray, there was no small chance that she would meet her match.

In a clash of blades—Shichika would likely realize he was at no disadvantage.

Meisai was not so doggedly opposed to throwing down as to avoid it at all costs—but she was hoping to get by without allowing Shichika to rally.

Fear and aversion.

Meisai was well versed in their application.

"What's it gonna be—"

While easygoing as ever, Meisai was adamant—persistent in her speech.

She was well aware these circumstances were not in fact so advantageous—but from her tone of voice, the sort taken toward a misbehaving child, you never would have known. Even if Shichika did not accept her ultimatum,[44] she was sure her domineering language would make him agitated—and start to think things.

Thinking—that was good.

He could think and think—until his brain went flop.

A man of Shichika's intelligence would not get far by thinking.

Which is why, regardless of his inclination, Meisai needed to spell things out.

"Why not call it a loss? I'm sure that for the shogunate, this Sword Hunt is no more than an amusement. It's not worth risking your life. Not for this mission. The Kyotoryu was no match for the Sentoryu. That's all there is to it—"

Shichika Yasuri. Island monkey. No combat experience.

Meisai Tsuruga. Thirteen years among brigands.

The disparity was insurmountable.

Unless.

"...You do eat meat, right?" Shichika asked softly. He had given up on

[43] 戦利品 SENRIHIN spoils of war

[44] 最後通牒 SAIGO TSŪCHŌ "final notification" translation of the Western word used in int'l relations

figuring out where Meisai was—and spoke looking nowhere in particular, as if to himself.

"Huh. Meat?"

"Yeah, meat—eating animals. I do."

Faced with this non sequitur, Meisai was bewildered—had she pushed him over the edge? That had not been her intention. Now she would never get him to plead for mercy—

With no regard for what she may be thinking, Shichika continued with his *gobbledygook*.

"Togame has no problem drinking that bitter water of yours, but then she goes and says she can't believe that I eat meat, like it's so gross... Me and sis did from the second we got teeth. Raw, fried, boiled, steamed...it tasted totally different from whatever plants we dug up or the fish we caught—I haven't eaten meat since I started off with her, and man, I miss it..."

"...? What's stopping you? Eating meat—is far from strange, at least among warriors. Not that I partake myself—"

"Back on the island too, beasts were quite nimble—you couldn't catch them just by chasing them. So they were a rare treat. You're fast, but it'd be hard for you too. If you really wanted some meat, you had to lay a trap."

A trap—a trap like the Thousand Sword Odyssey.

"But that's easier said than done for an idiot like me. Once, I set one near our hut...and sis got caught in it... That was crazy."

"..."

"Get it? Traps are for prey... You don't surround your house with them."

"What are you trying to say?" demanded Meisai, exasperated by his ramblings. "What is it that you've been trying to say this last minute? If you're ready to surrender, then—"

"One," Shichika stated emphatically. "One idea is all I've got."

"Huh?"

"I've been trying to figure a way out of this—Thousand Sword Odyssey. No matter how perfect it looks, there's gotta be a hole or—"

"No holes," Meisai interrupted. "The Thousand Sword Odyssey is invincible. The Sentoryū is the ultimate means of self-defense, and the ultimate—defense of the sacred."

"I want to test whether that's true—whether the Sentoryu is really better than the Kyotoryu!" yelled Shichika—before dashing off.

His choice of direction gave Meisai pause—*crap!* Instantly, she grew tense. Impossible—but with the way things were going, *impossible* no more.

Had the boy—figured it out?

Slow as he was?

"Nkk..."

In a mind game, Meisai dominated Shichika—that much was true.

How—ever.

In her desire to provoke and agitate, she had made the one mistake which, as Shichika's opponent, she would have done well to avoid—in passing judgment on the Kyotoryu, she should have accounted for the incompleteness of his personal development as a swordsman. She should never have condemned the school outright based on his performance.

You could also say she had made too much of his comment about killing his own father, the previous Master.

In any case, it was a genuine mistake—having thrown away her pride in her own school long ago, well over twenty years now, she no longer felt its absence, making the error practically inevitable. *The Thousand Sword Odyssey is invincible. The Sentoryu is the ultimate means of self-defense, and the ultimate defense of the sacred*—but since nobody believed this less than Meisai, sound judgment of another school evaded her.

The difference was this: while Meisai had ranked the Sentoryu against the Kyotoryu simply in order to define her strategy—Shichika regarded their duel as a true test of his school against hers.

After nineteen years of incessant training under his father, the pride that Shichika felt for the Kyotoryu was—extraordinary. Carefree as he appeared, his affection for his school was unimaginable.

Which is why Meisai should never have put down the Kyotoryu.

Along with fear and aversion—she had fostered anger.

She knew better—anger links to passion, and passion, dissolving fear and aversion, can even hatch a kind of miraculous intelligence.

"Whah—what the heck!"

Of course Meisai could not have known the reason for her error—lacking pride in her own school, the paradigm was lost to her. Without a clue—all she could do was pursue Shichika.

While nowhere near as muscular as Shichika, Meisai had higher odds, as the better runner and a master of the *game of tag*—if she could only catch up with him before he reached *it*, she could use one of the swords stashed here and there and slash him from behind!

But in the end, Meisai could not catch up with Shichika. Starting from the thicket worked against her in this instance—she certainly had the home advantage on these premises, but once they had plunged into the thicket, the gap between them narrowed—growing up on Haphazard Island, where almost everything was mountain, Shichika had lived for twenty years among the trees.

Wherever the earth was unmaintained, Shichika expanded his lead in the footrace, but such an easy rationale sounds forced—perhaps we should say that he was angry enough to overcome any difference in running ability. Bursting from the thicket, he made one last enormous bound and kicked up a cloud of dust where his bare feet touched down.

When Meisai saw him fly, she stopped.

Stopping was her only option.

No use catching him now.

Because—they had arrived at *an area where not a single Legion had been stashed*. Even if she reached him, she would have no sword with which to slash him.

"Yup...thought so..." Shichika said slowly, as if his suspicions were confirmed, before turning to face his foe. "Thousand Sword Odyssey or not—there's no way you'd stash any *here*...isn't that right, Meisai Tsuruga. Say what you will about me, but you gotta be real careful around Togame—"

They were standing at the place the guests had been staying for a week—the teahouse. Right in front of it.

■ ■

Terrain Effect: Thousand Sword Odyssey.

The Sentoryu in concert[45] with Sento the Legion—swords stashed all around the battlefield, Meisai could face her enemy unarmed. Thanks to this tour de force, Shichika felt like he was fighting one on a thousand.

It mattered that the thousand swords were Sento the Legion, that mass-produced masterpiece of Kiki Shikizaki. In the Sentoryu, it was not some trusty[46] weapon that was wielded, but the enemy's—thus it changed from one enemy to the next. Except in the Thousand Sword Odyssey, where all thousand of the swords were the same. Every sword could be wielded the same way.

Sento the Legion might have been made expressly for the Sentoryu—if a katana chose its owner, the Legion had most definitely picked the Sentoryu.

A custom fit, in every way.

But in spite of, or perhaps because of this—it was crucial to set up the Odyssey with the utmost care. A trap can only be effective if it is not discovered prematurely—which is why all thousand swords had to be stashed around the grounds the night before. And in such a way that neither Shichika nor Togame would catch on.

Hence the hole in the stash.

The teahouse—where they slept.

It may be going too far to say this was a defect[47] in her strategy. Expecting things would come to this, Meisai had asked them to sleep in the teahouse,

45 共同合作 KYŌDŌ GASSAKU joint effort, collaborative work
46 愛用 AIYŌ "lovingly used"
47 瑕疵 KASHI flaw; blemish

and not the honden, to minimize the area where no swords were stashed.

She had been positive the winner would be decided before Shichika—or Togame—noticed the defect. She had bolted when the duel began, luring her foe into the thicket and the vast number of Legions stashed therein—but her main objective was to create as much distance as possible between Shichika and the teahouse.

If she had not been so gratuitously provocative, he might never have realized. Or perhaps if she had retained a shred of pride for the Sentoryu—

But she was a day late[48]—if not a sword short.

Turning toward Meisai, Shichika assumed Form One—the Suzuran. He was tired from their tour of the thicket, and it showed—but the crushing claustrophobia[49] had dispersed.

He was no longer one against a thousand.

And the stifling situational disadvantage—was no more.

"Phew..." Meisai sighed morosely at the sight of Shichika in his stance. She had the mood of someone totally acknowledging, and accepting, her defeat. She spoke equally morosely. "Even if you win the sword, you'll still need to figure out a plan for shipping it back to Owari, right?"

"..."

"If I should lose the duel, the Kuromiko have been asked to cooperate, and will hand-deliver the Legion to the bakufu... Having each tote a piece will hide[50] the treasure in plain sight. Feel free to adopt the plan."

"...Tell me you're kidding."

Rather than respond, Meisai persisted. "In exchange, I ask the bakufu to safeguard the futures of the thousand Kuromiko—all but me—and the fate of Triad Shrine."

"Come on. That's—"

"In appointing my successor, they will need to dispatch someone with the necessary level of compassion and sensitivity toward matters of the heart. While the bakufu may be a swamp full of ghosts and goblins,[51] there must be at least one person who fills that description. The Kuromiko who has made the furthest progress in her recovery, whom I have already designated, will serve as a proxy until then—if you have questions, you can ask her."

"Does this mean—you forfeit?"

"Um, no?"

Meisai shook her head and reached down by her feet—to where a Legion had apparently been buried in the earth. She leisurely freed the sword from the soil and held it up at middle guard.

"But the possibility of losing has become too real to ignore—so much so

48 あとの祭り ATO NO MATSURI "post-festival"
49 窮屈 KYŪKUTSU hemmed in
50 偽装 GISŌ "fake attire" disguise, camouflage
51 魑魅魍魎 CHIMI MŌRYŌ evil spirits of the hills and streams

I feel obliged to get my affairs in order. But I am not forfeiting this match. I will stop at nothing to obtain the Leveler and the Razor."

"..."

"In my book, without due resolve nothing is gained—I say this risking everything, prepared to lose my life. Which is why I have no problem asking that much of the Schemer. Both of you are still too young to understand, but being outsmarted by someone younger than you is not such an awful feeling. Yet...yet. It may sound like I'm contradicting[52] myself, but I went into this duel ready to be defeated...it's like I said. Maybe I've been waiting for people like you to come here all along."

"..."

"As far as contradictions go—to think I used the katana's poison to help these women. Relying on those murdersome swords for life—I always believed it was a mistake. But also a necessary evil—"

"..."

"Poison or medicine, at the end of the day, the Legion is a butcher knife.[53] I would be lying if I said there was no other way. I mean, the old Meisai Tsuruga needed nothing like a Mutant Blade—because he knew how to run a shrine. I say I'm going to help these women—and then I give them weapons. But was that correct? If these women were abused[54] under the sword—how could giving them swords ever save them? They may be using the venom as medicine—but if I cannot bear to part with them, the medicine must be poison after all. Force is the only way you'd ever take them."

"..."

"But correct or not, perhaps I had no other choice. Because I was waiting, for people like you, who would crush my worthless views, and the necessary evil of the sword's venom—kindly negating my erroneous methods—"

Hold on though.

What if this was all part of her strategy too?

Diversionary tactics.

What if she was only being sentimental to stir up Shichika all over again, when he had finally calmed down—regardless of her intentions, with the way her story was developing, the outcome was highly probable. Meisai should have known from their talk the day before that such diversions rarely worked on Shichika—but he was not entirely immune.

However—Shichika was thinking something altogether different. He had been silent thus far not because he was processing what Meisai said—but because he was fixated on the Legion that Meisai had pulled out of the ground.

This sword—made him feel it.

[52] 矛盾 MUJUN "spear shield" (the word alludes to an imaginary contest between a spear that pierces all shields and a shield that blocks all spears)

[53] 人斬り包丁 HITOKIRI BŌCHŌ "man cleaver"

[54] 虐げられる SHIITAGE RARERU to be oppressed overtone of 虐待 GYAKUTAI abuse

The exact same sensation he had felt the month before beholding Zanto the Razor in the hands of Ginkaku Uneri, back at Gekoku Castle.

Shichika was positive.[55]

The sword Meisai Tsuruga was pointing was Sento the Legion—no.

The *original* Legion.

Togame's argument stood the test of logic—or at least was sufficiently persuasive—but Shichika now realized that she must have been wrong. Her "first piece" was not the original.

No matter how neatly the argument had stacked, her inference could not be absolute—what was absolute was this sensation.

In crafting the original Legion, Kiki Shikizaki had left no identifying mark, after all.

Doing so would have been antithetical to his abnormality.

But this—was the original.

The Legion's *template*.

That she would draw the piece here, at the final stage—a one in a thousand chance—Meisai Tsuruga...

The katana had chosen her.

Just like I chose Togame—Meisai was chosen, by the Legion.

That said everything. Shichika braced himself.

If gaining the advantage, once and for all, had spawned even the slightest negligence in Shichika, this purged it. In which case, drawing the original Legion against thousand-to-one odds was in fact luckless.

But this, too, was fate, and necessity, if she had been chosen.

Chosen to possess—Sento the Legion.

"I am Shichika Yasuri, Seventh Master of the Kyotoryu—bring it on."

Answered Meisai, "As Mistress of Mt. Taizan, Izumo's Triad Shrine...no." She broke off and closed her eyes. "I am Meisai Tsuruga, Twelfth Master of the Sentoryu—here I come."

It was hard to tell what she was feeling when she said this. She had neither regained her pride in her school, nor meant it as some mind game.

"Time to show you the secrets of the Sentoryu."

"Not if you're torn to smithereens."

Finally—the fight began.

A fair fight, with no strategies, or tactics, or mind games, or traps.

Meisai Tsuruga versus Shichika Yasuri.

The Sentoryu versus the Kyotoryu.

And Sento the Legion versus Kyoto the Diamond.

May the best sword win!

"Hah."

Just like at the beginning, Meisai threw her sword spinning through the

[55] 確信 KAKUSHIN "definite belief"

air at Shichika, and once again, he swatted it heavenward—as expected.

Against the exact same move in the exact same circumstances, he would respond in the exact same way, being no veteran—she had been certain that he would swat away the Legion.

And Meisai's next move was precisely the one Shichika had anticipated at the beginning. In other words, after her sword she shot forth, unarmed, and at terrific speed—but on her last step, she leapt into the sky and caught the sword midair.

The Sentoryu.

Even a soaring katana—belonged to it.

"Rolling Thunder!"[56]

Shichika countered her sword with a Fatal Orchid.

With the utmost respect, with the fastest move available to him at that moment.

A rigid stance, as if his legs had grown roots—paired with a twisting of the hips so furious they threatened to tear free.

In your face.[57]

The heel of his hand shot forth from Form One!

"Kyotoryu—Kyoka Suigetsu!"[58]

■ ■

"Huff, huff, huff, huff, ugh...huff, huff, huff, huff...ack."

Togame had lost sight of Shichika and Meisai no sooner than their duel began, but as her innately serious and scrupulous personality would not permit her to leave her post as official witness and referee, she wandered the grounds, nearly reduced to tears—until she found them.

By then, it was all over.

What she saw when she arrived in the vicinity of the teahouse was Shichika Yasuri in a relaxed stance, staring at his left hand, freshly drenched in blood, and Meisai Tsuruga lying on her back, clinging to Sento the Legion—the imprint of a hand forced through her ribcage.

"Shi-Shichika."

"Hey, Togame." Hearing her voice, Shichika looked toward her with an invigorated smile. "I won," he reported his victory with pride. "No room for a bad call, as you can see."

[56] 空中一刀・億文字斬り KŪCHŪ ITTŌ OKUMONJI GIRI (空中 KŪCHŪ midair, in the sky) slashing 億 OKU, the many-stroked character for "hundred million," using one aerial sword

[57] 単純にして明快 TANJUN NI SHITE MEIKAI clear and simple; often just 単純明快 TANJUN MEIKAI

[58] 鏡花水月 KYŌKA SUIGETSU "Mirror Flower, Water Moon" i.e. reflections, the mere image

Togame—gazed upon the body of Meisai Tsuruga.

By now, demonstrably a corpse.

Meisai Tsuruga—Mistress of Triad Shrine.

Former brigand.

Togame knew little of the woman's early years—but enough to hazard a guess. No, not just about her—the Schemer was certain that all thousand of the Kuromiko serving the shrine had personal circumstances rivaling, even surpassing her own *reasons*.

Parents murdered.

Families massacred.

Lineages eradicated.

Such tales—were common at this shrine.

And yet.

Togame had brushed it all aside, for the sake of her own reasons, her own ambition, her own revenge.

"Shichika, did you really—" she began to ask.

Did you really need to kill her?

She almost asked—her katana.

In her thirteen years among the brigands, Meisai Tsuruga had slain countless innocents—a crime that could never be forgiven no matter how she apologized or atoned.

No matter how many of the girls at Triad Shrine she assisted by turning the Legion's poison into medicine—her efforts were hypocritical.

No, apology and atonement were in and of themselves hypocrisy.

Meisai Tsuruga bore the burden—of a crime that could never be forgiven.

And yet.

Togame had no right to judge.

She was only here—to take the sword.

To further her self-centered[59] agenda.

"Huh? What's wrong? Togame."

The look on his face—was honest and undisturbed, not what you would expect from someone who had just taken a life.

A sword that could kill—without due resolve—relinquishing nothing.

A katana did not choose who to kill.

But—it chose its owner.

In which case—she had killed Meisai Tsuruga.

And this road—Togame herself had chosen it.

She had walked too far along it to turn off or turn back.

If her resolve could be compromised by such trifling disturbances—she would have given it up long ago.

"Shichika—"

[59] 自分勝手 JIBUN KATTE doing as one pleases

Togame stifled the emotion in her voice.

Swallowing her cowardice,[60] she spoke with bravado.[61]

"Well done."

60 弱気 YOWAKI "weak ki" timid
61 強気 TSUYOKI "strong ki" bold

EPILOGUE

■ ■

That evening, Shichika and Togame left Triad Shrine behind. The Kuromiko responded to the death of Meisai far more calmly than Togame had expected—you could even say coolly. Perhaps this should have come as no surprise, but faced with the loss of the guiding force behind Triad Shrine as they knew it, the girls appeared to have no interest in what might happen to them. This was no different for the Kuromiko whom Meisai had tasked with the aftermath—but for the single comment, a kind of a reflection, whereby she hinted at her thoughts: "So it has finally come to this." Togame had no way of knowing what this was supposed to mean or why it had been voiced at all.

"Okay, what's next?" Shichika asked Togame—walking beside her down the thousand steps.

"...Next?"

"You know...on the Sword Hunt."

"Ah—now that we have the Legion, along with the Leveler and the Razor, we have three of the Twelve Possessed—I think it's time we paid a visit to Owari. Three swords should make for a good present."

"Huh."

"It will be necessary for me to explain you to my superior—to be honest, I hired you without prior approval. But your track record speaks for itself. It's a done deal."

"Track record, huh. Three swords in three months—guess it does speak for itself. The hunt is going quicker than I thought—when I heard the Old Shogun failed to collect the Twelve Possessed for all his might, I couldn't imagine what that meant for us, but since we only have nine more to go, I'd say it's doable."

"Don't get comfortable. We live in a peaceful world. The current owners of the swords are not to be compared to those who owned them back in the Old Shogun's days. As a ruler and sovereign, he was tyrannical. Schemes like mine operate on the opposite end of the spectrum. Remember, we have the luxury of profiting from his mistakes."

"Makes sense."

"Not another arrogant word out of your mouth, you understand? Doing something someone else has failed to do is no excuse to brag."

"I understand. I just got a little excited, okay? Don't be so nagging. So what happens at Owari? Will we meet the Shogun?"

"You idiot." It was rare for Shichika to be so inquisitive, but Togame chopped his question in two. "I doubt the two of us will enjoy an audience with His Excellency until we have secured all twelve of the swords."

"Oh."

"Do you want to meet His Excellency?"

"No, I don't care."

I don't care—with those words, Shichika stopped that conversation short. Obviously all he had wanted to know was whether *Togame* was going to meet the Shogun, but since she would not touch upon this, he felt it was not his place to intrude.

Not yet.

"Anyway—what kind of place is Owari? Is it like Kyoto?"

"Similar in scale, but Owari is not as flowery[1] as the capital. Kyoto is like a carnival, all year round—and Owari is, well, a working city. More serious and solemn."

"Oh."

"The way that things have been arranged, it looks like we'll be reaching Owari Castle before all thousand pieces of the Legion have been delivered—but we'll make do."

"Yeah, but..." Shichika looked back over his shoulder—and, recalling the shrine's premises, brimming with a thousand swords, he asked, "Are you gonna be okay?"

"Excuse me?"

"I mean, that was kind of a rash thing to promise—safeguarding the futures of a thousand women. Can you do that when this shrine is—"

"I was merely exercising my abilities," Togame said. "If the Yanari Bakufu cannot accommodate another thousand women, it has no right to its reputation."

"Okay..." muttered Shichika, not really getting it. But as a sword, this was perhaps not something he needed to get—or profited from getting.

"Not such a bad deal for the bakufu, insofar as it would establish intimate relations with Izumo, which is otherwise autonomous. Now that it's lost the Legion—Triad Shrine will likely abandon its status as a fortress, but this would only mean returning to what it was before things changed."

"Before things changed."

"Before the katana—changed everything."

"Then maybe Meisai should have tried that from the beginning. Instead of being all greedy and trying to win the Leveler and the Razor."

Being all greedy, she had perished—

"She was far from greedy—but since she was ultimately the owner, Meisai could never free herself entirely from the venom of the Shikizaki blades. We were forced to pry them from her cold, dead hands."

"Yeah...but what would you have done?"

[1] 華やか HANAYAKA showy echoes 花 HANA flower

"Me?"

"If I had lost—would you have given her the Leveler and the Razor, like we agreed?"

"Mumble mumble."[2]

"Excuse me?!"

"I-I would have had to wait to see if—no, I was certain you would never lose!"

"...You really put your neck on the line, too—what's the word? Fearless? Fearsome?[3] Like that thing with the first piece."

"What about it?"

"Yeah...we'll talk about that later—I'm still trying to sort things out...but let's just say I felt for myself what makes these Kiki Shikizaki swords different from normal swords—totally apart from the venom or the medicine or whatever. What I really wanna know is, what does that mean?"

"Don't think too hard, Shichika. It didn't exactly help you out this time, did it? And of course, I wound up missing your Fatal Orchid, yet again. How am I supposed to write my report? Such a headache."

"First Komori Maniwa, then Ginkaku Uneri, and now Meisai Tsuruga... are you just not meant to watch me in action?"

"M-Mrg..."

Togame was unable to respond.

In light of the facts, he certainly had a point. In order to write her report, and to supervise Shichika, her katana—she needed to come up with a decent plan.

"Guess it's time for us to say goodbye to these stairs," Shichika noted. "Makes me kinda sorry to be leaving."

Vaguely aware of Togame's trouble[4] with the steps, he had kept apace with her, maintaining a steady footing. They were halfway down the mountain, having descended a great deal—around five hundred steps.

"You're sorry about the staircase, but not the shrine? You weirdo."

"No, it just makes me kind of sad to know I'll never carry you like that again. No matter where this Sword Hunt takes us, I'll probably never have a chance to hold you in my arms—"

"Ch-Cheerio!"

Hoping to teach him not to be so daft with women, Togame sent her fist flying. The fact that they were halfway up a mountainside, and on cruelly steep stairs, completely slipped her mind. They were descending them, too.

As expected, she lost her footing.

"Ah!"

"Whoop—"

[2] ごにょごにょ GONYO GONYO onomatopoeia for mumbling
[3] 大胆...不敵 DAITAN...FUTEKI usually used together as 大胆不敵 audacious
[4] 懊悩 ŌNŌ anguish

Shichika reached out to catch Togame—and caught her wrist midair, but in the process leaned perilously from the staircase. She was so sprightly that she weighed nothing compared to him, but when she tugged at his outstretched limb like that, he had no hope of staying balanced.

"—ps, oops, oops, uh oh."

"Wh—ah!"

Thus, hopelessly entangled, they tumbled down the remaining five hundred or so steps, rolling faster and faster.

■ ■

They had yet to realize, as they fell.

That they would not be returning to Owari without further ado.

That on the road ahead, the Strongest Swordsman in Japan, the Fallen Swordsman who had willingly fallen from his seat as the Strongest, who had tamed Hakuto the Whisper, the most unwieldy masterpiece among Kiki Shikizaki's Twelve Possessed—for whom nomenclature like Sword Master and Sword Saint[5] were intended—that none other than Hakuhei Sabi awaited his turn with them.

Sento the Legion: Check
End of Book Three
To Be Continued

[5] 剣豪剣聖 KENGŌ KENSEI terms applied to the best of them, e.g. Musashi Miyamoto

CHARACTER INDEX 3

MEISAI TSURUGA

AGE	Unknown
OCCUPATION	Servant of the Gods
AFFILIATION	Triad Shrine
STATUS	Miko
POSSESSED	Sento the Legion
HEIGHT	5' 10"
WEIGHT	115 lbs.
HOBBY	Drinking

LIST OF SPECIAL MOVES

HOLLOWED GROUND	←↙↓ KICK
ONE LINER	→→→ SLASH + KICK
DOUBLE CROSS	→↓↑← SLASH + THRUST
ROLLING THUNDER	←↖↑↗→ SLASH SLASH SLASH
TERRAIN EFFECT: THOUSAND SWORD ODYSSEY	↓↓↑↑ SLASH + THRUST + KICK

OPPONENT	Hakuhei Sabi
OBJECTIVE	Hakuto the Whisper
VENUE	Suo: Ganryu Island

AFTER(S)WORD

Well, regarding that, there are all kinds of ways of thinking about things, and no blanket statement is possible, but when someone does something wrong for instance, it's not so easy to say what they could do to earn forgiveness. Not to mention the problem of pinpointing what we mean by such a vague idea as *wrong*, and defining where it starts and ends—but as a working definition, let's call wrongdoing any action with a victim. Unless you're a perfect person,[6] in the normal course of everyday life, you're going to wind up doing something wrong to somebody, even if it never hits the level of a crime. So how should we make up for these wrongdoings? There are going to be times where it isn't good enough to apologize, or to be remorseful, or to suffer the same fate, because at the end of the day, asking for forgiveness is the epitome of arrogance. When you have a perpetrator and a victim, it certainly doesn't mean no wrongdoing occurred just because the victim sees what happened with complete indifference and doesn't even feel victimized, and a wrong is still a wrong even if the perpetrator is oblivious and shows no sign of compunction. Or rather, crime or not, no matter how we may regret or even forget the things we've done, they never go away, and if they get brought up for the rest of our lives, that doesn't seem so unfair. Atonement and punishment are done for the victim's sake, not our own, but we can't seem to keep ourselves from mixing this up, and it's depressing to think how humans, as a species, are unable to consider crime and punishment in anything but self-regarding terms. But that's enough slapdash philosophy for one sitting. If you do something wrong, go ahead and apologize.

Thus ends the fourth of the twelve *KATANAGATARI* books. Yikes, I mean the third. Sento the Legion, a thousand swords in a single bunch. The fact that it's only the end of one installment in a longer series makes all of these afterwords surprisingly difficult to write, but sluggish as these words may be, the story proper marches on. Sometimes I think thanking our illustrator,

[6] 聖人君子 SEIJIN KUNSHI "saintly prince"

take, is the only solid reason for these commentaries, but just as there are times when saying sorry isn't good enough, there are times when saying thank you isn't good enough. Demonstrating gratitude is never easy, but for what it's worth, I've tried.

Nine more books to go!

NISIOISIN

Palindromic **NISIOISIN** made his debut as a novelist when he was twenty. Famously prolific, he is known to publish more than a book per month at times.

Beloved illustrator **take** is also known for adorning the *Zaregoto* mystery cycle with striking visuals.

Sam Bett is a fiction writer and Japanese translator. His translation work has won the Japan-U.S. Friendship Commission Prize and been shortlisted for the International Booker Prize.